Dance With The Devil

A novel by Kris Lillyman

For Netty, Scarlett and Dexter.

Prologue

Hollywood, California 1948

Maria lay naked on the couch in the pool house, her body glistening with perspiration and tingling deliciously with the satisfied afterglow of sex.

The secret rendezvous with her lover, Armando, had been wild and steamy, much as it always was whenever they managed to snatch a few precious moments together.

But the secrecy, the fear of being discovered, made it all the more exciting, all the more intense.

Indeed, she was still breathing heavily, as was Armando, who lay beside her, at last, spent. His muscular, sweat-soaked body pressed against hers as they both recovered from the passionate throes of their clandestine liaison.

Maria's hastily discarded robe and expensive swimsuit lay on the floor alongside Armando's dirty work clothes and worn-out boots, emphasising the huge gulf between them; their lives at opposite ends of the social scale.

She had just turned seventeen and he was barely a year older yet their backgrounds could not have been more different.

She was an heiress, born into fabulous wealth whilst he was just another poor immigrant who worked for her father.

But the differences did not matter to them because they were in love.

Maria was feisty, passionate and smart; a rare beauty with lustrous black hair, striking green eyes and a figure to die for whilst Armando was darkly handsome with an impressive physique honed from hard outdoor work.

He was a fun, carefree joker but when it came to romance he was totally serious. He had been born in an orphanage near Naples, his parentage unknown, and had escaped at sixteen, stowing away on a ship bound for New York. He had no plan, no grand scheme for his future and took the view that life would be an adventure no matter where it took him.

Maria was from Italian stock too, although she was second generation, born and raised in America by her extremely strict, very protective father. Her mother had died many years earlier and Maria could barely remember her but in photographs, she looked extremely beautiful, just like her. Maria always wore a tiny gold necklace, given to her on the day of her Christening by her mother, to remind her that she would be forever with her.

Maria, like Armando, also thought life should be an adventure and wanted to live it to the full away from the strict rules set out by her father. She longed to be free; to travel, to explore and to make love to Armando whenever she pleased.

Their attraction had been instant, from the very first moment they laid eyes on each other. Their first kiss had been shortly afterwards, hurried and rushed in a breathless declaration of their feelings for each other. She had caught him stealing a cookie from the jar in the pantry and as she brushed past him to return it their passion ignited.

That was two months ago and since then they had made love at every stolen opportunity. Each time it was hot, passionate and torrid, neither one of them able to get enough of the other. They had become reckless, careless even. Maria did not dare think of what her father might do if he found out and Armando did not seem to care; the irresponsible flame of youth still blazing within him.

He intended to marry Maria. He would explain this to her father, declare his love for his daughter, tell him he would love her for as long as she lived. Italians were romantics and lovers by nature so surely her father would understand.

Maria, however, was less certain. She was sure of her love for Armando - had never been surer of anything in her life - but as for her father understanding, she seriously doubted it.

As they lay there together, revelling in their closeness, drinking in the simple pleasure of just being with each other, Maria thought she heard something outside.

Armando nuzzled her ear with his nose and kissed her gently on the cheek. "You want make love again?" he whispered, his accent strong.

"Ssh!" she replied, "I think I can hear someone."

"Tis, nothing, baby, don't worry. Your father he out for day, at work. We have house to ourselves."

"Ssh, no. I can definitely hear something, voices - my father!"

Suddenly Armando could hear it too. Voices and the sound of footsteps heading towards the pool house.

They were frantic then, panicked. Both of them shot up and made a grab for their clothes. Maria hastily pulled on her robe and Armando struggled to shrug into his dungarees. But it was too late.

The pool house door flew open and in the doorway stood Maria's father. His huge figure nearly blocking out the light. Behind him stood his assistant, Salvatore Falcone, grinning triumphantly.

Falcone, who had been with her father since the early days in New York, had long suspected the affair but had failed to prove it until this point. However quite by chance, he had been looking out of an upstairs window and witnessed Maria enter the pool house closely followed by the young gardener who was all the things Salvatore did

3

not like. Falcone had summoned her father home immediately and he had duly returned, furious, betrayed and disgusted.

Maria's father marched towards them. "Father! Please - I love him!" she pleaded.

"Grab him!" Her father ordered Salvatore.

"No Father, please don't, I—"

"Quiet, slut!" Growled Carlo Liuzzi as he raised his hand and struck his daughter hard around the face.

Briefly, Maria saw Armando's terrified face and then her world went black.

***

Sweat glistened on Nathaniel Kelly's brow and the warm California sun reddened the pale skin of the young Irishman's muscular bare arms as he polished the luxurious chrome of his employer's brand new Cadillac.

Nathaniel had dreamt of such marvels back in County Clare from where, just a year ago, he and his young wife, Megan, had embarked on their journey to start a new life in America.

Now they were here and he could not believe it. They were living in Hollywood of all places, in a huge mansion. There were palm trees and movie stars and houses bigger than any he could ever have imagined. The sun shone every day and with it the possibility of a better life.

It was Nathaniel's ambition to one day own a mansion just like his employer's and if he worked hard he knew he could. In America everything was possible. It did not matter how you started out or where you were born as America was a country that embraced ambition and nurtured enterprise and Nathaniel had bags of both. Here he could make something of himself, be a success, raise a family - maybe even become rich.

For now, though, he was a lowly chauffeur with a small one-room apartment above the garage that he shared with his childhood

4

sweetheart who worked as the maid. They were employed as a husband and wife package deal which suited them just fine for the present.

Their employer, however, was one of the most powerful and influential men in Hollywood, a studio boss whose fabulous wealth was matched only by his fearful reputation. But he, too, was an immigrant who had come to America with nothing. His route had been via the tough initiation of Ellis Island and the South Bronx - a baptism of fire as he entered the promised land of the New World. The loud, boisterous, vibrant surroundings of New York a complete contrast from his humble upbringing in rural Italy. But he had survived all the hardships America had thrown at him including The Great Depression and had been amply rewarded for his efforts.

Nathaniel dearly hoped to emulate this, to match his employer's meteoric rise to the top and to maybe get some tips or even a helping hand from him along the way. But there was a dark shadow looming which threatened to spoil his plans.

Megan was pregnant. It had not been intentional, just a stupid mistake but there was nothing they could do or were prepared to do, about it now. They had always planned for a family - a large one - but just not quite yet.

Even so, now the initial shock was over, they were both looking forward to it.

Nevertheless, Nathaniel hoped his wife's pregnancy would not hamper their ambitions or, indeed, threaten their position but, as yet, he had not dared to tell his employer for fear of what he might say. Their employer was not a man given to compassion or sentimentality but Nathaniel prayed his year of hard work and eagerness to undertake any task would serve him in good stead when the time came to break the news.

Megan was already four months gone but was prepared to work right up until the day she gave birth and then resume almost immediately afterwards. She and Nathaniel would take it in turns with the baby so it would not interfere with their work. This is what he intended to tell his employer in the hope he would understand and surely he would.

Nathaniel pondered all this as he finished polishing the car. Megan was not showing much of a bump at present but would be very shortly. His window of opportunity was closing and he knew he had to tell his employer before the man found out for himself. Although he did not relish the thought.

The Cadillac was gleaming, the black gloss paintwork shining like a mirror as Nathaniel admired his handiwork in the heavily buffed finish. The car's sparkling chrome and luxurious white-wall tyres perfectly illustrating all that he loved about his newly adopted country and bringing home to him just how much he wanted to stay.

He wiped his brow and swept the mop of curly red hair off his wet forehead then tucked the cleaning leather into the back pocket of his old dungarees before picking up the bucket and washcloth. As he strolled back to the large garage, Nathaniel enjoyed the heat of the late evening sun on the back of his neck. However, as an Irishman, sunburn was a regular problem although in recent months his white skin had browned just a little. But he would be sore tonight and would have to ask Megan to rub some of her soothing balm onto his neck and shoulders in order to ease the sting.

The garage was just one of three on the property that stood in a line at the rear of the house. Each contained four cars including a Buick Roadmaster, a Mercury Capri and a Rolls-Royce Phantom IV. These were in addition to the Coupe De Ville on the driveway that Nathaniel had just cleaned inside and out.

In fact, he had cleaned all but one of the cars that day as his services as a chauffeur had not been required, his employer opting to drive the convertible Roadmaster himself to the studio that morning, which he had returned in a couple of hours earlier than expected.

It was not usual for him to come home from work early so Nathaniel noted it as strange but thought little more of it.

Above each garage was a small apartment. Nathaniel and his wife had one of these, the maintenance man had another and the last one belonged to the gardener. The rest of the staff all lived in various rooms on the top floor of the main house. Nathaniel thought he and the other garage dwellers had the better deal. They had more freedom there than in the structured regimes of the house which suited him just fine.

As he walked to the back of the garage to put his bucket and washcloth away, Nathaniel noticed the rear door to the garage had been left open and from where he stood he could see that the garden hose had not been put away either. Instead, it been left out, unfurled on the patio. If his employer saw this he would go spare. Within his household neatness and order was of the highest importance.

Nathaniel cursed under his breath. Tidying up after Armando, the gardener was becoming a regular habit.

Armando was eighteen, just three years younger than Nathaniel and only one younger than Megan, yet whereas they were conscientious, hard-working people who abided by the rules clearly laid out by their employer, Armando was a wild and reckless dreamer who flouted authority and pushed boundaries to the limit.

He was a romantic, too, with looks that made women fall at his feet but he lacked the focus and drive needed to succeed in America as Nathaniel intended to.

Nevertheless, he was good company, a gifted raconteur and a natural free-spirit - three things Nathaniel definitely was not, but that was perhaps why they got on so well.

It did grate, however, when Nathaniel found himself having to clear up yet another of his friend's messes. Yesterday it was the garden tools, the day before that it was the oil from Armando's motorbike which had leaked all over the spotless flagstones of their employer's immaculate driveway and today it was the hose which would have to be put away in the garden store underneath the tennis courts before their employer saw it and reprimanded them both.

Nathaniel coiled the hose around one of his thick arms then carried it across the lawns towards the tennis courts. Needless to say, as usual, there was no sign of Armando when any clearing up had to be done.

The door to the garden store was located in a sunken area of lawn which was disguised from casual view by an immaculately manicured hedge at the far end of the tennis courts and was reached by a short flight of wooden steps. As Nathaniel trotted down these he saw the door to the store was already open and again cursed Armando, assuming it was he who had left it open.

Inside was a small area where spare nets and covers were kept for the courts and then beyond that, another door leading to the garden store proper. As Nathaniel crossed the outer area, he heard raised voices coming from behind the second door.

And then he heard a scream.

Nathaniel froze. Again he heard voices; his employer's for certain and possibly that of his assistant. They were angry, accusatory and menacing. Nathaniel then heard another voice; gruff and pained, obviously speaking with some difficulty. But Nathaniel would have known it anywhere as it belonged to his good friend, Armando.

Without thinking, Nathaniel opened the door and very nearly vomited with revulsion as he took in the macabre scene before him.

In the foreground, with their backs towards him, stood Nathaniel's employer, Carlo Liuzzi, and his assistant, Salvatore Falcone.

In the background was a barely recognisable Armando who was hanging naked from the ceiling by his wrists which were secured to an overhead beam by a chain. His face had been badly beaten and bloody drool dangled in long gooey strands from his split lower lip.

8

Yet what repulsed Nathaniel most was the large gash in Armando's stomach and the rivers of blood pissing from it, forming a grisly looking puddle on the floor beneath his dangling feet.

It was only then Nathaniel realised with horror, that Armando's testicles had been severed, too, and the sack that contained them was sitting in this large puddle of blood.

Suppressing the urge to throw up, Nathaniel suddenly felt light-headed. He staggered backwards and grabbed for the door handle in a bid to stop himself from falling. However, the sound of this disturbed Liuzzi and his assistant, interrupting them from their evil work.

They both turned to see the chauffeur standing there, his face grey with horror. Armando, too, managed to look up, his tear-filled eyes fixing on the appalled gaze of Nathaniel. The eighteen-year-old boy, who only that morning had been so full of fun and vigour was now just moments from death but somehow he found the strength to speak.

"Run," Armando croaked, "run for your life!"

But by the time his words registered through the shock of what he was witnessing, it was too late for Nathaniel to do what his friend had instructed. Salvatore seized him and threw him to the ground then slammed the store door closed.

As Nathaniel lay there looking up, the powerful form of his employer loomed over him. He was holding a dagger with a long, curved blade, Armando's blood dripping from it.

"I'm sorry, Nathaniel", said Carlo Liuzzi. "This was none of your business, but unfortunately your presence here cannot be ignored".

Nathaniel looked into Liuzzi's face and saw a murderer staring back. He felt suddenly cold. "But I'm going to be a father," was all he could manage to say.

"Then you have my sympathy", Liuzzi said. "Your wife, too. But she will be taken care of, as will your child. You have my word".

Then he raised the dagger and at that moment, Nathaniel knew his American dream was over.

Chapter One

Nine months later

Carlo Liuzzi had listened all night to the screams of his only daughter. He had not gone to her, had not sent word and had not enquired after her. He cared deeply for her but was not accustomed to displays of emotion. Neither was he a big advocate of forgiveness and Maria, his daughter, had shamed him beyond words. She had shamed herself, too, and no matter how much Carlo loved her he could not condone or forgive what she had done.

He stood now in thoughtful silence looking out on the vast lawns of his mansion, high up in the Hollywood Hills, from the tall windows of his very masculine study. It was after midnight but the full moon illuminated the grounds enough for him to see the gardens clearly.

Inside, the large fireplace crackled with smouldering logs, their glow providing the only light in the room.

The screaming had stopped several minutes earlier and all was now quiet upstairs. Then Carlo heard the bedroom door open and the sound of footsteps crossing the landing and coming down the stairs. A moment later, there was a slight cough at the open door of the study, "Mister Liuzzi?"

"Come."

The nurse, Megan Kelly, entered the room and stopped near

the fireplace, uncertain as to how close she should approach. Liuzzi cut an imposing figure in the half-light; tall and powerful with broad shoulders. His strong face, in shadow, looking as if it had been carved from granite and his black wavy hair swept back off his forehead shining silkily in the moonlight. The nurse knew there were traces of grey at the temples and in his thick black moustache but they were not visible at present as he faced away from her, gazing out across the lawns.

Her heart raced as she stood waiting, his impeccably cut suit hanging perfectly on his impressive form. Megan could not help but be enamoured by his looks and even more so by his wealth but remained fearful of his power and temper.

However, when she was left pregnant and widowed after the brakes apparently failed on a car her husband had been driving, sending him careening over the cliff on Mullholland Drive to his death below, Liuzzi had been unexpectedly supportive.

Nathaniel's accident had never been fully explained to her and she still did not know exactly why or how it happened but had it not been for her boss, things might have been a whole lot worse for her.

Indeed, Liuzzi had allowed her to remain under his roof even after the birth of her child which had been somewhat surprising. What is more, to enable her to nurse her baby, he had been most flexible with her working arrangements so she was extremely grateful to him for that.

"My daughter?" he said.

"She's well, sir. Very tired, but well. She was very bra—"

"Good." Liuzzi cut across her. "And the, er," he struggled to hide the unexpected tremble in his voice, "the child?"

"Oh, fine sir. Healthy and a good weight - a good set of lungs—" the nurse was smiling and was going to say more but then Liuzzi turned to face her and suddenly her words dried up as he stepped over to examine the small bundle she was holding in her arms.

The smile was fleeting as Carlo Liuzzi regarded the newborn child. The bastard offspring of his only daughter. "What is it?" he asked.

"Baby boy," said the woman. "A real handsome little fella too."

Again the fleeting smile. Of pride perhaps. A boy, of course. It would have to be.

Carlo had longed for a son and heir but none had arrived, only one precious girl.

Now, his seventeen-year-old daughter had given birth to a bastard; its father a lowly gardener with no prospects, no money and no respect for family.

The gardener was dead now, his mutilated body acting as fertiliser for the plants he once tended. Carlo had seen to it personally - the irony appealing to the dark beast that lurked within him.

His beloved daughter had been spared, but she would never forget the beating she received on the day her treachery was discovered.

Soon Maria would be sent to Italy to join a convent where she would learn the true value of chastity, which he had obviously failed to instil in her.

As for the child - the baby boy he was now looking at, he too would have to go. No matter how much Carlo would feel the pain. The shame, for him and for his daughter, would be worse.

Liuzzi raised a finger to the baby's face, as if to stroke its cheek, but stopped just short. He dropped his hand and turned swiftly back to the window. 'You've been paid?' he asked curtly.

"Pardon, sir? I mean, yes sir, thank you. Most generous."

"Everything's organised?"

"Yes, sir."

"Good. Then take it away."

"Sorry, sir?"

"Take it. Take it now. Get it out of my sight."

13

The woman opened her mouth to say more but thought better of it. She stood there, momentarily stunned, for just a second longer then turned and left the room.

And Carlo Liuzzi was alone once more.

***

Megan Kelly, a slim, wan woman with a round plain face and short auburn hair, closed the study door as silently as she could and glanced guiltily up the stairs. She could still hear Maria sobbing, pleading desperately to be allowed to see her child.

Yet it was Megan who held Maria's newborn son, with orders to take the boy to her own quarters.

She had been paid to take care of him until Maria was fit to travel. Furthermore, she had been given strict instructions not to let mother and son see each other until the car arrived to take them all to the station.

As Megan reached her small apartment above the garage, the newborn began to stir and fuss. He was ready for a feed and Megan felt her breasts swell with milk in response to the baby's demands.

Her own three-month-old son lay in his cot asleep and would be waking to take his turn at her breast in a few short hours but for now, Megan's milk was needed elsewhere. Sitting in her favourite old rocker, she cradled the baby boy in her arms and popped open her blouse allowing a plump, full breast to spill out. She guided her nipple towards the baby's mouth then let Mother Nature take it from there, relishing the gentle tingle as her new charge enjoyed his very first meal.

After giving the infant ten minutes on each side, she burped him and then settled him down in the Moses basket next to the cot. When she was certain he was asleep, Megan quickly changed into her nightdress and slipped into her small bunk in the corner of the tiny room. She needed to get some sleep because before long she would be awake again and then there would be two hungry mouths to feed.

**

Maria stirred from her deep slumber as the first rays of bright morning sun shone in through her tall bedroom windows. Her thick mane of glossy, black hair lay across the pillow as she turned her beautiful face to the light and blinked open her green eyes.

Just for the briefest moment, all was right with the world but then, as the soreness of giving birth made itself known, the hideous memories of the previous night flooded horribly back and she knew her world would never be right again.

Last night she had given birth to a son. Her baby boy.

Maria had caught just the briefest glimpse of him as he was carried off by Megan, as per her father's explicit instructions. She had screamed long into the night, begging to see her baby, begging to hold him just once, just for a minute. But her screams had been ignored and she had eventually given in to sleep, too weary to fight any more after the rigours of an eighteen-hour labour.

Now she had awoken and the horror of what was destined to happen caused fresh tears to spring from her almond-shaped eyes.

In two days time, she was to be shipped off to a convent in Italy and her son was to be taken from her to be raised by monks at a monastery in a location unknown to her.

The only consolation was that she would be travelling with her baby to Italy, accompanied by Megan and her son so she would, at least, get to see him, to be with him, for the duration of the journey. However, all motherly duties such as feeding, bathing and changing her child were to be carried out by Megan, not her. Her father's man, Salvatore, would also be travelling with them to ensure Carlo's instructions were carried out to the letter.

Until the day of their departure, Maria was to be confined to her room and have no contact with her son whatsoever which, in her father's mind, would prevent any bond forming. To further preclude this he had also decreed that the child should not be given a name so she would never be able to find him.

This seemed the cruellest punishment of all. How could a mother not know her own child's name?

But somehow, some way, before she was delivered to the convent, Maria was determined to escape with her son and then she would give him a name - a name that Carlo Liuzzi would, one day, learn to respect.

***

Two days later, Carlo Liuzzi watched from his window once more as preparations were made for his only daughter's departure for Italy. Her bags had been taken out into the driveway and the Bentley had been brought around from the garage in readiness to take her to the station.

However, Maria was to wait in her room, watched over by Salvatore, until Megan and the children were settled in the car. The last thing Carlo wanted was a big, dramatic scene on the driveway.

Maria had only packed three small cases as there would be no need for her glamorous wardrobe at the convent - not that she had any intention of ever going there. But for appearance's sake, she had to make her compliance look convincing.

Surprisingly, it was Megan who had the most luggage. Two cases for herself, one for Maria's baby and one for her own son, Nate, who had been born eight weeks prematurely and was still below the desired size and weight for a child of three months.

Nate, who had his father's red hair and pale skin, was a sickly baby and had nearly died several times in the first desperate weeks of his life. But, after a long drawn-out struggle, much of it without his mother by his side due to her heavy workload, he had made it through. However, he was not flourishing as well as he should which worried Megan greatly.

She loved her son dearly and would have liked nothing better than to have been with him during those long days and nights in the hospital as he fought for his tiny life. But with her husband gone, money scarce and an employer who was not the most understanding of men she simply had to keep on working. It was a dreadful wrench and she had hated every minute that she spent apart from her son, blaming her absence from his bedside as the reason he was not doing as well as he should be. But all that was soon to change as they were about to embark on a new life together.

In the weeks leading up to his grandson's birth, Carlo Liuzzi had summoned Megan to his study and told her what he required of her. Firstly, he wanted her to act as a nursemaid when Maria's child was born; she already had milk so he did not consider this to be a problem. Secondly, she would accompany Maria and her offspring to Italy; continuing her role as nursemaid until the child could be delivered safely to his new home at the monastery. And thirdly, if she carried out the first two tasks as instructed, Liuzzi promised he would organise passage for her and Nate back to New York and personally guarantee her work with a wealthy family on the Upper West Side.

There was also a fourth part of the arrangement, which was for Megan to train her replacement. Liuzzi had already employed another husband and wife team to take up residence above the garage as she and Nathaniel had nearly two years earlier. A woman, Mildred, and a man, Edmund would be the new maid and chauffeur - the new Megan and Nathaniel.

Megan could not help but think about this wistfully as she took her place in the car with the children and waited for Maria and Salvatore. She thought about her husband and all his grand plans for their fantastic new life in America which had all come to nought after the tragic accident that had so cruelly stolen those dreams away.

Nonetheless, since Nathaniel's death and Maria's own loss, the two young women had become close. Not only were their ages similar

17

but their shared tragedies had naturally bonded them together too.

However, unlike Megan who knew of Nathaniel's passing, even though the version she had been told of it was a lie, Maria did not know Armando was dead. She innocently believed he had just been sent away and warned, in no uncertain terms, never to return. And so, unaware of the truth, she foolishly hoped to be reunited with him someday.

Nonetheless, Maria did not resent the fact that Megan would be caring for her baby as she knew it was not her choice. Indeed, Maria was pleased it was Megan if it had to be anyone and delighted that she would also be accompanying them to Italy - which would give Maria an ally against the menacing presence of Salvatore.

***

Earlier that morning, Salvatore Falcone had taken his morning espresso with his old friend Carlo Liuzzi who, at forty-two, was seven years his senior. They sat in the heavy oak furniture of Liuzzi's office which was decorated in strong, bold colours.

The walls were lined with photographs which marked the short passage of time that had seen him rise from penniless immigrant to fabulously wealthy Hollywood studio boss. Arriving in America at just twenty-five, his journey to the top had been swift. He owed much of this meteoric rise to three things; his fists, his guile and his ambition. However, he also had Carmine Carboni to thank too.

Carboni was a respected and powerful New York godfather who took a shine to Carlo after being impressed by his quick intelligence and willingness to get his hands dirty. Taking the young man under his wing, he carefully orchestrated his rise through the ranks and took great pride in him finally becoming the youngest and most feared Consigliere in the Five Boroughs. Then, when Liuzzi saw an opportunity to expand The Family's interests on the West Coast, Carboni agreed to back him.

Starting small, Carlo muscled his way into owning part shares

18

in several studios then, little by little, bought out his partners by either fair means or foul. Eventually, he combined all these smaller studios into one enormous entity, calling it 'Gold Star Pictures' and instantly became one of the main players in Hollywood. The rest was history.

Salvatore had been with him every step of the way although he had never hit the dizzying heights his friend had assailed to. Nevertheless, he had always been by his side and liked to think of himself as the Consigliere's consigliere.

"You're all set?" Asked Carlo, sipping his strong espresso.

"Yes."

"You're clear on what to do with the nursemaid?"

"Yes. Don't worry, I'll handle it."

"There must be no witnesses, Salvo," Liuzzi warned, "Megan and her boy must die - and my secrets with them - in Italy before you return. No one must know about my daughter and her bastard. Understand?"

Falcone took a sip of his own espresso and smiled, "When have I ever let you down, my friend?"

"Never." Replied Liuzzi, raising his tiny cup in salute. "And let's hope you never do."

Both men were smiling but the underlying threat was clearly understood by Salvatore.

***

Maria was ready and had steeled herself for the emotion of seeing her son for the first time. She would not be allowed to hold him or to touch him, not with Salvatore in such close proximity but she was certain that somewhere on the journey a chance would present itself. It would be impossible for Salvatore to keep watch twenty-four seven and Maria intended to make the most of every stolen opportunity.

She sat at her dressing table in her bedroom waiting for the

19

knock on the door from Salvatore to indicate when it was time for her to leave. In the short time since she had given birth and her subsequent house arrest Maria had not been idle. She was far from stupid and knew that even though she planned to escape there was a possibility she might not. No matter how hard she tried there was still a chance she might end up at the convent with her son lost to her forever.

In the case of this eventuality, Maria had written her son a letter which she had hidden amongst the pages of a carefully cut-out section of a bible, that she would slip into his belongings. The bible was a leather-bound edition with a clasp so there was little chance of the letter falling out accidentally and, as it was a bible, it would not be seen as at all suspicious - particularly by monks.

Along with the letter, which she had placed inside an envelope addressed to *My Son*, Maria had also included a gold locket, bought for her on her sixteenth birthday by her father which was inscribed with the words *Always and Forever*. Inside was a picture of her as she was now together with a lock of her hair.

If she did end up at the convent, her hope was that her son would find the letter and, one day, come looking for her. In the letter, she had told him everything that had happened - about his father, about his grandfather, about her and about his heritage and rightful birthright. No matter what, no matter how awful, she was determined her son would know it all.

***

When everything was set outside, with Megan, the children and the luggage all loaded into the Bentley, the knock came on Maria's door. It was time for her to leave the only house she had ever known. Forever.

She stood and smoothed down her skirt, picked up her purse with the Bible tucked inside and left the room without so much as a backwards glance. She had quite done with her father's house and the memories it held for her.

Salvatore Falcone stood waiting on the landing; tall and thin with a receding hairline and a long, tanned face. He had a Roman nose and thick rubbery lips that spread into a leery grin when Maria appeared. He was a sinister, shadowy figure who had been with her father for years; his closest confidante, but he had always given Maria the creeps - always seeming as if he was imagining her naked whenever he looked at her. However, in her father's house he would never dare touch her - but away from there, away from her father, Maria could not be sure and this troubled her.

She ignored Falcone but heard him close behind her as she descended the wide sweeping staircase, her gloved hand gliding lightly on the polished marble bannister as she made her way swiftly down to the grand oak doors where, just beyond, her child was waiting for her.

She was nervous, excited, anxious, but was determined not to cry in front of Salvatore or her father who she knew would be watching from his study window.

Maria and her father had not spoken since the night he had beaten her - the night following the afternoon when she had last seen her beloved Armando. Since that night they had been strangers living in the same house, neither being able to quite believe what the other had done and neither able to forgive it.

It was this estrangement that had allowed Maria to disguise her pregnancy from her father until it was far too late for him to force her to terminate. It was a willful act of defiance that enabled her to keep something of Armando; a child that would be forever theirs. But Carlo Liuzzi had conspired to rid her of that too. In the battle of wills, he had emerged victorious, at least for the moment.

Once, not long ago, Maria had been the apple of Carlo's eye and she had viewed him as the man against whom all other's paled. But no more; she hated him and he had severed her from his cold, black heart and even though she was leaving and never coming back, they would not speak now. Indeed, Carlo would not even leave his study and she would not look for him as she passed through the doors and out onto the driveway.

Edmund, the new chauffeur, stood there in his smart black uniform holding the rear door of the Bentley open, the shiny peak of his cap and polished black boots sparkling in the sunlight. The Bentley was a one-off, built especially to Liuzzi's specific design and featured bench seats that faced each other in the elongated rear compartment. The plush leather and lacquered walnut trim emphasising the luxury and quality of the impressive automobile.

As Maria climbed into the limousine and took her seat opposite Megan and the children, her emotions threatened to overwhelm her as she laid eyes on her baby for the first time since his birth. She longed to take him up in her arms, kiss him, and tell him she loved him but Salvatore had already squeezed in beside her and had laid a slender hand on her knee to restrain her. However, there was no need, she would not give him the satisfaction and kept herself perfectly in check. But the journey ahead of them was long and soon enough, God willing, she would steal her boy back and be rid of Falcone and her father's controlling ways for good.

Only then could she set about finding Armando.

One day all three of them would be reunited; Armando, her and their beautiful son. At least that was the dream.

The Bentley started up and pulled away. As it sped down the drive towards the enormous gates that separated the property from the outside world, Maria did not even glance out of the window. Her focus was on her son and that is where it would remain.

***

Carlo Liuzzi watched from his study as the car carrying his only daughter and her newborn bastard departed. Maria had been his world once; the only truly good thing in his whole, entire life.

She was beautiful and innocent and he had loved her with all of his heart. But she had squandered his love, obliterated his trust and lost her innocence forever. Now she meant nothing.

Or at least that's what he tried hard to tell himself.

Liuzzi was not a man given over to sentiment or emotion, in fact quite the opposite. He was cold, hard and immovable. If someone betrayed him, or disappointed him, as Maria had, he had the ability to cut them out of his life for good.

Indeed, he had the ability to extinguish life also, as he had done in the case of Armando and Nathaniel. And, many years before that, Maria's mother, Olivia, too.

Olivia Liuzzi had tried to leave Carlo; sick of being ignored, belittled and punished by him for not being able to give him a male heir. Even though Carlo doted on his dark-haired, green-eyed daughter, Maria was not the boy child he so badly craved.

Olivia had made the fatal error of telling Carlo she was leaving him and in a fit of terrifying anger he had strangled her to death.

Thanks to Carlo's strong ties to the Carboni family, the murder was covered up and suicide recorded as the cause of death which was what Maria had always believed.

But it was all a lie. As was the denial of his love for his daughter, but he was too proud, too foolish and too stubborn to admit it either to himself or to her. All he had left of her now was her hatred and that only served to make him even more of a monster.

Carlo watched until the Bentley passed through the electric gates at the end of the long driveway, then poured himself a stiff glass of bourbon. Sitting in his leather-bound chair behind his heavy mahogany desk he selected a cigar from the solid silver box before him and rolled it thoughtfully between his fingers.

For a long moment he stared into nothingness, his mind running a cine film in his head, conjuring up images of Maria growing up; her first tooth, vacations they had taken together, him holding her in his arms after she had fallen off her pony, her sixteenth birthday when he had presented her with the locket. He thought, too, of the night he had beaten her and finally of her son; the much longed for baby boy. But the child had been conceived out of wedlock and the father was of unworthy stock. Carlo's shame had proved greater than his desire for a grandson and that realisation had shamed him even more.

He squeezed his eyes tightly shut, trying to block out the truth of it. But he could not.

Suddenly Carlo's mouth buckled into an ugly grimace and he let out a terrifying roar before scrunching the cigar up and mangling it between his fingers. Then he roared again as if releasing years of pent up, long suppressed emotion and violently flung the crystal glass tumbler across the room, smashing it into tiny pieces as it hit the fireplace with a loud crash.

Carlo Liuzzi then cradled his head in his hands and wept like a baby.

Chapter Two

The first part of the journey was from Los Angeles to Chicago on the newly refurbished Super Chief, nicknamed 'The Train of the Stars' because of the many celebrities who travelled on it. Its new streamlined sleeping cars and 'Pleasure Dome' lounge car were the epitome of elegance and luxury and were widely regarded as the only way to travel.

From LA to Chicago it would take a mere thirty-six hours and from there it was just another shorter train journey to New York before boarding the grand ocean liner that would be taking the Liuzzi party to Naples.

Once there, yet another train would take them on to their final destination of Messina on the eastern tip of Sicily.

Maria's father had spared no expense in her banishment, securing her first class travel all the way. However, it was not out of love for her that these arrangements had been made but for his own elitist pride. Whilst in transit and free from the confines of the convent, Maria still carried his name and no Liuzzi would travel in anything other than the grandest style.

Maria had kept her emotions under control incredibly well on the drive to the station. Just once, when her baby began to snivel and had to be calmed by a feed from Megan's breast, did the tears spill from her eyes but she took several deep breaths and held it together as best she could, berating herself for the brief show of weakness in front of Salvatore.

Feeling incredibly awkward, Megan had no choice but to feed the grizzling child but felt felt immense pity for Maria and hated herself for the part she was being forced to play.

Salvatore, however, merely smiled and made no attempt to avert his eyes as Megan discreetly opened her blouse and reluctantly suckled the infant.

They arrived at Union Station and were boarded on the Super Chief with speed and efficiency. Salvatore had a standard birth, Megan a roomette, which was enclosed for more privacy, and Maria had been assigned a full bedroom which featured a private bath amongst other luxuries.

The births had been reserved by Carlo Liuzzi's secretary who, without knowledge of the train's layout, had made the arrangements on the basis of who was travelling - which was the one slight oversight in Carlo's otherwise scrupulous plans. Therefore, Salvatore had been assigned a birth suitable for a single man, Megan had been booked one as a nursing mother and Maria, as the wealthy daughter of a powerful Hollywood mogul, had been reserved a First Class suite.

This meant Salvatore would be much further down the train than either Maria or Megan and, as such, could not maintain his vigilant watch on them all night. He had tried to change his birth and spent many minutes in a heated argument with the guard but it was to no avail, the train was full and no other births were available. He would have to stay put.

This news delighted both the women and soon after a gourmet supper, eaten in the spectacular dining car, they retired to bed. Salvatore protested and tried to stop them but once again he was powerless to prevent it without making an embarrassing scene. He had already angered the guard, who was now watching him closely, so had no desire to rile him further and risk being physically removed from the train as an unruly passenger.

The moment the two women were alone, Megan presented Maria with her son, allowing her the chance to hold him for the very first time. Maria was trembling as she took her baby into her arms, her eyes wet with tears at the sheer joy of it. As she cradled the small, perfect bundle, she kissed him and breathed in his wonderful scent.

Maria's breasts ached to feed him but her milk had all but dried up and gone away, her father having robbed her of that singular pleasure. All she could do was offer her finger as the little boy chewed it with his gummy mouth. It tickled and she laughed and then she began to cry in earnest. Deep, heavy sobs that had been threatening to come since the journey began, brought on by the knowledge that this moment, this time with her son, would be all too fleeting and unless she could change things, it would soon be gone and he would be out of her life forever.

Megan found herself crying too as she stood next to Maria with Nate, her own son, in her arms; crying for her friend; crying for herself and Nathaniel; the good, strong, reliable man her son would never know.

The women stayed with each other in Maria's bedroom until the early hours of the morning. Maria had spent the whole night with her son; holding him; playing with him and bonding with him. When he needed feeding she had pressed herself as close to Megan as possible to try and get a sense of what it would be like, imagining it was her full breast her child was nuzzling, not the nursemaid's. In doing so, Maria desperately hoped that if he should look up, it would be her face he saw smiling down at him and not Megan's.

Megan was extremely accommodating, fully understanding how her mistress felt and wishing things were different for her. However, she could not help the bond she already felt for Maria's baby. It was an instinctual thing which had just taken her over; feeding him and feeding Nate just seemed like the most natural thing in the world and she would dearly miss her surrogate son when he was placed in the care of the monastery, thus ending her involvement in the boy's welfare for good.

As the first rays of the morning sun came up, Maria reluctantly handed her son back to Megan, noticing that the two children could not be more different as the young Irishwoman held them both in her arms.

Nate was pale, fair skinned and tiny for his age whereas her baby was olive skinned with a messy bush of black fluffy hair and even though he was small, as all newborns were, Maria could already tell it would not be long before he surpassed Nate in both size and weight. He was destined to be tall and handsome just like Armando had been, although perhaps with her green eyes.

As Maria thought of Armando, she also thought of the Bible and the letter concealed within it. Seizing the opportunity, she quickly rifled through her purse and pulled out the leather-bound book.

"Take this," she said to Megan. "Take it and hide it at the bottom of my baby's suitcase - and please make sure Salvatore does not see it - ever."

"What is it?" Asked Megan, sensing by Maria's clandestine manner there was something more than just scripture contained within the book's bindings.

"Something for my baby, so he knows of me and what happened. Just in case—" Her voice trailed off but the implication was clear.

"Don't worry. Salvatore won't find it, I promise. But nothing will happen, things will work out for the best I'm sure of it," Megan assured her. "Somewhere between here and Messina, you will have a chance to escape."

"I hope you're right. I pray you are. But just in case, please take it. Hide it and let's never speak of it again. Salvatore is far too wily to be easily distracted and an overheard whisper could prove disastrous."

"Of course. I understand."

Maria bent and kissed her baby's head, holding her lips there for a long moment and breathing in his delicious scent one last time before saying, "Good. Now go. And make sure no one sees you."

A second later Maria was alone and already feeling bereft. How on earth would she be able to survive a lifetime without her son?

***

As the small party stood on the dockside at the Port of New York preparing to board the ocean liner, *SS Conte Biancamano*, en-route to Naples by way of Halifax, Lisbon, Gibraltar, Barcelona, Palermo, Cannes and Genoa, Maria could not help but notice Salvatore's complexion looked ever so slightly grey which was in stark contrast to his normally dark tan.

The reason for this, unbeknownst to Maria, was that Salvatore was not a good sailor and was viewing the ship with alarming trepidation.

Indeed, Salvatore had only ever been on a ship once before - the one that brought him to New York along with Carlo Liuzzi. The pair, having met on board ship, had been processed through Ellis Island's Immigration Centre together and had been friends ever since. However, apart from that chance meeting, Salvatore's memory of the voyage was not a happy one and he had suffered from extreme sea sickness even on a calm day.

When Carlo had instructed him to accompany Maria to Italy it had been Salvatore's one reservation. He was in absolutely no rush to repeat what had been one of the worst experiences of his entire life but it was a sacrifice he was willing to make.

With Maria out of the picture and no other heir to stake a claim on the Liuzzi fortune, Falcone was in line to inherit millions. In his view, it was only what he was entitled to for all his years of loyal service.

Friendship or not, Salvatore was not much better than a glorified errand boy to the older Carlo who had fared much the better in the hands of Uncle Sam than he had. Which was a fact that had always rankled. But he was also one for the bigger picture and once he caught wind of the affair between Carlo's precious daughter and the lowly gardener he suspected it was only a matter of time before good fortune, at last, shone on him.

It did not do any harm, of course, to inform Liuzzi of the sordid little tryst in the pool house which had ended so badly for Armando and the unfortunate Nathaniel and so well for Salvatore. In fact, things could scarcely have gone better if he had planned it himself, although this sea voyage was, admittedly, an unforeseen and most unwelcome blip.

He just hoped his resilience to the constant, unrelenting movement of the ship had strengthened with age.

Unlike the births allotted to them on the Super Chief, this time the arrangements were exactly as intended. Both Maria and Salvatore had been assigned First Class cabins adjacent to each other and Megan and the children had been allocated a small but private Second Class cabin two decks below.

This suited Falcone extremely well, particularly as he had harboured salacious designs on Maria since she was in her early teens. Yet now she had matured into an incredibly striking, very desirable woman and Salvatore craved her with every fibre of his being.

Originally it had been his hope to marry her, thus securing both her affections and her father's money but this had been a problematic plan. Firstly, it was abundantly clear Maria found him nothing short of abhorrent and secondly he seriously doubted if Carlo would ever consent to a union between him and the much younger, much more deserving, Maria.

Now, however, neither was an issue. Maria was completely under Salvatore's control and would be for the immediate future so he could take her whenever he pleased. Furthermore, once she was ensconced at the convent, her inheritance would rightfully be his upon Carlo's death - especially as the bastard grandson would no longer have a claim to it.

The monastery where Maria's child was destined to spend the next eighteen years of his life was the same one Salvatore, himself, had been brought up in, although the monastic life had proved too restrictive for a man of his needs.

Salvatore had known he was not cut out for the pious life of a monk since the first stirrings of puberty when wandering through the village close to the monastery he had seen the young girls of his age playing in the streets. Visions of their freshly sprouting bodies; firm and slender and ripe for the plucking had infiltrated his sinful dreams for many nights afterwards, giving him regular cause for self-gratification.

When he was of age he had left the monastery in a bid to find fortune and perhaps a girl with whom to satiate his sinful desires.

His search led him to a small town in the hills just south of Rome and a sweet, young, thirteen-year-old girl named Lucia Tartaglia.

Unfortunately, his feelings for her were unrequited. Yet, one night, unable to bear the humiliation and the thought of never being able to touch her in the way he so desperately wanted, he had followed her to town and spied on her with her friends. Afterwards, as she made her way home, alone, Salvatore sprang out from behind a tree and dragged her off the road and into a shallow gully. He clamped a hand firmly over her mouth to prevent her from screaming, then pushed open her legs and forced himself upon her.

But Lucia would not stop struggling, would not stop kicking and trying to throw him off.

Scrambling around in the dust, Salvatore's hand fell upon a small rock and his fingers closed around it. Then he hit her with it, hard, rendering her unconscious. With her finally silent he continued with the depraved attack unimpeded, finding it all the more pleasurable because she was powerless to prevent it.

When, at last, he had finished he studied her for several minutes, taking a mental photograph to keep in his memory for all time, ignoring the blood oozing from the deep gash in her forehead above her ruined left eye, lingering instead over her bare thighs and exposed breasts which were now clearly visible through the torn gap in her sundress.

Then he left her with her legs spread and her privates on display for anyone to see.

And then he ran.

He ran to Naples and to the sea, boarding the first ship he could find that was bound for America - the ship upon which he would meet Carlo Liuzzi and change the course of his life forever.

However, he knew it would be foolish to mention what he had done to the girl he had left for dead in the hills of Rome to anyone - including his new friend.

But Lucia Tartaglia would never forget the name Salvatore Falcone for as long as she lived.

Nevertheless, it had been Salvatore's memory of the monastery and its restrictions that had made him bring it to the attention of Carlo. Indeed, it was upon this suggestion that Liuzzi had chosen to send Maria's illegitimate offspring there - a decision that had worked out rather well for Salvatore, all things considered.

***

The sun shone in the late October of 1948 as the SS Conte Biancamano steamed out of New York Harbour, along the Hudson, to begin its month-long voyage to Naples.

The sea was calm as the huge liner sailed into the bay, passed the

Statue of Liberty and Ellis Island; the very same landmarks Salvatore had seen as he entered the United States seventeen years earlier. Back then his head was hanging over the rail, too busy throwing up to appreciate the magnificence of Lady Liberty or the significance of the Immigration Centre and now, as he passed them again, this time heading in the opposite direction, his stomach began to lurch once more.

Maria and Megan, on the other hand, were enjoying the brisk morning air as they stood on the upper deck admiring the cityscape that was growing smaller with every passing wave. Megan was rocking a baby carriage, loaned to her by the cruise line, and both the children were fast asleep in it.

Salvatore had been standing close by them when the first wave of nausea came over him and was forced to abandon his guard and run to the nearest bathroom, leaving the two women alone to giggle at his misfortune.

This became the pattern of the days that followed and allowed Maria and Megan to spend many happy hours together. More importantly, it afforded Maria a chance to spend some hugely important time with her child, which starkly contravened her father's orders to Salvatore.

However, Salvatore presently had more pressing concerns, spending days on end confined to his cabin with his head bent over the lavatory. He did not eat in the restaurant as the smell of food combined with the motion of the ship made him heave. He ate what meals he could in his room but nothing stayed down for long, not even the sea-sickness tablets the ship's doctor had supplied. It was a miserable, filthy existence and Salvatore hated every second of it. He was failing Liuzzi and squandering any opportunities he may have had with Maria and he prayed sometime soon, before the voyage was over, his affliction would pass and he could continue with his plans.

So far, what with the sleeping arrangements on the Super Chief and now this dreadfully debilitating sea-sickness, his assignment had been one unmitigated disaster after another and Salvatore knew he had to get it back on track quickly.

After a brief stop in Halifax, where none of the Liuzzi party disembarked, the Conte Biancamano made a leisurely seven-day crossing of the Atlantic. By the time they reached Lisbon Salvatore was a shadow of his former self, the weight had dropped off him and his complexion was sallow and sickly. The short time they spent ashore did wonders to invigorate him but it was all too brief and soon enough he was back on board with the rest of his party, steaming on to yet another destination.

Nonetheless, with every disembarkation, Salvatore grew stronger; the ports of call thankfully closer together now the horrendous, week-long crossing from Halifax to Lisbon was over. As the ship sailed out from each sun-drenched harbour, the sea-sickness became steadily less severe. Indeed, by the time they had called at Gibraltar, Barcelona, Palermo and Cannes, Salvatore was almost enjoying himself and managing to spend many hours on deck. He was even able to dine in the ship's excellent restaurant and, perhaps more remarkably, keep down what he ate.

As for Maria, each port of call delayed her arrival at the convent further, allowing her to spend more precious time with her son. Although she was extremely thankful for this, she was also painfully aware that it would only cause her more heartache when the time eventually came to say goodbye.

With that in mind, she had been desperately trying to plan some means of escape in the hope she would never have to give up her baby but, as yet, no clear way out had presented itself and her time was running out.

For Salvatore's plans, too, the window of opportunity was swiftly closing. And, as the ship steamed out of Cannes towards Genoa, the last port of call on their busy itinerary before they finally arrived in Naples, he knew there was little time left for him to enjoy the delights of Maria.

Soon they would be on a train bound for Messina where she and all the mouth-watering pleasures her firm, young body promised, would be lost to him forever.

If he was going to take her, then it would have to be in Genoa, whilst all the other passengers, including Megan, were ashore. But it would need careful planning.

Salvatore knew Maria would be keen to go into the town - her last gasp of freedom before being confined to the convent - so he would have to orchestrate a scene, contrive a situation to get her alone.

Then he would pounce.

***

As the Conte Biancamano docked in Genoa and her passengers thronged the rails, eager to disembark and see all the wonders the ancient city had in store, Maria, Megan and the children, again in the borrowed carriage, stood along with them, excited by the prospect of shops, restaurants and beautiful architecture.

Salvatore stood apart from the crowd, watching Maria, his palms sweaty and his pulse quickening, knowing his moment had almost arrived.

Once the gangway was in place, the passengers alighted from the sleek ocean liner; the Liuzzi party amongst the first to set foot on the dockside before climbing into a waiting taxi. Salvatore, speaking in his native tongue, then instructed the driver to take them to a restaurant recommended to him by the ship's purser.

Neither Maria or Megan were especially hungry but Salvatore was most insistent, claiming that now his appetite had returned he was keen to enjoy the food of his homeland. The women knew it was pointless to argue, neither suspecting Salvatore's appetite was not truly for food but for something much sweeter.

They arrived at the trattoria which was a small, unassuming little place but the purser had assured Salvatore it was family friendly and the food was excellent. Once they were seated, the waiter delivered a basket of freshly baked rolls and three hand-written menus that listed the day's specials. Whilst the women pondered, Salvatore ordered himself the signature ravioli and a decanter of house red. Megan and Maria both opted for a light salad, not wishing to fill their stomachs before a busy afternoon's shopping.

Megan was wearing her one summer dress which she wore only on special occasions whilst Maria had opted for a pretty blue sleeveless one that perfectly set off her tan.

She looked ravishing and the beast stirred within Salvatore. Not long now.

The wine duly arrived and Falcone poured himself an extremely generous glassful. He took a sip and then purposely placed the glass down near the edge of the table, close to Maria's elbow. Maria, herself, was looking the other way, admiring her handsome son as he slept in the carriage, snuggled up next to Nate.

As Maria turned, her elbow knocked the glass over, spilling its entire contents of dark red Chianti all down her beautiful dress, just as Salvatore planned. She squealed and quickly stood up, grabbing a napkin to press against the huge red stain. But it was immediately obvious the dress was ruined and she was going to need a change of clothes.

By now, Salvatore was also standing and barking orders in Italian at the restaurant staff. Then he turned to Megan and said, very firmly, "Stay here. Eat your food and tend to the children. We shall return to the ship so Maria can change. We'll be back as soon as we can".

Alarm bells were already ringing in Maria's head, "No, no - I can go on my own. I won't be long. You stay and have your lunch - I'll be fine," she said to Salvatore, desperately hoping to dissuade him.

"No". He said. "I'm coming". And that was final.

As he spoke, the restaurant manager was fussing around him apologetically. Then, to add to the commotion, his wife appeared from the kitchens with a damp cloth and began trying, unsuccessfully, to soak up the stain.

Amidst the confusion and with her fear of being alone with Falcone rising by the second, Maria took advantage of his momentary distraction and swiftly slipped something off the table into her purse without anyone noticing. Just as a precaution.

Two minutes later a taxi, called by the restaurant at Salvatore's insistence, arrived and he and Maria jumped in leaving Megan alone with the children and fearing the very worst for her friend.

***

The dockside was empty now and the grand ocean liner was like a ghost ship sitting all alone in the harbour. The gangway was deserted and all the passengers had vanished into streets of Genoa. The crew were nowhere to be seen as the taxi pulled up alongside and Salvatore and Maria got out. "No need to wait," Falcone said to the driver.

Maria, who thanks to her father had been speaking Italian fluently since she was very small, said, "But I'll be quick - I'll only be a few minutes".

The driver seemed to hesitate, uncertain of what to do until Salvatore spoke again. "Go. We'll get another cab later".

"No—" Maria tried again, her eyes pleading with the driver to stay but Salvatore cut across her.

"Go - be on your way. We'll be fine". He said.

The taxi driver nodded and the car sped off leaving Maria alone with Salvatore on the dockside.

Feeling incredibly ill at ease, with Salvatore following very closely behind, Maria led the way through the warren of passages on the ship to her First Class cabin, somehow sensing what was in the mind of her father's assistant.

She was frightened and the fact the ship was so deserted scared her all the more. She was starting to panic, knowing if she screamed no one would come running.

As they turned onto the passageway leading to her cabin, Maria's stride lengthened as she tried to put some distance between her and Salvatore but he merely adjusted his pace accordingly.

Nonetheless, with her key at the ready, she unlocked her cabin door the moment she reached it and attempted to squeeze in quickly before Falcone could rush in behind.

But Salvatore was too close and he thrust the door wide, throwing her off balance.

Maria spilt into her room and fell to the floor, her purse slipping from her fingers and sliding out of reach across the carpet.

"What are you doing?" She snapped at Falcone, "Get out!"

"Oh, I'm not going anywhere, sweetheart. I've waited a long time for this and now I'm going to enjoy it".

Maria immediately saw the bestial look in his eyes and a shiver of dread ran up her spine. "Get out now or I'll scream," she demanded. "I mean it!" Maria was terrified and tears were stinging her eyes but she was angry too.

The loathsome figure of Falcone loomed over her prone form. "Scream all you like, honey," he sneered. "See if I care - there ain't no one around to hear".

"You bastard!" She spat, "What do you think my father would do to you if he knew what kind of depraved animal you are?"

"In case you haven't noticed, he ain't here either," Salvatore shrugged. "So how about you shut your mouth and show me what's under that ruined dress of yours, huh?"

"Go to hell you sonofabitch!" Yelled Maria, scrambling to get away on all fours and trying to reach her purse. But it was too far away and Falcone was immediately on her. He forced her onto her stomach and pressed his body down onto hers. "That's it, little girl," he whispered in her ear, "Struggle, see what good it does you".

He pawed her body before reaching down and pushing up her dress. Maria cried out, "No!" and fought like a demon, hitting out with her elbows and kicking with her legs, but he was too strong, too heavy.

"Get off me!" She screamed again. The tears were now streaming down her cheeks but she was wriggling and scratching like a wild cat in a bid to throw him off. She kicked out with her foot and the heel of one of her white sling-backs caught Salvatore painfully on his upper leg just inches below his groin.

"Bitch!" He yelled, releasing his grip on her for just a second as he clutched his injured thigh.

Maria used the momentary reprieve to slither out from under him, managing to get within touching distance of her purse before he was on her again.

This time she span onto her back and slapped him hard around the face but it only made him more determined as he forcefully pinned her down and slid his hand up her dress once more; images of Lucia, the girl he left for dead all those years ago, flashing into his mind, serving to excite him further.

Yet Maria was still fighting furiously to escape him, the knowledge she was about to be raped fuelling her anger. With renewed vigour, she wriggled and twisted and somehow found enough space to power her knee up into Falcone's balls.

He yelped and recoiled with pain, allowing Maria to slither a few more precious inches towards her purse.

Her hand seized upon it just as Salvatore grabbed her again. He clawed at her breasts, ripping the stained fabric of her dress to expose her bra as she fumbled frantically with the clasp of the purse.

Finally, it burst open and with relief her hand seized upon the steak knife she had taken from the restaurant.

Suspecting Falcone's wicked plans, she had slipped it into her purse, knowing she might have a need to protect herself.

Her instincts had proven all too correct and as Salvatore's eyes widened at the sight of her naked flesh, he felt the sharp stab of the serrated edged knife as it pricked his Adam's apple.

"Get off me you filthy sonofabitch before I kill you - and don't doubt for a moment that I won't!"

Salvatore froze as he felt the sharp point at his throat, instinctively knowing what it was. "Now hold on—" He began, but Maria jabbed it in a little further, silencing him instantly.

"Move!" She said. "Now".

"Okay, okay," said Salvatore, slowly climbing to his feet, his head held back, trying to avoid putting undue pressure on the knifepoint. Maria stood too, very carefully, so as not to give Falcone an opportunity to overpower her again, yet never once did she let the knife leave his throat.

Finally, they were standing, facing each other. She held the steak knife at arm's length, still pushed against his Adam's apple as a little trickle of blood ran from the sharp steel tip down to the collar of his shirt.

He was looking at her with defeat and fear in his eyes, but there was hate there too. He had squandered his chance and doubted he would get another, although there were still many miles to go before they arrived in Messina.

"Now get out", she snarled with disgust, "And if you ever try that again I swear I will kill you".

Salvatore backed away but as he reached the open door he smiled. "We'll see," he said.

Then a voice behind him said, "Everything alright here?"

Falcone turned to see a young officer standing in the doorway, his expression quizzical and concerned.

"Yes, thank you," said Salvatore, "The lady's had a small accident

40

with some wine I'm afraid. She was just about to change".

The officer saw the blood on Salvatore's neck and then the knife in Maria's hand. He also saw her bra through the torn and stained dress. She looked dishevelled and tearful and he read the situation instantly. "Are you okay, Miss?"

"Yes. I mean, I think so, thank you," she said, before adding, "But Mr Falcone is just leaving. Would you mind just waiting outside while I quickly change and freshen up - then perhaps arrange a taxi for me back to the town?"

"But of course," said the young officer, "It would be my pleasure". Then he looked knowingly at Salvatore, regarding him as the disgusting pig he was, and said, "I'll let you get on your way, sir. I can look after the young lady from here".

Falcone looked at Maria and then back at the officer. "Yes, thank you," he muttered before flouncing out of the cabin clearly humiliated and disgruntled.

Once he was out of earshot, the officer turned to Maria once more and said, "Take all the time you need, Miss. I'll be outside". Then, as an afterthought, added, "If you don't mind, I'll also arrange for someone to keep an eye on you for the rest of the trip - you never know when another accident might happen".

Maria smiled, conveying her understanding and gratitude. "That would be most welcome. Thank you."

The young officer then shut the door and she locked it behind him.

Then the tears came.

Chapter Three

With the awe inspiring sight of Versuvius looming ominously in the background, the Conte Biancamano at last sailed into the Bay of Naples. But as Maria stood at the rail, she did not appreciate the staggering beauty of her surroundings and instead saw only a life of solitude and heartache ahead.

The chance to escape had not yet presented itself and now, with their final destination so close, it seemed far less likely she would be able to.

Nonetheless, the young officer had been as good as his word and for the remainder of the voyage she had not been troubled by Salvatore even though he was an ever present feature of her remaining days on board. However, soon they would be in port and the last leg of this long journey would begin. In less than twenty-four hours they would be in Messina where she would be confined to the nunnery and her son would be on his way to a location unknown to her. Megan, too, would be lost to Maria; her one friend whom she had come to love like a sister in recent weeks would be returning to New York to start a new life. Maria, her baby and Megan scattered to the wind, lost to each other forever and all because of the twisted pride of Carlo Liuzzi.

After the ship had docked, a cab drove them to the railway station to catch their train onto Calabria where, upon arrival, they would board the ferry to Messina.

It was hot, even for late November and the air was still and heavy. Maria and Megan were perspiring as they struggled admirably with the children and cases; Salvatore resolutely refusing to help, his demeanour sour and morose. The trip had proved entirely fruitless and now he was eager for it to be over; any chance he may have had with Maria had all but evaporated and he held little hope for the situation to change now.

By the time they were all seated on the train and it began to roll out of the station, they were extremely glad of the cool breeze that filtered in through the open window. The carriage was deserted, so they made themselves as comfortable as possible and let the gentle rhythm of the train lull them to sleep.

It was Nate who woke first, late in the afternoon. He was hot and hungry and feeling thoroughly miserable in the stifling conditions of the carriage; the cool breeze now more of a warm wind as the train rattled along the tracks at considerable speed. He began to snivel and then he started to cry. Before long he was bawling loudly and Maria's baby, woken by Nate's hollering, had decided to join in too.

Everyone was awake now and the two women were fussing over the children. Indeed, even though it went against his boss' specific orders, Salvatore no longer cared if Maria had any involvement with her child or not.

He took the view that Liuzzi was not there and soon Maria would be parted from her sprog for good - the wrench probably all the more painful for her having known her son, so what could it hurt?

The incident onboard ship had caused him to lose all interest in his assignment and he had been in a foul mood ever since.

As the babies screamed, Salvatore pulled the brim of his fedora down over his eyes and tried to go back to sleep, attempting to ignore the awful din.

43

Nate, however, would not be calmed. Megan offered him her breast but he had worked himself up into such a state that he refused to feed. His cries were deep and loud and his little lungs were bellowing relentlessly. Megan was up with him, walking the length of the deserted carriage and back again, rocking him and singing to him trying to settle him down. But it was not working.

Maria, meanwhile, was consoling her own baby who, although not as loud as Nate, was voicing his disapproval equally well.

Salvatore was becoming more annoyed with every wailing cry and making his irritation abundantly clear with a constant stream of huffs and shrugs amid his growling displeasure.

"Can't you shut that goddamn brat up!" He finally yelled at Megan, snatching off his fedora and throwing it on the seat opposite. "A little bit of peace and quiet - is that too goddamn much to ask?"

Megan looked down at the floor, avoiding his gaze, not wishing to anger him further. "Sorry," she said meekly, "I'm trying, I really am."

"Yeah, honey?" Salvatore sneered, "Well not fuckin' hard enough!"

Maria glared at Salvatore, her green eyes flashing, "I'll thank you not to talk to Megan like that," she said, "and certainly not in front of the children."

"Ha!" Falcone scoffed, contemptuously, picking up his hat once more and plonking it down on his head, again pulling it firmly down over his eyes as he made a big show of going back to sleep.

Maria glanced over at Megan and nodded reassuringly although Nate was still squealing loudly, as was her own little boy.

"I think he might have a bit of tummy ache," whispered Megan in her soft Irish brogue, trying hard not to disturb Salvatore any further even though he was clearly not asleep.

"Bring him to me, let me try," said Maria, placing her own son carefully down on the seat beside her. "You can take care of this little man for a while - I think he's settling down a bit."

Megan smiled her thanks, knowing Maria was trying to protect her from Falcone's wrath and she wandered back down the carriage towards her friend. But, as Maria reached out her arms to take the child from Megan and she, in turn, held the baby out to her, Nate let out a ferocious belch and then vomited a stream of hot, white puke all over Salvatore's expensive hand-made suit.

Salvatore shot up, throwing his fedora off yet again, his anger erupting like Versuvius itself, just as Maria took hold of Nate. "You stupid Irish bitch!" He yelled, before slapping Megan hard around the face. She staggered backwards, stunned, but Falcone marched towards her and swiped her violently again with the back of his hand. This time she fell against a seat but raised her arms up to protect her face.

"I'm sorry, I'm sorry - please—," she cried.

But Salvatore was not to be put off and with his eyes murderous, he shouted, "You dumb fuckin' whore - do you know how much this suit cost?" Then he punched her full in the stomach with devastating ferocity.

Megan collapsed like a folding chair as she fell to the floor and curled up in a tiny ball, badly winded from the blow, unable to breathe.

"I'll kill you!" Falcone raged, "Just like we killed that schmuck husband of yours!" Then he kicked her, his foot connecting with her head, stunning her, but she could still hear him yelling. "Carlo told me to kill you as soon as we'd dumped the kid at the monastery - but who the hell cares if I do it a couple of days early!"

Maria had been unable to help Megan until she could safely bundle Nate into his moses basket but, once she had, she rushed to help her friend. However, when she heard Salvatore boasting about killing Nathaniel and then revealing he was supposed to kill Megan too, she was shocked to the very core.

Terror shot through her as she immediately thought of Armando. Had he been killed as well? Had he not been sent away as her father previously led her to believe?

It was as if a light had been clicked on in her brain and she suddenly knew the dreadful truth of it. How could she have been so naive? If her father was capable of banishing her and having Nathaniel and Megan killed then he was certainly capable of ordering Armando's death too. But she had to know for sure.

Suddenly, Maria was incensed, her body fuelled with rage and she leapt onto Salvatore's back; wrapping her arm around his neck and punching and kicking him with all her might. "You goddamn evil bastard!" She screamed, as Salvatore struggled madly to throw her off. "What about Armando? Did you kill him too?"

Yet at that moment Falcone managed to grab a handful of Maria's dress at the back of her neck. Then, exerting an immense amount of strength, he physically hurled her over his head. She flew through the air like a rag doll and landed with an awful crunch against a seat some distance away, squealing in agony.

For a moment she was still; stunned by the impact, however when she did eventually try to move a sharp pain shot up the length of her left arm. It was broken, and one of her ribs too, yet her green eyes were still aflame, her anger still boiling as she forcibly blocked out the pain. "Did you kill him?" She demanded again, staring unwaveringly at Salvatore. "Did you kill my love?"

Falcone smiled victoriously. What could it hurt now? Why not tell her the truth?

"No. I didn't kill him," he said, relishing the opportunity to hurt her more than physical violence ever could. "But your father did."

Maria suddenly felt sick but it made no difference as her father's vile lieutenant was clearly enjoying himself.

"Carlo hung Armando up in the garden store under the tennis courts and gutted him like a fish."

Salvatore smiled at the memory, "I watched as he sliced off your lover's balls," he said triumphantly.

Then he began to laugh as if it was some big joke and he had just delivered the killer punchline. "You wanna know what's even more funny?" he giggled, "The guy said he wanted to marry you. Can you believe it? Just as your old man was cutting off his balls, he actually begged to marry you! Now that takes balls - or it would've if he had some!"

Falcone then collapsed into a fit of hysterical laughter as Maria slowly, deliberately, climbed to her feet.

She stood and painfully walked to where the two babies lay who, remarkably, were now both silent and staring up at her with big, innocent eyes.

As Salvatore laughed, Maria reached for her purse and surreptitiously took out the steak knife that had been hidden there since the incident onboard ship. She took a firm grip on the handle then turned and charged forward. "You murdering bastard!" She screamed, fully committed to plunging the knife into Falcone's black heart.

But Salvatore had been a scrapper all his life and had beaten men twice the size and many times more dangerous than Maria. With lightening speed he grabbed her wrist and the knife span from her hand as he twisted her arm up and around her back before butting her on the forehead, knocking her nearly senseless, ending the attack almost as soon as it had begun.

The sound of the train running over the tracks changed slightly as they steamed over a bridge, the rhythm suddenly more high-pitched, more erratic, but Salvatore did not care. He was mad now, insane even, a wild look in his evil eyes as he grabbed Maria by the hair and jerked her head backwards.

"Yes, I'm a murderer," he growled, his voice like gravel as he stared at her without remorse. "I helped Carlo murder the chauffeur and in a minute I'm going to murder your friend - but right now I'm gonna murder you!" His boss' orders meant nothing to him at that moment, nor did the fact she was Liuzzi's daughter. The red mist of madness had descended and the violence that was never far from the surface had clouded his judgement.

Megan was still curled on the floor, her breath only just returning, but she had heard all Falcone said and she, too, was now filled with hatred and thirsty for vengeance after, at last, discovering Nathaniel's true fate. She tried desperately to get to her feet, to help her friend who had so bravely tried to help her. But her body would not respond quickly enough and she could do nothing but watch helplessly as Salvatore dragged the dazed Maria along the centre aisle of the carriage towards the door.

Maria was a dead weight as she hung heavily in Falcone's grip, her legs still unresponsive as she slowly began to rouse.

Salvatore was ranting as he dragged her, "I've just about had enough of you, honey," he raged. "And convent or not, you're gettin' off this train now!"

The sweat was dripping off him as he spoke and his previously slicked back hair was now hanging wildly around his thin face as he struggled with her along the rickety railway car.

Upon reaching the end of the aisle, he flung open the carriage door, causing a ferocious blast of wind to rush in, the force of it nearly knocking them both over.

That, coupled with the deafening noise of the clickety-clack as the wheels sped over the tracks, spurred Maria's body into life. Suddenly her feet found purchase and her fight returned but it was almost too late. Salvatore had her positioned perfectly in the door opening and was preparing to push her forcefully off the train and into the clear blue water of the estuary many feet below.

Megan was now crawling towards the doorway, frantically hoping to prevent the awful thing that was about to happen. Her hand fell on the steak knife and she grabbed it up, but the distance was too far and there was no hope of stopping Salvatore in time.

Maria wedged her feet either side of the door and clung desperately onto the framework with her one good hand; her other arm limp and useless. With Falcone in front of her and a clear drop behind, Maria knew she was just seconds from being ejected from the train and plummeting over the edge of the bridge to an almost certain death.

It was too much of a drop, the water too far below and she felt sure no one could survive it. She hated Salvatore, wanted him dead, but now, with the wind tugging at her body, trying to pluck her from the fast moving locomotive, she pleaded with him, hoping to find just the tiniest shred of humanity in him. "Please," she shouted over the thunderous noise of wind and motion, "Please let me see my son, I beg you!"

Once more Falcone smiled; an evil, vicious grin. "Oh, you'll see him," he sneered triumphantly. "You'll see him in Hell!" Then he kicked her firmly in the centre of the chest, jettisoning her from the train; her body hanging in clear space just for an instant before dropping like a stone into the void below.

Megan watched aghast from where she now stood having managed to at last climb to her feet just a few tantalising steps away.

As Maria was ejected from the train, Megan briefly saw the look of absolute horror on her battered face before she suddenly disappeared from view.

Staring in disbelief, it took Megan a few seconds to register what she had just witnessed, but slowly the dreadful reality dawned and, as impossible as it seemed, she realised with gut-wrenching sadness her friend and mistress had actually gone.

***

Salvatore hung out of the carriage door for a long moment, his greasy hair flapping wildly in the breeze as he tried to see where

Maria entered the water, but he could not as the train had already left the bridge and was speeding back onto solid ground.

Disappointed, he closed the door and turned back into the carriage, which was when Megan thrust the knife deeply into his shoulder.

Falcone looked at her in disbelief, then down at the wooden handle sticking out of his shoulder, the steel buried completely within him. He staggered slightly and stumbled forward but Megan had not finished.

Back in Ireland, her father had been a champion bare knuckle boxer and had regularly given her lessons in how to defend herself just in case she should ever need to. Now she did, and even though she was a slender, waif of a woman she knew how to throw a punch and she balled her hand into a fist and let one fly.

The punch landed in the exact place she aimed it, right where her da had showed her. The shot stung Falcone and the surprise was clear to see in his eyes. He reached out to grab her, but this time she was ready for him and she punched him twice more in quick succession with a blistering one-two jab that caused his nose to crack and his head to spin. Suddenly Salvatore was seeing stars and he toppled backwards, landing badly with his back against the door and his legs sprawled out awkwardly in front of him.

"I'll slit your fucking throat you Irish whore, just like Carlo did to your husband", he slurred, still dazed. "Just you wait".

"So it was all a big lie?" Megan hissed, already knowing the answer but unable to prevent herself from wanting to know the truth of it. "Nathaniel didn't die in a car wreck? He didn't plummet to his death on Mullholland Drive like Mister Liuzzi said?"

"Ha!" Sneered Salvatore as he eyed Megan with gleeful disdain, "You stupid little woman. How ridiculously naive you are. No, your husband didn't die in an accident - he died under the tennis court at the mansion with his eyes as big as golf balls as Carlo slit his throat from ear to ear. I held him down until he stopped screaming - until the only noise we could hear was that of his filthy Irish blood as it splashed all over my brand new shoes!"

Megan had heard more than enough and without even thinking about it as she bent down, took hold of the knife handle and twisted it viciously. Salvatore cried out in pain, tears erupting from his eyes. "Aaaaaah!" He wailed in agony, "I'm gonna fucking kill you!"

With him writhing in pain, Megan placed her lips close to Falcone's ear and said, "I don't think you'll be doing anymore killing today, laddie!"

Then she reached up, opened the door and Salvatore cartwheeled out of the carriage backwards. Hitting the ground hard, his body somersaulted over the grassy scrub verge, bouncing several times before at last coming to rest.

Megan hung out of the door to watch, just as Salvatore, himself, had a few minutes earlier, the wind billowing through her hair.

She was anxiously searching for any signs of life as the distance grew between her and the man who had killed Nathaniel and Maria. But she saw none.

There was no way she could have seen, as Falcone lay face down in the dirt, the slightest twitch of his little finger.

Eventually, when Salvatore was nothing more than a tiny speck, she shut the door. It was only then she noticed she was still holding the knife, its blade slick with bright red blood. Revolted by the sight of it she quickly opened the door again and threw it out as far as she could, then after closing the door once more she went back and sat with the children.

They were both sleeping.

Chapter Four

Hollywood, California 1951

It had been two and a half years since Maria's tragic death, which Carlo Liuzzi had been led to believe was the result of suicide.

He had been told she jumped from the train bound to Messina, taking her son, Carlo's grandson, with her.

Maria had reportedly tried to take Salvatore with her too but somehow, miraculously, he had survived. Although his injuries had been severe and included a large scar on his chest where Maria had evidently tried to kill him with a knife, missing his heart by a hair's breadth.

But he had lived and after spending several months convalescing in hospital in Messina he had at last returned to America to give Carlo a full explanation of what had happened.

Yet he knew Liuzzi would kill him if he ever discovered the truth of what had actually transpired so Salvatore conceived a fabricated version of events which Carlo might find somewhat more palatable.

In his fictional account, Maria had become emotionally unstable during the sea crossing and had concocted a desperate plan to escape, somehow convincing the weak minded Megan to help her.

Her plan, as told to Carlo, was to overpower Salvatore then jump with Megan and the children from the train, which Carlo thought to be ludicrous in the extreme, especially with two babies. But Salvatore said Maria had been acting manically and irrationally for many days prior to that and this was just the culmination of her increasing insanity - brought on by the disappearance of her lover and the imminent loss of her child. As Falcone related this, Carlo squirmed only slightly, his conscience not hindered by long-lasting bouts of remorse.

Nevertheless, Salvatore went on to relate how Maria and Megan had attacked him on the train; how Maria produced a knife from nowhere and tried to kill him. Naturally he had attempted to defend himself and during the ensuing struggle managed to eject Megan and her child from the train. They had, according to Falcone, fallen to their deaths as the locomotive clattered over a bridge.

But Maria would not give in. In a state of utter madness she had picked up her baby and run towards the open carriage door, ready to jump into nothingness, to kill not just herself but the baby, too. Salvatore said he rushed after her and grabbed her by the arm but still she struggled. As he desperately fought to save her they all spilled from the train and into a deep ravine.

The last thing Falcone said he remembered was seeing Maria and the baby plummeting towards certain death in the narrow estuary hundreds of feet below. And then, for him, everything went black.

As he told Carlo this wholly invented tale, Salvatore wept; his performance worthy of an Academy Award as he attempted to convey his deep regret at the death of his best friend's daughter and his failed efforts to save her.

However, the remainder of his tale was mostly true. He went on to say that the next thing he knew he was in the back of a truck where he briefly regained consciousness before waking up in a hospital bed in Messina, having been out for the best part of a week.

Upon regaining consciousness, he had pleaded with the

orderlies and the local authorities for any news of Maria - more for his own sake than hers - but no trace of her could be found, although he did not reveal how relieved he was to hear this.

Liuzzi listened to his friend's story without interruption and when it was finished he thought for a long time. As his mind ran through the story again, he scrutinised Salvatore, regarding him carefully as his long time friend snivelled apologetically in the opposite chair. Carlo studied the walking stick and the sling upon which Salvatore still relied, as well as the poorly constitution which had dogged him since the incident in Italy.

Clearly his injuries were genuine and his ill health no act, but something about the story did not ring quite true; Maria's madness for one, that just did not seem like her, she was stronger mentally than that. Also, the fact she jumped from the train with her child, again did not sound like something his daughter would do. But Carlo had no proof upon which to base these doubts and no matter what his reservations there was no questioning Salvatore's remorse or the injuries he sustained whilst apparently trying to save Maria.

Salvatore had been a good and reliable friend and in honour of this Carlo had no choice but to believe him. But the trust he had in Falcone now would be limited and only time would tell if it had been previously misplaced.

At long last, Carlo finally looked up at Salvatore and said, "Maybe it was for the best." Liuzzi then stood and walked to where his friend sat and placed a hand firmly on his shoulder. It was a gesture that could easily have been mistaken for kindness but Salvatore knew it carried more sinister overtones; this time he had been given a reprieve but it would not do to give Carlo a reason for doubt again as next time he would not be so forgiving.

In the two and a half years since that day, Salvatore had done his utmost to regain his friend's trust but was still not convinced he had been successful.

As for Liuzzi, himself, he had not so much as mentioned his daughter since hearing Falcone's rather unconvincing explanation of her death.

Today, however, would have been Maria's birthday and he could not help but think of her.

He lay alone in the darkness of his enormous bedroom. It was morning but the curtains were still drawn. He had awoken after a fitful night's sleep and had lain there in his navy monogrammed silk pyjamas beneath the black satin sheets of his huge oak four-poster trying to ignore the significance of the day's date.

Indeed, Carlo had been trying to think of anything other than that; trying to put the memory of her and any regret he may have had about his treatment of her out of his mind. He knew from bitter experience it served little purpose to linger on the past. It was done and that was that, or at least that was what he kept telling himself. But still the persistent niggle remained.

However, on this, her birthday, Carlo always thought of his daughter; especially how she was as a little girl and the love he felt for her then would flood his empty heart. But those thoughts would do him no good and he made a conscious effort to expel them from his brain and concentrate on matters of the present.

At which point, Mildred knocked on his bedroom door and entered without waiting for a response. She was carrying a breakfast tray. "Good Morning, Sir!" she said brightly before placing the tray down at the end of the huge four-poster bed and crossing to the heavy velvet drapes. She threw them open and the sun burst into the room silhouetting Mildred momentarily and highlighting her hour glass shape.

She reminded Carlo of a young Jane Russell; dark eyes, large breasts and long legs - an enticing combination especially with the maid's uniform emphasising her very womanly figure; smart black dress pulled tight at the waist by a lacy white apron and a little white cap perched on top of her glossy brunette tresses to finish the look perfectly. The sight of her instantly extinguished any lingering thoughts of Maria and ignited ideas of an entirely different nature.

Sitting up in bed in his blue silk pyjamas, Carlo watched her hungrily as she picked up the tray again. "Where's Edmund?" He asked. It was the question he asked whenever he desired her - not that he really gave a damn where her husband was as it had never bothered either of them before.

"What? No 'good morning?'" She teased, her eyes flashing with mischief as she placed the tray down firmly on his lap.

"Good morning." He said, sardonically, as she bent over the bed and made a pretence of plumping his pillows. However, he completely ignored the cooked breakfast and neatly folded LA Times on the tray before him and instead ran his hand up the back of her thigh, her skirt crumpling up as his fingers travelled higher until, at last, they found the gartered tops of her nylons and her naked bottom beyond; her lack of underwear fuelling his desire even further.

Mildred smiled slightly, her excitement building as it had done on many such mornings prior to this one.

"Now where's Edmund?" Carlo said again, but this time with more impatience.

Without speaking, she again lifted the tray and backed away from the bed, forcing him to move his hand. This time she placed the tray down carefully on his dressing table. "Oh, he's washing the cars," she said, snapping open the top button of her dress and returning to the edge of the huge bed, "He'll be hours out there. I just don't know what I'll do in the meantime."

Then Mildred kicked off her shoes, hitched up her skirt and climbed onto the bed.

As she straddled Carlo Liuzzi and lowered herself onto him, it was not long before she was screaming with utter delight; her cries of pleasure echoing around the walls of the vast mansion with neither she nor her lover caring a jot what either the staff or, indeed, her long-suffering husband might think.

***

Edmund paused for a moment as he polished the Cadillac, his face set with resignation as he listened to his wife's lustful screams which could be clearly heard outside on the driveway. It was longer than he could remember since she had made those sounds with him, reminding him all too painfully he had lost her for good.

Furthermore, aside from what the rest of the household might think of Mildred's scandalous behaviour, she clearly had no regard for his feelings on the matter. Worse still, such was his obvious insignificance, Liuzzi went about his business as if nothing had changed even on the occasions when Mildred had been with him just minutes before.

But Edmund was not a confrontational man and not a particularly brave one either. Mildred had often called him 'spineless' and that was what he was proving himself to be.

Everything he did seemed to irritate her. Their conversation had all but dried up and any sort of intimacy was a thing of the past. But Edmund felt powerless to act. He was never a particularly sexual man and not what anyone would describe as dynamic but Mildred had been attracted to him once and their sex life, for what it was when they first met, was relatively rewarding - although it was always her that instigated things in the bedroom.

Mildred and Edmund Peyton came from a small town in Iowa - a nothing little place where there was very little work to be found. Mildred had been very popular at high school amongst the boys - who regarded her as extremely pretty and just the right side of slutty, but most of her admirers were not in her league physically and she mostly just toyed with them to pass the time.

Edmund, although not ambitious was a relatively handsome young man with wavy blonde hair and finely chiselled features.

57

He was also reputed to be rather well endowed. This made him something of a catch amongst the local girls and for Mildred, too, who was also keen to find out if the rumours of his God given gifts were true. So, not one to be outdone by her friends, set her sights squarely on him.

Before long they were a couple but with money scarce, Edmund thought it might be a good idea to give Los Angeles a try in a bid to earn a living and Mildred, desperate for a better life, eagerly tagged along.

Agreeing it would be cheaper if they lived in one apartment not two, they got married and moved in together. Briefly they were happy and Mildred fell pregnant very quickly but living in LA was expensive and they needed both their wages just to make ends meet. Neither of them could give up work to look after the baby.

So, when their baby girl was born, they reluctantly sent her back to Iowa to be raised by Mildred's mother until they were in a secure enough position financially to look after her properly.

Shortly afterwards, Mildred and Edmund were offered the maid and chauffeur jobs at the Liuzzi mansion and for a time, life for the two of them was good. They were earning a decent living and managing to save a little money each week. Before long, Mildred asked Liuzzi if their daughter could come and live with them at the mansion and much to their delight he agreed. Carlo already had designs on Mildred and was happy to agree to anything if it might get her into bed.

Indeed, she was already giving him signals that led him to believe she would be more than willing.

Needless to say, within eighteen months Edmund and Mildred's marriage had crumbled and she had begun an affair with their employer. What is more, Carlo seemed as enamoured with Edmund's daughter as he was with his wife and Edmund, himself, had been left out in the cold.

All he was good for now was to look after their child whenever Mildred could not, which was something, even she had to admit, came naturally to Edmund. He was an excellent father and his daughter was his one joy; his only reason for living.

Her name was Ava.

***

Mildred Peyton was unlike any other woman Carlo Liuzzi had ever known. He was even beginning to think he might be in love with her.

She was undoubtedly more than just another conquest. His position as a studio boss ensured him a steady stream of ambitious young starlets who were willing to throw themselves at him in pursuit of fame, but Mildred was different.

Firstly, she was not intimidated by him, which most women seemed to be. Furthermore she did not just fall at his feet like the others did; she made him chase her, made him do all the running, even though she clearly laid the breadcrumbs which gave him the impetus to pursue her. He, of course, knew she was toying with him but that's what made it all the more delicious when he finally caught her.

Aside from that, though, she was strong, ambitious and intelligent as well as extremely sexy. She may only have been a maid but Mildred would be at ease in any social situation without being the slightest bit fazed. In fact, she would thrive.

Edmund had been merely a means to an end and he was now of little use and of even less importance to either Mildred or Liuzzi. However, his daughter was. Which was the second thing which attracted Carlo to Mildred.

Ava was Maria at the same age. At two and a half she was the beautiful little girl Maria used to be, all wavy dark hair and pretty pink bows with boundless energy and a giggle that was just a delight. Every time Carlo looked at her he got a warm feeling inside and

59

could not help but spoil her just as he had with his own daughter all those years before. Yet, when Maria was a little girl Carlo had been busy building his empire and could not spend the time with her he wanted to but with Ava he could get that time back. Now he was rich and successful time was easier to find.

He had a romantic vision playing in his head of him, Mildred and Ava becoming a family; a second chance to put right what once went wrong. Mildred was not weak like his first wife and Ava was still young enough to be moulded by him - the mistakes of the past could be rectified this time around, he was sure of it.

Soon, it would be Ava's birthday, too. In just a few short months she would be three years old and Carlo had promised her a pony, causing her little face to light up with the biggest smile. Mildred was delighted, too, but when she told Edmund of this he merely shrugged giving her cause to sneer at him derisively. How else did he think Ava was ever going to get a pony?

It was the catalyst that spurred Mildred to move into the main house with Ava, leaving Edmund to spend his nights alone in the small apartment above the garage.

Ava had been given her own room in the mansion, decorated in pretty pastels and stocked with more toys than she could ever play with. Her bed was huge and she felt a little bit scared in it and longed to be back in the apartment with her daddy but Mildred had told her to stop snivelling and be grateful for the lovely room she had been given.

Mildred, herself, also had her own room and was still, ostensibly, the maid but she rarely fulfilled the duties she had been employed for and the rest of the staff had taken to treating her deferentially because of their employer's obvious feelings towards her. Secretly they regarded her as something of a conniving slut but they all valued their jobs and knew to upset Mildred was to upset Liuzzi himself.

Along with her own room, Mildred had been given a completely new wardrobe full of stylish clothes and only wore her uniform occasionally for appearances sake. However, Carlo liked her to wear it in the mornings when she took him his breakfast as he loved to see her in her crisp black dress and starched white pinafore.

The lack of underwear had been her idea but it was a very welcome omission as far as her lover was concerned and he had forbidden her to wear it ever again which had brought an even greater intensity to their lovemaking.

The passion between them frequently ignited at the merest touch and whenever it did Mildred was always ready, much like she had been on that particularly morning.

However, when at last they were spent, laying satiated and exhausted on the bed, Mildred turned to her lover and said, "Carlo, my darling, I could definitely get used to this."

Liuzzi smiled and thought for a moment. "You know what?" He finally replied. "I could too. So why don't you marry me?"

***

The house had been abuzz with the news ever since it was announced. Hushed conversations between the staff had taken place all over the mansion - although always well out of ear shot of either Mr Liuzzi and Mildred - or, indeed, Mrs Peyton, as they had now been instructed to call her. It was all so deliciously scandalous but they had to be careful; heads would undoubtedly roll if their employer got wind of what they were saying.

Things had happened swiftly upon Mildred's acceptance of Carlo's proposal and preparations for a huge wedding were soon well underway. She had set about planning the whole extravagant event, proving to Carlo, if he ever had any doubt, she could thrive no matter what was thrown at her and adapt to any new change of circumstance with skill and efficiency. She, of course, had stopped being 'the maid' the moment she said 'yes' and immediately took to her new role as lady of the house like a duck to water - happily barking orders to her former colleagues as if she had been born to it.

The small, seemingly rather insignificant fact that Mildred was already married had hardly been seen as any hurdle at all.

Carlo Liuzzi had summoned Edmund to his very grand, very masculine study; the very heart of his power base where his chauffeur could scarcely feel less at ease, and spelled out the situation to him in no uncertain terms.

"Ah! Edmund," he had said, as his fiancé's husband shuffled in, still wearing the smart grey uniform and polished leather boots of his traditional chauffeur's livery. "Sit down a moment would you?"

Edmund doffed his cap and did as instructed whilst Carlo finished off some paperwork on the desk in front of him, obviously far too busy to give the other man his full attention for the moment.

As Liuzzi signed this and that and studied various documents before him, Edmund sat uncomfortably in his seat, uncertain of exactly why he had been summoned but fearing the worst until his employer finally looked up and removed his black framed reading glasses.

"Ah, yes, Edmund," he said, as if suddenly remembering he was there. "Good, thank you for coming."

Edmund nodded and attempted a slight smile, Liuzzi intimidated him, scared him somewhat, and this situation was not something he was at all comfortable with. He was quite happy showing his back to Liuzzi whilst chauffeuring him around Beverly Hills with a thick pane of privacy glass between them, but face to face in these austere, grandiose surroundings, he felt truly out of his depth and extremely overawed.

Edmund also knew how taken Liuzzi was with his wife and how those feelings were reciprocated. Mildred had never felt the need to tiptoe around the subject - indeed the whole house knew what was going on. Edmund, however, had preferred just to bury his head in the sand, to concentrate on his duties and ignore the issue. As long as he had Ava that was all that counted, he did not need to know the rest.

"Now look here," Carlo continued, "The fact of the matter is this. Mildred and I are in love and we intend to be married as soon as possible. I know that may seem brutal but it's simply the way it is."

Edmund's face reddened with embarrassment as he squirmed in his seat, praying this ordeal would be over shortly. He wanted to clamp his hands over his ears to block out the sound of his employer's voice but he had no choice but to listen.

"Put simply, she needs a divorce and she needs it quickly," added Liuzzi, "And I hope I can count on you not to stand in her way."

For the first time Edmund looked up and stared into the hard chiselled face of the powerful man before him, sitting there in his finely cut handmade suit and surrounded by the opulence of his immense success. Carlo's face was emphatic, to disagree was not an option.

"Yes, of course," Edmund muttered, unable to maintain eye contact any longer and quickly averting his gaze. "I mean, that's to say, no - no, I won't stand in the way."

"Good man," Carlo said, "I knew you would see the sense of it."

"Will I, er, will I still have a job here?" Edmund added, suddenly afraid that he would lose that too, along with any chance he might have of still playing a permanent part in Ava's life.

"Sure, why not?" Liuzzi said, already moving onto other matters as he slid his reading glasses back on and pulled a stack of important looking documents towards him, "A good chauffeur is hard to find. Unless of course you're gonna have some problem with addressing your ex-wife as Mrs Liuzzi and respecting her new position as your boss?"

"Er, no sir, none at all," Edmund said almost apologetically.

"Good, then it's settled," replied Carlo, unscrewing the lid of his gold-plated fountain pen and bending to the work in front of him. "Please - shut the door on your way out, I don't wish to be disturbed anymore."

"Yes, of course, sir. Thank you," said Edmund springing to his feet and heading swiftly for the door.

Just as he turned the handle to make his escape, Liuzzi looked up from his paperwork and snatched off his glasses once more. "Oh, Edmund! Just one other thing…"

"Yes, sir?" Edmund said, cracking the door in his haste to be gone.

"We'll discuss what's best for little Ava at a later date, alright?"

"Yes, sir," Edmund replied hesitantly, his heart suddenly sinking as he contemplated the ominous implication. "Of course."

"Excellent," said Liuzzi. "Now shut the door behind you, there's a good man."

***

Nevada state law allowed couples to get 'quickie' divorces in just seven days; the only stipulation being that they had to be resident in the state for a minimum of six weeks. So, Carlo uprooted his whole household, including Mildred, Ava, Edmund and Salvatore, and transferred them all to a ranch just outside Las Vegas for six weeks in order for the divorce to be granted as soon as possible.

When it was finalised and Mildred was a free woman once more, everyone headed back to Hollywood to prepare for her and Carlo's big day.

On the morning of the wedding, Salvatore Falcone sat in a lounge chair on the wide veranda at the rear of the mansion trying to keep warm even though it was beautifully sunny outside. He was finding it difficult to breathe and trying hard to keep his cough at bay. Salvatore had been plagued by long bouts of pleurisy since his time in Italy, brought on, doctors thought, by the trauma to his chest, courtesy of the knife Megan had thrust into it. This debilitating illness affected him in many ways; sometimes he just had a painful cough and a sore throat; at others he could be bed ridden for several days with a high fever, night sweats and violent diarrhoea. But most of the time he just suffered from an annoying shortness of breath. Although the illness had caused his weight to plummet and his clothes now hung off his boney physique.

Aside from the pleurisy, Salvatore had fractured his wrist in his fall from the train. The break had been so bad that all the nerves in his right hand had been severed, rendering it completely useless. A cracked hip would also ensure he walked with a limp for the rest of his life.

Ultimately, he was lucky to be alive. But he did not feel particularly lucky as he silently watched an army of staff put the finishing touches on what was sure to be a spectacular garden wedding.

On one side of the vast lawn, carpet was being laid over the freshly cut turf and fancy white chairs were being set out in rows to accommodate the two hundred or so guests, which would comprise mainly of movie stars, studio executives and a few very close friends. Beyond that was an ornate rose covered canopy where the happy couple would exchange vows, and in the background an enormous marquee had been erected which was in the process of being elaborately decorated. A whole team of wedding personnel paraded in and out with beautifully over-the-top flower arrangements, magnificently garish candelabras and mock roman sculptures. To Salvatore's amusement, a couple of very effeminate looking men were chasing several white swans which had decided to make a last minute dash for freedom. *What on earth had the world come to?*

On the other side of the lawn, Salvatore could see Carlo Liuzzi standing beside a pure white Shetland pony, holding a very uncertain looking Ava in the fringed, rhinestone saddle. The little girl looked absolutely adorable in her satin and lace bridesmaid's dress although her eyes were beginning to fill with tears as the pony refused to stay still beneath her.

The new maid, dowdy and unattractive in appearance, as purposely chosen by Mildred, was standing in close attendance keeping a careful watch on her new charge.

Carlo Liuzzi looked every inch the rich, Hollywood success story in his immaculately cut tail suit which was perfectly displayed on his tall, broad frame. His ruggedly handsome face was tanned and his black wavy hair was turning a silvery grey at the temples which gave him the air of an Italian Clark Gable.

Liuzzi had it all; looks, power, wealth - a beautiful woman about to become his wife and a new daughter to replace the one that had turned out to be such a disappointment.

How was it he had everything when Salvatore had nothing?

Falcone watched his friend as he laughingly lifted Ava off the pony and put her down safely on the ground. The very picture of a happy family man.

But as Salvatore watched, dressed, too, in his wedding tail suit, he knew the suave and charming image Carlo portrayed was all just a show and deep down he was a monster. Just like him.

The very same man who was speaking so sweetly to Ava was the very same one who had strangled his first wife to death; the same man who had cut off Armando Calabrese's balls before slicing open his gut and spilling his intestines; and the same one who had slit Nathaniel Kelly's throat. Indeed, Carlo Liuzzi was no kind benefactor at all but an evil, dark, twisted individual who had clawed himself up from the gutter using whatever means necessary.

Knowing only too well of Carlo's murderous temper, Salvatore had thought long and hard about returning to California after the incident in Italy for fear of what his friend's reaction might be. After all, no matter how much he changed the facts to suit his own needs, the simple truth was he had been responsible for Maria at the time of her death.

In the end though, Salvatore decided to roll the dice and put faith in their friendship and fortunately his gamble had paid off. He felt certain though that Carlo had not been entirely convinced by his tale and knew he had lost much of Liuzzi's trust because of it. He also knew it would take a great deal of effort to win it back.

But Salvatore was not the man he once was. Three years earlier he had been fit, healthy and in the prime of his life with one eye on the Liuzzi fortune and a keen desire to be its next keeper.

Now though, he was afflicted with ill health, had a gammy leg and a lifeless hand. The fight had left him, or at least temporarily and his designs on Carlo's fortune had, for the time being, faded along with his friend's trust.

In short, the madness of his acts in Italy had ruined his life leaving him permanently damaged and filled with resentment for all the good things Liuzzi had.

However, as Carlo left Ava in the care of the maid and headed back towards the veranda to join him, Salvatore put a smile on his face and slipped easily back into the role of 'friend.' Only time would tell if he ever became a trusted one again. And if he did, well maybe by then his health would have improved and his current apathy might have lifted.

"She's beautiful isn't she?" Said Carlo, referring to Ava, his Italian accent almost non existent now after years of vocal training.

"She is indeed", replied Salvatore, his accent still very much in evidence. "Not sure about the horse though - I've seen bigger rats!"

"Haha, it's not a horse, Salvo, it's a pony - but yeah, you might be right".

"Hey, horse, pony, they're all the same to me - just big dumb animals that leave a trail of shit wherever they go!"

"That's true. But have you ever seen Ava more happy?"

Salvatore had scarcely seen Ava at all as he did everything he could to keep out of the brat's way, but from where he was sitting she had looked far from happy when sitting on top of the pony. However, he thought it best not to mention it and said instead, "No, I haven't." Then added, "But I thought you were gonna buy the kid a nag for her birthday - when she was three you said, so what happened? That's not for a couple more months is it?"

Suddenly Salvatore saw Liuzzi's mood change, as if a switch had been flipped in his brain and the jovial, happy Carlo transformed into the psychotic, crazy one. When dealing with him, it was a very fine balance and Falcone immediately knew he had pushed the conversation too far.

"What happened?" Carlo echoed. "I couldn't resist, that's what happened. She's a beautiful little girl, this is my wedding day and I thought I'd buy the kid a little present - that okay with you?"

"Hey, Carlo, that's great, just great - you're right, she's a beautiful kid - you're a very lucky man. The horse was a fantastic idea."

"It's a fucking pony!" Yelled Liuzzi with unexpected violence, the loud outburst causing the people working on the wedding to stop and stare at the two men on the veranda. "How many goddam times you gotta be told? And are you sure it's a fantastic idea? I mean, God forbid I have to ask your fucking permission!"

Salvatore raised his hands in defeat, "Sure, Carlo, of course. You're right, I'm sorry, I didn't mean to—" And then the coughing began. Deep, breathless coughs that prevented Falcone from saying anymore as he bent over in his chair and hacked away at the floor, little specks of blood spattering the flagstones and his shiny black shoes. Quickly he produced a clean white handkerchief from his pocket and brought it up to his mouth to catch the spittle.

"Ah, that's right, cough it up, goddamit! Just when you're about to apologise. It really sticks in your fucking throat doesn't it?"

Liuzzi was looking at Falcone incensed, the red rage of anger still burning within him, his temper not yet spent. But Salvatore was too occupied with the coughing fit that had suddenly overtaken him to pay attention. This only served to infuriate Carlo more and he was just about to launch into another manic tirade when he noticed bright, wet blood on Salvatore's handkerchief. Then more of it on the floor and on his shoes.

As quickly as it erupted, the anger left him and he became instantly attentive, his voice suddenly full of concern.

"Oh, my dear friend, I'm so sorry. Are you alright? Please tell me." He begged.

Salvatore looked up at him and nodded although his eyes were watery and blood was dribbling down his chin. But still the fit did not relent as he continued to cough and fight for breath.

"Quick, one of you!" A shocked Carlo shouted at the effeminate pair chasing the swans, "Fetch this man a glass of water - do it now, this second!"

Both men ran off in the direction of the house, eager to comply with the very angry, very frightening looking gentleman on the veranda.

By the time they had returned, each of them holding a glass of water, Salvatore just about had the coughing fit under control.

"Thank you," Carlo said, once more charm personified. "Now please, don't let us keep you from your duties." The two men took their cue and hastily made their retreat, leaving Liuzzi and Salvatore alone once more.

"Here, my friend," Carlo said, proffering Salvatore a glass, "Drink. It'll make you feel better."

Salvatore took it eagerly, still wheezing heavily but only coughing slightly now in between breaths. "Thanks," he said hoarsely before taking a sip. Then another.

"I had no idea this disease of yours affected you so badly," Carlo remarked.

"Only sometimes. When I get excited," said Salvatore, dabbing his mouth with the bloodied hankie. "It's been worse. Just something I've got to live with I guess."

Carlo had not seen first hand the effects of the illness that regularly seemed to ail his friend. He had known him to spend days in bed, or be out of breath sometimes but he had dismissed it all rather off-handedly, thinking Salvatore may have been feigning to somehow prove how much he had suffered in his attempt to save Maria. But the blood on the handkerchief had not been faked, it was real and it had made Carlo think again about what his friend had been through.

Carlo sat with Salvatore as he drained the glass of water and studied him as he drank. It was the first time he had really looked at him since he had returned from Messina almost three years ago when he was still reliant on a walking stick and a sling. When Carlo, himself, was still numb from the death of his daughter as he fought to suppress any emotions he may have felt about her passing. He had known then that Salvatore was ill and his injuries were severe but somehow in the intervening years he had dismissed them; forgotten about them even. And in suppressing his emotions he had also suppressed his trust.

Looking at his friend now he suddenly felt guilty.

Salvatore had always been lean and slender but he was skinny now, just a bag of bones really. He looked pale and ill, his pallor grey and sickly. Then there was the dead hand; useless and unmoving. Previously Liuzzi had not really considered this a disability as it looked normal enough and did not seemed to hinder too much but upon reflection he realised what an awful injury it was. He imagined for the first time how much his own life would change if he only had the use of one hand.

He had never truly believed Salvatore's tale previously, about how Maria died, but now he felt forced to reconsider. Surely no one

70

would go through so much if they did not have to. Had he misjudged his old friend? Perhaps maybe, in retrospect, he had.

"Salvo", he suddenly said, "You must forgive me".

"For what, for that?" Replied Salvatore, referring to Liuzzi's recent outburst. "Hey, please, don't worry about it - I was way out of—"

"No, Salvo, you misunderstand," interrupted Carlo, "You must forgive me for the lack of respect I've shown you over the last three years and for the doubts I've had about you. I've done you a huge disservice, my friend, and for that I humbly apologise."

Salvatore was stunned and had no clue as to where this was coming from. Carlo's behaviour had always been somewhat erratic and his mood swings were legendary but this - where on earth was it coming from and why now?

"Er, thank you, Carlo", Falcone said, a little dumbfounded. "That's very generous of you and, of course, I accept".

"No, that's not good enough," Liuzzi said, a brilliant idea flashing into his mind. "Not only must you accept but you must stand beside me at the wedding this afternoon and be my best man".

"But I thought you and Mildred had agreed not to have a best man?" Said Salvatore, still reeling with shock.

"We had, but I'm changing the plan." Carlo was extremely animated now as the idea blossomed in his head. "Now say you'll do it. As my best and longest friend I demand you say yes."

"Er, yes. Yes, of course I will," grinned Salvatore at last standing and shaking Carlo's hand. "I'd be very proud to indeed".

Liuzzi pulled his friend towards him and embraced him warmly. "Thank you, my friend. You do me a great honour," he said.

Salvatore hugged him back. He said nothing but the cogs in his brain were already whirring. Perhaps it would not take so long to regain Carlo's trust after all.

Chapter Five

Hell's Kitchen, New York 1955

The small group of youths were laughing and smoking as they congregated in their usual spot just a block away from the Hudson River and a stone's throw from the bright lights of Broadway.

42nd Street may only have been a short distance from where they stood but it was a world away from their lives and their reality.

These boys, who ranged in age from as young as ten to as old as eighteen, were the 'Westside Dukes' and their small patch of turf extended from the Hudson in the West to 10th Avenue in the East. Eight square blocks which each one of them would willingly give their lives to protect.

The neon sign of 'Red's Diner' flickered intermittently like it did every night as the boys gathered outside. Tonight there was just ten of them but sometimes there could be as many as thirty or forty. Their full strength was somewhere around seventy but they were rarely seen in force. Nonetheless, their youthful appetites certainly kept Red busy. Although not tonight it would seem.

Teenage street gangs were a frightening new phenomenon of New York and the Dukes were just one of many. Amongst them were the Mau Maus of Brooklyn and the Fordham Baldies from The Bronx; Harlem had the Dragons and Washington Heights the Jesters to name but a few. Indeed, in addition to the Westside Dukes, the residents of Hell's Kitchen also had the Lincoln Playboys and the Majestics to contend with.

Between these rival factions fights or 'rumbles' were commonplace and the authorities were finding it increasingly hard to keep a lid on a pot that was forever boiling over.

But tonight everything was calm.

It was approaching midnight and the cobbles on the blackened streets were still wet from a brief summer shower but the air had remained warm, almost unbearably so. The only building illuminated amid the dark tenements and empty alleyways was Red's Diner which was lit up like a Christmas tree and shone like a beacon of hope in this very poor, very working class area of Lower Manhattan.

Inside the diner the over-worked air conditioning unit was turned up high and the juke box was turned down low as Red swept the floor and emptied ash trays. His white apron was covered in grease from a day spent flipping burgers and feeding the fryer. But the evening rush had died down at around seven and it had been unusually quiet since.

However, it was relatively cool in the restaurant after the stifling heat of the kitchen and he made the most of the insufficient air con as he pushed the broom around the black and white chequered floor.

All the booths were empty and Red was thinking about closing up for the night; he was tired and it had been a long, gruelling day. The Dukes had not seemed particularly hungry tonight and the earlier rain had kept other customers away.

Then, just as he was thinking of turning the sign on the door over from open to closed, he heard the tinkle of the bell above the door and felt a rush of warm air as Rebel and Double J entered the diner.

"Hey, Red," said Rebel, the taller, pug-faced one, "You still open?"

Rebel, at eighteen, was the undisputed leader of the Dukes and

73

a seasoned campaigner. No one argued with him as he had proven himself many times in battle and had an enviable 'rep' amongst his peers who feared and respected him in equal measure. The same went for Double J, his younger brother by a year. John James O'Riordan or 'Double J' as he was known, was the more restrained of the two, some would say the more sensitive, particularly amongst the girls who also found him eminently more attractive. But it was Roddy or 'Rebel' who called the shots.

The O'Riordan's were second generation Irish just like all the Westside Dukes. Whereas Patrick 'Red' Tierny, on the other hand, was the real deal; an ex-prize fighter and ex-racketeer, he was a Dubliner born and bred and as such was held in high esteem amongst the boys.

A predominantly Irish community populated much of Hell's Kitchen and there was perpetual conflict with the influx of Puerto Rican and Italian immigrants who were also making it their home. Particularly amongst the youth.

To the Dukes, Red was a kind of father figure and his diner represented a little piece Ireland. Therefore it had become the very centre of everything they strove to protect, whether Red had asked them to or not. But he liked the boys, at least most of them, and regarded them as good lads even though they were what he rather generously described as a bunch of scalawags. He chose to ignore the knives, bats, pipes, studded belts and, in some instances, guns they regularly used to hurt or maim people. Indeed, in his time, when he was a younger man, he, himself, had been much like them and had fought tooth and nail for what he wanted so he did not begrudge them a little rough and tumble. Besides if they helped rid the neighbourhood of all the spicks, wops and niggers that were moving in by the boat load every day then what could it hurt?

"Sure boys," replied Red genially, in his gravelly Irish brogue. "Come in, siddown, what can I get you on this fine hot, summer's

74

eve?"

"I'll take a strawberry shake," said Rebel, "And a double cheeseburger with fries."

"Sure. And you, Jay?"

"Can I just get a soda, Red?" Replied Double J. "I just ain't hungry tonight, it's too damn hot to eat."

"No problem. They'll be coming right up boys!" Said Red, glad of some customers at last and feeling revitalised by the prospect of putting a few dollars in the register. "Meggie!" He yelled, calling to the only waitress still on shift, who had been busily wiping down the counter and waiting impatiently for midnight when she could at last turn her apron in for the night.

"Yeah?" She replied, looking up, her pale blue waitress uniform damp under the armpits and clinging to her back.

"Get these gentlemen their drinks would you? I'm gonna go and fire up the grill!"

"Sure, Red, will do. Same as usual boys? Strawberry shake, Reb, and a soda for you, Jay?" She asked them.

"Yeah, thanks Meggie!" The boys' said politely in unison. As well as being highly thought of by Red, Meggie was also born and bred in Ireland so therefore warranted their respect.

"You want me to walk you back again tonight, Meggie?" Asked Double J. It was the same question he asked her every night and she always answered it the same way.

"If it's not too much trouble. That would be kind, thanks."

"Hey, no trouble," said Rebel, speaking for his younger brother, "It's late and you gotta stay safe, right."

"I have at that," smiled Meggie.

However, there would be little chance of her not being safe on Dukes turf but Rebel liked to flaunt his authority.

Nevertheless, Red did not like her walking home on her own after midnight and had quietly asked Rebel if he could always make sure one of the boys was available to accompany her. He had agreed, although none of the others ever had to be asked as Double J had willingly taken on the role of her nightly protector.

As for Meggie, she found it comforting to be so well looked after.

Turning away, she opened the freezer to get the ice cream for Rebel's shake, leaving the door open a few seconds longer than absolutely necessary to enjoy the benefit of the delicious chill.

After nearly six years at the diner, it still felt nice to be called 'Meggie'. It was what her da used to call her when she was a little girl back in County Clare and what her late husband occasionally called when he was feeling playful or amorous.

She had grown to like the name Meggie Malone now, which she had chosen for herself after arriving back in The United States. In fact, it seemed almost inconceivable she had ever been called anything else. But she had.

For the first twenty years of her life she had been called Megan Kelly.

Deep down it was who she still was and she would never forget the terrible events that had brought her to this place in her life and who was responsible for it.

***

Six years earlier, Megan had arrived in Messina with two babies, a suitcase and a small amount of money which she had found amongst Salvatore's belongings. This was just enough to buy her passage back to America and sustain her for a very short time afterwards.

Briefly she considered returning home to Ireland but there was nothing for her there now as her beloved mam and da were both dead and her two older brothers had each been killed in the war.

She was alone with two young boys to bring up and New York seemed as good a place as any to make a fresh start. Regardless of what had happened to Nathaniel, she still believed America was where her future lay, so arrived back in New York in the early Spring of 1949 using the new name of 'Meggie Malone'.

She thought it unlikely Carlo Liuzzi would concern himself with someone so lowly as her but he had ordered her death just a few months earlier so she considered it prudent not to use the name 'Kelly' any longer, just in case Liuzzi ever tried to trace her.

So, with a new name and barely enough money left for two months rent, she moved into the cheapest little apartment she could find in the largely Irish part of Hell's Kitchen on Manhattan's West Side.

Deeply engrained racism was endemic in 'The Kitchen'. The Irish, Puerto Rican, Italian and black communities all felt completely boxed in by one another. Combined with the lack of jobs and cramped living conditions it all added up to a spicy mix of anger and resentment that frequently boiled over into violence.

So for Meggie, living in a completely Irish building, on an almost exclusively Irish block, having such an obviously Italian child was not ideal and did not go unnoticed by the other tenants.

Nevertheless, desperate for work, Megan set out to find any kind of legitimate employment that would put food on the table. But, with no child care available, she had to take the two little boys with her to interviews which did not impress prospective employers. Megan found they were either put off by the sight of two screaming infants or, more commonly, just the sight of the very dark haired, very olive skinned one.

Before long, she was down to her last few dollars and beginning to wonder how on earth the three of them were going to survive. As it was, Nate was already worryingly under weight.

Then, purely by chance, she was passing Red's Diner when she saw a sign in the window asking for a waitress, which was when her luck changed.

Red took an immediate shine to 'Meggie' and loved little Nate at once. He was not so enamoured by the more Italian looking child next to him but when Megan explained his mother had died in childbirth and she had taken the boy in to raise as her own, Red's racist heart thawed somewhat and he gave her the job.

The pay was not great but she got to keep her tips and although Red was bigoted and racially intolerant he was also a surprisingly kind and understanding boss.

Red had even introduced her to other mother's in similar situations - those who had been widowed in the war and some whose husbands worked shifts - who helped each other out with child care. This meant whenever Meggie was at work, someone was available to look after her two boys. In return she would look after their children when she could. But it was clear from the start the other women thought little of her. A young woman such as she with no husband and two babies clearly by two different fathers, one an Italian of all things, was not someone they were eager to be associated with no matter what sob story she told.

Many of the young mothers disliked taking care of Meggie's adopted son and would often leave him neglected whilst they attended to the needs of Nate or the other Irish children in their care. Indeed, many was the time Meggie had returned home from a long shift at the diner to find her Italian son's diaper had not been changed all day.

Neither was it just the little boy who suffered. Meggie's reputation was in serious question too. People did not bother to ask how it was that a young Italian baby came to be in her care and just assumed she had given herself willingly to the boy's father. And how could any good, God-fearing Irishwoman lie with a filthy Italian let alone give birth to their offspring?

Meggie found herself spurned by her detractors and life in the tenements became extremely difficult. She found herself with very few friends and to be thought of as a slut or a fallen woman was incredibly hard for her to deal with - especially as she was so devout. However, even though raising an Italian child had been problematic almost from day one, Megan had never once considered giving him up. On the contrary, it did not matter that she had not given birth to him, he was her son now and she loved him every bit as much as she did Nate.

Meggie knew it was Maria's wish to give the child an Italian name, but along with all the other hardships the boy would have to endure in this entirely Irish block, she could not in good conscience comply with that wish. It would be just too much provocation for those already set against him. But he would need a name nonetheless.

Meggie decided to name the boy after her elder brother, Daniel, whom she had always been particularly fond of. He was kind and strong and a loyal protector, just as she hoped her adopted son would be for her and Nate whom he was already much bigger than.

So the child became Danny Malone; a very Irish name for a very Italian looking child but it was Meggie's hope it would help him fit in.

And in time it did.

Almost six years on from arriving back on American soil, Meggie and Nate had become accepted members of the Irish community and without the hindrance of an Italian name to constantly remind people of his Mediterranean roots, Danny had finally been accepted too, albeit rather cautiously.

With Red's help and support, people had come to learn that Meggie was not an evil harlot after all but a kind and thoughtful woman who had made the best of the difficulties she had striven to overcome. Furthermore, those who had been so set against her when she first arrived in Hell's Kitchen had now all reversed their opinions and most had become good friends. Nevertheless, those same women who had so badly misjudged Megan would be very quick to turn against her again if she did not conduct herself in an appropriate fashion.

As a devoted catholic, Meggie was acutely aware of this, which made her increasingly more sinful thoughts seem all the worse.

Indeed, sometimes, for a woman on her own, life in Hell's Kitchen could be very lonely and any distraction was a welcome relief even for a religious and God-fearing woman such as Megan.

Furthermore, temptation was never very far away and for Meggie, this temptation took the form of John James O'Riordan - The Westside Dukes' very own Double J.

***

Meggie was twenty-six and Double J was only just seventeen yet he had been wooing her for the past six months and her resolve was slowly crumbling.

Jay was not a boy by any means; he had seen and done things in his life that put Meggie's very sheltered existence to shame. His sexual exploits alone made him far more experienced than her who had known only Nathaniel in that way.

But she could not help but be flattered by Jay's attentions.

Meggie knew that Red, too, held a torch for her and would make an extremely willing suitor. He had never made a secret of the fact he admired her and seemed to assume she would one day be his wife, although she had never given him reason to think such a thing. On the contrary, she had tried to put him off but nothing seemed to work and his affection for her only seemed to grow stronger.

Red was in his fifties and thick around the middle. His face was weathered and lined and his hair was grey. He represented stability and maturity, almost in a fatherly way, but he did not, in any way, represent excitement or fun and she could certainly not imagine ever going to his bed.

Although Nathaniel had been much younger, he too had been a very straight arrow. But she had loved him and admired him and had been extremely happy before fate intervened. Now, however, after seven years of hardship and of raising two young boys alone, she wanted some excitement, maybe even a little danger.

As such, she found herself thinking more and more of Double J and what he would be like as a lover, even though she knew it to be wrong in the eyes of God.

Since becoming a mother, Meggie had filled out somewhat and her figure had become more curvaceous. In addition, her formerly wan complexion now had more of a healthy glow and even though she was not a natural beauty she had blossomed into an attractive young woman with flowing red hair which she kept neatly tied in a bun.

Jay, in comparison, was tall and lean without an ounce of fat; his muscles hard and tight. He had light brown hair which was greased back at the sides and quiffed like Elvis Presley's. A cigarette and a smile were never far from his lips and he exuded the confidence of invincible youth. Forever in jeans and sneakers he always wore an emerald green letterman jacket with white sleeves and a white 'D' on the left breast that each of the gang members wore. The jackets had the owners name embroidered on the opposite breast and the words 'Westside Dukes' arching across the shoulder blades in white, gothic lettering.

Street gangs, although from rough neighbourhoods and poor families liked to look good and each gang had its own identity - whether it be matching jackets, sweaters, hats or waistcoats - very often custom made. And the Dukes were no different. Their jackets were prized possessions; their gang colours, and they would never be seen on the streets without them.

Double J in particular was obsessive about his appearance and was forever running a comb through his slicked hair or checking his reflection in a store window. But it was all part of his considerable charm and Meggie, even though she had tried hard not to, was finally

81

falling for it.

Jay was also extremely good with Nate and Danny. Especially Danny whom he took a real shine to, seemingly unconcerned about the lad's Italian heritage - but it would not do to let Rebel see as he was not so easy going as his brother. Indeed, Rebel ran the gang with military precision and had laid down a strict set of rules that specifically forbade members from fraternising with other ethnic groups.

Gangs, no matter what creed or colour, were mostly racist, particularly the leaders who sometimes also bordered on the deranged, and Rebel was a prime example.

Rebel, of course, knew about Meggie's younger child and respected what she had done. She was a good, honest catholic woman with a decent heart and he did not judge her for taking the boy in. In fact, he liked Meggie very much but that did not mean he had to have anything to do with her child and, in his view, neither should Double J.

But Jay felt differently and what Rebel did not know would not hurt him so whenever he was away from his brother's scrutiny Jay was his own man.

Sometimes, when he was allowed into Meggie's cramped apartment, he would play with Danny for ages. Jay liked Nate, too, but he always seemed much more fragile, more breakable than his sturdier younger brother who was always up for a bit of rough and tumble. He was bigger than average for a child of his age and already stronger than he knew.

But it was Meggie with whom Jay was primarily interested. There was no doubting Double J was a ladies man and he certainly made the most of it, but Meggie was different. She was not silly and giggly and prissy like the others. She was older, more mature; more sensible. Even though she had not told him much about her former life, Jay sensed there was sadness, too, and he had an overwhelming desire to comfort and protect her.

Of course, it did not hurt that he was easy on the eye and charmingly witty either; just two reasons why Meggie's resolve was weakening.

It was past one in the morning by the time Meggie actually left the diner. Red was still there as business had picked up a little after midnight with a few of the other Westside Dukes wandering in to order food, but he could manage well enough on his own so told Meggie to get off home.

As requested, Double J was accompanying her. The rain had long since moved away and the moon was now clearly visible in the cloudless sky; its light playing off the windows and fire escapes of the towering tenement blocks. Wet laundry that had been caught in the shower had been left out to dry in the warm summer's night and hung in the cat's cradle of lines that criss-crossed between the darkened buildings, the clothes hanging from them limp and lifeless in the still air.

They walked in easy silence along the cobbled streets, passed the mesh enclosed basketball courts, the small family run stores and dilapidated tenements that made up the majority of Dukes turf; the small patch of real estate that represented all that they had. There was nothing else. At least not for most.

But for Jay and Meggie there was the chance of something new, no matter how ill-advised or mis-matched they may have been. Something was building and they both sensed it.

Meggie was tired tonight; weary from her shift and not particularly talkative but she was content to be there with Jay beside her and did not resist when he took her hand softly in his. It was the first moment of intimacy they had shared and the significance of it was not lost on either of them.

Eventually they came to a halt outside Pat Flanagan's butcher's shop which was on the ground floor of Meggie's building. She lived six floors above in a modest little apartment that was reached by a narrow and unforgiving flight of stairs.

"Want me to come up?" Jay asked as he stood facing her, smiling wickedly and already knowing the answer to his question.

Meggie looked up into his kind brown eyes, genuinely tempted for maybe the first time and smiled back. "No. I don't want you to come up. Nate and Danny will be asleep."

"Hey, that's okay. I won't wake them up if you won't," he grinned.

"Sure you won't, you great clumsy lummox. Any excuse to play with those kids and you'll use it."

"It's not the kids I was hoping to play with," said Jay, looking down at her meaningfully.

"Hmm," she replied softly, "I sort of guessed that. You do know I'm eight years older than you don't you? Practically an old maid."

"So you've told me. Many times - and you're nothing of the kind. Besides, I don't care. I think maybe I—." Suddenly he choked on his words and looked slightly embarrassed.

Meggie stared at him sharply. "What? What is it that you think?"

Jay was suddenly lost in her face, drinking her in as her innocent blue eyes searched his features for a meaning. "I think I love you," he said at last.

"You do?" She said huskily.

"I do," he replied, bending towards her upturned face which was now just inches from his.

"Oh my," she said a second before his lips touched hers.

They kissed tenderly for a moment, each tentatively relishing what they had secretly imagined for many weeks. Then, his arms were around her waist pulling her close and her hands were at the back of his neck guiding him, keeping him where she wanted him as the passion ignited and their kissing became more urgent.

As his probing tongue wriggled into her eager mouth thoughts both delicious and sinful flooded her brain. She knew what had started in that moment could only end in trouble down the line yet still she submitted herself willingly, deciding to worry about the possible repercussions some other time.

Chapter Six

Cadiz, Spain 1955

The sumptuously appointed Hermes IV circled the private airstrip as it prepared to land; the famous Matador motif painted red on the plane's gleaming silver tail fin.

Diego Del Toro, multi-millionaire owner of the Matador Hotel chain, paused his monologue for a moment as he nervously fastened his seatbelt. Then, when it was secure, he turned back to his secretary and resumed dictating the last letter of the day.

As the plane began its final approach, Diego shut his eyes and gripped the arms of his luxuriously upholstered leather chair. Flying was not one of his favourite pastimes but it was a necessary evil. With a business empire as large as his, and with hotels in locations as far apart as Berlin to Bombay and from Manilla to Monaco, it was the only efficient way to travel.

To make it more bearable he had bought the large, four-engined Hermes and had it completely re-fitted to suit his specific needs whilst, of course, using the finest materials and craftsmen available. No expense had been spared and the sleek interior cabin of the airliner now included two bedrooms, two bathrooms, a large galley, a spacious lounge area complete with bar and movie screen and a fully equipped office.

However, none of this made Diego feel any easier as the plane touched down on the tarmac and rumbled noisily along the runway; his fingernails buried deeply in the armrests.

Thankfully, it came safely to a complete halt and Diego could at last relax.

Even though the Matador Headquarters were based in Cadiz, this was an unscheduled visit. Instead of being there, Diego should have been in Waikiki opening another Matador hotel but his plans had changed at the very last moment following a phone call from Cadiz.

Miguel Degollado had contacted him at the Geneva Matador with the news he had been waiting to hear for the last seven years and his heart had soared with delight. So rather than flying from Geneva to New York, en-route to Waikiki as planned, he had flown directly to Cadiz.

Within minutes of landing, Diego was in the back of his personal limousine, speeding from the private airfield towards the ancient city just a short drive away. The hospital and, more importantly, the recently constructed 'Del Toro Medical Centre,' was located in the newer, more modern part of the beautiful old town and lay in lush, exotic parkland amongst the giant trees supposedly brought to Spain by Columbus from the New World.

But today, Diego could not have cared less about the surroundings as all he could think about was getting to the hospital and her.

***

Seven years earlier, Diego, then aged just twenty-five, had been holidaying on his family's three-hundred foot yacht, *Corrida*, in the Mediterranean. It was intended to be a preparatory trip in advance of him taking control of the Matador Corporation; a position he had inherited after his father's fatal heart attack some weeks before, which had effectively made Diego one of the richest men in the world - and one of its most eligible bachelors.

However, no matter how ready he was to take on the responsibility, having been groomed for it from an early age, he was still struggling to come to terms with his loss. If he could have traded all the huge resources he now possessed to have his father back then he gladly would have. But sadly he could not.

As it was, the enormous yacht had just up-anchored and was preparing to get underway as the sun rose on another glorious Mediterranean morning when it was flagged down by a fishing trawler out of Palermo; the crew calling frantically for help.

The captain of the Corrida immediately heaved to and upon hearing their tale thought it best to wake Diego who was still asleep in his quarters.

Bleary-eyed and wearing a robe over his silk pyjamas, Diego arrived on deck; his dark hair unbrushed and his sharp jawline rough with stubble.

"So, what's going on here?" He said, pushing his glasses up the bridge of his nose, "How can I be of service to you gentlemen?"

Upon hearing his words, the small group of burly fishermen, decked out in their greasy yellow oilskins, together with several Corrida crew members in their crisp, spotlessly white uniforms, parted before him to reveal what they had all been looking at.

Diego stared in disbelief, temporarily dumbfounded by the sight before him. But as he rallied his thoughts, the captain of the trawler stepped towards him and removed his wooly hat deferentially, as if in the presence of royalty.

"If I can explain, sir," he said in Italian, but Diego was fluent in several languages so could easily understand.

"Yes, of course, please do," he replied in the same tongue.

The captain then proceeded to explain how his trawler was headed for the deep waters off the tip of Africa to hunt for tuna when it had encountered a large mass of flotsam floating across their bow. They were about to take action to avoid it when one of the crew saw something which he thought resembled a body.

Carefully they came up alongside and pulled the mass of broken debris towards them with a boat hook to get a better look. Sure enough, as the crewman had thought, amongst the mangled netting and broken remnants of what appeared to be a small vessel was the bedraggled, sodden corpse of a young woman.

Gently they pulled the body on board before setting the flotsam adrift once more. However, as they lowered the dead girl onto the deck; her dress torn and filthy and her soaked skin almost black with dirt, the same eagle-eyed crewman who had originally spotted her floating on the ocean suddenly cried out with amazement.

"She's alive!" He declared triumphantly. "Look, she's breathing!"

However, the trawler was in the middle of the ocean, miles from the nearest port, racing against time and tide to catch their haul of tuna from which the much needed profits would help feed their families for several weeks. They could not turn back, they had to push on, but that did not solve the problem of what to do with the half-dead young woman laying unconscious in the stern.

Then, at first light the next morning, the captain of the trawler saw the Corrida on the horizon and knew precisely what he had to do.

By the time the captain had finished relating his tale Diego had regained his composure and was now kneeling down beside the young girl. The trawler men had cleaned her up a little but she still looked grey in pallor and her long dark hair was matted with filth and detritus.

Nevertheless, grey and filthy or not, she was still the most beautiful creature Diego had ever seen.

Miraculously, a thin gold necklace still hung around her neck with a tiny pendant attached. He was not to know, but it had been a Christening gift from the girl's mother and she was never without it. Diego picked it up and examined it carefully; a picture on the face depicted the Virgin Mary holding the baby Jesus. On the back was an engraving covered with green slime from the sea and impossible to read. He rubbed it with his thumb, wiping it clean, enabling him to see the inscription clearly.

It said simply; *To Maria with love.*

***

Diego immediately took responsibility for the girl, whom he now assumed to be called 'Maria' from the inscription on her pendant.

He also thanked the fishermen and assured them he would do everything in his power to see that she lived.

Safe in the knowledge he would be as good as his word, they set off once more whilst Diego instructed the captain of the Corrida to set a course for the nearest port. This turned out to be Sfax in Tunisia where Maria was transferred immediately to hospital by ambulance.

The hospital found her to have a broken arm and collar-bone, four fractured ribs a dislocated shoulder and numerous cuts and bruises which were all treated and re-set as necessary. However, Maria remained unconscious throughout and further tests revealed her to be in a coma. She had clearly sustained some kind of head injury and although not life threatening, the doctors could not say for certain when, or even if, she would regain consciousness.

Yet this mysterious girl provided Diego with a much-needed distraction from the grief of losing his father and it inspired him to put all his efforts into taking care of her.

So, in the weeks that followed, he had Maria transferred to Cadiz where he hired the very best medical staff to give her twenty-four hour care. He specified she must have fresh flowers in her room every day and have her long dark hair brushed each morning and night.

As often as he could and at least once a month, Diego made time in his busy schedule to visit her in Cadiz, demanding to be notified immediately of any change in her condition.

Whenever he stopped by, Maria always looked the same, her beautiful face fresh and clean and her eyes closed as if she was merely sleeping. He would talk to her and share his thoughts, mostly about anything which popped into his brain; business, the latest hotel project; his purchase of the Hermes IV and progress of its re-fit. He somehow found it relaxing.

He would also discuss his feelings and over the weeks, months and years that followed he began to realise he was in love with her and probably had been since the very first moment he set eyes on her.

In time, he paid for a new wing of the hospital to be constructed specifically for the care of victims of coma and their families. Upon completion, Maria was given her own suite and her own personal physician, Dr Miguel Degollado, who was a world-renowned coma specialist.

Degollado was a good man and Diego was certain Maria was in excellent hands. However, the doctor was not one to give false hope, so when he telephoned Diego in Geneva on the eve of his trip to Waikiki, there was no mistaking the news to be anything other than truly miraculous.

Indeed, after seven long years, Maria had finally awoken.

***

At first Maria did not know her own name and it was only when she was shown the inscription on the necklace which still hung around her neck that she learnt it. However, the name was as alien to her as the surroundings in which she found herself or the language the nurses were speaking. She was confused, muddled, and was having difficulty forming basic sentences. Her muscles had weakened and her mobility was limited. What is more, it would be several weeks before she would be able to walk and even then possibly not strong enough to do it unaided.

91

All of this, according to Dr Degollado, was only to be expected and completely normal for a patient who had been in a coma for so long. He also found it encouraging that Maria's brain was functioning within the desired parameters and there were no obvious signs of impairment or retardation, which upon Diego's arrival at the hospital, came as very welcome news.

He was met at the entrance by Degollado and updated on Maria's progress as they walked, taking note of everything the doctor said and asking pertinent questions as and when necessary. Over the years, Diego himself had become something of an expert on the effects of coma so nothing Degollado told him came as a particular surprise. But what no one could have known until Maria actually awoke was how badly her brain had been hurt and what, if any chance there was of her leading a full and normal life.

As it was, her prognosis was good and she was responding extremely well to treatment. But she would need time to recover fully and it could be years before she regained all she had lost. She had absolutely no knowledge of who she was or from where she came and no idea how she ended up floating amongst a mass of torn netting and wrecked sea debris somewhere in the Mediterranean.

Although she did not speak Spanish, Degollado's most important patient did understand English, Italian and French and, even though she could only string a few words together at present, she spoke each with equal proficiency. Yet knew not why.

Because of this it was difficult to determine even which country she was from. Maybe when she was able to speak a properly cohesive sentence, in either tongue, then they would all find out more. But for now it was enough to know she had all her faculties and had, at last, taken her first tentative steps on the long road to recovery.

As Diego and Miguel Degollado arrived at Maria's private suite, Diego suddenly stopped outside the door to take pause. Trying to control his nerves, he ushered the doctor ahead of him, saying he would join him in a moment. Degollado nodded his understanding, knowing the importance of this moment for the young man beside him, whom he had come to hold in the highest regard over the years. Then he opened the door and left him alone.

Diego Del Toro was far from most people's idea of the typical tycoon. He was well-educated certainly and extremely privileged of course; he also dressed in the finest clothes and lived in fabulous style in houses all over the world. But he was no playboy and not prone to a rich man's acts of whimsy - although his obsession with Maria was an exception to the rule.

If anything he was an intellectual. A deep thinking, quiet man, more bookish and thoughtful by nature than a tough boardroom battler. But he had an edge of steel and a streak of icy determination that made him very formidable in business. Indeed, since his father's death, Matador had positively thrived under Diego's masterful helmsmanship and its share price had almost quadrupled. He had diversified the company's interests and now as well as the hotel chain Matador had large stakes in shipping, newspapers and the automobile industry. It also owned an American television network and was seeking the right opportunity to expand into the potentially very lucrative movie business.

Diego was slender in frame and of medium stature, he had a mop of untameable dark hair that never seemed to sit neatly on his head - maybe because he was forever running a hand through it; a mannerism that betrayed his underlying social unease. Attractive and boyish in appearance with sharp, studious features, he wore black horn-rimmed spectacles which he polished regularly with his tie; a habit that was yet another sign of his natural awkwardness. However, at his heart, Diego was a kind and considerate man who had garnered much respect from his employees and the business world alike since his father's passing.

But none of that mattered at present and as he stood outside

Maria's door he suddenly felt a little foolish.

He was in love with a woman who had never even looked at him; never spoken to him. A woman from he knew not where - who could be married, or engaged, or who may even be a mother. For seven years he had taken care of her, providing everything he could to make her life more comfortable whilst she slept, even though she was oblivious to his very existence.

But that was about to change.

Without any further ado, Diego swept a hand nervously through his hair, took a deep breath to steel himself, then pushed open the door.

***

Diego slipped into the room as discreetly as possible, positioning himself in the shadows against the back wall behind Doctor Degollado who was standing in front of Maria's bed flanked by two nurses, who in turn were busying themselves with various things, and a junior doctor who was taking notes and hanging off every word the great man said. For a moment Diego thought he had managed to enter unseen, his presence unnoticed, but as the doctor spoke Maria's attention turned from Degollado to the awkward, slightly scruffy looking young man standing behind him.

Embarrassed, Diego searched the floor and every corner of the room, trying everything he possibly could to avoid her gaze but finally he could not resist the temptation and at last he looked up and stared directly into her large green eyes, momentarily entranced by their beauty.

Her dark hair was neatly brushed as it tumbled in loose curls around her shoulders and for the first time she looked not only awake but unbelievably alive. Her eyes were bright and inquisitive and her face was full of colour. Yet the most remarkable change was that she was no longer still and lifeless but alert, curious and aware.

More specifically, she was aware of Diego and briefly their

eyes met before Miguel Degollado spoke up in broken English. "Ah, Maria," he said, following her gaze. "May I introduce your saviour, Señor Diego Del Toro, the man who rescued you and the one who built this facility to enable your care." A small ripple of applause spontaneously erupted from the two nurses and the junior doctor making Diego wish the ground would open up and swallow him whole.

"Please, please," he said holding up a hand to quieten them, "It was nothing, really. Please stop."

The applause died and Diego stood there with his face bright red, suddenly the centre of attention and feeling very foolish indeed. "I'm sorry," he said. "My apologies for interrupting, please carry on." He turned and made a rush for the door, eager to be out of the room to hide his acute embarrassment; to go somewhere where he could quietly die. However, as his hand reached for the door handle a small, hoarse voice spoke up.

"Señor Del Toro?"

Diego opened the door, pretending he had not heard but then the voice spoke again, this time slightly louder. "Señor Del Toro, please, wait."

Diego stopped in his tracks and slowly turned.

Maria was looking at him again, this time her eyes brimming with tears. "Señor Del Toro," she said once more, clearly straining to speak from so many years without practice, "Thank you. Thank you so much. You've been—," she stopped and corrected herself, "—you are extremely kind."

Diego smiled bashfully and ran a hand through his unruly hair. "Please Señorita," he replied quietly, "It is nothing. It is my pleasure. The very least I could do."

"You saved my life," said Maria.

Diego shrugged awkwardly, "No more than any man in my position would do I'm sure."

"I disagree. But thank you again."

Diego forced a shy smile, acknowledging her thanks. "You are comfortable?" He said, changing the subject.

"I am, yes. Very."

"That is good to know, Señorita - and you are being looked after well by these fine people?" Diego gestured to the assembled medics.

"Extremely. Thank you."

"Good, good. Excellent," said Diego, wishing he could find more words to say but feeling very conspicuous with all eyes upon him. "Then I wish you a speedy recovery, Señorita. Now if you'll excuse—"

"Maria, please," she insisted.

"Pardon?" Queried Diego.

"My name is Maria, or so it seems. Please, I would like it if you would call me that."

"Diego smiled again. "Of course. And I am Diego."

Now it was Maria's turn to smile but she was tiring and she sunk back into her freshly plumped pillows as the nurses scurried about her, fussing with her blankets and smoothing her sheets. "It was nice to meet you, Diego. Please, come and visit me again soon. I would like that."

"As would I," said Diego. "Until then, I leave you in excellent hands." He then nodded curtly and rushed from the room, his face still flushed with embarrassment but his heart bursting with joy.

***

It was two whole weeks before Diego dared to go back.

In the intervening time he had cancelled almost all of his appointments, sending his personal assistant, Juan Pablo Clemente, in his place. Clemente was a trusted confidant and a good friend - he was also a better and more confident public speaker than Diego could ever hope to be so Matador's reputation was in safe hands.

Diego, meanwhile, had taken to working from his main office in Cadiz, in between trips to the hospital where many times he had intended to visit Maria but had always lost the courage to do so. Each time he had ended up just chatting with Miguel Degollado and receiving status updates from him. And the news was encouraging.

In the fortnight since Diego had last seen her Maria's progress had been steady and Dr Degollado was particularly pleased with the results. Maria's voice was now much stronger and time had shown her to be more fluent in English than any other language. She had also responded well to physiotherapy and was getting stronger everyday in the gymnasium. Her arms and legs were still extremely weak and she could not yet walk unassisted, indeed, she almost had to learn to walk all over again as the memory of how to do it seemed to elude her. Nonetheless, she was able to manoeuvre herself quite easily in a wheelchair and with the use of a walking frame was able to get dressed and use the toilet without help.

Basic functions were having to be re-learnt, like buttoning a dress, tying a ribbon in her hair and eating with a knife and fork. Such simple, every day things but Maria had to master them all over again. It was infuriating and exasperating but she never complained and just set about each task in turn.

She also still suffered from spells of confusion and sometimes had difficulty grasping what had happened to her and how long she had been lying in her hospital bed. Seven years of her life had gone in the blink of an eye and accepting that was proving a difficult pill to swallow, as was not knowing who she actually was.

This was all completely normal and she was doing exceptionally well under the circumstances. Time would ease her confusion and help her to accept the years she had lost. Dr Degollado also felt she should regain at least some if not all of her memories within an unspecified period of time. It could be weeks, it could be years, there was just no telling.

As it was, Maria still had absolutely no memory of what had caused her to be floating in the Mediterranean and no recollection of her life prior to that and, more than anything else, she was finding this particularly hard to come to terms with.

She was also desperate for companionship. Of course, the nurses were friendly enough, as was Degollado but they were always busily efficient and engrossed in their work. So when Diego at last showed his face again Maria was more than pleased.

She had liked the look of him immediately; his shy embarrassment and his awkward boyish manner. But he had kind eyes and was clearly a very benevolent and selfless person. He had saved her and had it not been for him she would have undoubtedly died. Maria found herself eager to know more about this mysterious, kindly man and was delighted when two weeks after their first meeting he finally knocked on her door again.

She looked up to see him there and smiled. Diego was leaning against the door frame as he tentatively peered into the room, "Hello, Señorita. Do you mind? Am I interrupting?" He asked shyly.

"No, no, please - come in," she replied, "sit down. And it's Maria, remember?"

"Yes, of course. Thank you, Maria." Diego said, stepping immediately over to the wing-backed chair beside the bed and sitting down. Looking into her deep green eyes Diego very nearly lost his train of thought, transfixed once more by her staggering beauty, but he quickly regained his composure before speaking again. "So, Dr Degollado tells me you are doing well. That is very good news."

"It is, yes."

"And you are feeling better in yourself?"

"Much, thank you."

"Good, good..." Diego's nerves were getting the better of him, especially as she was now studying him intently. He was not a natural conversationalist nor especially good at chatting to women in general but he usually managed well enough. However, Maria had come to mean so much to him over the years so he was momentarily tongue tied and knew not what to say next for fear of it possibly being the wrong thing. "That is good news indeed," he said, then realised immediately he was repeating himself and assumed she must think him a complete buffoon. "Sorry," he said, brushing a hand through his hair, making it stick out at odd angles. "May I have a sip of your water?"

"Of course, please do," said Maria smiling.

Diego reached for the water jug and spare glass on her bedside table. With an unsteady hand he hurriedly poured himself a drink and took several long sips. Instantly he felt calmer.

"Better?" she asked.

"Better."

"I make you nervous?"

"A little, yes." He replied. "Actually a lot," he laughed. She laughed, too, in a kindly way. She had a magical, tinkling little giggle which somehow relaxed him.

"I don't know why. I'm supposedly a captain of industry, an international businessman responsible for the livelihoods of thousands of people, yet here I am, a blithering idiot. It's truly ridiculous is it not?"

She laughed some more. "It is a little," she said. "But there's no need to be nervous, I'm not a monster, I won't bite your head off."

"That is reassuring to know," he said, placing a hand on his heart and tapping it with mock relief.

"I am cross with you, however," she said.

"You are?" Diego spluttered, suddenly mortified. "I'm deeply sorry, Señorita, why so?"

"Because two weeks ago you said you would visit me again soon and yet it has taken you all this time." Even though her voice was stern she was smiling, maybe even flirting a little, but she meant every word she said - not that she was actually cross with him but she was desperate for company and he did intrigue her very much. She felt he would be an ideal companion for her whilst she convalesced.

"Señorita—"

"Maria".

"Yes, Maria, sorry, please forgive—"

"No, Diego." She interrupted. "I will not forgive you. Not unless you promise to visit me every day or at least as often as your work allows." She may have sounded like a petulant child but there was a mischievous glint in her eye and a playful grin on her face that told Diego she was only teasing but he was most happy to play along.

"Why of course. You have my word of honour. I will visit you every day from now until the day you wish to leave. Would that please you?"

"It would," she said earnestly. "But what about your company, your commitments?"

"Ah, well," replied Diego, now feeling much more at ease in her company, "That is the great benefit of being a wealthy man. I have many people I can rely on who will keep things running smoothly in my absence."

He was underplaying his importance to Matador considerably. People like Juan Pablo Clemente were indeed loyal, talented and eminently capable but none were so naturally gifted at global business as Diego Del Toro. But for him nothing was more important than Maria. Her recovery was first and foremost in his mind and if that meant him taking a temporary leave of absence then so be it. He could still keep his hands firmly on the tiller of Matador, it would just have to be from Cadiz. Juan Pablo had already done a sterling job representing him over the past two weeks and Diego was certain he would be more than happy to continue.

"That is indeed a significant benefit."

"It is. I am an extremely lucky man. So, Maria, do you accept my offer?"

"You'll visit every day, you promise?"

"Ten o'clock every morning for at least an hour, I swear it."

"An hour?"

"At least. We'll have to be guided by Dr Degollado - we must not hamper your recovery and you may find me—" he searched for the right word - he spoke English fluently but it was not his first language. Then he smiled and said, "Tiresome."

Maria could not help but laugh. He was very modest but also extremely likeable. "You are right," she said, "I might. But somehow I doubt it."

"Those are my terms. Do you accept?"

"I do."

"Excellent. Then, Señorita Maria—" he said, rising to his feet and taking her hand in his, "I bid you farewell until tomorrow when I will be back here at ten o'clock sharp." He bent and very lightly kissed her hand then moved towards the door.

"Until tomorrow," Maria said, feeling strangely flushed.

"Indeed," said Diego. Then he was gone.

***

Diego was every bit as good as his word. Each morning he would arrive at Maria's room at 10am and stay for at least an hour. Their time together was limited by Dr Degollado at first as Maria did tire easily, although not of Diego's company. Even though he did not consider himself to be a natural conversationalist he found he could talk to Maria for hours without ever running out of things to say and in turn she found him witty, smart and wonderfully entertaining.

She was always eager to spend more time with him but she also needed her rest. Her day did not only consist of Diego's visits but of recuperation too. Physiotherapy, exercise, mental stimulation, bodily co-ordination and motor skills; all were regular parts of her day and each were important to recovery.

However, as the weeks passed and Maria became more competent, she and Diego did spend more and more time together. Initially his visits would take place in her room, then over time he would push her around the grounds in her wheelchair and then finally, as she grew stronger, they would stroll together with her using his arm for support. Eventually she no longer needed Diego's supporting arm but it became a comforting habit and she would link arms with him as they headed off for their daily walk.

They circled the grounds for a time, always chatting happily, enjoying each others company, then after consulting with Degollado, they were allowed to wander further afield and often took to ambling around the streets of the old town. Sometimes they would even go shopping where Diego would delight in buying Maria a dress, or a purse or a pair of shoes - sometimes all three. She would always protest but he would hear none of it, it was his pleasure.

With Maria long since having re-learnt how to use cutlery, they would occasionally go to a restaurant for lunch, although wine was never an option as the doctor thought it may inhibit recovery. Afterwards they would usually go to a park and sit under one of Columbus's huge old trees where Diego would read to Maria, soon discovering she was partial to the romances of Jane Austen and the wit of Oscar Wilde. She was now easily able to read a book from cover to cover by herself but she so liked the sound of Diego's deep, calming voice that she would lie down on the grass beside him and let his dulcet tones wash over her.

For nearly a year it was an almost idyllic existence. Maria had all but recovered from her horrific ordeal and the debilitating after-effects of the long coma. She was still under Dr Degollado's care although he now granted her a great deal of freedom and instead of spending her nights at the hospital she now had a room of her own at Diego's mansion. However, this was all above board as Diego had hired a woman named Delores Morales to act as both a chaperone and companion for her. Delores was also a fully trained nurse who had been approved by Miguel Degollado himself.

This idyllic existence, however, was not quite perfect. Maria still had no memory of her life before Cadiz, no clue as to who she was aside from the necklace with her name on it and it was starting to irritate her. She had a niggling feeling in the back of her brain that told her she was missing something important - not just who she was or where she came from, something more than that, something deeper, more vital and this bothered her more with each passing day.

Also there was the question of Diego. He was a wonderful, generous man; intelligent, too, and very wise. He was also madly in love with her. She knew it. Even though he did everything he could to try and hide his feelings, it was clear to see. He would do anything for her. In fact he had done everything for her and she was incredibly grateful.

She was extremely fond of him, too, and liked him a lot. More than a lot; a huge amount. She liked his company, his personality, his conversation, but did she love him? She suspected she did as her instincts told her as much.

But what if she was already in love with someone else? Perhaps even married? When she was found in the sea she was not wearing a wedding band which indicated she was not but there was no way of being absolutely certain.

How could she give her love fully to Diego until those questions had been properly answered? She prayed her memory would be restored soon so they finally could be. She suspected Diego would declare his feelings for her before too long and, should that be the case, she had to be in a position to give him the answer he truly deserved.

She decided to give herself another year. If her memory had not returned by the end of that time then she would agree to marry Diego should he ask her. If he proposed before that year had ended then she would ask is she could defer her answer until the twelve months had run out.

She felt that would be fair to him, to her and to any other persons as yet unknown.

Nonetheless, she could not help but hope no other suitor would come forward as her feelings for Diego were growing stronger by the day.

Chapter Seven

Hollywood, California 1957

Nine year old Ava Peyton sat on the staircase in yet another frilly satin party dress waiting to be called into the dining room by her step-father, Carlo Liuzzi.

She was, as he liked to put it, his 'little star' and at each gathering she became his party piece. At a certain point in the evening, Carlo would call Ava, who would be waiting patiently on the stairs for her cue. He would then take her up in his arms and parade her around the party, showing her off to his guests like some prized possession. They, in turn, would be expected to say how pretty she was, or how cute, fearing Carlo's displeasure if they failed to sound convincing.

Ava, herself, enjoyed the attention when she was just a little girl but now she hated it. However, she, too, knew better than to upset her 'Daddy Carlo' as he insisted she call him.

Ava had tried to defy him once, when she was six years old and feeling a little under the weather. She had asked him sweetly if she really had to go downstairs to the party that night as she was feeling poorly. Carlo's mood immediately blackened and he insisted she did as he asked. She, in turn, begged to stay upstairs in her room as she just wanted to go to sleep but Carlo shook her violently by the shoulders and told her not to be such a spoiled little brat and to do just this one thing he asked of her.

Ava began to cry and ran off to her room inconsolable, her mother nowhere to be seen. At the appointed time that evening, when Ava was due to make her appearance on the stairs, she instead shut herself in her closet and hid behind the dozens of fancy dresses hanging inside.

However, when she failed to make an appearance, Carlo flew into a wild rage. He burst into her bedroom and when he did not immediately see her he began throwing her possessions about the room, breaking ornaments and toys - even tipping her bed upside down assuming she might be hiding underneath.

When he eventually found her cowering in the closet he pulled her up and threw her over his knee. Ripping off his leather belt he whipped her six times violently across the buttocks and demanded she never defy him again. Ava was hysterical, the guests downstairs could all hear the ruckus but dare not speak up and Mildred merely stood in the doorway of her daughter's bedroom, a glass of bourbon in her hand watching her husband beat her little girl. The look on Mildred's face as she stared into the tear-stained eyes of her daughter was one of bitter disappointment. How could Ava ruin such a lovely evening with such a selfish display of defiance.

When Carlo had finished, he and Mildred left Ava alone in her debris strewn bedroom, clutching her favourite dolly and crying silently, her bottom lacerated with welts.

Later that night, Carlo returned to her room, righted her upturned bed and lay the now sleeping Ava upon it. She awoke as Carlo was pulling the covers over her and was immediately filled with terror. But Carlo was calm now, gentle, his voice no more than a whisper as he said, "You promise not to disobey me ever again?" The little girl tentatively nodded, tears brimming once again in her eyes. "Good," said Carlo, "Then let's not speak of it any more." He then kissed her on the forehead, tucked her in and shut the door behind him as he left her room.

As the six year-old Ava lay there in the darkness she wished with all her heart that she could be asleep in her bed above the garage with her real daddy watching over her. But even at that young age she knew it was a forlorn hope. Carlo Liuzzi had claimed her as his own and for some reason she did not understand, her mother seemed to have let him.

She felt sorry for her daddy, Edmund, and knew instinctively he was no match, either physically or financially for Liuzzi. She did not blame Edmund but wished above all else it could be just her and him alone. No Daddy Carlo and no mother to constantly keep telling her what 'a lady' she should be.

However, in the three years since the night Carlo trashed her bedroom, nothing at all had changed - or at least nothing for the better. In fact, he was now even more domineering than ever and her mother had all but given up. Moreover, Ava only seemed to see Mildred at meal times and only then briefly. The rest of the time she was either being watched over by her nursemaid or doing something with Carlo, invariably accompanied by the loathsome Salvatore.

Carlo would often take Ava with him to the studio or the polo club or to screenings of his latest pictures - as if she was a trophy for him to show off. Ava hated it. At the studio she often had to sit and wait for him in an anteroom whilst Carlo and Salvatore held meetings in the main office. At the polo club she was forced to sit with Salvatore whilst Carlo played seemingly endless chukkas and at the movie screenings, the pictures were rarely suitable for her to watch so they did little to hold her attention.

The best part, by far, of being with Carlo was the ride in his limousine to and from wherever they were going because it was one of the only times of day she got to see her real father. And even though she could not talk to him, she could see him through the privacy glass.

Often he would catch her eye in the rear-view mirror and when

Carlo, or more likely, Salvatore, was not looking he would wink at her. She lived for these brief moments as well as the few hours she got to spend with Edmund on his day off.

Recently Ava had taken to sitting on her bedroom windowsill at night when she should have been asleep. From there she could see the the light above the garage emanating from Edmund's apartment. Often she would sit and watch and wish things were different until his light went out. Sometimes she would wake in the early hours, still perched on the windowsill, having fallen asleep where she sat. She was careful, however, to always be in her bed in the morning when her nursemaid entered to wake her as it would not do to be found by the window pining for her father. If Carlo found out Ava felt sure both she and Edmund would be punished.

Edmund, himself, was an excellent father when he was allowed to be by his employer and his ex-wife. However, shortly after Carlo and Mildred got married, Edmund was summoned to Liuzzi's office once more to find himself in the presence of not only his boss but Mildred, too, and a high-powered lawyer. There and then he was required to sign a document which in effect made Carlo Liuzzi Ava's official guardian. If Edmund agreed to surrender all parental rights to his little girl he would be allowed to see her unsupervised for one afternoon per week. At all other times he must treat her as he would his employer - which meant with reverence, speaking to her only in his capacity as chauffeur and employee of the Liuzzi household. In short, Ava was now above his station and should be treated as such.

Edmund had no money, no savings and lacked the wherewithal to challenge Liuzzi. He needed his job and needed to see his daughter and suspected that if he did not sign the agreement he would end up losing both. It was a dreadful, gut-wrenching decision but left with little choice he duly signed.

But it was a decision he regretted almost before the ink was dry.

In the six years since, Edmund had slipped into a deep depression. He despised his spinelessness, hated himself for not having fought harder for Ava and for having given her away so easily.

But he was a weak man. Hard working, reliable, but weak. Liuzzi knew it and capitalised on it, as did Mildred. Edmund's relationship with his ex-wife now was almost non-existent. She treated him like a piece of shit on her shoe and that is exactly how he felt. In his own opinion he was a worthless waste of space; a man so afraid of his own shadow he could not even fight for his own daughter.

Deeply unhappy, Edmund knew he must make an effort to change. If he wanted to play a bigger part in Ava's life then he had to stand up for himself and for her. He loved seeing her on his days off even though he was not permitted to take her off the estate. But he could talk to her privately, have fun, watch TV, play games and be a proper father. But one afternoon a week was not enough, seeing her every day through the glass partition in the limousine was not enough. He was Ava's father dammit, and it was high time he acted like it.

No matter what Carlo Liuzzi said, or Mildred, or some high-priced fancy lawyer. Edmund had had enough. It was time for him to stand up and be a man.

**

It was the night before the Oscars, the 29th Academy Awards, and a big occasion for Gold Star Pictures who had two movies in the running for Best Picture as well as one for Best Actor and one for Best Director. As the head of Gold Star it was biggest night of Carlo Liuzzi's career and to celebrate he was throwing a huge pre-awards party at the mansion.

It was a wonderfully glitzy occasion; movie stars were everywhere - leading men, leading ladies, pretty starlets and handsome young wannabes keen to rub shoulders with influential producers and directors.

Tuxedos, mink stoles, fabulous evening gowns and sparkling jewels were de rigueur with guests dancing to the music of a thirty-piece orchestra - accompanied by the sound of a thousand champagne corks popping.

The driveway was filled with a shining array of automobiles; Rolls-Royces, Bentleys and Cadillacs - all highly polished, the acres of chrome gleaming in the moonlight. Indeed, every aspect of the glittering occasion had been meticulously planned and everyone who was anyone was there.

Mildred had truly outdone herself, her talents as a hostess and organiser could not be more evident and she had choreographed it all to perfection.

Mildred, herself, looked simply stunning in burgundy satin. The tight-fitting gown was cut low at the neck to make the most of her impressive cleavage and even lower at the back to reveal an enticing expanse of smooth bare flesh. The dress left very little to the imagination and every man in the room had noticed her.

Even amongst the cream of Hollywood's leading ladies Mildred stood out.

Since marrying Carlo she had made the most of what God had given her and what He had not she made sure a very good, very discreet surgeon had. A little nip here, a little tuck there, a slight lift or two - nothing too drastic, nothing too extreme, just enough to enhance what nature had already given her, but the results were nothing less than spectacular.

Even though Mildred was an incredibly beautiful woman, she had long since come to terms with the fact that she had become a distant second to Ava in Carlo's eyes. She knew her husband loved her, as much as he was capable of loving any woman but to him it was Ava who was important, not her.

Mildred had never been particularly motherly and since marrying Carlo her interest in her daughter had waned significantly.

If anything now, Mildred saw Ava as competition and resented her for it.

Nonetheless, without her daughter to keep her occupied, Mildred had become bored and to alleviate this she had taken to drinking. Bourbon was a particular favourite but vodka was a less conspicuous choice and she spent most days in a blissful, semi-drunken haze. Nothing to alarm her husband but enough to keep her mind off the tedium of daily life.

She still enjoyed the benefits of being Mrs Carlo Liuzzi; the riches, the jewels, the glamorous lifestyle but her days were dreadfully boring and lacked any hope of excitement. She had no hobbies and few real friends; all her acquaintances tended to be the wives of Carlo's business associates - prim housewives who spent their days and their husbands' money attending charity functions and sponsoring good causes. This type of existence made Mildred gag. Even though she, herself, was an excellent organiser - as she had more than proved with the party that evening.

As the wife of a studio boss she was expected to host her fair share of events, although few were as grand as tonight's glittering occasion. Most of the events were held in the daytime and mainly attended solely by women; charity galas, auctions, fundraisers and the like. It was what the women of Hollywood did when their movie executive husbands were at work.

However, Mildred was not naturally at home in the company of women and only came alive when men were around but she had to be wary of Carlo.

Mildred thrived on male attention, loved the lascivious looks and the drooling desire she inspired in the men she met. She used to like the fact, too, that she was unattainable because she was married to one of the most powerful men in Hollywood. Knowing what Carlo would do to them if he caught them looking used to thrill her but not so much anymore. Now she just found it frustrating and impossibly constraining.

Mildred used to like nothing better than to tease, to make men think she wanted them. It used to be a big game she loved to play. Now, however, she genuinely did want them. She wanted them to make her feel alive, excited, free.

Carlo was once an incredible lover but not anymore. He was still prone to great charges of desire and would usually inflict himself on Mildred at least once a day and she found this mildly stimulating although barely satisfying.

Her lack of underwear also made their encounters more spontaneous and urgent which helped keep some sort of spark alive. But these liaisons were becoming more and more about what he needed and much less about her own gratification.

He wasted no time with foreplay, caring not if she was significantly aroused and when he was done he would leave her like a discarded toy and move onto more pressing matters with scarcely a kind word or a backward glance. Not until the beast stirred within him again.

She still loved him - or his power and money at least - but he was now fifty-one years old and his sexual appetite, and indeed, his prowess, had decreased significantly whereas hers was at an all time high and she craved the attentions of a man like a starved lioness craved meat.

Mildred ached for a younger man. Someone who could thrill her, make her pant and sweat and cry out with pleasure. A young stud who could satisfy her every need.

Sex had become something of an obsession and the thought of finding a fresh thrill excited her more and more with each passing day.

Tonight, at the party on the eve of The Oscars, Mildred had been playing the part of the perfect hostess. She had welcomed the guests, made polite conversation and ensured that everything was running smoothly. However, since before the party began she had been drinking and was now more drunk than she knew.

She had become overly flirtatious with many of the men, particularly the younger ones, telling them she was wearing no underwear and guiding their hands so they could feel for themselves. So far her behaviour had not been noticed by anyone other than the men concerned but she was getting more reckless with every sip of champagne.

The alcohol had made her lustful and her conversation lewd. She was on the prowl; a sexual predator basking in a sea of prime masculinity. Carlo was nowhere to be seen, he was mingling with his peers, entertaining the elite of the invited guests and soon he would be bringing in Ava, his 'little star', showing her off to all on sundry.

His attention was far from Mildred, who tonight was hungry for a man. Although it was not her husband she had a taste for but any one of the young studs she had been flirting so outrageously with. Maybe more than one if she was lucky.

Burning with salacious intent she had a need to be sexually fulfilled and tonight, with Carlo's focus elsewhere, she was on a lustful mission to satisfy her most indecent desires.

∗∗

The party spread from the magnificent ballroom, out through the open doors, onto the enormous patio and into the lush gardens beyond. The grounds were lit by tiny romantic fairy lights strung between dozens of ornate, gold-painted street lamps that had been especially flown in from Paris. Waiters in bright red tunics zig-zagged effortlessly through the throng of finely dressed guests with silver trays laden with flutes of champagne.

The house itself was also heaving with revellers; the lobby, living room and staircase, all packed with wealthy, influential people chatting, laughing and schmoozing. Everyone was having a wonderful time and the party was in full swing.

Only one man appeared to be separate from it all.

Salvatore Falcone moved stealthily amongst the guests, his limp now barely visible and his lifeless right hand covered with a black leather glove. He nodded and smiled here and there to people and spoke to a select few; always in whispers and only to those who may be interested in a new side venture he was planning.

Primarily, however, his job tonight was not to mingle but to watch. His bright, quick eyes mentally taking note of everything, making certain nothing was awry. Carlo had told him he wanted things to run like clockwork tonight, the eve of the most important night of his life. The party was a celebration of all Gold Star had achieved; a testament to him and the success he had earned.

Salvatore had filled out some in the last few years although he still remained inexorably slim. The debilitating bouts of pleurisy that had dogged him for so long had, at last, relented and he had not suffered so much as a slight cough for many months. Indeed, he felt healthier now than he had in very long time.

Since Carlo and Mildred's wedding, Salvatore had once again become a trusted confidant to his old friend and it felt good to be back in the fold. As an act of good faith, Liuzzi had also made Salvatore a partner in Gold Star Pictures by giving him a ten percent stake in the studio so he now had his own source of income and some form of reward for all his years of loyalty.

This meant, for the foreseeable future, Falcone's designs on Carlo's fortune had been shelved. Not least because Mildred, for one, stood in his way, as did Ava and both would be problematic to remove - although certainly not impossible. In fact, Salvatore had already noticed Liuzzi's interest in Mildred had waned considerably and as for the little girl, well there was plenty of time for something to happen to her. But nothing may need to as yet because Falcone had plans in the pipeline that could quite possibly make him independently wealthy and no longer reliant on the scraps from

Carlo's table.

So for now he was biding his time, enjoying the income he was receiving from his stake in Gold Star and diverting much of those funds into a new business scheme that did not involve Carlo Liuzzi or rely on his 'Midas touch' to make it a success.

Salvatore had a source from back East who could supply vast quantities of cocaine. This source, a man named Bruno Barca, had ties to a mysterious and very secretive family in Italy who, it was rumoured, had a female capofamiglia - a lady boss.

Barca neither denied or confirmed this but did promise they could offer an unlimited supply of top quality coke.

Falcone and Liuzzi had both been embedded with the Carboni family during their time in New York and still had strong ties to them, so it was a risk for Salvatore to involve himself with another family, but the rewards could be immense and made it well worth his while.

Barca had recognised in Salvatore the overlooked talent and untapped ability that Carlo had failed to see in him and, tentatively, an ongoing conversation had been struck up between them. After trust had been established the pair decided to go into business together; a clandestine little enterprise that they would run in secret behind Carlo's back.

Barca would deal with his friends in Italy, who would be supplying the merchandise, as well as running his end of things on the East coast, and Salvatore would take care of the big money to be made in Hollywood.

All Falcone needed to do was create a market amongst the Hollywood A-listers who would happily pay top dollar for high quality blow, and within such circles it would be easy. Salvatore had already sent out a couple of samples and the feedback was good. Tonight, too, he had cultivated several leads and sensed he was just skimming the tip of a very large iceberg. It seemed, for the first time in his life, all his ducks were lining up neatly in a row.

Tonight, however, his objective was to remain alert, eliminate any potential problems that may arise and ensure Carlo's big night went off without a hitch.

Salvatore moved stealthily through the throng and navigated his way around the clusters of beautifully attired guests that were clogging the steps of the grand staircase. As he made his way upwards, he caught snippets of numerous conversations; such as starlets shamelessly flattering fat, old producers, actors hitting on actresses and writers pitching plots to uninterested directors but all were of little consequence to him. Eventually, however, Falcone arrived at the huge galleried landing where he positioned himself beside a tall marble pillar. This vantage point allowed him an excellent view of the party below whilst remaining partially hidden from most of the guests.

Salvatore stood watching the goings on, thinking about all the monied people gathered there and wondering how many of them would willingly give up some of that money for a regular supply of his addictive white powder. He was delighted to conclude there would be quite a few.

After several minutes his eyes fell on the back of an extremely shapely woman in a tight fitting burgundy gown who was surrounded by a clearly bewitched group of young actors.

He knew instantly the woman was Mildred and he could not help but think, as they obviously did, how incredibly sexy she was. Salvatore studied her for a long moment, his eyes lecherously travelling up and down her immensely desirable body as he thought about what he would give for just a few hours alone with her. But she was off-limits, at least for the time being, until Carlo tired of her fully.

As it was, she and the four young men were standing towards the rear of the lobby, in front of the doorway that led to the library, which had been declared out of bounds for the night's festivities. Beside them, was a large, highly polished cabinet which had a huge ornate flower arrangement standing on top of it, effectively concealing them from the majority of other guests. Salvatore thought little of this as there were huddles of people all over the mansion, gathered anywhere that allowed them a bit of free space and was just about to turn away when he noticed something so blatant that he had to look again to be sure he had not been mistaken.

One of the young men had placed a hand on Mildred's behind, quite deliberately. Salvatore was amazed by the guy's insolence and was just considering how best to handle the situation when he saw Mildred discreetly remove the hand and smile sweetly. For a moment he thought she had most expertly defused a potentially explosive scenario and was inwardly applauding her.

However, as Falcone looked on, he was staggered to then see Mildred purposely reposition herself so that she now had her back against the library door. This meant the four young men were now in front of her, effectively blocking her in and disguising her from the prying eyes of other guests. But from Salvatore's viewpoint he could see everything and he watched aghast as Mildred took hold of the offending guy's hand and directed it invitingly to her backside once more. Upon this obvious, most unsubtle cue, another man slid his hand down her stomach towards the junction of her legs and a third slid his fingers around the curve of her right breast. Only the fourth man, the shorter, chubbier one of the group, kept his hands to himself. However, his eyes were busy watching out for others around them, making sure his friends were not interrupted.

Mildred, herself, looked wanton, clearly revelling in the attention and the touch of the much younger men.

Salvatore was transfixed, a surge of jealousy running through him as he wished it was his hands touching her so intimately.

He was unable to drag his eyes away, knowing he had to do

something but sensing too, that what he was witnessing would give him power. He did not quite know how yet but instinct told him he could gain from it.

Almost as he thought this, things seemed to suddenly get more heated between Mildred and the four men; the fondling had swiftly been replaced by genuine desire and heightened urgency and Salvatore could do nothing but watch as Mildred surreptitiously reached behind her and opened the door to the library. A moment later, she and three of the young actors had vanished inside the room, closing the door hurriedly behind them and leaving the shorter, chubbier one to stand guard outside.

Suddenly, Salvatore's brain flipped into gear and, fighting down his own jealous urges, he bolted from his high position, rushing as inconspicuously as possible back downstairs. He had to find Carlo Liuzzi. Quickly.

Chapter Eight

Ava had been waiting patiently since the party began but it was way past her bedtime now and she had finally fallen asleep. She had snuggled down in the large leather wing-back and drifted off listening to the gentle crackling of the fire in the enormous stone hearth and the muffled sound of party guests talking beyond the study door.

Tonight, amongst the hubbub, there was no place for Ava to sit on the stairs and wait for 'Daddy Carlo' to come and collect her, so she had been placed, out of harm's way, in his study instead. But the warmth of the fire and the perpetual murmur of conversation had lulled her and she was now curled up in a ball, fast asleep in the comfy chair.

The study adjoined the library with a door leading from one to the other. This was ajar, but Ava continued to sleep peacefully as four revellers spilled into the library from the party outside.

Indeed, Ava only roused after hearing a loud crash in the next room - the sound of a vase being swept urgently from the table - which woke her instantly.

For a moment the little girl thought it was Daddy Carlo coming to fetch her at last. However, when she realised it was not, she rubbed the sleep out of her eyes, slipped off the chair and went to investigate.

***

Bobby and Wyatt Bodene were proud Texans; good ol' boys with an easy line in homespun charm that had won over many a pretty country girl. Bobby, the older of the brothers by a year, used to be the star quarterback of the high school team with a promising career in college ball ahead of him until a popped knee put paid to that. Wyatt was also a gifted player, a wide receiver, who could have had some sort of future in the game, too. However, an affair with the Principal's wife promptly ended both his high school and footballing careers when he was caught in bed with the said lady by the Principal himself, on the night of the Spring Hop.

Bobby and Wyatt were both tall and square-jawed with blonde hair styled and quaffed like their idol, James Dean. They could almost have been mistaken for twins although Bobby was considerably taller and walked with just the slightest trace of a limp. The brothers were near inseparable and rarely seen apart; they were a double team that shared everything from bar tabs and liqueur to cigarettes and women - of which there were many.

The third member of the gang was Donnie Hunter, the Bodene's closest friend whom they had known since childhood and regarded, in everything but blood, as their brother. But Donnie was no jock, no golden boy football hero. On the contrary, he had dropped out of high school, his low grades belying his ability whilst accurately reflecting his lack of interest in class. Donnie was from the wrong side of the tracks with an absent mother, a no-good father and a bad boy reputation. He was a drinker and a brawler with very few true friends, except for Bobby and Wyatt who, for the most part, kept him out of any real trouble. However, like the Bodene boys, Donnie was popular with the girls; his dark, smouldering looks the natural antithesis, to his blonde, all-American, best friends'.

After high school, the three friends hung around town for a couple of years, bumming about mostly and getting into scrapes. However, the fame from their footballing days which had won the

Bodene's so many fans during their time on the team soon soured and along with Donnie Hunter they quickly gained a reputation as troublemakers. Bobby and Wyatt had never known their father who had died serving his country at Pearl Harbor and when their beloved mother suddenly passed away from a brain haemorrhage, their lives seemingly plummeted into free fall, strewn with drunken bar fights and one-night-stands.

Before long, the townsfolk made it clear that it was time for them to move on and they were inclined to agree.

With a view to capitalising on their good looks and obvious appeal to the opposite sex, they decided to head to Hollywood to become movie stars - just like James Dean.

But in stark contrast to their lives in Texas where they were big fish in a small pond who knew all there was to know about the people they met and the places they frequented, in Hollywood they were greenhorns, completely out of their depth amongst the big bucks and power players of Tinseltown. Three simple country boys lost in a world beyond their wildest imaginings.

They had been in town just a week when they met a young Nebraskan Jew named Ira Levenson. Ira was a writer desperate for a break in the movies who had moved to the West Coast a month earlier. Chubby and nervous with tight, curly, brown hair, he had rented an apartment with two other guys but, for one reason or another, they had both bailed, leaving Ira alone and unable to make the rent.

After sparking up a conversation with the three Texans and taking an instant shine to Bobby, Ira invited them to move in and share the expenses, which they eagerly did. Ira soon became the unlikely fourth member of the group and all of them set about taking the movie world by storm.

A month later, a young starlet who had succumbed to Donnie's charms, introduced the three handsome Texans to her agent, Rosalee

121

Rourke, who, after recognising their box office potential, signed them up immediately. She grudgingly also took a risk on Ira at the behest of the other boys.

Wanting all her new signings to be noticed by the great and the good of Hollywood, Rosalee had scored them all invites to the hottest party in town at the home of Carlo Liuzzi.

None of them knew what Liuzzi looked like, just that he was some wealthy studio bigwig and the people attending his party could greatly influence their careers. So, dressed in their freshly rented tuxes, they duly turned up at the Liuzzi mansion for the pre-Oscars party, not having the slightest inkling of how their night would end.

***

Salvatore had frantically scanned the party for Carlo, trying to appear calm, not wishing to alert the guests to any kind of problem. However, unable to find Carlo in the house he was now out on the patio that led off from the east wing, desperately searching the groups of glamorous revellers but having no luck. He had roped in two of Liuzzi's other employees, Frankie and Vito - both former associates from New York - who had now joined in the search for their boss, too.

Suddenly, Vito appeared in front of Salvatore, magically emerging from a dense throng of guests. He sidled up beside him conspiratorially and said, "Some guy just told me he'd seen the boss down on the lawn."

"Okay, good," said Falcone, "I'll go get him. You and Frankie wait here - and keep an eye on that library door - whatever you do, don't let 'em escape."

***

The mansion had a large, industrial kitchen, separate from the every day one, which was used specifically for occasions such as this, and it was a hive of bustling activity. The chef and his army of staff preparing enough canapés and hors d'oeuvres to feed a small African

122

country. Waiters in red bolero jackets swept in and out through the heavy swing doors to the non-stop accompaniment of pots rattling and silver platters clanging; everyone marching to the tune orchestrated by the Head Chef who was forever barking his orders above the constant din.

Edmund stood by the trash bins outside the open back door, smoking a cigarette as he watched the organised chaos within. A cup of coffee, made for him by a kindly member of the kitchen staff, sat steaming on the edge of one of the bins, for the moment too hot to drink. Edmund was not officially working this evening but he was on stand-by, just in case any of the guests were in need of a limousine. Some of the other chauffeurs were also assembled in small groups around the back of the mansion, hoping for some spare scraps or a hot drink as they kept out of the way, waiting for the party to end and their services to be required once more.

But Edmund stood alone. He was not a conversationalist at the best of times but tonight he was in a particularly unsociable mood. He was feeling very low, sickened by his own weakness, wishing he could run away with Ava, take her from this place and start a new life with her far away from either Mildred or Liuzzi. Sadly, though, he knew that was a forlorn hope. Just a few days earlier he had resolved to demand a greater role in Ava's life, but so far he had not been able to summon the courage.

He knew he should fight his employer's will and his ex-wife's seeming indifference to her own child. He should make an attempt to be the father Ava deserved, yet no matter how much he wished it, he simply could not and he despised himself for it.

Edmund blew on his coffee and took a sip. It was still too hot but his thoughts were elsewhere. He would make a stand. He had to. Next time an opportunity arose, he would take it. Ava was his daughter and he would make sure Liuzzi knew that, no matter what the consequences.

He had no way of knowing the opportunity he was waiting for would arrive that night.

***

Time had run away with Carlo. He had been chatting and mingling with his guests all night and in the excitement of the pre-Oscar buzz, which had been the subject of almost all his conversations, he had forgotten about little Ava waiting for him in the study.

His circulation of the guests had taken him from the house, across the patio and far down onto the lawn where the music from the orchestra was just a distant sound and he could speak easily without shouting. He was in deep conversation with a producer, talking animatedly about the other movies in his awards category, discussing their merits and flaws and how they stood up against his own studio's two exemplary offerings. The producer knew better than to pass criticism but champagne had made him careless and he was making a good case for the other pictures. Carlo could feel his hackles rising, the alcohol in his own system unnecessarily stoking the furnace of anger that constantly burned within him. He bit down hard on his half-smoked Cuban cigar and puffed frantically as he listened to the man's drunken diatribe.

The producer did not know quite how lucky he was when he was saved from annoying Carlo further by a rather distressed and out of breath Salvatore.

"My apologies, gentlemen," panted Falcone, "please excuse me. Carlo, may I have a word?"

Carlo's eyes were black with fury as he turned to face his associate, "What?" He snapped.

For a moment Salvatore hesitated, then leaned in and whispered quietly in Liuzzi's ear who seemed to visibly swell with rage at every word spoken. When Falcone had finished speaking, Carlo stared at him, his expression murderous. Then without another word he barged him out of the way and marched off towards the house with

Salvatore limping along behind.

The drunken producer was left standing alone with an empty champagne flute. "Jumped up little greaser," he said under his breath as he watched Carlo striding away across the lawn determinedly, ignoring any guest that dared speak to him.

Yet all Carlo could think about was getting to the library and killing everyone in there.

***

Mildred had been enjoying the attentions of the four young men surrounding her. Three were extremely handsome and very sexy, each clearly as attracted to her as she was to them. However, the fourth man, the little Jewish one, did not interest her in the least. After all, she had been in Hollywood long enough to recognise a homosexual when she saw one. But his particular preferences were none of her concern as she had her mind firmly set on the three Texan studs who could not keep their eyes, nor indeed their hands off her.

Her conversation with them had started off innocuously enough, just casual chit-chat about nothing in particular, but as their youthful naivety fed her drunken desire for male attention the dialogue had quickly deteriorated into something far more suggestive and entirely more slutty.

She had been flirting with them outrageously for over half an hour and leading them on by rubbing herself up against them at every given opportunity. Each provocative move signalling her brazen intent.

Furthermore, in the course of their salacious small talk Mildred had successfully managed to steer them all into a secluded little spot within the foyer where their sexual overtones could not easily be overheard.

She had learned that the tall one was Bobby, whilst Wyatt was the youngest and the dark, brooding one was Donnie. To Mildred, however, all of them looked absolutely delicious regardless of their names or ages and to stir things up she purposely let slip that she was not wearing a stitch of underwear.

Upon hearing that tantalising snippet of information, all of them became visibly more aroused and Bobby, unable to stop himself, reached out and grabbed Mildred's curvaceous behind.

Nonetheless, intoxicated as she was, she knew she was positioned with her back to the party and someone could easily notice Bobby's hand upon her, even though she relished the touch. Deftly, she removed his hand, although the salacious glint in her eyes did little to discourage him.

Indeed, she then stepped between the four boys and repositioned herself so her back now rested against the library door where she could no longer be seen by a casual observer. Once there, she took Bobby's hand again and placed it back on her rear end, her excitement building as his fingers explored her shapely derrière.

Taking their cue from this, Wyatt and Donnie were keen to join in the fun. Wyatt slipped his hand under one of her breasts and squeezed it firmly, whilst Donnie pushed his fingers into the 'V' at the top of her legs, making Mildred gasp with delight.

For a moment she was lost; her whole body consumed with desire, then with a jolt of fear, she snapped back to her rightful senses. Somebody might see her. Moreover, Carlo might see her and she could not risk that. Not if she valued her life.

Nevertheless, she now wanted these men desperately and could not bear to wait a moment longer.

Swiftly Mildred reached behind her and turned the door handle to the library. The room had been declared off-limits for the night so no one would disturb them. As for Carlo, he was off schmoozing with his high-powered guests so there would be no danger of him accidentally stumbling in on proceedings.

Bobby, seeing Mildred's intention, turned to Ira and said,

"Watch this door. Make sure no one comes in, okay?"

"Sure, Bobby, yeah," said Ira, "no problem." However, he could not help but feel a little sad. If only Bobby would look at him the way he looked at that woman. But he knew it was never to be.

Nonetheless, as Ira watched, Mildred and all three of his friends slipped silently into the library and closed the door behind them.

Once inside, Mildred snapped on the light to reveal a magnificently appointed library with high shelves that ran floor to ceiling, all crammed with sumptuously bound books. An ornate rolling ladder stood at one end to enable readers to reach the uppermost shelves whilst several comfortable armchairs were scattered about for them to settle themselves into once they had found the tome they were looking for.

But no one cared about any of those things tonight and now Mildred was finally alone with her admirers, she cast all caution aside, allowing herself to be pawed and fondled and caressed by the eager young bucks who were suddenly all over her.

As a group they moved further into the middle of the spacious room where a large, polished oak table stood pride of place. Several books were scattered on it and a vase of white lilies made a pretty centrepiece.

Mildred obligingly lay back on the table, impetuously sweeping away the books and knocking the vase of flowers onto the floor in her lustful haste, smashing it into large jagged pieces.

The crash was loud but no one would hear it above the din of the party. Besides the four people in the library were oblivious to the noise, seemingly deafened by their wanton desire as Mildred hungrily pulled Wyatt towards her. Hoisting up her dress, she kissed him deeply and wrapped her long naked legs around his waist.

Then, as the other two boys looked on, impatiently waiting their turn, Wyatt took her.

Mildred, however, merely closed her eyes and willingly

submitted to his masterful technique, eagerly anticipating all that was yet to come.

***

After Wyatt had done with her, it was Bobby's turn who seemed even more practiced than his brother. Mildred was now glowing with perspiration; her dress draped loosely around her waist as she gave herself up to him.

Bobby was hard, rough - almost crazed but Mildred found it even more thrilling and bucked and writhed beneath him like a wild mustang.

When Bobby was finished Donnie eagerly took over; his dark, brooding presence looming over her as the other boys watched with carnal delight.

They had saved the best for last as Donnie was an expert lover and utterly insatiable but Mildred was more than up to the challenge.

However, as a wave of incredible pleasure rattled through her fabulous body, her eyes fell upon the gap in the door that led through to the study.

Kneeling at the bottom of the gap was Ava, a horrified look on her innocent little face.

For a second Mildred could not compute what she was seeing, still lost in a haze of sexual delirium.

But then, as Donnie let out a triumphant growl; his passion finally spent, Mildred's head at last cleared.

"Oh, God no. Ava—" she whispered, as she looked straight into her daughter's terror filled eyes.

But her voice was drowned out by the sound of the library door as Carlo Liuzzi burst violently into the room.

Chapter Nine

"Hey!" Donnie yelled, turning towards the door half naked, his trousers around his ankles. "This room's occupied, okay?"

"Yeah, buddy," Bobby chimed in, "Give us a break would ya? We're kinda using the room if you get my drift." He hurriedly buttoned his pants and zipped up his fly, clearly annoyed at being robbed of a second turn on Mildred.

Liuzzi had entered the room accompanied by three other men as well as Ira Levenson who was looking decidedly sheepish and most uncomfortable.

Bobby glared at him and said sarcastically, "Thanks for keeping a look out, man - I mean, good job!"

Mildred slipped quickly off the table, her naked body slick with sweat and her dress like a screwed up rag as she tried desperately to pull it back on. Somehow, even without looking back, she knew it was her husband who had entered the room and dread flooded through her body.

Guiltily, she turned, shaking with fear. Carlo was standing there his expression as black as thunder. Salvatore, Frankie and Vito were positioned behind him. Vito had closed the door and was standing guard in front of it to prevent anyone else from entering or leaving. Salvatore had hold of Ira's arm; he was not going anywhere.

"Carlo, please! It's not how it looks - they forced me, honestly they did, I swear it - it's not my fault. I couldn't stop them, please, please, don't hurt me—." Mildred begged pathetically. Her eyes were filling with tears as she struggled to shrug on her dress and cover her nakedness but she was sticky and wet and it was proving to be a difficult task.

"Hey! That ain't true," protested Donnie.

"Yeah! Whoa, there! Hold on a minute, lady!" Yelled Wyatt, busily pulling up his pants. "What do you mean we forced you? You damn near dragged us in here, remember? And who is this guy anyway, your old man?"

Strangely, Carlo Liuzzi seemed to calm. His body became visibly more relaxed and the thunderous expression suddenly vanished. Indeed, he was almost genial as he spoke, his voice not much louder than a whisper.

"Yes. She is my wife and I trust you enjoyed her—"

"Carlo, please!" Whimpered Mildred, tears now running in rivers down her cheeks, mingling with the perspiration.

"Ssh." Carlo said softly to his wife as he walked towards Donnie.

"Hey, man - I'm sorry," said Donnie, pulling up his trousers and tucking in his shirt, "We didn't know she was your wife - we don't know anyone here. We're just good ol' boys from Texas out for a good time - hell, we don't even know whose party this is!"

Donnie was well-practiced in the homespun charm and it had got him out of more than a few scrapes in the past. Maybe it would work again tonight. Yet the sheer terror on Mildred's face was infectious and Donnie's stomach stirred with dread.

In fact, she was distressed in the extreme and this made him very uneasy.

Nevertheless, Carlo waved a hand dismissively. "Why would you know whose party it is?" He said. "But I can tell you this. It is mine. And my house." He then looked Donnie straight in the eyes, the malevolence undisguised, "And the things in it belong to me."

"Like I said, man - we're really sorry, we didn't—" Donnie stammered.

Again Carlo held up a hand, instantly silencing the boy as he bent down and picked up a jagged shard of the broken flower vase.

As he straightened back up to his full imposing height, he studied the broken piece lovingly, as if it was some precious gem he had just uncovered.

He regarded it for a moment longer as he tightened his thick fingers carefully around it. Then he looked up once more and moved closer to Donnie.

Mildred, her nakedness now covered, was behind the young Texan, pinned against the table, paralysed with fear.

"This was a party for me," Carlo said, his tone still calm and convivial, "to celebrate all I have achieved in Hollywood. It was supposed to be one of the biggest nights of my life. Can you imagine that?"

Donnie nodded meekly. He, too, now feeling extremely scared. He was a big, strong guy but not in the same ballpark as the powerful, brooding presence that stood close to him now. There was also something chilling about the man, something dark and dangerous. The men with him were also extremely sinister and Donnie's bowels shifted as the horrific notion struck him that he might not live to see the end of this night.

Everyone could sense that something was about to happen, the atmosphere thick with menace and the tension palpable.

"Hey, buddy!" said Bobby, trying to defuse the situation and deflect focus from his friend. "He said we were sorry. We didn't know."

"Yeah, it was your wife, man," added Wyatt, "she started it—"

"Silence!" Liuzzi roared. His voice suddenly angry and incredibly loud as he pointed behind him to quieten the two other boys whilst his focus remained unswervingly on Donnie. "Keep

131

quiet or I'll silence you myself - understand!"

Neither Bobby or Wyatt dare answer as they watched Donnie, their best friend since childhood, the bravest and toughest of the three of them, trembling with fear; tears flooding his eyes.

"Salvo," Liuzzi continued, "If either of them interrupt me again, shoot the Jew would you?"

"Glad to," replied Falcone, releasing his grip on Ira before reaching into his jacket and pulling out a shiny Browning 9mm. He pressed the muzzle hard against Ira's temple, pushing his head to a tilt. The boy whimpered with fear, like a scolded dog, but he did not utter a word, knowing for certain if he did it would be his last.

"Now where was I?" Carlo continued. His voice immediately calm again. "Oh, yes. I was telling you how this was my party - my very special party. And how this is my house - it's wonderful isn't it? I own all the amazing things in it, including the woman you have just fucked and the rather nice, very expensive vase that now lies in pieces on my carpet."

"Please, I, I, I'm sorry, mister..." snivelled Donnie, his bladder involuntarily emptying and its contents running down his leg to form a puddle at his feet.

"You come into my house uninvited and you're sorry?" Carlo said with incredulity, his voice rising by an octave. "You ruin my party and fuck my wife and you're sorry?" He was louder still now as he laughed, looking round at the others in the room for them to share the 'joke', but there was no humour in it and everyone stayed resolutely silent, no trace of a smile on any of their faces.

He turned back to Donnie with his face now transforming into an ugly, hateful grimace as he shouted, "You break my goddamn vase - this fucking vase—" Carlo showed him the large jagged piece of pottery in his hand, "—and you're sorry?"

Donnie was crying now, weeping openly, tears streaming down his face, knowing for certain he was about to die.

"Well I don't accept your fucking apology you piece of shit," Liuzzi hollered, "and as for this goddamn vase you can keep it as a reminder of my generous hospitality!"

With that, Carlo stabbed the shard violently into Donnie's neck, slicing through his jugular like a knife through butter. A tall fountain of bright red blood erupted from the hideous wound, spraying everything within the immediate vicinity - including Carlo and Mildred.

Yet Donnie's face did not show any sign of pain, merely a questioning expression, as if asking 'why?' But then his eyes rolled upwards, his lips parted and a thick stream of blood gargled up his throat and spilled out of his mouth.

As Carlo pulled out the shard Donnie dropped to the floor, his body convulsing grotesquely in the last throes of death. Liuzzi growled like an animal and threw himself down onto the boy, stabbing him again and again repeatedly in the face.

Quickly Donnie's handsome features turned to mush but by then the young Texan was way past caring.

"Oh God, oh God! Cried Bobby, panic running through him as he watched his best friend being butchered by a mad man.

"No, no, no," Wyatt kept saying, unable to comprehend the horror of what he was witnessing.

Mildred said nothing as Donnie's blood spattered over her, soaking her skin and staining it red. She merely wept, knowing the same fate almost certainly awaited her.

Finally, Carlo stood. He was panting from exhaustion, his shoulders heaving. He was covered almost entirely in the dead boy's blood. But his temper was still not sated and he turned his attention on Mildred who stood cowering just feet away. Carlo raised the bloodied shard above his head and prepared to thrust it deeply into his wife's treacherous heart, when suddenly she screamed out. "Carlo, please - Ava!"

"How dare you speak that angel's name you filthy goddamn whore!" He snarled, mere seconds from striking her down with his makeshift dagger.

"No! I mean, Ava— she's there, watching, by the door to your study, please don't let her see you kill me!" Mildred pleaded urgently. She had momentarily forgotten about the child when her husband burst into the room, thinking only of herself, but as she stood awaiting her imminent death, she suddenly remembered - desperately hoping that somehow, the daughter she cared so little for, would turn out to be her last hope of salvation.

Carlo was stunned, the rage vanishing from his eyes as he span towards the door.

And there she stood. Little Ava.

The door was now open and she was standing on the threshold of the library with her dark hair in glossy ringlets and tied with powder blue ribbons. She was wearing a pure white party dress with frilly lace petticoats underneath that made her look like an ornate China doll. The white dress was speckled with tiny red droplets; fresh and wet from the bloody shower that had sprayed from the gash in Donnie's neck.

Her face was blank, completely without expression, but as her 'Daddy Carlo' glared at her, the whites of his eyes shining evilly in a face smothered with blood, he could have been the devil himself. The terrifying vision before her was the final horror. She could not bear any more after all she had witnessed in that room that night, and all of a sudden she was light-headed. The room began to spin wildly before she passed out, slumping unconsciously to the ground.

Carlo threw the shard aside and ran over to her. He very nearly picked her up but was suddenly aware of the blood that soaked him from head to foot.

"Frankie!" He barked. "Quickly! Pick her up and take her somewhere safe - not up the stairs, there's too many people. To the kitchen - that'll be the closest. Stay with her until she wakes - I'll be there as soon as I can. Is that clear?"

"Yes, Boss," Frankie said with certainty. Quickly he crossed to where the little girl lay and scooped her up in his arms. Carlo turned away, he could not look at her, not like this, not whilst he was covered in blood and not when there was still more to be spilled. He would not set eyes on her again, would not allow her to see him again, until he was clean and washed and finished with all the murderous work he had yet to carry out that night.

Vito cracked open the door to check it was safe and nodded to Frankie who carried the little girl across the room and out of the door, which was then shut again behind them.

Liuzzi stood with his back to the room, all eyes on him. There was silence for a long moment, as the gears whirred in his brain. After maybe a minute or so, he walked through to his study and retrieved something from his desk drawer. With the mystery object concealed behind his back, he returned to the library and said in a voice only slightly louder than a whisper, "Salvo, ask all of my party guests to leave would you? Tell them my wife has been taken ill and I cannot leave her side. Get them out as quickly as you can but do not alarm anyone. Get the staff out, too."

"Of course, capo," replied Salvatore, addressing Liuzzi as he would have back in New York when the movie mogul was Carmine Carboni's consigliere.

"Vito?" Said Carlo.

"Boss?"

"Watch the Jew."

"Si, capo," replied Vito, also using the same Italian form of address whilst pulling out a .38 from the back of his pants. He aimed it at Ira's head whilst Salvatore returned his own 9mm to its shoulder holster and exited the library.

Carlo then smiled genially and addressed the room, seemingly

135

unconcerned that he was caked in blood and the brutally disfigured body of the boy he had just murdered was lying at his feet. "Whilst we wait for the house to empty, so that we might be afforded a little more privacy," he said, licking away a stray dribble of Donnie's blood which had run down onto his lips, "I'd like to tell you a story, if you would permit me."

No one uttered a word in reply. The three remaining boys were all weeping silently, grieving for their dead friend and seriously fearing for their own lives. Mildred had stopped crying now and was just staring glassy-eyed at the mutilated mush that used to be Donnie's face. She had begun to shiver uncontrollably as the shock of what she had just witnessed fully hit her. Nothing she said, nothing she did, would ever change what had transpired or, indeed, what was still yet to happen, as that was already a forgone conclusion. So why not let her husband talk - there was nothing she could do to stop him anyway.

Taking his cue from the silence, Carlo started to speak. "When I was a small boy I lived with my father in a tiny fishing village in the south of Sicily." He began. "My mother died in childbirth so I lacked a woman's guiding hand. We were very poor and my father, a fisherman by trade, was often away for many days at a time trying to earn enough to put food on the table, whilst I was left alone to fend for myself.

"Well, as you can imagine, I grew up wild and undisciplined, but I was tough, too. Very tough indeed. I fought for any extra scraps I could find and stole whatever else I needed. It was a very... how do you say?" He searched for the right phrase for a moment and when he found it he smiled. "Ah, yes - it was a very hand to mouth existence. But I hated being poor and hated my father for not being a wealthy man. What can I say, I was an ungrateful child, but such is life. I am not proud of it, but I simply believed I deserved more.

"One day, a man of considerable affluence came to the village

- an Arab; a Turk, in fact. He was dressed in brightly coloured robes of green and orange silk and wore a red turban on his head. He had a deeply tanned face and a black pointed beard that smelled of perfumed oils, I recall. Tied around his waist was a thick silken sash, also bright red, and tucked into it was a long curved dagger in a jewel encrusted scabbard.

"I remember watching the Turk showing the dagger to my father as they drank wine together, with many of the other men in the village on that sunny afternoon. As he pulled it from the sheath, there was an audible gasp from the assembled crowd. My father was particularly impressed and the Turk allowed him to hold it.

"The dagger had a carved gold handle, which had clearly been decorated and finely worked by a master craftsman. It sparkled in the sunlight and appeared to be embedded with tiny diamonds and larger emeralds and rubies. The long blade was forged from Damascus steel, as I learned later, sharpened on both edges and lovingly oiled and polished to a bright, gleaming shine.

"It was the most magnificent thing I had ever laid eyes on and I wanted it immediately. More than that, I knew I absolutely had to possess it. In my mind, it already belonged to me.

"The Turk was a trader, en-route to Genoa or Florence or some other such place to do business and was staying in our village, at the local taverna, for a few days rest.

"Nonetheless, that night, when the whole village was sleeping, I snuck into the Turk's room and took the dagger. Elated, I ran home in the darkness and hid it, wrapped in an old cloth, at the back of our wood pile where I was convinced no one would find it."

Briefly, Carlo paused in his monologue and grinned broadly, the whiteness of his teeth contrasting brightly with the deep red of his gruesome, bloodied face. "Hey, I was young and stupid, what can I say?" He said, before continuing. "Anyway, I hid the dagger but next morning the Turk and many of the villagers came knocking at my father's door, remembering his keen interest in the weapon. He denied everything of course but after the most rudimentary of searches the dagger was soon found.

"My father was— what's the word you Americans use?" Again, he thought for a moment, then said, "Yes. 'Flabbergasted'. My father was flabbergasted and loudly and violently protested his innocence. But no one believed him - he had been caught, as they say, red-handed.

"They took my father and bound him to a tree in the village square and then sent for the capofamiglia - the head of the local Cosa Nostra which you Americans might better understand as the Mafia."

Upon hearing that word both Bobby and Wyatt looked up at Liuzzi, their eyes still wet with tears and their faces ashen with terror. But as Carlo met their gaze they quickly looked away.

"Ah, gentlemen, I see you recognise the term, so you know what weight this man carried amongst the people of our village. As for myself, I remember Don Pio Allegretti, for that was his name, as a fat, pompous man who wore a white fedora and a red, silk cravat. He was a bloated, flabby peacock who I certainly didn't respect. Nevertheless, this self-important oaf passed judgement on my father - there was no trial, no hearing, no opportunity for him to defend himself. He was simply pronounced 'guilty', just like that—" Carlo snapped his fingers to demonstrate. "What was the sentence Don Allegretti deemed suitable for this most heinous of crimes, you might wonder? Well, the answer to that, gentlemen, is stoning.

"That very afternoon, as I watched amongst the amassed crowd, my father was stoned to death in front of my eyes. However, my thoughts were not with him, but with the Turk - or more specifically, with the dagger. All I cared about was getting it back.

"After the stoning, the crowd dispersed and I was left alone. No one cared about me - to them I was just a wild, untamed animal. I didn't blame them as I had given them no reason to like me but the fact remained I was now on my own and had to make a future for myself.

"That night, I visited the Turk again. He had not learnt his lesson from the night before and the dagger was in full view on his bedside table, unguarded as he slept. As the Turk snored soundly, my father's death of no consequence to a man such as he, I knew I had to make the dagger mine permanently and could not risk losing it again. The Turk would surely come looking for it when he awoke and this time it could be me tied to the tree. So I slid the blade out of the scabbard and admired it as it shone in the moonlight. Then I held it against the Turk's neck and slit his throat."

Carlo paused here for dramatic effect, before adding, "I was eight years old."

At this point Mildred turned and looked at him, stunned. She knew very little of her husband's past and had never heard this tale before. It shocked her - on a night when she thought she had experienced all the shock a person could take.

Carlo continued, "It was my first ever kill and it felt strangely good. The Turk had taken what I knew rightfully belonged to me and he paid the ultimate price.

"After that, however, I had one more person to visit. Using only the light of the moon, I left the village and took the mountain path high up into the hills where Don Allegretti's spectacular villa looked out over the bay. The guards were all asleep and it was simple for a small boy to slip into the grounds unobserved. Quickly I was inside the villa itself, my bare feet silent on the tiles as I searched for Don Allegretti's bedroom. I found it soon enough and approached the huge four-poster bed where the fat fool slept. There was no guard, no security, it was easy.

"I took the dagger from my pocket and carefully climbed up onto the bed - I was just skin and bone, so weighed not enough for him to notice. Nevertheless, as I pulled the dagger from its sheath it made just the tiniest sound of metal on metal and Don Allegretti's eyes flew open. He saw me there, over him, with the dagger raised but, as he opened his mouth to scream, I stabbed down into it, pushing the curved blade down his throat, silencing him for ever.

"The man had killed my father, whom I hated, but he was my father, he belonged to me and nobody was going to take what belonged to me ever again."

Carlo looked at the three boys before him, the significance of what he had just said not lost on any of them. "I see you understand me, gentlemen," he said. "But let me finish my story, I owe you that much at least.

"I left Don Allegretti's villa as silently as I'd entered it, not disturbing a soul, and again took to the mountain path. I walked all night and most of the next morning until I reached another villa in a neighbouring territory that was governed by yet another wealthy capofamiglia whose family had been locked in a bitter feud with the Allegretti family for many years.

"This man, however, was much more honourable than his adversary, with a widely respected reputation. His name was Don Caseareo Liuzzi—" Mildred shot him a glance. "—Ah, I see, Mildred, you recognise the name.

"Well, as I say, I went to Don Caseareo and told him all that I'd done. Can you imagine it? An eight year old boy who had just killed two men - one of them a capo? My God, I must have had balls of steel! Anyway, I told Don Caseareo everything and said if he wished to take over Allegretti's territory then now was the time to do it.

"He laughed at me and asked me what I required in payment for this information and for this service I had done for him.

"I told him simply that I wanted two things; the dagger and a home. He granted me both and in the years that followed he gave me much more than I could ever have hoped for - his guidance, an education, even enough money to buy my passage to America when the time came for me to leave him.

And when I did, I took his name also.

"Don Caseareo became the father I always wanted; the father I deserved.

"And all of this because I fought for what was mine."

Carlo then showed them all what was concealed behind his back and held it out to show them.

"Because I fought for this dagger," he said proudly.

It was just as he had described; truly magnificent with a jewel encrusted handle and a long curved blade. Bobby, Wyatt and Ira all felt compelled to look and even through their terror, they could not fail to be impressed. "It is my most prized possession and I cherish it above anything else. More than my house, more than my fine automobiles and certainly more than my wife - which I'm sure you young gentlemen can now understand. With it, I have killed many men, most recently my daughter's lover, who tried to steal her from me, and his unfortunate friend."

Carlo paused again, admiring the dagger with an almost insane reverence - as if it was the Holy Grail itself, before adding, "Tonight I will use it again."

Chapter Ten

When Edmund had finished his coffee, he wandered around to the front of the mansion and stood alongside his boss' immaculately maintained Fleetwood limousine, which had been brought out this evening specifically for the use of any guests who may require it.

To keep himself amused and to preserve the Caddy's perfect shine, Edmund had taken a rag from the glove compartment and was busy polishing out any blemishes that may previously have escaped his notice. His fastidiousness and attention to detail had been one of the reasons Liuzzi had kept him on after marrying Mildred as no one had ever looked after his fleet of automobiles with as much care. Not even Nathaniel.

As Edmund worked he noticed people gathering on the driveway as they swarmed through the grand front doors of the mansion. He glanced up and saw limousines driven by the chauffeurs who had previously been with him at the back of the house now queueing in a line around the curve of the drive, their owners pouring out and into the waiting vehicles.

Edmund was confused as it was way too early for the party to be over. Yet hordes of guests were suddenly leaving and he could not understand why. He spotted Salvatore Falcone amongst the gaggle and heard him apologising for the 'unforeseen circumstances'. He also overheard many of the guests wishing Mildred a 'speedy recovery'.

Had his ex-wife been taken ill? Edmund wondered. It seemed clear to him that the party was now over and gradually, as he looked on, the driveway slowly cleared. He thought maybe his services might be needed, so he put on his cap and stood to attention by the driver's door of the Caddy but everyone seemed to be well catered for. The sparkling limo would not be required after all.

It took maybe half an hour for all the guests to leave until the only people remaining were Falcone and Edmund. Salvatore looked over at him and shouted, "Go to bed, Peyton, you're not needed tonight. Make it quick, man - or else Mr Liuzzi will have something to say about it."

Edmund despised Salvatore. He did not trust him and did not like the way he looked at Ava. There was something rotten about the man which he could not quite put his finger on, but he always felt uneasy when Ava was alone in Falcone's company.

Nevertheless, Edmund nodded his compliance and turned towards the Caddy. He would put the car away then get a well deserved early night. However, several minutes later, as Edmund shut and locked the garage door, he felt a niggling sensation that told him something was not quite right. So rather than go up to his apartment above the garage, as ordered, he went back around to the kitchen instead.

He could tell something was wrong immediately. As he looked through the window he could see the kitchen was now deserted and the army of staff that had been there just a short while before had all gone. Furthermore, there were dirty pans, pots and plates everywhere. None of the work surfaces had been wiped down and the dishes had just been left piled up in the sink.

Making his way to the back door, which he could see had been left open in the staff's apparent eagerness to leave, he heard the sound of voices.

"Hey, be quiet kid," a voice, which Edmund recognised as Frankie DeLuca's, said. "You gotta wait here, the boss says so. It ain't no good bawling, there ain't nothing I can do about it."

As Edmund stepped into the light of the open doorway, he saw Ava sitting on a stool by the door and sobbing her heart out as Frankie stood helplessly over her, a handkerchief held pathetically in his hand as he tried to stop her from crying.

"I want my daddy!" She wailed. "I want my daddy, now!"

"Your daddy's busy honey, busy with his guests in the library," replied Frankie helplessly.

"Not him!" Ava scowled through gritted teeth and streaming eyes, "my real daddy."

Edmund felt as though his heart was going to break as he burst through the doorway and into the kitchen. "It's okay baby, I'm here. Daddy's here. Everything's going to be alright now."

Ava turned and flew off the chair into his embrace, flinging her arms around his neck and gripping him tightly as if she never wanted to let him go.

"Hey, Peyton!" Frankie yelled, "This ain't your place, you ain't supposed to be here. Boss says the house has gotta be cleared." Frankie DeLuca was not usually an unreasonable man, and was normally quite affable, but he had been given the directive by Salvatore, himself. The house had to be vacated as quickly as possible. And that meant everyone.

Summoning his courage from God knows where, Edmund glared at Frankie and said, "Go to hell! Can't you see my daughter's upset?"

Frankie was temporarily stunned. Edmund was usually so meek and mild. A real pushover.

"What is it, baby?" Edmund asked Ava softly. "What's happened?"

The little girl was trembling, her whole body aquiver, something was obviously deeply wrong. "It's Mommy," she started, "she and three men, they were doing… they were doing bad things—"

"What kind of things, sweetie? Tell me."

"Bad things. Very bad. They all got undressed and… and—"

"And what, Ava, what is it you saw?" Edmund pressed, although he could make a good guess.

"Daddy Carlo, he—"

"Okay, kid! That's enough," said Frankie cutting her off. "No more, alright. You didn't see nothing, okay?"

"Be quiet, man!" Edmund barked. "Let the girl speak!"

Frankie DeLuca was a tough Italian New Yorker and a former member of the Carboni crime syndicate. Very few people spoke to him as Edmund just had but the chauffeur was the girl's real father so Frankie was inclined to let it go and promptly shut up.

"Sorry, sweetie. What was it you were saying?" Edmund continued, "what happened with your Daddy Carlo?" Even now, when his daughter was in so much distress, he could barely bring himself to utter the words 'Daddy Carlo', but he had to find out what had happened as she was evidently traumatised by what she had seen.

Ava, sniffed and wiped her tears on Edmund's jacket. "He killed one of the men," she sobbed, "I think Daddy Carlo's the devil!"

Edmund was stunned. He did not question what his daughter had said as she wept into his chest, her shoulders heaving with deep, breathless sobs. Mildred had always been flighty, always very promiscuous. Some of the guys back in Iowa used to rib him about it, saying what a good lay she was, but he ignored them and put it to the back of his mind. But he knew they were not lying. Knew they had all been with her.

Furthermore, he knew it was only a matter of time before her licentious nature got her into trouble in Los Angeles too.

As for Carlo Liuzzi being the devil, Edmund did not doubt it for a moment. There was a thick streak of evil running through that man and tonight he had obviously shown it. But Edmund did not care about him or Mildred, he only cared about protecting Ava and a passion burned within him now that he had never felt before.

Tonight he was strong, tonight he was invincible and God help anyone who got in his way.

***

Salvatore watched all the guests leave and bade them a heartfelt goodnight, passing on his employer's apologies in the most sincerest way he could without actually meaning a word. When the driveway was clear, he barked his instructions to Edmund and then went back inside to do one more sweep of the house; there could be no stragglers, no witnesses. No loose ends.

When he was certain the house was clear, he crossed the now deserted lobby and knocked lightly on the library door. "It's me," he called.

A second later, Vito cracked open the door and peered out. "It's okay," said Salvatore, "everyone's gone."

Vito nodded and let him in.

"Ah," said Carlo Liuzzi, as if greeting the arrival of the port and cigars after a leisurely banquet, "just in time." He then looked at Falcone and asked, "We are alone, I assume?"

"Si, Capo."

"Good. Then, Salvatore, kill the Jew, would you? It's high time we got things started."

Suddenly Ira Levenson looked absolutely panic-stricken. He let out a fearful high-pitched whinny and pleaded, "No, no, please–" as his bowels voided.

Even Vito, who had been holding his gun on the chubby, curly haired boy for sometime looked quite taken aback and lowered his weapon, not quite sure if he had heard Liuzzi correctly. But in the time it took him to do this, Salvatore had pulled out his own Colt

9mm and pushed it against Ira's temple. Swift, precise and deadly.

Then he fired.

The sound was like the crack of a bullwhip, although much louder. The bullet exited the opposite side of Ira's head and buried itself deep within a bookcase several feet away. Chunks of skull, flesh and brain matter, sprayed out across the room like the discarded bark and sawdust from an industrial woodchipper as the boy's lifeless corpse dropped to the floor and bled out on the carpet.

Bobby fell to his knees and wept. Mildred leant over and vomited on the carpet and Wyatt just looked on incredulously, utterly stunned by the abhorrent act he had just witnessed.

"I think my library may be in need of some re-decorating, don't you?" Carlo Liuzzi said to nobody in particular, his manner light, almost jovial. "But my apologies, gentlemen," he added, now addressing Bobby and Wyatt specifically, "I have kept you waiting long enough and now we've ridden ourselves of the dead wood - I'm afraid your chubby little Jew friend was not worth my attentions - we can now get onto the main event of the evening."

Both the Bodene brothers, these two proud Texans, who had come to Hollywood seeking fame and fortune in the movies, looked up and stared into Carlo's cold, black eyes and knew, with absolute certainty, they would never see Texas again.

Liuzzi smiled, almost sympathetically, then said, "Salvo, Vito, please escort these fine young men out to the garden store, underneath the tennis courts, would you? I would like a few moments alone with my wife."

***

Edmund and Frankie heard the gunshot from the kitchen, both recognising it for what it was. Ava heard it too, the loud 'crack' startling her, making her jump. "What was that?" She cried through floods of tears, her head still buried in her father's chest.

"Nothing, baby. Just a champagne cork popping - just people

enjoying the party, that's all," Edmund assured her.

But as he said it an icy chill ran down his spine. What in the hell was going on? He had no idea but whatever it was, for his daughter's sake, it had to stop. Ava was already scared out of her wits, convinced that her step-father was the devil and probably traumatised by whatever it was she had witnessed that night for the rest of her life.

Well enough was enough. Edmund was going to have it out with Liuzzi. Now.

Delicately, he peeled Ava's arms away from his neck and gently placed her back down on the stool by the door. "Stay here, sweetie," he said, "Daddy will be back in just a moment."

"No, Daddy! Don't leave me, please don't leave me!" Begged the little girl.

"It's okay, honey," he said, kissing her gently on the forehead, "I'll be back before you know it, just you wait and see. I promise."

Ava snivelled, tears still streaming down her face. "You swear?"

"I swear."

As Edmund made to leave, Frankie stood in his way.

"Really?" Edmund said incredulously. "Here? In front of my daughter - after what she's been through already?"

"Just following orders."

"I don't give a damn about your orders, I care about my daughter and I'm gonna see Liuzzi whether you like it or not." Edmund made to barge past but Frankie grabbed his arm.

Edmund glared at him, anger burning in his face. "Take your hand off me," he snarled, "or so help me I'll lay you out."

Frankie stared back and after looking into the chauffeur's eyes he did not doubt it. Frankie had a daughter too, back in New York, and he understood how Edmund felt, even sympathised. However, he still did not let go.

Sensing the other man's empathy, Edmund said, "Look, stay here with my daughter. Do your job. Take care of her like you were told to by Liuzzi. I won't be but a minute. You have my word."

Against his better judgement, Frankie released his grip allowing Edmund to snatch his arm away. He then marched down the length of the huge kitchen heading determinedly for the library.

However, as he reached the kitchen door, he spotted Salvatore and Vito approaching. He stopped abruptly and pressed his back against the wall to the side of the doorway, hoping not to be seen. He did not need a run-in with Falcone, too, as he would not be as understanding as Frankie.

Salvatore and Vito were escorting two other men, rather roughly, and for a moment Edmund thought they were heading for the kitchen but, instead, Falcone opened the French doors that led through to the morning room and out onto the sun deck by the pool. Unbeknownst to Edmund, who remained unseen, they were on their way to the tennis courts that were situated to the west of the enormous garden, far away from the fairy lights and Parisian street lamps that still illuminated the eastern lawn.

Nevertheless, when they were gone, Edmund continued down the hall and, with considerable trepidation, silently opened the library door to confront Carlo Liuzzi once and for all.

***

When Salvatore, Vito and the two doomed Bodene brothers had left them, Carlo and Mildred stood in the library alone, amongst the blood and gore of what had so brutally transpired there.

Mildred felt certain she was going to die at any moment. Indeed, she had scarcely felt more sure of anything in her life. She was terrified, yet almost resigned to it. Carlo was an evil, vicious man, a murderous, sadistic maniac - the extent of which she had not truly realised until now. She had known him to be quick tempered, volatile and passionate - a man she should have known better than to cross. But it was too late now and she was destined to pay the ultimate price for disrespecting him with her whorish behaviour.

149

She felt her husband's gaze burn into her, but was too afraid to face him, standing there, as she was, dishevelled, caked in the blood of the dead boy lying by her feet. She knew he had died as a result of her own selfish, extremely foolish actions but she was numb to the guilt and feared only for herself, knowing she would be joining the boy in the afterlife very shortly.

Carlo stepped closer her to her now, so that his mouth was just inches from her ear as he spoke. "You are the mother of an angel," he said, which took Mildred somewhat by surprise and she turned her head very slightly to look at him. He then picked up her left hand gently, almost tenderly. "Were you not - or should I say, had I not been reminded of that so horribly tonight, then you would now be dead. Please be certain of that."

Unexpectedly, Mildred felt a glimmer of hope - *would the little girl be her salvation again? Could she really be that lucky?*

"After what Ava saw here I cannot in good conscience kill you," he continued, "God knows I want to, but she must be traumatised enough after seeing you rutting like a slut with all those men - and after I—" he paused momentarily to phrase it properly, "—after I put an end to it so permanently."

Mildred felt relief wash over her and very nearly passed out, her legs almost giving way beneath her, but she held steady. Carlo was still holding onto her hand, turning the heavy gold wedding band that he, himself, had placed on her finger seven years earlier. Till death do us part.

"It would be too cruel. Too much for her to take." He went on. "How could I ever look into Ava's little eyes again knowing that I had killed her mother?"

Mildred whimpered slightly and a tear trickled down her cheek, almost overcome with emotion after this unexpected reprieve.

"No. You cannot die. You must go somewhere safe from harm, where you can live out your life free from any further temptation -

150

somewhere that allows me to look into your daughter's eyes with a clear conscience and tell her you're alive and well, but where you'll never be able to hurt her again."

A chill ran through Mildred now. What did this mean? Where must she go - surely not to a nunnery where he supposedly sent his real daughter? Mildred remembered the day, shortly after she and Edmund arrived, when Maria left the mansion escorted by Salvatore. She had also heard the staff whispering about it, although she had never discussed it with Carlo directly as it had not concerned her. On the contrary, having Maria out of the way had worked extremely well in her favour.

But it concerned her now. "Carlo, please— I can't go to a convent - I won't survive, I'll die—" she pleaded.

Liuzzi chuckled, a cold, mirthless laugh. "Don't worry, my dear, I won't be sending you away anywhere. You have my word. I have got something much more appropriate lined up for you."

Mildred felt her bowels shift as she saw the malicious glint in her husband's evil eyes.

"But, I digress," he said. "Naturally, we can no longer remain married. It would not be fair to me. I am a man with needs after all and I may wish to re-marry once this whole sordid affair is behind us. And I refuse to be married to a whore - I'm sure you understand. It would not befit my status."

Mildred's head was spinning. What was going on, what did he have in mind for her, where on earth was she going to end up? With her mind awash with panic, she did not notice as Carlo stretched out her ring finger. Neither did she feel him place the curved blade of the bejewelled dagger beneath it, between the ring and the knuckle.

"So, I'm afraid," he said, with a menacing rasp, I must declare us divorced". With that he violently pushed the blade upwards, slicing it effortlessly through her flesh and sinew, before forcefully cutting through the delicate bone. Mildred screamed out in agony and struggled to free herself but Carlo held fast until the slim digit was finally detached, blood spurting from the ugly stump that remained. He looked at the severed finger victoriously, which was still encircled by the solid gold wedding band, delighting in Mildred's anguish, as he held it in front of her face as if it was some macabre trophy that he had won.

"Now I am free of you," he said, as the door behind him opened and Edmund walked in.

***

Edmund entered the room, full of intention, full of courage but as soon as he took in the macabre scene that was laid out before him, it all evaporated. It was as if he had walked into hell and Carlo Liuzzi was presiding proudly over it - the very picture of Lucifer himself.

Ava's words suddenly came rushing back to Edmund, 'I think Daddy Carlo's the devil', she had said, and now he did not doubt her for a second.

Edmund's face drained of colour as he looked about him. A young man's corpse lay close to where he stood, one side of his face blown completely off. Another body lay further away, mutilated and ruined beyond all recognition. Blood was everywhere, masses of it, in pools and in spatters.

He then saw Mildred; dishevelled, tear-stained and clearly in pain. Blood was pouring from her hand and he was convinced that she, too, was about to die. She looked at him, imploringly, begging him to save her, clinging to the slightest hope that Edmund, the good man she had once loved yet so readily discarded, would come to her rescue.

As Edmund stared at her; filthy, bedraggled and desperate, suddenly the years of resentment melted away. He saw once again the beautiful girl from Iowa he had married and the mother of his darling daughter. Any ill feeling he had towards her vanished, instantly replaced by pity and compassion. She needed him now

152

again. More so than she ever had before and he had to save her.

Without thought or care for himself he rushed forward, focused only on her and blind to Liuzzi who had turned to face him, the curved dagger in his hand.

Edmund did not feel the knife enter his stomach, only Liuzzi's arm upon him as he tried to prevent him from reaching his wife. He heard Mildred scream and briefly registered the utter shock on her face as his body went cold and he sank to his knees. He could not comprehend why his legs and arms would not respond as he desperately tried to struggle forward to save Mildred.

Only when he was laying on his back, looking up at the blurred image of Carlo Liuzzi standing over him, the dagger dripping blood in his hand and the sound of Mildred crying in the background did Edmund finally understand.

"Oh, my poor Ava," he whispered with his last dying breath.

***

Forty-five minutes after his murderous rampage, Carlo Liuzzi was standing under the hot, almost scolding jets of his shower, washing off the caked on blood of his victims.

Bobby and Wyatt had been killed in the same monstrous way as Armando Calabrese; chained up naked in the garden store under the tennis courts, their manhoods severed and their stomach's sliced open so that their intestines spilled out over the floor.

Their bodies, together with those of Donnie and Ira would be driven out to the desert and buried before the sun came up. Salvatore and Vito would see to it. The library would be cleaned and re-decorated by a specialist crew who would leave no trace of the horrors that had taken place there.

As for Mildred, she had passed out moments after Edmund's murder and had awoken to find herself locked in a soundproof room deep under the mansion.

This was to be her new home. A life of imprisonment and

solitude with time enough to think about how she had wronged her husband.

When Carlo designed the mansion many years earlier, he had included a 'safe room' in the plans, thinking it only prudent after making so many enemies during his time in New York.

However, until that night only he and Salvatore knew of its existence.

The room was accessed via a narrow staircase which was concealed behind a sliding bookcase in the study. The steel stairway led down two storeys under the house with the safe room sitting at the end of a slender corridor on the lowest level.

The room itself was fully air-conditioned and contained a double bed, a television, a small shower enclosure and a toilet. There was also a large larder and a substantial refrigerator - both presently empty. The near impregnable walls and door were made from ten-inch steel - the extreme thickness guaranteeing that no one would hear Mildred's screams. Ever.

As Carlo lathered his powerful, hairy body, the blood running in rivers down his naked legs and into the drain, he thought only of Ava and how he was going to regain her trust.

She had witnessed some hideous things that night and he was somehow going to have to explain them away. His plan was to tell her the three Texan boys were attacking her mommy and he had acted as he had to save her. It would be hard for her to swallow at first but time was a great healer and he felt confident he could win her over eventually. He would tell her that her mother had gone away somewhere safe to recuperate.

He could look Ava in the eyes and legitimately tell her that Mildred was not dead and the girl would be able to see the truth in it.

Edmund, however, was a different matter. Ava was much closer to him than Carlo would have liked, much closer than she was with Mildred and the little girl would feel his loss keenly.

It had not been Liuzzi's intention to kill Edmund but the man just charged forward straight onto the knife and there was nothing Carlo could do about it. Indeed, with the red haze of madness still burning he had just reacted instinctively.

However, mean it or not, he had to deal with the consequences but he could not, under any circumstances, let Ava think he had killed her father.

So he would have to convince her of a different scenario.

Unfortunately, this would mean the little girl being hurt even more but he would be there to comfort her and help her through it.

After all, he would be her only father now.

He would be her daddy, not just her 'Daddy Carlo'.

Nevertheless, he would arrange for Ava to find Edmund hanging in the apartment above the garage, a typewritten suicide note close by, explaining that he could no longer go on living life as a failure. The note would also instruct Ava to put her trust in her step-father, to rely on him and to love him.

Edmund's wounds would be bound and concealed and he would be dressed in his spare chauffeur's uniform, so Ava would not suspect Liuzzi's part in his death.

Carlo knew it was cruel, that the little girl would be grief-stricken and traumatised all the more after what she had seen in the library, but he could see no other way of explaining away Edmund's death without implicating himself. Ava had to see it with her own eyes. But she was a strong child and with Carlo's help she would make it through.

***

When he was thoroughly clean and impeccably dressed once more, looking, as always, like an Italian Clark Gable, Carlo went down to the kitchen to talk to Ava who he found asleep on Frankie DeLuca's lap. Frankie was sitting on the stool by the back door, his arms wrapped around the girl protectively. They had been waiting there over two hours and when Edmund failed to return Ava had cried herself to sleep in her bodyguard's arms.

Carlo studied the little girl. She looked like a sleeping angel and rather than wake her up he instructed Frankie to take her up to bed. Liuzzi followed at a slight distance as his underling did as asked, watching as DeLuca gently lay her head on the pillow and pulled the blankets up over her.

There was a look on Frankie's face that Carlo had not seen before; a caring, almost fatherly expression and a twinge of jealousy stirred in Liuzzi's gut. But he let it go, the girl had already been through enough and tomorrow she was going to have to go through a whole lot more. She would need all the support and understanding she could get and maybe Frankie could prove useful in that regard.

As Carlo closed her bedroom door, his thoughts again turned to the Oscars and he felt a little frisson of excitement at the prospect of picking up his very first Academy Award.

But he would not win.

Chapter Eleven

Hell's Kitchen, New York 1957

Nate and Danny were an odd couple; as tight as a pair of brothers could possibly be but polar opposites in almost every way. The only thing in which they were similar was that they were both smart. They got good grades and did well in school. At home, the two nine-year-olds helped with the chores, rarely talked back and mostly did as they were told. Megan could not be more proud of either of them and even though only Nate was hers by blood, she treated them both equally.

But out on the streets where they played it was different. Nate, whilst not particularly seeking approval, was generally accepted by the other boys whereas Danny, who couldn't have given a damn anyway, was not. But he had Nate and that was more than enough.

Nate was small for his age and skinny. He had a shock of bright red, curly hair, with kind, blue eyes and a pale complexion that was liberally sprinkled with freckles. Understanding and compassionate by nature, Nate was softly spoken and unassuming. A regular at the local church and deeply religious like his mother, he always said his prayers before bedtime without fail. He was also incredibly pleased to have recently become an alter boy.

Conversely, Danny was tall and dark with green eyes and a tanned complexion. An extremely good looking boy with broad shoulders and an athletic physique. Even at nine it was clear to see he was destined to break the hearts of many women. Danny was naturally tough, good with his fists and a fiercely loyal ally, but cross him and you would find a formidable enemy. He was fiery by nature; more passionate and intense than his brother but he was quick to smile, too, and had an irresistible charm to which few females were immune - including Megan and his fourth grade teacher - who both found it impossible to stay mad at him for long.

However, Danny was not particularly comfortable in his own skin. He didn't fit in somehow, but also never really felt the need to. He knew he was not like the other boys - certainly not like the Irish ones anyway and he never truly felt like he was 'Danny Malone'. He could not put his finger on it but he knew deep down, even at such a young age, that was not who he was meant to be.

Unlike Nate, Danny was not particularly religious. He supposed he believed in God but he definitely did not feel the need to go to church to prove it - much to the chagrin of Megan. On Sunday mornings, he'd much rather be shooting hoops or helping Double J fix his motorcycle than kneeling in some church praying.

Nevertheless, despite their obvious differences, the boys just somehow gelled and the weaknesses of one tended to perfectly compliment the strengths of the other.

Whilst Danny was the more hot-headed of the two, Nate had a calm air of serenity about him. Indeed, out on the streets, if anyone picked on Danny, which they invariably did because of his less than Gaelic looks, then Nate could often diffuse the situation. He would readily step in front of his brother and calm things down.

It was almost comical to watch as this small, weedy looking child stepped up in front of the taller, stronger and physically more imposing one.

But in spite of this obvious irregularity, the other boys, although all much bigger than Nate, mostly respected him and left him alone.

Not least, he suspected, because he was watched over by Red Tierny, the owner of the diner where his mother worked, who had taken it upon himself, unbidden, to become the boy's unofficial guardian.

However, Red had no such interest in Danny, who only had Nate to speak up for him. Nonetheless, when diplomacy failed, it was Danny who stepped in front of Nate and put an end to things with his fists. Few of his peers would tackle him on their own for fear of getting a beating, but when they were in a group it tended to be open season. But Danny always put up one hell of a fight.

Danny's natural protector and mentor was Double J. But Jay could not be seen to be sympathetic to the boy as it was against gang law and against Rebel's specific orders. But away from the pack or behind closed doors, they were the best of friends.

It was Jay who taught Danny to fight; how to throw a right hook and how to render an attacker defenceless by kicking him the balls. It wasn't from the Marquis of Queensbury's rule book but rather from Jay's unwritten handbook of street-fighting one-o-one, at which he was a master. There was only one other better in the whole of The Kitchen and that was his own brother, Rebel.

Jay also showed Danny how to strip an engine and re-build it, how to make a perfect layup shot and how to pop the cap off a beer bottle on the edge of a table. Needless to say, Megan did not wholeheartedly approve of all he taught him - but she was grateful he took an interest when others around him did not.

Jay was great with Nate, too, but it was with Danny that he had a particular bond.

Megan's two boys were not officially affiliated with any gangs although each, in their own way, had links to the Westside Dukes. However, most of their contemporaries had already been conscripted and could be seen around The Kitchen showing off their 'colours' - even though they were still only in third or fourth grade. Gang leaders liked to recruit their troops early and Rebel was no different.

159

Nonetheless, Nate was off limits upon Red's say-so and Danny was unwanted - not even by the Italian gangs. He was a wop by birth and a mick by upbringing and as such was considered a mongrel by both groups.

But neither boy saw much of a future for themselves as part of a gang. Nate was already considering going into the priesthood and Danny had his sights set on a life far away from Hell's Kitchen.

Nate expressed it best when he said he felt as if he'd been put on the earth to do something worthwhile. God, he said, had told him so.

Danny knew what he meant - although it wasn't God speaking to him, but his own sense of purpose.

***

Megan lay in the centre of the ancient bed which had been included with the apartment and bit her lip to suppress a gasp of pleasure. As she surrendered willingly to Jay's masterful attentions, she prayed their sinful lovemaking could not be heard through the paper thin walls, the guilt of her wicked existence washing over her again, as it did on most afternoons at around the same time.

She and Jay writhed together on the lumpy mattress, stained with the filth from God knows how many previous tenants, but neither of them cared in the heat of the moment. Yet as the bright afternoon sun shone in through the thin cotton drapes to flood the small bedroom with light, it exposed further the squalid conditions in which Megan and her two children were living.

Large patches of damp, which over the years had crept relentlessly across the walls were clearly visible in the sunlight through the tired paintwork, as were the scratches and chips on the cheap secondhand furniture and bare floorboards.

However, there was little Megan could do to improve her surroundings but she knew, at least, the sheets were clean - changed once a week without fail by her own fair hands. The apartment was clean, too, and spotlessly tidy, but it still did not disguise the general state of disrepair the low rent accommodation was in, yet it was all she could afford.

She was between shifts at the diner. The lunchtime rush was over and she now had a couple of hours free until the boys came home from school. Later on, after she had made them their dinner, she would head back to the diner and work until gone midnight. Then, after a few precious hours of sleep, she would be back there again, just before sun up, to work the breakfast shift. So she was grateful of the free time she had each afternoon. But it did little to assuage her guilt.

As she lay there, gripping the bars of the brass bedstead, with Double J sending her to a heaven quite unlike the one she imagined back in County Clare, Megan knew their affair was wrong and that it was against God's holy lore, but she could not stop herself. He made her feel so good - so free, so alive. But their liaisons were fraught with risk for both of them.

Megan and Jay had been lovers for almost two years now and remarkably they had managed to keep their romance a secret but things were becoming difficult. Even though Megan knew she was not in love with Jay, she did like being with him and was fairly certain he felt the same way about her. But both of them were under pressure from outside forces which would possibly put an end to their regular afternoon dalliances.

Jay had been asked by Rebel to step-up and take control of the Dukes. Whilst Rebel, now twenty and too old to be running with a street gang, intended to move on to bigger, better things. He wanted to get into the rackets, become organised and make some real money.

Recently he had been hanging with Andy Loughlin, a twenty-eight year old ex-con and ex-member of the Westside Dukes, who was a well known local thug and small time operator. Loughlin, broad and thick set with wiry blonde hair and a big square face, was the son of one of Red Tierny's old enforcer buddies from back in the day, and into anything that turned a profit. He and Rebel had big plans to get into the drugs trade and thought the Dukes would make ideal soldiers and traffickers in their new venture.

And who better to keep the Dukes in line than Rebel's own brother, Double J, who was more than up to the task, for a decent share of the profits, of course.

Jay, himself, viewed these anticipated profits as a means to get out of Hell's Kitchen someday; a way of earning enough to build a life for himself in a less God forsaken part of the world. But in order for that to become a reality he had to make sacrifices.

He knew that Rebel simply would not tolerate his paternal interest in Danny and if he found out Jay was investing so much time in the boy it would cause immeasurable damage to the brothers' relationship.

Furthermore, Rebel and Loughlin were hoping Red would put them in touch with a few of the right people as he was still well connected and, more importantly, well respected by those who could help them get their plans off the ground.

So upsetting Red, at this point, was not an option.

And that was why Jay was playing with fire.

Red had made no secret of his feelings towards Meggie and had somehow assumed, with no encouragement from her, that the pair of them would be married one day. Indeed, even though he had not so much as kissed her, he already considered them to be all but betrothed. And as for the issue of intimacy, Red confidently felt that would change soon, upon the day she would undoubtedly say 'yes' to his long planned proposal.

Which is exactly the reason why Meggie was feeling under pressure, herself.

Already racked with guilt over her sacrilegious affair with Double J, fearing God would judge her as an unholy sinner and banish her to Hell for all eternity, she was also concerned she may have unwittingly been sending Red the wrong signals concerning her feelings towards him.

But when she thought back over her time at the diner she was almost certain she had not.

There was no denying Red had been good to her, especially when she first arrived in Hell's Kitchen, when he was the only one to offer her a job. He had also helped her to organise a sitter for the boys whilst she was at work and to become more accepted within the community, for which she would always be grateful. But over the last few years he had become something more than just 'friendly'. He treated her with an unwarranted familiarity which made her feel uneasy. Furthermore he gave customers the impression that he and she were a couple and after a time the whole neighbourhood just assumed they were, especially when he insisted on escorting her to church every Sunday as if they were engaged.

Also, at the diner, when she did something well, he would often give her a congratulatory pat on the behind. Occasionally his hand would linger there gratuitously and sometimes, even more disgustingly, he would rub himself against her in the tight walkway behind the counter as he passed. Often she could feel his manhood as he pushed himself against her bottom as she worked the register or fixed a soda on the pretext he was squeezing by; his hot breath upon her neck as he savoured the light scent of her perfume.

Red would also speak to her quite openly about their future together as if it was a forgone conclusion and even more irritatingly offer her his unsolicited thoughts on what was best for her children when he and she eventually set up home together. This was by far the most infuriating aspect of Red's over familiarity as his view was so unbalanced and biased.

Nate was a source of great pride to Red and he would speak of him in glowing terms. He took pleasure in planning the boy's future within the seminary and his eventual acceptance into the priesthood. He dreamt of a time when 'Father Nate', his boy, would be the local priest administering to an awed flock and he, Red, would be responsible for bestowing such a man upon them.

Danny, however, in Red's vision of the future, did not fare so well. He was to be sent off to Jersey, to a strict boarding school, where his tanned complexion could be hidden from view and cause the least amount of embarrassment to Red and his bride. Out of sight and out of mind.

This, of course, was completely abhorrent to Meggie, as was any future with Red as her husband, but she did not know how to discourage him.

She could not even understand why he thought they might be a suitable match. After all, she was twenty-eight and supposedly in the prime of life, whilst he was thirty years her senior and heading towards retirement. Maybe that was it; perhaps he wanted someone to look after him in his old age - to do his washing, cleaning and cooking - someone to keep him warm in bed at night and make him feel young again.

But she could not bear the thought of his rough, liver-spotted hands pawing at her flesh or to feel his naked, heavy body upon her. The very idea of it repulsed her.

However, he was not an easy man to turn down. He was a powerful figure within the community and many people acted upon his say so. Meggie was reliant on Red for her livelihood and if she was to spurn his advances then it may well impact on that, too. Few would employ her if she lost her job and if she could not find work then it would only be a matter of time before she and the boys found themselves homeless. The friends she had made, with Red's assistance, would just as quickly turn their backs on her and things could go from bad to worse very quickly.

As Meggie slid out of bed, leaving Double J dozing lazily within it, at last spent after their afternoon exertions, she suddenly felt trapped.

She crossed naked to the tiny bathroom and looked at herself in the small, cracked mirror that hung on a nail above the sink.

Her hair was ruffled and her cheeks were still a little flushed from the afternoon's exertions but there were dark rings under her eyes and she looked tired. Even though she was exhausted she was not sleeping well, her mind awash with worry about the predicament she now found herself in. She had asked God, many times, what she must do but had been given no answer and she prayed He had not abandoned her for being so sinful.

It was at times like this she missed Nathaniel's wisdom but thinking of him only made her feel more guilty about the nineteen year old boy laying in her bed.

Was being with Jay so wrong?

If it was, then surely marrying a man she did not love was worse?

Her mind was filled with questions, her thoughts confused and jumbled.

What the hell was she going to do?

***

When Jay was gone and the boys had returned from school, Meggie once again put on her pale blue uniform and headed back to the diner for her evening shift.

When she got there, a few of the Dukes were loitering about outside, as per usual, but thankfully Double J was nowhere to be seen. She did notice just how young some of them appeared to be though and was grateful to God that neither of her two boys were mixed up with them. It was bad enough Jay was.

Nevertheless, she nodded to a couple of them and walked on past.

She felt more fatigued than usual this evening and her head ached from all the thoughts swirling around inside it but as soon as she pushed open the door, hearing the tinkle of the little bell above it, she forced a smile and put her game face on ready for work.

The diner was empty as it was too early for the evening trade as yet and Red sat in one of the booths reading the newspaper, drinking a cup of coffee, taking it easy before the rush began.

"Ah, Meggie darlin', there you are," he said, in his lilting Irish brogue as he peered at her over his wire-framed reading glasses.

"Yep, here I am again," she replied with false enthusiasm. "Things pretty slow still I see."

"Aye, but it'll pick up in a while, same as always and in a couple of hours we'll be glad for a slow spell."

"I guess. You want me to switch on the grill?"

"No, no darlin', that'll wait. Come sit with me, have some coffee - make the most of the quiet."

"Don't be silly, you enjoy your coffee - I'll have a runaround with the broom." She didn't really feel in the mood for a chat and besides, she was trying to avoid situations in which he might find an opportunity to propose. It was only a matter of time, Meggie sensed, before he officially asked her to be his wife and the longer that could be avoided the better.

"Nonsense, lass," said Red, "I won't hear of it. You come and sit down with me - there's something I've been meaning to ask you anyway and now seems like as good a time as any."

Meggie's heart sank and suddenly she felt a bit weak at the knees. This was it. This was the moment she had been dreading. With rising panic, she slowly walked over to the booth where Red's bulky frame was parked. His shirt, pants and apron were all white and liberally stained with grease and his sleeves were rolled up to expose his meaty forearms. Red's eponymous hair was mostly grey now with just a bit of faded orange in the receding curls on top and his big square face was speckled with brown freckles which contrasted starkly against his pale skin.

He smiled as she reached the booth. "That's it lass," he said as he closed his newspaper and folded it neatly. "Siddown, siddown, take the weight off."

Much against her better judgement and filled with a sense of impending doom, Meggie made a move to do as instructed. Yet when she glanced down and saw the folded newspaper before her, her eyes suddenly sprung open as if she had seen a ghost. A second later, her head started to spin wildly and she lurched backwards unsteadily, clutching futilely at the air as she tried to save herself from collapsing.

"Meggie?" said Red, concerned, tossing his specs onto the table top and leaping to his feet as he tried to catch her.

But before he could reach her, Meggie's eyes rolled upwards, her legs buckled and she dropped to the floor like a stone.

Immediately Red was out of the booth and kneeling by her side. "Oh, my darlin' girl, what on earth is the matter?" He was saying as Meggie's eyes fluttered open briefly and she saw his blurry form looming over her.

"Are you sick, lassie? Have I been working you too hard? What in God's name have I done to you?"

But it was nothing Red had done or, indeed, anything he was about to do that had caused Megan to faint.

It was the shock of seeing the photo on the front page of the newspaper. The photograph that had been taken just yesterday at LaGuardia airport.

The photograph of Maria.

Chapter Twelve

Lake Como, Italy 1957

Diego Del Toro was nervous. He checked his reflection in the enormous gilt framed mirror that hung on the wall of the spacious hallway in his beautiful 17th century lakeside villa and prayed everything would go as planned.

The Villa itself was set upon a lush, tree lined peninsula that jutted out from the shoreline. It had been built on the uppermost level of four, fastidiously maintained, man-made terraces, each lined with beautifully sculpted stone balustrade. Narrow stairways, again with carved stone balusters, led down from one tier to another. Each terrace offered spectacular views of the lake and featured immaculately cut lawns with borders full of sweet-scented azaleas, rhododendrons and other dazzling blooms. There were also many trees such as pine, soaring cypress and oak to give shaded and fragrant respite from the afternoon sun. At the base of the lowest terrace there were moorings for several boats and two sizeable motor launches were tied up beside a small, stone jetty. To the side there was a boathouse and slipway.

The villa was a large, high-sided, three story dwelling with tall, shuttered windows. A grand, columned porch extended over the main entrance and a covered veranda, again regally columned and sculpted by ancient craftsmen, lay along the lake side of the property.

Most of the upper rooms featured french windows with ornate iron balconies decorated with climbing flowers.

In short, it was a fabulously impressive property in an absolutely idyllic setting, which Diego hoped may help in some way to create the right mood.

Eight months earlier, the day after Maria had been given a clean bill of health, Diego had summoned up the courage to ask her to marry him.

But it had not gone well.

Whilst Maria was deemed fully recovered by Dr Degollado, she still had no memory of her life before Cadiz and this troubled her greatly. With this in mind, she had told Diego that she loved him, too, which he found extremely reassuring, but asked if he would wait several more months before receiving her answer.

She told him she had given herself a year for her memory to return. Enough time, she believed, to honour anyone who may be standing in the shadows of her past who could potentially get in the way of her and Diego's future happiness. If her memory had not returned at the end of that time and if no one had come forward to lay claim on her, then she would consider herself free to move on with her life.

Maria's instincts told her there was no one else but she did have a feeling of great loss within her which she just could not explain. Some niggling suspicion that someone, somewhere needed her.

Diego told her he completely understood and would happily sacrifice the remaining eight months of the year she had allowed herself if it meant he could spend the rest of his life married to her. However, he dare not think of how he would feel at the end of that year if it was found she was married to another. But he vowed not to stand in her way should that be the case.

Nevertheless, in the intervening months, Maria had been his almost constant companion. With her health fully restored the pair of them, along with Delores Morales acting as chaperone, had flown around the world in the Hermes IV visiting many of the Matador hotels.

Cairo, London, Rio, Helsinki, Delhi, Monaco and many more. The trips were largely to ensure every aspect of the chain was running smoothly but often they were for ribbon-cutting ceremonies for the opening of a new hotel. A celebrity or local dignitary would usually be the person holding the scissors but Diego always liked to be there to represent The Company's interests. It was good business and he was exceptional at it. Maria had come to respect him all the more as she watched him work and proudly stood alongside him whenever he asked her.

Sometimes they were accompanied by Juan Pablo Clemente but mostly Diego had him working on other projects; laying the groundwork for future Matador ventures primarily in America where interesting opportunities awaited.

But that was all for discussion at some later date. For now Diego had other things on his mind.

Eight months had now past since his proposal. The clock had run down a week ago. Maria's memory had still not returned and no trace of her former life had been found. She was a woman with no past, only a future and as Diego polished his glasses on his pale blue tie and tried to smooth his wayward hair, he hoped the time would now be right for her to accept that her future was with him.

Two days earlier, Maria had accompanied Diego to the opening of the Portofino Matador and the two of them had driven up from there in Diego's bright red Maserati Spider. She had looked so beautiful in the passenger seat when he glanced at her; a cross between the sophistication of Audrey Hepburn and the sexiness of Gina Lollobrigida. Her green eyes sparkled and she had a big grin on her face as the wind blew through her long, dark hair. She looked utterly adorable and he thought his heart might burst with love for her.

It was nine years to the day since he first laid eyes on her. Exactly nine years that he had wanted her to be his wife and tonight he hoped that would at last become a reality.

Delores and Juan Pablo had flown up to Como ahead of Diego and Maria to make the preparations. Maria, herself, had been booked into a hotel a few kilometres away from the villa, unaware of its existence, on the pretence that Diego had business elsewhere but she was assured he would join her again soon. Maria had been kept occupied by Delores in the short time he had been absent but now she had been asked to dress for an evening out.

Juan Pablo was to accompany her and they would apparently meet up with Diego later. It all seemed very mysterious but Maria happily went along with it as Diego had never given her cause to doubt him.

Maria put on a simple, calf-length, white dress with a wide cowl neck. The dress, nipped in at the waist to emphasise her striking figure, was teamed with white satin court shoes and a pair of pearl earrings that had been a gift from Diego. To complete the look, she wore her hair up, piled high on her head to enhance her long graceful neck. The finished effect was stunning and she was the picture of understated elegance.

At the appointed time, Juan Pablo and Maria arrived at the magnificent villa in its stunningly picturesque setting. It was dusk and the warm evening air was blowing gently off the lake. The full moon was already glowing in the darkening sky and the slight lulling of the waves as they lapped at the shore could just be heard above the evening chatter of the nightingales.

Juan Pablo escorted Maria through the wrought iron gates that led onto the property and then, most oddly, ushered her onwards alone. The trees lining the drive had been strung with tiny lights that cast their glow on the ancient flagstones under her feet and lit her way down the short winding approach to the villa. Delores was waiting for her by the front door under the wide columned porch and escorted her over the threshold into the high ceilinged foyer.

"What's going on?" Maria asked nervously.

"Nothing child," replied Delores. "Señor Diego is waiting for you on the veranda, follow the candles to find him."

Maria looked at her former nurse who had now become her trusted assistant and friend with a curious expression but Delores' face was inscrutable and she merely waved her forward.

The grand hallway was lined with candles and Maria tentatively followed the illuminated trail trying not to be awed by the valuable paintings that were displayed on the walls.

Eventually she came out onto a magnificent veranda which gave way to stunning views of the lake. The moon shone on the water and a thousand lights from the shore dotted the coastline making the whole scene seem magical.

Flowers were in abundance and the air was filled with their perfumed scent. As Maria noticed Diego standing nervously by the stone steps that led to the garden, a string quartet began to play a romantic melody and she knew then why she was there.

She smiled and a little squadron of butterflies began to flutter their wings in her stomach.

Diego looked handsome, yet endearingly awkward in a navy silk suit that he was wearing over a crisp white shirt and powder blue tie. He resembled a young, slightly more studious, rather more nervous, Stewart Granger and Maria knew without doubt that she loved him.

He smiled as he approached her and ran his fingers through his dark hair. Then, when he was facing her, he stood stiff-backed and straight, keeping his restless hands forcibly by his side and his expression earnest and sincere.

"Maria," he said quietly, staring directly into her big green eyes,

"It is nine years today that I first saw you and nine years today that I have loved you. You are my world. You are my heart." He paused to swallow down his emotion as he saw a tear trickle down Maria's cheek, her eyes now brimming.

Then he went down on one knee and took her trembling hand in his. "I love you. I always have and I always will. Until my dying breath. Please, I beg you, will you do me the enormous honour of becoming my wife?"

She gasped at the words, tears now running down both cheeks in tiny rivers as he pulled a small box from his pocket and opened it, offering the contents to her. Inside was a gold ring with a diamond the size of a rock sitting on top which was encircled by a cluster of eight smaller diamonds. Nine in all; one for every year he had loved her.

"Marry me, Maria. Marry me please." He said.

She looked down into his deep brown eyes, the emotion clear to see. "Yes," she replied. "Yes, yes - a thousand times yes. I will. I will marry you, Diego Del Toro - it will be my greatest pleasure to be your wife.

＊

Delores was, indeed, a most valuable assistant. She knew to the nth degree Maria's exact measurements and her very specific taste in clothes. The wedding dress she had chosen for her was stunning; a narrow bodice with a shallowly scooped neckline, tight at the waist with a ballerina style, full skirt over numerous petticoats that fell just below the knee. The dress was sleeveless and cut from the finest silk. The simple veil was held in place by a pretty white band with a small bow on top.

Four hours after her acceptance of Diego's proposal, at a quarter to midnight, Maria stood in the vestibule of the small hillside church that looked out over Lake Como as the wedding music began to play.

Diego had pre-arranged everything. He had not wanted to wait a moment longer for Maria to be his bride and she was in complete agreement, they had already wasted too much time.

Diego stood by the alter wearing the same blue suit he had on earlier with his hair, for once, impeccably brushed and neat. His nerves were much less intense now she had accepted his proposal. Juan Pablo Clemente stood beside him in matching attire, proud to be best man.

The church, even though it was all but empty, looked extremely romantic. Lit entirely by candlelight with flowers lining the aisle and rose petals sprinkled on the floor. It could not have been more perfect.

Miguel Degollado had been flown in for the ceremony, in the hope that Maria's answer would be favourable, and he had taken up duty as 'father of the bride'.

Delores was fussing with the veil but as the second verse of the music struck up, she went to find her seat on the 'bride's side' of the church.

Slowly, Maria and Miguel made their way down the aisle until, at last, she stood shoulder to shoulder with Diego. He took off his spectacles and slipped them into his breast pocket as he smiled at her with his eyes full of love and said in a whisper, "You are beautiful."

Once Degollado was seated next to Delores, the priest took his place in front of Maria and Diego and, after a suitable pause to allow things to settle, he began to speak to the tiny congregation.

A short while later, as the church bells chimed the stroke of midnight, he declared Diego and Maria to be 'man and wife'.

Then they kissed.

***

They honeymooned at the villa for another wondrous week then transferred to Diego's yacht, *Corrida*, which was anchored off the island of Capri, for an additional fortnight. It was upon the yacht he had first laid eyes on Maria and it seemed apt to both of them that the luxury vessel play its part in their union.

It was a blissful time, which was spent making love, sun-bathing, laughing, eating and just happily being in the company of one another.

The Corrida had a sizeable crew and an excellent chef so the newlyweds wanted for nothing. Matador was temporarily in the capable hands of Juan Pablo Clemente and Delores was enjoying a well-earned rest back in Cadiz. So Maria and Diego's existence on board was trouble-free and without unwanted interruption.

Over dinner one evening, Diego was speaking about his business passionately and shared his views on how he saw it progressing.

Matador had rapidly growing concerns in the shipping, newspaper and automobile industries. Its burgeoning involvement with an American television network was also evolving quickly and, in addition to this, a much sort after route into the movie business had recently opened up.

It was a little known fact that the ageing boss of 'Viscount Studios', an enormous privately owned movie studio in Hollywood, was dying of cancer. As such, he had been in top secret discussions with Matador for some time about a possible buy out. Those talks had now come to fruition and a deal was imminent.

It was a bold move that would turn the movie business on its head and shake-up the ever-so comfortable, happily complacent power players of Hollywood. The deal would encompass all aspects of the business, meaning that the contracts of the actors and production crew currently signed to Viscount would automatically transfer to Matador.

Of course, success would all be reliant on output but Diego felt confidant that Viscount, under his guidance, could become one of the strongest studios in Hollywood.

Maria did not doubt him in the slightest.

175

***

Two days before the end of their honeymoon, Diego and a couple of crewmen took the dinghy off to Capri. They needed one or two supplies and Diego needed to make a couple of phone calls.

Whilst he was gone, Maria took a book up to the sun deck and topped up her deep tan whilst reading a few more chapters of her book.

She could not have been happier. It mattered little to her now that her memory had gone as her future was with Diego and together they would make new memories - and, if they were lucky, maybe even a couple of kids, too. Maria smiled at the thought.

To be a mother would be wonderful and Diego would be an excellent father, she just knew it.

But as she lay there, thinking about babies, she had that strange, empty feeling in her stomach once more; the feeling of loss, as if someone needed her or as if she had abandoned them.

Such was the strength of this feeling she began to cry. It was inexplicable as she was weeping for something unknown, but the pull of it was immense.

Nonetheless, Maria quickly pulled herself together and resolved not to tell Diego what had happened for fear of him thinking she was losing her mind. Besides, she was probably only feeling emotional due to it being her time of the month, as was usual for her.

Even though they were only just married, Maria could not help but feel slightly disappointed by the prospect of her period as deep down she had hoped, after all their love-making, she might find herself pregnant. Yet it was clearly not to be as she could already sense the onset of her cycle.

However, there was always a next time.

***

Diego returned shortly before lunchtime with a big grin on his boyish face. He leapt barefoot out of the dinghy and onto Corrida with a bag full of shopping - a long, crusty baguette protruding out the top.

"Guess what?" he said excitedly as he pecked her on the lips. "I have good news - very good news, at least I hope you'll think it is."

"What? What is it?" she said, his excitement contagious.

"I have just spoken to Juan Pablo and he tells me that Matador have just been granted permission to build a brand new hotel on Fifth Avenue!"

"You mean Fifth Avenue, New York?" Maria asked.

"Yes - a prime site that looks out directly over Central Park - it's going to be fantastic - a flagship for the whole Matador chain."

"Wow! That is great news. I'm so proud of you, so pleased."

"But that's not it, my darling. That is just the beginning." He ran a hand through his hair and pushed up his glasses. He looked so adorable to her in that moment; so excited, so thrilled, in his baggy white shorts and pale yellow T-shirt.

"So—" Maria was still a little confused.

"So we will have to move to New York - live there - at least until the hotel is built - maybe even longer."

"Live in New York?"

"Yes, it will be perfect. From there I can easily manage our other interests in America - the West Coast is only a few hours away by plane, which is perfect for what's happening with Viscount Studios. And Europe's only a hop away in the Hermes!"

"Wow, New York!" Said Maria, surprise now giving way to joy. "Saks Fifth Avenue, Bloomingdale's, Macey's—"

"Yes, yes, my darling. All of those," Diego laughed. "But do you know what I think you'll enjoy the most?"

"What?"

"Finding us an apartment there. The biggest, best one you can find and decorating it from top to bottom exactly how you like - it will be my wedding present to you."

"Oh, Diego," she gasped, "I don't know what to say—"

"Just say 'yes," he said.

And so she did.

***

A week later, after a brief stop in Cadiz to pack up their affairs and to collect Delores. Maria and Diego landed at LaGuardia to start the next stage of their life together.

As they descended the steps from the Hermes IV and set foot upon American soil, a flashbulb popped. An opportune photographer from the New York Times had got himself an exclusive picture of hotelier and business tycoon, Diego Del Toro arriving in the city with his beautiful new bride.

The photo would be printed on the front page of the newspaper the very next day.

Chapter Thirteen

New York 1957

Meggie had been sent home by Red, escorted by two of the Dukes to ensure she got there safely and without further incident.

After witnessing her pass out in the diner, Red assumed she had been pushing herself too hard; struggling to cope with two children whilst working three gruelling shifts a day. He had ordered her to bed, insisting she did not come back to the diner until she felt completely rested.

Meggie protested but he would hear none of it. "I've got to have you healthy, darlin'," he had said, "I'll not hear it be said that I worked any woman o'mine into an early grave!"

Meggie just smiled meekly. Now was not the time to raise any objection to his assumptions about 'her' being 'his' as she was still reeling from the shock of what she had seen on the front page of The Times.

When the two gang members had deposited her outside her apartment building, she waited until they disappeared from view and then went to the newsstand on the corner of the block to buy her own copy of the newspaper, before slipping it under her coat, out of sight.

She opened her apartment door expecting to see the boys but they were not there. She was surprised at first before realising it was still early. She was home much earlier than usual and the boys were still out playing. But tonight she was pleased to be alone with her thoughts.

Megan shrugged off her coat and took the newspaper through to her bedroom, shutting the door behind her. Sitting on the bed, she steeled herself before looking at the photo on the cover of The Times again. The photo was below the fold in a throw away article made up of only a few paragraphs about a business tycoon - a hotelier, it said - named Diego Del Toro who had landed in New York yesterday to oversee the building of a new flagship hotel on Fifth Avenue. However, the only line in the story that interested Megan was the one that read, 'Mr Del Toro was accompanied by his new bride, Maria.'

There was no other mention of her but the photograph left Megan in no doubt. Maria was alive and well.

She was also in New York.

Megan was stunned. Struggling to believe it, she had seen Maria ejected from the train by Salvatore with her own eyes; watched helplessly as she was swept away over the bridge and into the steep canyon, plummeting to certain death in the waters below.

But somehow she had survived.

And not only had she survived, she had seemingly thrived.

In the nine years since Megan last set eyes on Maria, what had become of her? Had she been pining for her son? Searching for him, thinking he was maybe imprisoned in the unknown Italian monastery he had been destined for?

Maybe Maria had already discovered he was not in Italy and that she, Megan, had in fact taken him as her own.

Was that why she had come to New York, to find her son, to take him away from the only mother he had ever known?

Suddenly Meggie was panicked. Maria had been her friend and when she died - or at least when Megan thought she had died, she had been overcome with grief, unable to bear the thought of that little boy all alone in the world without a mother.

So Meggie became his mother. She had raised him, loved him as her own, given him everything she had, exactly as she had with Nate, her own flesh and blood.

Danny was nine now - nearly fully grown and she loved him with all her heart. The thought of losing him was too great to even imagine. Yet how could she, a woman of deep faith, knowingly keep another woman's child from her - especially someone like Maria who was so kind and so caring.

Megan clearly remembered how devastated Maria had been by the prospect of losing her baby boy to the monastery all those years ago on the explicit orders of her violent, unforgiving father. She had not been much more than a girl herself back then and knew how incredibly hard it must have been.

But then for Maria to be stolen away from him in such a terrible way, even before their allotted time together was over, Megan knew it would have been utterly soul destroying.

She could not even contemplate how Maria would have coped.

In the nine years that Megan had been his mother, she had never told Danny the truth.

She knew Danny felt he was different and that he did not fit into the Irish 'ideal'. She even suspected he knew he was Italian although she had never sat down and physically told him - but was in no doubt the boys at school had.

Furthermore, she had never explained how she came to be his mother or why his brother was so markedly different in appearance.

It was not that she never intended to tell him, more that she had never managed to get around to it, forever putting it off until he was older or wiser or until, perhaps, he asked her himself.

Megan started to cry. Partly for the joy of knowing Maria lived, but also with despair at the prospect of losing her son.

She sobbed silently for sometime, sad for what her life had

become; she was in a relationship that was going nowhere; being pressured into marrying a man she did not love; and raising a child that in the eyes of God belonged to another.

After a while, she dried her tears and crossed to the shabby chest-of-drawers that had been included with the apartment. She stooped and pulled open the bottom drawer; the place where she kept her most prized possessions. In it was the veil she wore when she married Nathaniel as well as a velvet box which housed the gold cufflinks he had been given by his father. There was a shawl of her mother's and photographs of her two dead brothers along with several other cherished items she had picked up over the years - none with any real monetary value but priceless in all other ways.

Tucked at the back, under her mother's shawl, was a small, leather bound bible with an ornate metal clasp which kept it tightly shut.

Megan had thought of this many times in the years that Danny was growing up; the last trace of his real mother who had entrusted it to Megan's care, to hold for the child she had never known until he was old enough to understand the truth.

Her hands trembled as she pressed the button that sprung the clasp and tentatively opened the bible. She turned the pages until she found the hollowed out section in the middle. Sitting there, exactly where Maria, herself, had placed it, was the envelope she had addressed to *My Son*. Alongside it sat the gold locket, inscribed *Always and Forever*.

Megan snapped open the locket and saw the small, oval-shaped photograph of Maria as she had been at seventeen. She looked just as youthful in The New York Times photo taken yesterday. The years had clearly been kind.

On the opposing face of the locket, opposite the photograph was a lock of jet black hair. Maria's hair. And as Megan delicately ran a finger over it, she burst into tears once more.

182

This time her sobs were deep and unrestrained; hard tears running in rivers down her cheeks as she struggled to gasp for breath.

She was crying for Maria, for Danny and also for herself. Again, as it had been so often recently, her mind was spinning in a maelstrom of uncertainty as she desperately considered her options.

She knew what she should do, knew what God would tell her to do - which was what any good, honest catholic woman should do.

But the question was, could she?

As she mopped up her tears and sniffed away her sobs, she heard the apartment door burst open and the cries of Danny and Nate as they tumbled through it.

Quickly, she snapped the locket shut and tucked it back into the secret hollow within the bible, then she closed the book and re-fastened the clasp.

As she was about to tuck it back under her mother's shawl, Danny opened the door and stumbled boisterously in. "Oh? Hey, Mom," he said, surprised. "You're home already - thought you'd still be at work?"

"Hey, Danny boy," she replied, hastily trying to conceal the bible. "Nope, Red gave me the night off so I'm all yours."

"Great! Does that mean we can have ice cream?"

"Yeah, does that mean we can have ice cream?" Echoed Nate from the other room.

Meggie smiled. "Well, yes. I guess it does."

"Cool!" the two boys yelled in unison before Danny looked at his mother quizzically. "What's that you got?" He said, noticing the tale end of the bible as Meggie at last tucked it under the shawl and closed the drawer.

"Nothing. Nothing at all. Or, at least nothing to concern you anyway."

Danny just shrugged and said, "Oh, okay. You coming to get the ice cream now?"

"Yes, yes. I'm coming," smiled Meggie as she followed her beloved son from the bedroom and closed the door firmly behind her.

It appeared her decision had already been made.

***

Just over one and half miles away uptown, and a mere thirty minute walk from where her long lost son was growing up, Maria Del Toro, blissfully unaware of his existence, was discussing cushion fabrics with her interior designer.

It had taken Maria six weeks of extensive searching to find 'just the right place' and a further two to finally get the keys. Renovations and decorations took another eight weeks before everything, at last, was finalised - aside from a couple of cushions that Maria had decided perhaps did not match the drapes after all.

Diego had been as good as his word and had left it completely up to her to choose where they were going to live in the city.

What she had eventually settled upon, was the sprawling penthouse suite of The Greyling Building on the lower half of Manhattan's Upper East Side, which she had fallen in love with immediately.

Occupying the top two floors of a twenty storey, majestically styled, pre-war building on one of the most sort after and exclusive boulevards in the world, the classically designed apartment was just what Maria had been looking for. The imposing, grey exterior stood like a proud old gentleman on Park Avenue, just below East 61st Street.

It was the perfect location for her and Diego - Lexington Avenue to the East, Madison Avenue to the West and Fifth Avenue just a two block stroll. If Diego so desired, he could walk to the site of the new Matador which was presently under construction a short distance away.

The vast interior of the apartment was a masterpiece of design.

Ostensibly a large four bedroom, eight bathroom family home, it was, in reality, so much more. The focal point was a grand double-height limestone entrance rotunda with a glass roof which flooded the apartment with natural light.

Spread over two spacious floors, the extravagantly styled apartment also featured two living rooms, both with spectacular views of the city, a library, study, games room, a huge kitchen with an outdoor terrace so Diego could enjoy the daily newspapers with a coffee in the morning sun, an impressive dining room with seating for over thirty guests and a lush roof garden complete with swimming pool, koi pond and ornamental fountain.

For Delores, there was a separate, two-bedroomed annex with private dining and living quarters complete with its own small garden. This was accessed from the entrance rotunda in the main apartment.

Along with all this considerable grandeur came a private elevator, around the clock security, concierge services and six, generously-sized, private spaces in the underground parking garage.

Furthermore, The Greyling Building was situated just steps away from Central Park.

All in all, it was absolutely perfect and Maria could not have hoped to find anything better.

Diego was so proud of her when he saw the apartment for the first time and the fittings, furnishings and fabrics she had chosen more than validated his faith in her. She had a sharp eye for detail and an exquisite sense of style - so beautiful and yet so talented, too. He was, indeed, a lucky man.

Whilst Maria had been apartment hunting, Diego had been busy with the new Fifth Avenue construction, spending long hours pouring over the plans with the architect; adding an extra touch here or taking out certain things there, that he felt did not work. Alongside this he had been travelling back and forth to Los Angeles to finalise negotiations for the control of Viscount Studios which were taking much longer than expected. He was also flying to Europe for a couple of days every two weeks to ensure everything was running smoothly at Matador headquarters in Cadiz as well as at the various hotels within the chain around the world.

Whatever free time he had he spent with Maria. Even though both were busy in their own separate ways, they were still very much in the 'newlywed' phase of their relationship and spent most of their time together in bed, especially now they had moved out of a hotel and into their own apartment.

They made love at every available opportunity, revelling in the time they had together and hoping maybe, sooner or later, it would result in Maria becoming pregnant. Diego was eagerly looking forward to becoming a father and Maria could not wait to present him with an heir.

However, after almost three months of married life and many, many nights trying, their efforts, so far, had been unsuccessful.

Although it was still early days and it was possible Maria could fall pregnant at anytime, Diego had taken the liberty of consulting with Dr Degollado to see if the difficulty in conceiving may have something to do with Maria's long coma.

Degollado was almost certain it was not related but he did say a lack of conception could be as a result of whatever trauma had induced her coma in the first place. He suggested, just as a precaution, that Maria undergo some tests to rule out any such problem.

He recommended they see a specialist of his acquaintance by the name of Dr Richard Cornell who was a leading figure within the gynaecological field and highly respected the world over. He also happened to be based in New York.

Diego and Maria listened to what Degollado had to say and took his advice on board but decided not to act in haste. Instead, they chose to give it two more months to see if nature would eventually take its course and try to put any thoughts of possible complications out of their minds.

However, by the end of that time their most concerted efforts had still not born fruit, so they both agreed it was time to make an appointment with Dr Cornell.

They met with him the very next day at his consulting rooms in Queens, finding him to be a middle-aged, smartly dressed, intelligent looking man with pointed features and a clipped European accent of indeterminable origin. Nevertheless, he was kindly and understanding and agreed with Miguel Degollado's opinion that Maria should have some tests to see if there was any possibility she was infertile.

He also suggested Diego should be tested to eliminate any question that the issue might be with him.

After a thorough examination and numerous tests, Maria and Diego were sitting back in Cornell's well appointed, scrupulously clean office one week later, anxiously awaiting his findings.

"I have good news, some not so good news and some news you might find somewhat surprising," Cornell said. "Although the overall picture is encouraging."

Maria and Diego felt a weight leave their shoulders but were yet to hear all the doctor had to say.

"The not so good news, which I'll get out of the way first," continued Cornell, "is that you, Señor Del Toro, have a slightly lower than average sperm count. This does not preclude you from having children but could make it somewhat more challenging."

Diego's heart sank and Maria squeezed his hand to comfort him, knowing what a blow this must be.

"But please, try not to be disheartened as I've seen many men with much lower counts than yours go onto father children - several children in some cases - but it can tend to rely a little on luck," said Cornell. "But there's no reason to think you won't be lucky."

Diego brightened a little and managed a smile.

"And me Doctor?" Asked Maria meekly, "Am I alright?"

"Physically yes. You are as strong as a horse—" He stopped to correct his unflattering analogy. "—A very pretty, very feminine horse," he chuckled awkwardly. "If you will forgive me for saying so. But I can find no reason why you should not be able to conceive. There are no internal injuries to indicate a problem and your monthly cycle is regular and consistent so everything appears to be in good working order."

It was time for Diego to squeeze Maria's hand as she felt a little rush of relief.

"The fact of it is," continued Cornell, "there are no medical reasons why neither of you could not become parents."

Both of them smiled. They would just have to double their efforts. Luck would be on their side, it had to be.

"Thank you, Doctor," said Diego, "that's a relief."

"I'm sure," replied the doctor, a look of hesitation on his face which Maria instantly picked up on.

"What is it Doctor? What aren't you telling us?"

Again, Cornell looked pensive, unsure of how best to proceed.

"Before that," he said. "Would you allow me to share a theory of mine with you. It is not medically recognised but a growing number of my more forward-thinking colleagues are finding themselves in agreement. Again, though, I must advise you, this is not fact, merely hypothesis."

"Please," said Diego, bidding him to continue.

"Thank you, Señor." Said Cornell, before directing his gaze at Maria. "Forgive me, Señora, but I believe you are suffering from memory loss, is that correct?"

"It is, yes," she replied, slightly puzzled by the question. "I have no memory of my life before 1955. None whatsoever. It is a total blank. Why do you ask?"

"Because I believe you may be suffering from emotional trauma. Emotions are extremely complex things and if something happened to you in your past, the effects of it could have serious repercussions on your emotional well being. It may cause a blockage, if you will, which could potentially impact on your ability to conceive, even though your body is physically able."

"You mean the coma? But Doctor Degollado has already ruled that out - he said it was most unlikely that—"

"No, Señora, not the coma but whatever happened to you prior to that."

"But I don't know," said Maria. "I have no idea what caused it - no idea of how I came to be found as I was, so how can I possibly fix something I have no knowledge of?"

"Like I say, it is just a theory," said Cornell. "But it leads me on to the more surprising news I mentioned earlier.

"There's more?" said Maria, slightly ruffled.

"Yes, I am afraid so. And it might be better if I speak with you alone at this point."

Maria was stunned. A feeling of dread creeping into her stomach, what on earth was he going to tell her. Was she ill, was she dying?

She looked at Diego for support, seeing that he, too, was as surprised as her. "No," she said, "I want my husband here. We keep no secrets from each other. Whatever you have to say to me, you can say to him too."

"Very well," said Cornell. "If you are sure?"

"I am," she said.

"In that case you must both prepare yourselves for a shock."

The pair of them shifted uneasily in their seats, their minds racing with unknown possibilities - each one worse than the other.

"As you know," continued the doctor, "we have done extensive tests and examined you thoroughly, Señora Del Toro, and our findings are certain. There can be no doubt. I have checked them twice myself to be absolutely sure."

"What? What is it?" Maria could bear the suspense no more. "What have you found?"

Cornell cleared his throat apprehensively before saying. "It's my belief you have given birth before. In fact, it's a certainty."

The colour drained from Maria's face as Diego looked at her aghast. She squeezed his hand hard, her nails digging into his flesh as she tried to take on board what the doctor was saying.

"You mean… you mean—"

"Yes, Señora," he said. "You are already a mother."

Maria was stunned. Suddenly it made sense, the feeling of loss, the feeling of abandonment she so often had in the pit of her stomach, now she knew the reason for it.

It was because she was a mother.

Chapter Fourteen

Try as she might, Megan could not forget the image of Maria in the newspaper nor ignore the rotting feeling of betrayal and dishonesty that was steadily gnawing away at her conscience.

For many weeks she had gone about her daily business, trying to maintain the appearance of normality when, in truth, all around her, her world was crumbling.

Not only was it the discovery of Maria's survival and the subsequent fear of losing Danny that troubled her but also her affair with Jay. Her relationship with him had been thrown into uncertainty by his accession to gang leader now Rebel had moved on, leaving them at something of an impasse. Indeed, until today, she had not seen Jay for many days, and neither had Danny, which had left the boy thinking he had perhaps done something wrong.

Meanwhile Red was an ever-present shadow in Megan's life, prowling menacingly, impatiently in the wings. So far, ever since her fainting fit some weeks before, she had managed to keep him at arms length, but he was keen to press his suit and his advances could only be put-off for so long.

Meggie felt as if God had deserted her. She could neither hear his voice nor feel his presence and her prayers for His spiritual guidance had been unanswered. Every night she knelt down to pray for His forgiveness but, as yet, her burden had not been lifted.

She knew confession would help to cleanse her troubled soul and absolve her of her sins but she had stayed away from Father Thomas' confessional for the shame of revealing the dreadful things she had done.

Meggie's weight had plummeted. She was not eating properly and, as a result, her cheek bones now stuck out sharply from her pallid face. Her breasts had lost their plumpness and her once finely upholstered behind had lost much of its padding. As she stared at herself in the dressing table mirror, each of her ribs were clearly defined and her sunken belly looked starved of food. But she was not hungry; her appetite was gone and all that filled her stomach was guilt.

She stood there braless, wearing nothing but an off-white girdle and tan stockings, regarding herself numbly in the reflection. Her bra and uniform were laid out on the unmade bed ready for her evening shift.

The bed sheets were still mussed up from an afternoon of illicit, sinful sex. The first time she and Jay had been with each other in over two weeks.

Jay, still not satiated, was behind her now, naked except for a T-shirt; his arms encircling her as his hands cupped her shrunken breasts.

"You're looking thin, Meggie," he said without thinking. "You should eat more, y'know?"

She looked at him blankly but said nothing, feeling him grow hard against her bare buttocks.

"You're still sexy though, baby. Very sexy."

Meggie shut her eyes, revolted by her reflection, disgusted by the feelings of heightened arousal that still rushed through her body; astonished by how this could be when she knew, all too well, the sickening guilt that would surely follow.

Yet she could not resist and that was her curse. Which was why

God had abandoned her, she knew it.

She lifted her bottom slightly and pushed it towards him. Despite herself, she had become wanton, a harlot; a woman who knew exactly how she wanted to be pleased.

Jay responded instantly, needing no further encouragement, and they made love once again. Yet his mind was elsewhere, troubled by what he must do and being so distracted, he forgot to withdraw at the appropriate moment. He realised his mistake almost immediately but said nothing.

There was already much that needed to be said today and any mention of this stupid slip would just complicate matters all the more.

Jay had hardened in the last few weeks; the carefree boy he had been before had been replaced by a more reserved and calculating man. Meggie meant a lot to him, so did her boys but the opportunity had arisen to considerably increase his wealth and social standing and he could not afford to let sentimentality or childish ideals stand in his way.

He was now the leader of the Westside Dukes and, as such, had to conduct himself accordingly. The gang lived by a code, a set of laws that each member must abide by and he had to be beyond reproach.

Which meant his relationship with Danny must come to an end.

Likewise, with Red Tierny being such an important link from the life Jay had to the life Jay wanted, he had to end his affair with Meggie, too.

Double J had been mulling this over in his mind for several weeks, trying to see away around it - trying to figure a way of still seeing Danny and still being with Meggie but he simply could not. If either Red or Rebel found out what he was up to then that would be the end of any dreams he had of escaping Hell's Kitchen.

So it all came down to today. This was where he ended it with Megan. It was what Jay had come here to tell her.

Their affair was over and they had just made love for the last time.

***

When Meggie emerged from the small bathroom, having washed away any trace of their sexual union, she crossed to the bed and picked up her bra. Jay was now fully dressed, a cigarette dangling casually from his lips as he sat on the bed tying the laces of his dark blue sneakers.

When he was done, he stood and watched as Meggie put on the bra. He thought, again, how skinny she had become and how the life seemed to have drained out of her. When they were first together she smiled often but it was a rare sight now and the last few times he had seen her she always seemed a little sad.

Nonetheless, she would always have a place in his heart and it was with great regret that he eventually said, "It can't go on Meggie."

"What can't?" She replied absently, wriggling into her pale blue waitress uniform and fastening the zipper at the side, above her left hip.

"This."

"This what?"

"This. You and me. It's got to end, Meggie, today. It's over."

Strangely, Megan felt little except for a hint of relief. "Oh," she said flatly, her expression blank as she glanced over at him. "Okay."

"Okay? Is that all you've got to say?"

It would have been easy for her to take him to task, to accuse him of being selfish for having his way with her one last time before plucking up the courage to end it. But she could not be bothered, she felt dead to any emotion other than guilt and numb to any additional blows she might be dealt. Besides, they both knew this had been a long time coming - his absence from her bed for the last couple of

194

weeks had all but confirmed it.

"What do you want me to say?" Was all she could muster.

"Dunno. Somethin' I guess. Somethin' other than just 'okay.'"
He stubbed his cigarette out on a cracked saucer by the bedside,
clearly irritated.

"But there is nothing to say, we both know that. It was good
while it lasted but now it's over. That's that. Just the way it is."

"You don't care?"

"Sure I do, I guess. But it's run its course - we both know it,
don't we?"

"Yeah, but-"

"No 'buts', Jay. It's over. There's nothing more to say."

As she spoke, it seemed as if an enormous weight was being
lifted from her shoulders. As much as she would miss Jay and his
skilled attentions in the bedroom, her life without him would mean
she would be committing one less sin. Sex out of marriage was
against God's lore and sex with a boy who was significantly younger
would surely be considered much worse. Maybe now the affair was
over God would be more forgiving of her other transgressions.

"Fine," Jay said, picking up his green and white Dukes jacket
and pulling it on over his white T-shirt. "I guess that's it then, huh?"

"Yep. I guess."

For a second he looked like a little lost boy, no trace of the tough
gang leader he had become, but it was only fleeting and a moment
later his expression hardened. "See you around then, I s'pose?" he
said coolly as he crossed the room and opened her bedroom door.

"I'm sure you will," said Meggie, with more indifference than
intended.

Before leaving, Jay turned and looked back at her as if he was
about to say something important or meaningful - it occurred to
him that he should perhaps mention what had happened earlier,
about his failure to withdraw in time - but, as he opened his mouth

to speak, he suddenly decided against it and in the end, he just said, "Bye, then."

A second later Meggie heard the sound of the front door closing behind him.

And she was alone, again, once more.

***

Three weeks later, whilst working a busy breakfast shift at the diner, Meggie had been in the middle of serving a burly construction worker a plate of eggs, sunny side up, when an overwhelming sense of nausea swept over her. She had all but thrown the plate in front of the poor unsuspecting guy, causing him to spill his coffee down his plaid shirt, as she dashed off to the restroom to be violently sick.

That should have been her first indication, but instead she put it down to being over-worked, over-tired and under fed.

But the next morning, she had to jump out of the shower to vomit in the toilet. She was sick again during her breakfast shift and once more at lunchtime - the smell of all that grease making her feel suddenly nauseous.

Fortunately Red had not noticed her sudden jaunts to the bathroom. But as she sat in the tiny cubicle in the ladies restroom, wondering where on earth she could have picked up this nasty little bug, the realisation suddenly hit her.

Her period was over ten days late. Somehow she had been too busy or too tired to notice. How could she have been so remiss?

When she had been carrying Nate, almost ten years earlier, she suffered from dreadful morning sickness during her first trimester. It had started early on and continued until at least her twelfth week.

It was the same now. The same feeling of nausea, the sudden urge to throw up. There could be no doubt about it.

She was pregnant.

***

It was raining hard on Megan's first full day off in weeks

and her old woollen coat and hat were simply not up to the task of keeping her dry. She had ridden the subway from Columbus Circle to Lexington Avenue but had walked the rest of the way in the pouring rain, on foot, in her best shoes. Now, aside from having blisters on her feet, she was also sopping wet, shivering and cold. Despite this, she had been waiting there, on the opposite side of the street from the Greyling Building for almost four hours just to get a glimpse of Maria.

Indeed, this was the only time, since Megan had been living in New York, that she had ventured further uptown than 42nd Street - the first time she had taken the subway or seen a skyscraper up close. But now she was there on swanky Park Avenue, standing in the rain looking like a half-drowned, country mouse, feeling out of place and way out of her comfort zone.

She did not even know why she was there exactly. Was it to ease her conscience by finally confessing to Maria about Danny? She knew deep down it was not, as much as she also knew that was the right thing to do.

Was it then to ask Maria what had happened nine years ago on the way to Messina and how on earth she had survived the fall from the train? Again, Megan suspected it was not, although she was curious.

Or was it merely to see Maria with her own eyes, in the flesh - and not just a picture of her in some newspaper?

Perhaps that was it. Perhaps it was because Maria represented a friendly face, someone she had once been close to, who she could talk to and confide in and Megan was desperately short of people like that in her life at present. In fact, aside from the boys, she had no one she could talk to at all, but for obvious reasons she could not burden them with her woes.

For all intents and purposes Megan was alone in the world; her spirits low and her faith in God shaken to its very foundation.

197

She was desperate; trapped by circumstances beyond her control, lost in a swirl of worry and uncertainty.

Yet for all the potential heartbreak she brought with her, Maria represented hope - a lifeboat in an increasingly stormy sea. And Megan found great comfort in that.

In the three weeks since discovering she was pregnant, Meggie had done all she could to avoid situations that might prompt Red to declare his feelings. But he would not be easily put off and kept pestering her to join him for a quiet dinner one night, just the two of them, after her shift.

To deter him, Megan had feigned migraines, blamed a lack of babysitters, pretended she had to help the boys with a school project and had even stopped going to church on Sundays to avoid spending time with Red - stating that she was feeling too exhausted to attend.

This had been an effective ploy so far as Red clearly remembered Meggie passing out at the diner and was still berating himself for working her too hard.

But Megan was running out of excuses and in the last couple of days Red had been pressing her to spare him a few moments for a 'little chat'.

It was an impossible situation as even if she wanted to marry him she could not do so because of the baby she carried inside her.

As for Double J, Meggie had seen him around quite often and had noticed him surreptitiously eyeing her. She sensed that he wished they could still be together but his new status would not allow it. Rebel and Andy Loughlin's fledgling drug business was just getting off the ground and he did not want to jeopardise any profits he might receive from his part in it - especially as they represented any chance he may have of a better life.

He was moving on but it did not stop him from wanting what he could not have no matter how much he tried to convince himself otherwise. He told himself Meggie was too old, too plain, too religious; a mother of two who was marked for another, but still he could not stop thinking about her.

But to Megan, all Jay represented now was more worry. He was the father of the baby that was growing rapidly inside her and sometime, either sooner or later, he was going to have to be told. And that could only result in trouble.

For the present though, Meggie still waited in the rain opposite Maria's building.

After another hour, however, when Megan could no longer feel her feet nor stop her nose from running, she was just about to give up her surveillance when a shiny, black limousine pulled up to the kerb in front of The Greyling Building. A top-hatted doorman, wearing a double-breasted green coat with polished brass buttons, rushed out with a huge umbrella and opened the car's rear, kerbside door. A moment later, a glamorous, strikingly beautiful woman stepped out of the limo and ducked under the waiting brolly. She was wearing a fitted camel coat with a flowing, orange silk scarf draped casually around her neck. Her long dark hair was immaculately styled and hung loosely upon her shoulders.

Megan would have known the woman even at twice the distance, indeed she looked scarcely different from the last time she had seen her, all those years ago in Italy. Maria was as beautiful now as she was back then - possibly even more so - and it did Meggie good to see her friend - her beloved ex-mistress - looking so well.

As Megan craned to get a better look, a handsome, intellectual looking man with black rimmed spectacles and dark, untamed hair, stepped out of the limousine to join Maria, temporarily blocking Megan's view. Megan recognised this man as Diego Del Toro, Maria's Spanish, multi-millionaire husband. He, too, was stylishly dressed in an impeccably tailored blue suit and a beige, lightweight overcoat.

Together they looked the perfect couple.

Megan turned her gaze from Diego back to Maria and in that

instant, from across the busy street, their eyes suddenly locked; Maria's green and bright, Megan's red-rimmed and sickly, but she could not break away.

Then a large Coca Cola truck obscured her view as it slowed before her in the heavy traffic. But in her mind she could still see Maria's inquisitive, caring eyes and the sensitive, compassionate nature they revealed. Meggie, engulfed by a sudden rush of guilt, stumbled backwards, feeling suddenly faint once again. Her legs threatening to give way under her, but she forced herself to stay upright and fought to keep control.

As the strength returned to her legs, Meggie turned on her heels and ran. Desperate to hide her shame from the innocent gaze of the woman whose child she had stolen, cursing her stupidity for actively seeking Maria out.

She kept running, heedless to her blistered feet, numb to her frozen body, until she reached the subway, the overwhelming anxiety she was stricken with not easing until she got home to her apartment. However, the moment she walked in, she threw herself down on her knees, clasped her palms together and begged God for His forgiveness.

***

It was as if a thick veil had been pulled aside to expose the brilliance of unimpeded sunlight as the fog lifted from Maria's memory.

Suddenly, she remembered everything; Armando, her father, Salvatore, Italy - even her fall from the train.

And she remembered her son, too.

It all came back to her in a flash as soon as she set eyes upon Megan. In an instant she knew who she was, where she was born, where she lived - her likes and loves, and all of the traumatic events that led her to be floating, like flotsam, in the Mediterranean sea.

The shock of it hit her like a blow to the chest and she toppled backwards in the rain, outside her apartment building, prevented from falling to the ground only by the quick reactions of the doorman.

But Maria could not speak as she fought to regain her feet and just kept pointing wildly across the road as if she had just seen a ghost.

Which, indeed, she had. A ghost from her past.

Diego was fussing around her, searching for what she might be pointing at, but he could see nothing except for a lot of traffic and a sidewalk full of people all rushing to get out of the rain.

Diego and the doorman escorted Maria inside, worried she might be sickening for something. Diego said he would call the doctor immediately but she insisted he did not, declaring herself to be fine but revealing nothing more as she tried to regain her composure.

When Diego was satisfied his wife was fit to go on, he thanked the doorman and several other people who had gathered around them in the foyer to enquire after Maria's wellbeing, and pressed the button for the elevator.

As the elevator doors pinged and glided shut behind them, Diego turned to Maria and said, with his voice full of concern, "Are you sure you are quite well, my darling?"

"No, Diego, I don't think I am."

"But I thought you said you were fine?"

"I am, yes, physically. It's just that—"

"What, my darling? What is it?"

"It's that I now know who I am."

"What? I don't understand."

As the elevator reached its destination, it pinged again and the doors slid open to reveal the large white entrance rotunda that was bathed in the natural light from the circular glass dome above. The sound of the rain unheard as it pelted silently against the ornate pattern of thick panes.

As they stepped off the elevator into their apartment, Maria took Diego's hand and turned to look him in the eye. For all his intelligence and business acumen, he seemed like a little boy lost, his love for her etched deeply on his concerned face.

"My memory has come back, Diego. It happened in a flash, down there on the sidewalk." She snapped her fingers, "Just like that."

"You mean?" Diego was flabbergasted, flustered almost, finding the news too amazing to fully comprehend. "You know who you are?" He said at last.

"I do." Maria smiled nervously, uncertain of what this wonderful man, who she was deeply in love with, would think after she told him all that she knew.

"Tell me," he said, excitedly, "tell me who this beautiful woman is that I'm married to."

She took a deep breath. "My name is Maria Liuzzi. I am twenty-six years old and was born here in New York, but moved to California when I was just six. I was brought up in Hollywood."

"Hollywood?"

"Yes. My father is a rich man. He owns a studio there."

"Your father? My father-in-law you mean?" Diego smiled but Maria's face remained solemn. "And what of my mother-in-law, will I get to meet her, too?"

"No, my love. She is dead and I wish my father was, too."

"What? But surely—"

"No, Diego. He is an evil man. A terrible man. But he's not who I want to tell you about - we can discuss my father another time."

"Who then? Who do you want to discuss?"

"I have a son, my darling. I'm sorry to break it to you like this, so suddenly, but Doctor Cornell was right, I am a mother, I had a baby when I was just seventeen - he would be nine now."

"You were married?"

"No, Diego. I was not - I wanted to be, we were in love but

Armando, my son's father, he… he…"

"What? What did he do?"

"He was killed." Maria was unaware of the tears now streaming down her cheeks as she regurgitated all of these long hidden memories, finding them shocking, even to herself, as they spilled from her lips. "And our baby, our little boy - he was taken from me, my father, he—"

Suddenly she broke down as visions of her baby boy flooded into her mind's eye. His little face looking up at her as she held him in her arms for the first time on board the Super Chief en-route to New York.

Diego took her in his arms, "It'll be okay, my darling, I'm here now and together we'll find him, I promise. If he's out there, we'll find him."

"He is, I know it," Maria snivelled. Again, she looked up into her husband's kind, understanding face, his deep brown eyes full of concern. She knew he must have a million questions and, in time, she would answer them all, but for now, all she could think about was finding her son.

Seeing Megan had been the catalyst for her memories to be unlocked. She had been there, across the street, watching her, staring right into her eyes. Although Maria was a little unsure of why she had vanished so quickly as they had obviously recognised each other - shocking as it was.

Nevertheless, Megan was in New York, close by, she would know something, anything that might lead her to her long lost son. She would at least know what happened immediately after that fated train journey in Italy.

"My son is out there, somewhere in the world, I can feel it in my heart," she sniffed. Then, thinking of Megan once more, she added, "And I know exactly who might tell us where to look."

Chapter Fifteen

The next day, all through Meggie's breakfast shift, and at lunchtime, too, Red was acting very strangely. As she tried to concentrate on her work, her mind still harking back to the events of the day before, she kept feeling Red's eyes burning into her and whenever she turned to look at him he would just smile knowingly and occasionally give her a subtle wink. Something was going on and she did not like it one bit.

She felt ill today; shivery, feverish, her head ached and so did her body. The morning sickness had relented a little but she was still finding it difficult to keep anything down - not that it mattered as her appetite had all but vanished.

Her uniform, once snug fitting and emphasising her womanly curves now hung loosely from her. The small, swollen bulge in her stomach, which would have been so noticeable against her shrunken frame, was concealed by a tight corset which kept suspicions to a minimum and the wagging tongues of the local gossips at bay. But it was constricting and made her feel even worse.

Even though she was half the woman she used to be, her pallor sickly, her hair lank and her health clearly questionable, Red seemed not to notice. She was still 'his Meggie' - his blinkered, rose-tinted opinion of her unwavering, which would have been sweet had his hands not been so regularly fond of finding her butt or if his feelings had been in any way reciprocated. But they were not. Indeed she had done everything she could to discourage him but he would just not let her alone and his very handsy attitude towards her made her feel cheap and dirty.

She knew if she told him she was pregnant it would put him off and longed to shout it in his face to make him leave her alone. But she knew, too, that would unquestionably mean the end of her job and most likely the loss of her apartment. Red carried great sway within the community and his influence was far reaching.

Also, bubbling under the surface, there was a streak of violence in the man and Meggie suspected those that crossed him did not fair well. This, on top of everything else she was dealing with, was probably the thing that terrified her most.

She could not marry him. Not just because she didn't love him - indeed he repulsed her, but also because of the baby. Red would be disgusted and appalled if he knew she was pregnant. For all his sins, and there were many, he was a man of devout faith and an illegitimate child would just not be acceptable to him.

Nate and even Danny, to a degree, were different. Meggie had been married to Nate's father and Danny, in Red's view, was somebody else's bastard who she had taken on out of the goodness of her heart. Besides, when they were married, the little wop would soon be gone.

But a baby? There was just no way.

So what was Meggie to do? Sooner or later there would be no disguising her bump - and even before that she suspected Red would propose. An abortion was out of the question; apart from it being against everything she believed in, she had no money to pay for one.

It was a hopeless quandary that played constantly over and over in her mind and God, it seemed, could not have cared less.

***

That night, as Megan walked up the cobbled street towards the diner to start her evening shift, she was puzzled by the fact that all the lights in the low, single-storey building were off. The neon sign above the restaurant, that intermittently traced the words *Red's Diner* in garish red light and the green four-leaf clover that was usually flashing brightly above it, were both, most unusually, switched off, giving the place a haunted, eery appearance.

Surely the diner was not closed.

Several of the Westside Dukes were outside, wearing their unmistakable green and white letterman jackets, smoking and chatting and generally just clogging up the sidewalk but she was not intimidated by them. They would never dare to lay a finger on her as they all believed her to be 'Red's gal'.

However, she did feel a slight knot in her stomach when she saw Double J. He was squatting by the side of the road, also proudly wearing his gang colours, and talking to Rebel who was leaning out the passenger window of an aged Oldsmobile. A man Meggie recognised as Andy Loughlin was wedged behind the steering wheel.

Loughlin, blonde-haired and stocky with a broken, flat nose, wound the window down as she approached. "Hello, Meggie darlin'" he said, in a much too familiar voice, "You'll find the man, himself, inside."

Of course she would, where else did he think Red would be? But she just smiled her thanks and walked on past the car.

She caught Jay's eye, who was handing a package to Rebel, no doubt filled with cash, but his face was filled with concern and Meggie could have sworn she saw him shake his head slightly, as if trying to alert her to some hidden danger.

The diner certainly did seem strange, all in darkness, and suddenly she was scared. She flashed another look at Jay but his attention had been snatched away by Rebel who was asking him how much money was in the package. Loughlin was still eyeing her though, his smile wide and knowing.

Megan turned away from him as she reached the door and hesitated momentarily before pushing it open. As she stepped inside the diner her heart sank and she knew instantly what Jay had been trying to warn her about.

This was it. This was the moment. Red was going to propose.

The whole diner was in darkness except for one candlelit booth in the centre. The table was covered with a red gingham tablecloth, on top of which sat an ornate, tri-pronged candelabra. There was also a small bunch of flowers in a little glass vase, two crystal tumblers and an open bottle of fine Irish Whiskey Red had been keeping for a special occasion.

Standing beside the booth was Red. All done up like a dog's dinner in his Sunday best; bottle green plaid suit and bright red tie. His red/grey hair was oiled and slicked back and a goofy, lop-sided grin was on his big, square face. He reminded her of the self-important, slightly ridiculous local squire who frequented her father's tavern back in County Clare, behind whom's back all the regulars secretly laughed. But this was no laughing matter.

The juke box was playing *True Love* by Bing Crosby and Grace Kelly and Meggie wanted to be sick.

"Ah, Meggie, my sweet girl," Red said, his voice dripping with syrupy blarney, "Come here, siddown, would ya, darlin'."

Temporarily at a loss for words as her brain desperately tried to think of how on earth she could extricate herself from this predicament, she slowly stepped over to the booth.

As she moved closer to Red the overpowering smell of his aftershave permeated the air, its distinctive odour nauseating and she had to resist the urge to gag. She also noticed on his neck a small dab of tissue paper that was stuck to a tiny splodge of blood where he'd nicked himself shaving - indeed, she had never seen him with such a close shave, even at church on a Sunday.

"We're not opening tonight?" She at last said, her voice

trembling slightly.

"No lassie, not tonight," he replied, his breath thick with the scent of liquoricey mouthwash; its pungency mingling with the aftershave and the perfumed aroma of his hair oil, making a potent cocktail strong enough to fell a charging rhino.

Meggie tried to breathe only through her mouth, the smell of him too offensive for her delicate nostrils as she said, "But won't you be losing lots of money?"

He smiled as he ushered her to her seat, making certain she was sitting comfortably before replying. "Sometimes there's things more important than money, darlin', and tonight's one of them occasions."

"But I don't understand?" She bluffed.

"Oh, I think you do, lass. I think you know all too well and I suspect you must be very excited. I'm sure it's a very big thing for a girl when a fella sets out his stall for her."

"But—"

"It's okay, Meggie, darlin' - it's good that you're a little overwhelmed. I understand it. But all of this is for you. The tablecloth, the candles - hell, even this suit I'm wearing - you deserve it."

"But I—" was all she could stammer again.

"It's all so you know I'm serious about you being my bride. I know you perhaps thought I'd never get round to asking you, that maybe I took you for granted and, dammit, I'm sure you wish I'd asked you years ago - hopin' I could be a father to that lovely lad of yours."

"I've got two sons."

"Whassat? Oh, yes, course you have, I know that, darlin' and that other boy will be well taken care of as you know - there's this wonderful school in Jersey - perfect for his kind—" He paused for a second, realising now was not the time to go into that. "Anyway," he continued unabashed, "lets not worry about that now. The point is I know I've been tardy, but now it's time for me to make an honest woman of you."

"Please, Red, no - you don't have to—"

"Hush, lass, it's okay. Let me finish my big speech - let me do it properly - it's only right that I do."

"There's no need, honestly!"

"Ssh," said Red, as he went down on one knee, taking her tiny left hand between both of his liver-spotted, dinner plate-sized paws. He cleared his throat and then said loudly, "Sweet Meggie Malone, my darlin' girl, light of my life, would you do me the pleasure of becoming my wife?"

***

As Double J squatted beside the car listening to Rebel, he felt distracted by thoughts of Meggie as he watched the door of the diner close behind her. He knew, or at least strongly suspected, what was about to happen inside but was powerless to do anything about it - especially with his brother and Loughlin right there beside him.

As he stewed on this, his eyes fell upon a solitary figure down the street, maybe two hundred yards away, who had just wandered casually out onto the sidewalk from the concrete basketball court down the block. It was dark and the figure was in shadow but Jay could see he was slim and tall and was carrying something long and shiny in his hand. Something prickled at the back of Jay's neck; his sixth sense giving him a warning.

Then, as the lone figure crossed the cobbled street and stood in the light cast by a nearby streetlight, straight legged and facing towards him, Jay knew why his senses were going so crazy. The figure was a young Puerto Rican man of around Jay's age known as 'Javier'. He wore jeans and sneakers but he was naked from the waist up except for a bright purple satin waistcoat with a yellow 'P' on the left breast and on his head, tilted at a jaunty angle, was a matching purple 'newsboy' cap - the unmistakable uniform of the 'Lincoln Playboys', the Dukes' arch rivals.

Javier, as the leader of the Playboys, was muscular and toned with not an ounce of spare flesh, his arms thick and well developed; indeed, a fine specimen of youthful masculinity in its prime.

On his face was a wide, menacing grin and in his hand was a long, highly polished machete.

By now, the other members of the Dukes had also seen him, as had Rebel and Loughlin - all their eyes fixed on the intruder, Javier.

When he was certain of their attention, Javier put his thumb and forefinger in his mouth and whistled a loud signal. Immediately an army of similarly dressed youths, all Puerto Rican, their ages ranging from about twelve to twenty, streamed out from where they had been concealed within the mesh-fenced basketball court. There was at least fifty of them, all armed to the teeth with an array of bats, clubs, chains, knives and even car aerials. It was also quite likely one or two of them were carrying guns.

Fifty of them against eleven of the Dukes. Unless reinforcements arrived soon, Jay knew it was going to be a massacre.

He looked directly at Rebel who read his thoughts instantly. Nodding his understanding, he, in turn, spoke quickly to Loughlin who immediately jammed the Oldsmobile into reverse and backed it hastily around the corner. Then, with its wheels screeching loudly on the cobbles, it sped off in the opposite direction.

Upon witnessing the car driving away, a spontaneous cheer rose up from the assembled Playboys, the smell of victory already in their nostrils.

Javier let his troops enjoy the moment for a few seconds before raising his fingers to his lips once more. Another short whistle brought them instantly to silence. Then he stepped away from them, two or three paces towards the diner and stopped, his eyes never leaving Jay's. He stood there posturing provocatively for a moment, the challenge unmistakable. Then lifted the machete, pointing it back in the direction of the basketball court, designating it to be the place where their two tribes should fight.

Double J nodded his approval slowly, then watched as one by one the Playboys silently disappeared back into the basketball court followed, at last, by Javier.

Jay had a switchblade in the back pocket of his Levis and a small leather cosh tucked inside his letterman jacket.

At home he had a .38 Special concealed in a drawer and if Rebel had understood him correctly, then he would shortly have that, too.

He looked around at his small band of soldiers in their uniform of green and white, all armed in a similar fashion to him. Of the ten there with him, six were seasoned campaigners - all over sixteen and spoiling for a rumble. The other four were younger, aged between eleven and fourteen, but they were all tough and had proved themselves in battle at least once before and Jay was pleased to have them with him. All they had to do was hold the line until Rebel could spread the word.

But fifty versus eleven? It was a tall order but this was their turf. Dukes turf. And they would defend it until their very last breath.

"Ready?" Jay asked, and in return received several silent but determined nods.

"Okay then. Let's do it," he said. "And keep it tight, all we've gotta do is hold the line until Reb gets back here with the others. He's rounding them up now and will be back any second, I promise."

Slowly, in a line stretching out across the street, they made their way down the block until they stood grouped outside the entrance to the basketball court.

The court itself was positioned between two high tenements with a mesh fence at the front that ran parallel with the sidewalk and another identical to it that ran across the back. It could be entered either through the gate on Jay's side or through a similar one on the far side of the court, making it the perfect arena for street gang gladiators to do battle.

"Okay, boys," Jay said, pulling the switchblade from his pocket, "Let's go show 'em how we do things on Dukes turf." He then led them through the open gate and into the court to face the waiting horde lined up on the far side of the concrete killing field.

***

After months, maybe even years of anticipating and dreading this moment, Meggie still had no answer prepared. Her head, of course, was loudly screaming 'No!' And her heart absolutely concurred, but her voice had temporarily left her - which was fortunate as she could not just blurt out the word 'no', she had to try and let Red down gently. But so far nothing was springing to mind.

Red, still down on one knee, saw the concern on her face but, instead, read it as shock. "Oh, my darlin' girl," he said, "I can see you're all of a flutter. Your poor little heart must be beating ten to the dozen, eh?"

Meggie managed a slight nod.

"Not to worry lass," continued Red, climbing to his feet. "It ain't like I don't know what your answer's gonna be. After all, it feels like we've been courting for so long already. So you just sit there and get your thoughts together and I'll go and rustle up the food. I've got a coupla nice T-bones lined up to celebrate our engagement. Won't be long."

He then strode off, in the direction of the kitchen, the waft of his cologne following along behind, leaving Meggie alone with the candles, the flowers and the open bottle of whiskey, her mind trying to conjure some suitable response that would placate Red.

She sat there with her elbows resting on the table, her head in her hands. There was nothing for it, the time had come and she had to let Red down the best and gentlest way she could. But it did not make her feel any less nervous when a few minutes later he returned from the kitchen holding two large plates.

He slid one down in front of her. On it was an enormous,

barely cooked T-bone steak, blood still oozing out of it and running into the generous dollop of creamy mashed potato that sat beside it. "I hope you like it rare," Red said, "it's the best way to taste the meat - brings out the true flavour."

But with her already delicate stomach and ultra-sensitive nose which had arrived with the onset of morning sickness, the sight of the bloody steak nearly made her vomit on the spot. Yet somehow she fought against the instinct which, in turn, made her eyes water. Again, Red wrongly interpreted this as a sign of emotion and said, "There, there, lass. No need to cry, tis only a piece of beef. When we're married we'll eat like this regular and often."

Meggie forced another smile as she inspected the huge hunk of meat in front of her, reluctantly picking up her knife and fork without any idea of how she was going to manage to swallow even a mouthful.

However, as she pushed her fork into the tender T-bone, Red spoke again, sliding a little faded blue, velvet box with the lid open in front of her as he did so. In the box, sitting in a small slit in the navy silk was an antique engagement ring; silver, with three small diamonds in an ornate setting sitting across the top. It looked like it hadn't been polished in decades and appeared to be far too big too fit any of Meggie's fingers but it was pretty.

"Before we eat, Meggie darlin', might I hear you say the words? It'll do me heart the power of good to hear you say 'yes' and to watch you put on me Mammy's ring."

Meggie tentatively put down her cutlery and then, hesitating just slightly, picked up the box containing the ring.

She looked at it for a long moment, steeling herself for what she must now say. Then with her eyes still cast down, she whispered, at last, in a voice barely audible, "I can't."

"Whassat, Meggie, m'darlin', I didn't quite catch it?" Replied Red, leaning in, the pungent whiff of his cologne mingling nauseatingly with the bloody aroma of under-cooked meat.

Megan took a deep breath then looked Red directly in the eyes. "I can't marry you. I'm so sorry," she said, sliding the ring back across the table.

Red stared at her for a second or two while the information trickled slowly into his brain. "You can't? Why not?" He eventually said.

"I'm flattered, I really am - it's so kind of you to ask - and I know how fond you are of Nate. It's just that I... I—"

"What?" Red looked genuinely flummoxed and a little forlorn.

"It's just that I... I don't... I don't—"

"Don't what, Meggie? Please, tell me darlin'"

"I don't love you, Red. I'm so sorry." She braced herself for what he might say, hoping he would not be too annoyed or too hurt, but at least she had told him the truth and it was a relief to have finally done so.

Again, Red stared at her, his eyes completely blank, giving nothing away and Megan held her breath as she awaited his reaction.

Several seconds passed before Red began to smile. Then the smile turned into a chuckle and then a loud, throaty guffaw as if someone had just told him an extremely funny joke. Tears of delight running down his face as he rocked backwards and forwards in his seat, clearly enjoying the moment.

"Oh, my dear, sweet Meggie. My darlin' girl," he said at last getting his humour under control and wiping the tears from his eyes. "I know you don't love me. Of course you don't - I mean how could you? We don't know each other intimately enough yet. That will take months, maybe even years. But, darlin', when we're married, when we've laid together as husband and wife, when we know each other in every possible way, inside and out - only then can we truly find love. Love takes time, lassie, lots of time - but I'm willing to bet you and me will find it before long. I'm willing to gamble on our future

214

together, is all I'm saying - it's what that ring will be saying if you put in on your finger and if you're willing to walk down the aisle with me by your side.

"Life's a lottery, darlin', but I'm putting money on us and I hope you will too. Now, no more of this 'I don't love you' nonsense and give me a proper answer. Whaddaya say?"

Megan was shocked. Of all his possible reactions she least expected this one and had no idea how to deal with it. "I'm sorry, Red. My answer's still no I'm afr—"

"No? Why not? I've just told you, girl, love don't mean a jot - we can work on that. So the answer is 'yes'. Yes, you will marry me." Red was trying to keep a lid on his frustration as he could tell Meggie was getting upset.

"I can't, Red, I'm sorry." A tear slid down Meggie's cheek, how could she make him understand. "I just can't—"

"Whaddaya mean, 'you can't'? I just told you didn't I? It don't matter - hell, I don't care that you don't love me. So what else can it be? You holdin' out for better, is that it?

"No."

"Cos, I'm telling you, it don't get no better, not round here. You ask all the widows and divorcees, I'm as good as it gets. Heck, I could ask any number of women and they'd all say 'yes' - but I chose you, Meggie. You."

"It's not that. I know I should be grateful," she was crying now, tears streaming down her face. "It's just—"

"What?" What is it?"

"It's just that—"

"Tell me, Meggie. Tell me what it is."

She couldn't take this badgering. After all the stress of the last few weeks - of the last twenty-four hours, she just couldn't take it anymore. She felt fragile, alone, desperate. Her resistance crumbling under his persistent questioning.

"Tell me!" He finally demanded, his voice sharp and angry.

"I can't marry you because I'm pregnant!" She blurted loudly before instantly wishing she hadn't.

Suddenly there was silence. Red just seemed to freeze, his face fixed in disbelief.

As Megan looked at him, she could see the information slowly registering, the shock of it infiltrating his thought pattern, sending his perfectly worked out plan off kilter and spinning it wildly out of control.

She opened her mouth to speak, but at that moment she heard what sounded like gunfire in the distance, from somewhere beyond the diner, but dismissed it, thinking it must be just the sound of a car backfiring - Loughlin's shabby looking Oldsmobile possibly. Ignoring it, she said, "Red, please, I'm so sorry. I didn't mean—"

"How can you be pregnant?" Red's voice was a whisper.

"It just… It just sort of happened—"

"How can you be pregnant!" Red suddenly roared, springing to his feet and violently sweeping the table clean with his thick, chunky forearm; the plates and glasses smashing on the black and white tiles, the engagement ring spinning somewhere out of sight. The bottle of Irish Whiskey also hit the ground and shattered, spilling its entire contents far and wide all over the floor, splashing liberal measures of single malt over the surrounding booths and tables.

The river of alcohol was spreading dangerously, like a trail of gasoline, towards the still lit candelabra which had also crashed to the ground, its flames eagerly licking the drooping folds of the tablecloth.

Megan jumped up, scared out her wits, the anger on Red's face clear to see. "I'm sorry, Red! Please, it was an accident."

"Whore!" He growled. "Filthy goddam whore!"

"Red, please!" She cried in floods of tears, backing away from the big, burly Irishman whose face was flushed scarlet with anger.

"Who's the father. What dirty bastard put his cock in you - who dared to fuck my woman?" He spat. "Or did you come on to them? Did you open your whorish legs and invite them in - eh? Is that how it was?"

"No... please. It wasn't like that—"

"Tell me! Tell me who it was!" Then, almost as if a lightbulb had flickered on in his brain, he suddenly knew. "Double J." He growled victoriously. "That's who it was - wasn't it? He's the one you fucked?"

Meggie could not speak but her eyes gave her away and in doing so she saw something terrifying on Red's livid face. Quivering with fear she backed away even more but came up against another booth and was unable to retreat any further.

Red marched forward and grabbed hold of her throat in one of his meaty paws. "That's who it was, wasn't it you slut? That boy - nearly half your goddamn age - he's the one isn't he?

"Please—" Meggie choked, Red's fingers digging into her windpipe, "Please, stop!"

"Quiet, whore!" He yelled, slapping her hard around the face, landing a clattering blow with the back of his hand. Meggie's head rocked sideways and she briefly saw stars as she collapsed backwards over the table top before everything suddenly went black.

***

Meggie stirred a short time later, her jaw throbbing from the hefty blow that knocked her out.

As she slowly roused, she became aware of a heavy weight pressing down upon her, the force of it juddering her body violently.

The unbearable stench of cheap aftershave filled her nostrils and she could hear the sound of panting close to her ear, like a weary dog after a long run.

Then the awful truth dawned.

Instantly she remembered where she was; disgust and revulsion filling her senses as she realised with unspeakable horror what was happening.

She opened her eyes and stared directly into Red's crazed face, contorted with lust and rage as he forced himself upon her.

As his hot breath seared her cheeks, a piece of spittle from his drooling mouth fell onto her lips to make her gorge rise.

"Get off me!" She screamed. "Stop this, please, stop!"

"But this is what you want, darlin' ain't it?" He growled. "Whore's wanna be fucked, that's their job ain't it? So I'm just making the most of your services."

Red's voice was hoarse with effort and thick with carnal desire as he pinned her to the table.

He had seen his chance whilst she was still unconscious; years of pent up desire and vicious aggression suddenly springing to the fore.

Unable to resist, he ripped open the front of her blue uniform then tore away her bra, tugging it manfully from her limp body. He then hauled up the hem of her dress to reveal the nylon corset that disguised her pregnant bulge, ripped off her flimsy underwear and forced her legs apart.

Then he dropped his green plaid trousers and thrust himself into her whilst she lay there, unknowing and inert.

But before he had satiated his despicable lust she had awoken.

And now she was conscious she fought.

With everything she had she fought, using all her strength but she could not shift his vast bulk; the weight of him completely immovable. His hands were clamped over her arms and she tried desperately to wrestle them free but it was impossible.

So she kicked with all her might but Red was seemingly immune.

"Get off me, you filthy brute - get off!" She screamed hysterically at the top of her voice, "Please, you're hurting me!" She wept loudly.

But her hopeless pleas fell on stony ground.

Megan, crying loudly, repulsed and unable to bear the thought of what was happening, tried desperately to focus her mind elsewhere.

Attempting to block out the depravity of her situation, she focused on an orange glow that seemed to be dancing in the air beyond the extent of her vision.

It seemed warm and welcoming and for the briefest moment she thought God had come down from the heavens to save her.

But then, as she blinked away tears, she realised what she was actually seeing was fire and in her dazed, damaged state, it occurred that she had been summoned straight to Hell.

However, she soon realised, as Red huffed and puffed, spent and exhausted on top of her, that what she was actually seeing was a large unwieldy blaze that had taken hold of the booth where she and Red had recently been sitting - the flames of which were now angrily licking the ceiling of the diner and scorching it black.

Immediately Megan saw her death and was more than ready to meet it. Indeed, with her body aching from brutal violation and her life it tatters from the ungodly mess it had become, she positively welcomed it.

But then she heard a familiar voice shout from somewhere near the entrance of the diner, the voice of someone who had at last come to save her, although the knowledge she might yet live did little to comfort her.

Chapter Sixteen

The four youngest members of Jay's small band of Westside Dukes had already fallen; one was lying lifelessly, face down on the concrete in a large pool of blood; another was on his side, being set upon by a pack of Playboys - kicking, punching and stabbing. He was out of it, maybe for good. A third was sitting off to the side, tears streaming down his bloodied face, his arm clearly broken and the fourth was on his knees, doubled over, spitting up blood.

Jay and the five other boys were holding their own although all, bar Jay himself, had sustained injuries - some of which looked quite serious.

Jay found himself in the centre of a large circle of baying Playboys, facing the leader, Javier. In his periphery he could see his other gang mates but they were all locked in battles of their own.

Javier and Jay had already gone several rounds and both were looking battle worn, their clothes ripped and bloody. Javier had lost two teeth courtesy of a tremendous left hook from Double J and he also had a long slash across his chest as a result of stepping too close to Jay's switchblade.

But Jay was unhurt, aside from some bruising on his face and a slight nick above his right eye and he was easily getting the better of Javier whose bark, it seemed, was much worse than his bite. The Puerto Rican was, however, still in possession of the machete and Jay had only narrowly missed being sliced by it several times - too many times for comfort.

He knew, too, that if he managed to despatch Javier, the rest of the Playboys would simply swarm in and overwhelm him and even as proficient as he was at fighting, he could not beat off an army.

As he eyed Javier, who was wielding the machete once more, readying for yet another brutal clash, Jay prayed Rebel would arrive soon with reinforcements.

Then, as Javier charged with his machete held high, a gunshot rang out and one of the Playboys dropped to the ground.

In the ensuing melee, Jay ducked under Javier's outstretched arm and stabbed upwards, thrusting the thin blade of his knife into the other boy's ribs. Javier went down as Jay span to see the wondrous sight of maybe fifty Westside Dukes, in their green and white jackets, swarming onto the court led by Rebel who was holding a pistol aloft.

In the background, Andy Loughlin cruised slowly up the block in his elderly Oldsmobile.

Behind Jay, too, even more of the Dukes were entering the court from the rear and the Lincoln Playboys had disintegrated into panic.

Rebel reached Jay, a big, wide smile on his face; this was what they lived for, it was what they knew and what they excelled at. He handed his brother the .38 Special he had taken from Jay's drawer, just as he'd asked - even though no words had passed between them.

"Thought you might be needing this," Rebel said with a grin.

Jay smiled back, "Welcome to the party," he said, looking about him and seeing his loyal troops going about their well-practised business. "Although looks like the party's nearly over!"

"Then I'd better go get me a taste before it's done," Rebel said, sprinting off into the fray, whooping with glee as he went.

As Jay watched his brother launch himself headlong into the action, it was clear to see The Playboys were being routed and dark-skinned teenagers in purple waistcoats and caps were going down all over the court. Those that weren't were either on the run or fighting for survival against superior numbers of Dukes.

The battle was almost won and most of Jay's original band of warriors had survived. It was a good day.

Then he turned back to face Javier, expecting to see him writhing on the ground in agony, but instead saw him standing right in front of him with the machete raised murderously above his head. Jay saw it in the briefest instant just a second before Javier swung it down on him.

Swiftly he stepped aside, although not quick enough to dodge a hard blow to the shoulder. But with no time to think and acting purely on instinct, he brought up the pistol and fired two shots in quick succession straight into Javier's muscular torso, felling him instantly.

The leader of the Lincoln Playboys collapsed like a puppet with its strings cut and bled out on the cold concrete of the basketball court. Dead. He had paid the ultimate price for invading Dukes turf.

As Jay stared down at the body at his feet, he heard someone cry out in Spanish and then the sound of another shot. Suddenly he felt as if he had been stung and he twisted in pain. He looked up and saw Rebel running back towards him. He saw, too, the shooter of the gun; another Puerto Rican youth with similar features to Javier, clearly his brother. The boy was still holding the gun outstretched, pointing it at Jay, its barrel smoking.

Jay could do nothing but watch as the youth readied to fire again but before he could, Rebel pushed his own .38 into the boy's ear and blew his brains out.

As the boy went down, Rebel continued onwards, a look of horror on his face as he approached Jay.

"Jesus, man - what the fuck...? You okay, man?" He shouted.

Jay looked quizzically at him, "Yeah, sure I am, why?"

"Why? Fuckin' look at yourself, man! You're hurt - hurt fuckin' bad!"

Only then did Jay become aware of an intense pain.

He looked down to see blood oozing from a bullet hole in his right side, staining his jeans and sneakers red. Then he moved his head to the left and his eyes widened with shock and disbelief. Javier's machete was buried in his shoulder, stuck like a butcher's cleaver double the depth of the blade, having severed through his jacket, his flesh, his bone and his muscle to inflict an almighty wound. Blood was pouring like a waterfall from the grotesque fissure, transforming his green and white gang jacket to dark red.

His left arm was completely unresponsive, he couldn't move it and the pain now was all consuming.

He rocked on his feet, suddenly weak, "Fuck!" He said, with an almost calm disbelief, tucking his pistol into the pocket of his custom made letterman jacket, seemingly unaware his face was now ashen and he was swaying like a drunk on a Saturday night.

But then, a second later, he steadied himself, and a look of steely determination appeared in his eyes. With his pallor almost grey, he looked at his brother and said, "Get it out, get it out of me, now."

Rebel looked mortified. He had never seen such an appalling injury - and he'd seen and been responsible for many. "But it'll kill you - the pain, man - it'll be fuckin' huge!"

"I don't care. I want this fuckin' thing outa me - if you don't do it, I'll do it myself!"

"Jesus, Jay! Think about it will ya—"

"Enough! No more talking. Just do it. Get it over with - do it now!"

Rebel knew there was no changing Jay's mind and knew, too, that he had to do what he had been asked. He studied his brother's pained expression; their eyes locking for a second, once again understanding each others thoughts. Then Rebel nodded and very gently took hold of the handle of the machete.

Jay immediately winced with agony, but nodded vehemently and through gritted teeth growled, "Do it!"

In that moment Rebel pulled the blade free as quickly and smoothly as he could, but it had to be dragged through meat and sinew and muscle which all seemed unwilling to give up the steel without a fight; sucking at it as Rebel tugged it clear.

Jay was screaming at the top of his voice, crying out in excruciating agony as the machete was drawn from his shoulder.

Then, when at last it was out and Rebel was holding it free in his grip, Jay staggered again, woozy from losing so much blood, his mouth sagging open and his eyes half closed as he struggled to remain conscious. But the darkness was rapidly closing in on him and he knew he had to fight it. If he was to have any hope of surviving he had to stay awake.

Nevertheless, try as he might to remain standing, his legs buckled and he dropped to his knees.

Rebel, full of concern, quickly ripped off his own jacket and pressed it to his brother's gaping wound in an effort to stem the bleeding. But soon that, too, was soaked through.

All about them the Playboys were running, the arena now dominated by the Dukes as their opponents desperately tried to flee from the court and return to the safety of their own turf.

In the distance, but not too far away, police sirens could be heard. Soon they would be arriving to take control of the gruesome scene, certain to arrest anyone left standing.

"We gotta go, Jay!" Rebel said. "Gotta go now."

Double J nodded and lifted his good arm for his brother to help him to his feet. Rebel slipped it around his shoulders and held his hand firmly then as gently as he could he hoisted Jay up.

Again Jay cried out in pain, but then, once he was up on his feet, he nodded. "I'm good, I'm good - let's go," he exclaimed through panting breath. "The diner, take me there. We'll be safe there."

As quickly as they could, whilst they watched the rest of their gang mates scatter, the brothers made their way out of the court and back up the block, the sirens getting louder with every step they took. Jay was surprisingly sprightly considering his injuries, willing himself onwards, one step after another, relying only on Rebel to help keep his balance.

They reached the diner just as the first squad car screeched to a halt beside the basketball court, swiftly followed by three others. An ambulance turned up too, but they would need a lot more than just one.

Andy Loughlin had parked the Oldsmobile around the corner from the diner, out of sight from the army of cops who were now dashing into the court.

"Can you manage to get inside by yourself?" Rebel asked Jay. "I'm just gonna get Loughlin, okay?"

Double J nodded. "Sure, man. I'll be fine." Although he looked anything but as Rebel carefully removed his arm from his shoulders.

"Take it easy, Jay. I'll be there in a minute - okay? Hold on, man, till we can figure out what to do."

Again Jay nodded through the excruciating pain as he placed his one good hand on the door of the diner, looking at the deeply concerned expression on his brother's face as he did so. "Go, get Loughlin," he said. "I'll see you in a second - and I ain't plannin' on going nowhere, so stop worryin.'"

He then pushed open the door and staggered inside.

***

For a moment Jay thought he was delirious as it seemed he had walked in through the gates of Hell.

But it was no mirage.

Tall, angry flames were licking the ceiling of the diner burning through the wood-paneling like the dry kindling of a parched forest. Fire had also taken hold of several booths as well as the bar and dancing flames of orange, gold and amber were blistering the walls.

And in the centre of the restaurant, almost at the very heart of the inferno, Jay saw Meggie, on her back, her stockinged legs forcibly spread apart, and the animalistic, rutting form of Red between them, pushing himself into her.

Meggie was clearly in distress and from where Jay stood, even though near blinding pain was surging through his body, it was obvious Red had forced himself upon her.

Momentarily Jay forgot all about his hideous injuries as his blood boiled with anger.

"Hey! Get off her you fat prick!" He yelled.

Red, now spent, raised his head at the sound of Jay's voice and turned towards the door to see the boy standing there.

But Red's eyes were not those of a sane man and he seemed almost not to recognise Jay at all.

Red pushed himself off of Meggie and stood beside the booth with his trousers round his ankles, as if in a daze.

The fire was burning out of control just feet behind him and the intense heat of it, as it scorched the hairs on the backs of his bare legs, suddenly snapped him out of his reverie.

He span around quickly to be faced by the raging wall of flame that had already engulfed much of the area surrounding him. His livelihood, his life for the past twenty years, literally going up in smoke in front of his eyes. He was stunned, momentarily frozen as he tried to take in the horrific reality of what was happening.

His first thought was to fight it; to get water, buckets, pots, pans - anything that would help to get the inferno under control, but almost instantly he realised how futile the attempt would be, instinct telling him it had already burned beyond the point of salvation and his diner was all but gone.

Even if he could somehow, miraculously, put the fire out, too much of it had been damaged and the cost of refurbishing would be astronomical. He was ruined, the restaurant finished, and it was all Meggie's fault.

Red turned back to Jay, thick, black smoke billowing around him as he pulled up his plaid pants and fastened his belt buckle; anger burning on his face.

"What the fuck have you done, Red?" Spat Jay with disgust over the loud roar of the raging fire. But the answer was all too clear as Meggie, at last able to move, rolled herself off the table and onto the bench seat of the booth, hurriedly trying to cover her nakedness with the torn remains of her uniform and shield herself from the blaze.

Red regarded Jay for a moment, not quite believing what he was seeing; the boy was soaked with blood that was steadily seeping from an atrocious wound in his shoulder, his life clearly sapping away as it dripped relentlessly onto the black and white tiles of the diner.

"You tell me, boy!" Red growled. "You're the one who fucked my woman, you're the one who caused all of this - you and her - that whore, there—" He pointed at Meggie as she lay cowering in the booth, coughing violently as toxic smoke found its way into her lungs. "—The deceitful slut that's pregnant with your bastard child!"

"What?" Jay said, incredulous, uncertain as to whether he was lying or not. "She's pregnant?"

Meggie, almost overcome by smoke, crawled out from the booth and staggered to her feet. She felt weak and battered, everything ached. "Red, please - don't!" She coughed. Then she looked over at Jay, dreading his reaction; the awful truth of her situation now revealed, the flames licking at hers and Red's heels.

"You're pregnant?" Jay asked again as she came into view through the smoke. "You're gonna have a baby?"

Then Meggie properly saw him; her lover, the father of her child, the kind hearted boy who had taken such an interest in Danny and Nate, and realised, with horror, that he was dying.

"Yes," she said simply, her heart breaking for him, all her injuries, the brutal violation by Red and the raging inferno instantly forgotten as she desperately tried to go to him.

But as she moved, Red fastened his hand on her neck once more. "Where the fuck do you think you're going, slut? You're staying right here with me - this is all your fault and I ain't finished with you yet, darlin.'"

"Leave her alone, Red!" Jay shouted. "Let her go."

"Or what, boy? What are you gonna do, eh? You're nearly fuckin' dead!"

"Or I'll kill you," Jay said softly, pulling the .38 from his pocket as he swayed on unsteady legs and aimed it in the general direction of the other man.

Red considered the gun for a minute, then smiled derisively, "Pah! I'd like to see you try," he scoffed before turning back to Meggie and tightening his grip on her throat, unaware that flames were now clawing the turn-ups of his green plaid pants.

A shot rang out just as Rebel and Loughlin rushed into the diner. At the same time Jay's legs gave way and he dropped to the floor, the .38 skittering away across the tiles.

Momentarily, Rebel was stunned by what he saw; the whole restaurant aflame, its walls blistering under the volcanic heat and thick, black smoke everywhere. The noxious smell of it burnt his lungs and stung his eyes whilst waves of rolling flames were sweeping the length of the ceiling; its timbers crackling like logs on a bonfire.

Rebel saw Jay fall, then looked beyond him, to the centre of the restaurant where his mentor, Red, stood holding Meggie by the throat.

"Holy shit!" Rebel exclaimed as Red slowly released his grip on Meggie and turned to face his protégé, exposing the small round hole in the centre of his chest where the bullet had entered his body; fresh, bright blood just beginning to ooze from it. Shock registered on Red's face as Meggie, now free from his clutches, ran towards Jay.

In the same instant, Rebel watched, appalled as flames climbed Red's legs. "Stay with Jay!" He barked at Loughlin as he sprinted to save Red, passing Meggie as he went and reaching the dying Irishman in several long bounds.

"Help me, son," Red pleaded, his voice a rasping whisper as tears streamed down his blackened face and blood pumped from the hole in his chest, the acrid smell of his own burning flesh filling his nostrils as the flames roasted him alive.

"Careful!" Loughlin shouted as he watched his business partner attempting to rescue the man who was absolutely key to their lucrative ambitions.

But Rebel was heedless as he pulled Red from the brink of the inferno and lay him down on the ground, flames engulfing the old man's body.

Without thought for his own safety, Rebel threw himself down on top of Red to smother the flames but instead of putting them out, they caught hold of his own arms and torso and he screamed in agony. He rolled away, desperately fighting to extinguish them, but they only took a greater hold and Rebel could feel his own skin blistering and popping excruciatingly as the flames grew ever more fierce.

Red's whole body was now engulfed in flame. His hair was gone and his skin was covered head to foot in hideous, boiling pustules of burning flesh. He screamed maniacally, a wild howl through the excruciating pain of it all. "Meggie!" He yelled as an almighty cracking sound rang out above his head.

Beside him, Rebel, who was still fighting madly to snuff out the fire on himself, looked up in terror, and instinctively knew it was the end for both of them.

In that instant, there was a thunderous crash and a huge molten chunk of ceiling collapsed down on top of him and Red, burying the two of them under several tons of mangled debris.

***

"No!" Loughlin yelled, as he saw the two men so vital to his long-planned success, die so horribly in front of his eyes. His dreams of wealth and a life of easy luxury buried along with them.

But Meggie was oblivious to his woes and everything going on around her as all she could think about, all she cared about, was Jay.

She had his head cradled in her arms now and he was looking up at her, barely conscious, unaware his brother was dead.

Meggie's face was streaked with black soot and tears, both of emotion and from the toxic smoke that billowed about them, streamed from her eyes.

Jay's shoulder wound was horrifically gruesome; a deep crevice that exposed open flesh, sliced muscle and severed bone. He'd lost so much blood from it, as well as from the bullet wound in his side, that he was now as white as a ghost. He lay on his back, panting for breath, fighting for life that Meggie knew was slipping away rapidly.

His eyes were glassy as he spoke with a hushed, pained voice, barely audible as the roaring fire raged all about them, but Meggie leaned in close so she could hear what he had to say. "It's true? You're pregnant?" He asked. She nodded, her tears dripping onto his youthful face. "Mine?" He said.

"Mmm hmm," Meggie nodded, her heart breaking as he smiled with pride at the thought of being a father.

"There was no one else. Just you." She said.

"And Nathaniel," Jay said.

"Yes."

"I'll be seeing him soon, Meggie."

"Yes." There was no point in her denying he was going to die as they both knew it to be a certainty.

"Anything you want me to tell him?" Jay asked, his voice fading.

"Tell him I loved him," Meggie sobbed loudly, "tell him I loved you both."

Jay looked up into her tear-stained face and smiled; his kind, caring, irresistible smile and said, "You know what, Meggie Malone? I loved you, too."

Then he died in her arms.

***

"What the fuck did you do here?" Loughlin snarled at her.

Meggie, overcome with emotion, not comprehending his anger, looked up at him and said, "What?"

"What did you do here you stupid bitch - what did you fuckin' do?" Loughlin was livid, the rage and bitterness of lost opportunity etched on his big, square face. He stood over her, his T-shirt and jeans speckled with soot as sparks and molten embers rained down upon them.

"What?" Said Meggie again, wracked with grief and unable to focus her mind on anything other than Jay's passing.

"I said what did you do here!" Shouted Loughlin, grabbing her roughly by the arm and pulling her physically to her feet so Jay's head slipped from her lap and cracked down on the hard floor. "What did you fuckin' do!"

"I... I didn't do any—"

"Don't fucking lie to me, bitch!" Loughlin yelled, whacking Meggie across the jaw with a devastating back-hander, knocking her sideways and causing her to spill from his grip as she struggled dizzily to stay upright.

"I promise," she begged, blood dripping from the side of her mouth, I didn't do anything - it was Red, he—"

"Liar! You've ruined everything!" He coughed as he punched her with all his considerable might in the centre of her stomach, folding her in half, the pain tearing through her frail body, the air sucked from her scorched lungs.

Meggie sank to the floor, yet Loughlin was still screaming at her, his unbridled wrath finding no bounds, his eyes red-rimmed and sore from all the smoke, giving him a devilish appearance as he glared down at her.

"You've killed it - you've killed everything - it's all fuckin' gone and it's all your fault!" Then he kicked her, as hard as he could, the steel toe-cap of his big, chunky work boots connecting with devastating force against Meggie's ribs sending her sprawling at full stretch across the tiles, leaving her fingertips mere inches from the fire as even more pain exploded within her.

With blackness threatening to overwhelm her, Loughlin loomed large once more. With him standing directly above her, Meggie's fingers closed around something hard and metallic and near scolding hot at the furthest extent of her reach. She could not see the object through the deadly black smoke that was crawling like a poisonous monster across the floor. It blinded her and scorched her lungs, but she realised instantly what it was.

Forcibly she shut out the severity of the volcanic heat as the handgrip of Jay's discarded .38 seared into her palm and branded her soft flesh with its scolding imprint.

"I'm gonna fuckin' kill you, bitch," Loughlin growled.

"No, you're not," Meggie snarled back, "As God is my witness, you will not!" Then she rolled onto her back and fired.

The bullet tore through Loughlin's right eye and exited through the top of his head, taking a huge chunk of skull, brain and blonde wavy hair with it. He took three or four zombie-like steps before finally tumbling headlong into the flames where he fried to a crisp.

∗∗∗

Meggie somehow managed to stand, the fire almost surrounding her as she limped slowly, agonisingly back to the entrance of the diner; her heart aching with sadness as she watched Jay's ruined body being claimed by the flames. But there was nothing she could do, the heat of the inferno was so intense, so strong, that her own skin was blistering and bubbling as it literally burned away. Much of her hair had been badly singed and she was almost overcome by smoke inhalation. If she did not escape now then she would undoubtedly die there too, along with Jay and everyone else. Meggie had seconds not minutes to get out and as she pushed the door open and almost fell into the clean night air, another vast chunk of ceiling crashed down immediately above where she had been standing a moment before. Had she idled just one second longer she would have been killed for sure.

As she breathed in deeply, trying to flush the toxic smoke from her lungs, she wretched and threw up a large quantity of what looked to be black oil before succumbing to a convulsive coughing fit. When it had passed, she wiped her mouth with the back of her hand and noticed the same black oily substance which, upon closer inspection, appeared to be congealed blood.

However, even though her whole body was consumed with pain, she forced herself to move.

Police, who for some reason unknown to Meggie, were swarming down the block, had begun to move up the darkened street as they noticed the glow of fire from the diner. Indeed, somebody had already raised the alarm as Meggie could hear the wailing sirens of fire trucks as they sped toward the burning restaurant.

But she had no wish to linger or to answer unwanted questions. Needing, instead, to get home to be with her boys.

So, wrapping what was left of her torn uniform around her, she slipped quietly into the shadows, limping and hobbling as she went.

She was bruised, battered and the insufficient material of her uniform barely covered her naked flesh. But she made her way back to her apartment by just concentrating on placing one foot in front of the other, oblivious to blood seeping from her private parts and of the bloody trail she was leaving in her wake.

Chapter Seventeen

It was only eight-thirty by the time Meggie staggered in through the door to her apartment and thankfully her boys were still out playing on the streets; no doubt fascinated by all the police cruisers and fire trucks that were clogging up the area around the burning diner.

She was in a bad way. Even before she had gone to the diner, supposedly to start her evening shift, she had felt shivery and feverish; a result of the previous day's vigil standing opposite The Greyling Building on Park Avenue in the cold and rain. But now she felt like death, her whole body, every single inch of it, hurt like hell and all she wanted to do was curl up in a ball and cry.

Jay was dead, she had watched him burn, his injuries so awful that she could not even bear to think about them. But he had saved her. Had he not entered the diner when he did then she, too, might have died in the blaze along with Red.

The thought of Red, of what he had done to her, made her feel sick and ashamed. The wounds she had sustained at his hands and the beating she had received from both him and Loughlin had caused something inside her to burst. There was a piercing, almost unbearable ache in her stomach now, as if something had ruptured within her and she instinctively knew the trauma of it all had ended her pregnancy.

She wanted to give up, to succumb to her injuries, so the pain would at last subside.

But she had to fight, for her boys' sake, she had to be strong. But as she limped awkwardly, painfully, into her small bedroom and caught sight of herself in the mirror, Meggie was horrified by the ghoulish, ruined figure staring back at her.

Her hair was almost gone and the left side of her face, including her ear, were burnt and raw; the skin blistered and pustulant; the ear itself was little more than a curl of fried flesh with a gaping hole at its centre. Her neck had been severely scorched too and her left arm was shining red with exposed, raw tissue from deep, angry burns.

Her pale blue uniform had been singed black, all down the whole of the left side, and had all but seared itself to the damaged skin beneath, whilst her left leg, below the knee, was just one huge mass of ugly, popping blisters.

Aside from the obvious injuries, Megan's insides throbbed incessantly and as she stood, appalled by the sight of herself, she could also see a dark puddle forming on the floor between her feet and the constant drip, drip, drip of fresh blood as it dribbled from her torn and throbbing innards.

It seemed to her that God had finally given her His answer and the dreadful injuries were the levy she had paid for her sins.

She began to cry but that only triggered another coughing fit which, in turn, made her charred lungs burn all the more. She put her hand to her mouth in an attempt to contain the violent, hacking cough and when it had, at last, subsided, she looked at her palm and saw, worryingly, that it was covered with treacly black blood once more.

She was aware now, from the extent of what she had seen in the mirror and what she actually felt inside, that her time in this world may be short. But the realisation did not fill her with dread, merely sadness that she would be leaving her boys whilst they were both still so young. There was also the question of what would become of them when she was gone.

She also had to put right what she had done so terribly wrong; to cleanse herself fully before passing into the next life if she had any chance of God accepting her into Heaven. But even as she thought it, she could feel her strength fading and it was apparent her window of opportunity was closing fast.

Firstly though, she had to prepare herself for Danny and Nate as she could not let them see her like this.

Working as quickly as her damaged body would allow, Meggie hobbled over to her dressing table and found an old full-length white, linen nightgown. Then she carefully, very gently, pulled it on over her head, draping it completely over the burnt nylon uniform which had now become intrinsically melded to her skin and could not be removed without a great deal of pain. Then she lifted out her mother's white shawl, her most prized possession, and wrapped it gingerly around her shoulders.

After that, she found a fine silk headscarf that had been amongst Maria's belongings, it was green with a delicate, light pink floral pattern. She draped it over her head and around the sides of her face, tying it softly under her chin to hold it in place.

Finally, she checked her reflection again in the mirror. Her injuries now were all but concealed. Her face still revealed some bruising from where Red and Loughlin had struck her and her skin was reddened from the intense heat of the fire. But all the major burns and blisters were completely hidden from view.

She laid an old cloth over the small pool of blood on the floor before very carefully putting herself to bed, pulling up the covers around her shoulders to stop the uncontrollable shivering which had now taken her over.

And there she waited until her boys came home.

***

Danny and Nate woke her maybe an hour later as they burst into the apartment full of news, desperate to report what they knew of the big gang fight between the Dukes and the Playboys and the huge fire at the diner - certain their mother would already be home because of it, hoping she would have yet more information about it.

But as they stumbled, excitedly, into her bedroom they both stopped in their tracks as they saw Meggie laying there in bed all wrapped up in a headscarf and shawl.

She attempted a smile but she looked gravely ill and the boys would not be fooled into thinking she was not.

They were both smart enough to realise she had been injured in the fire and they rushed to her and sank to their knees beside her bed. "What happened, Mom?" Nate asked, "Did you get burned bad?"

"We saw the fire at Red's," Danny added, "But we didn't think you were hurt - we kinda just thought you'd got out okay."

"Yeah, we thought you'd got out okay?" Nate echoed.

Meggie smiled again and attempted to speak but her voice was weak, nothing more than a whisper, her whole body tightening now as the injuries dried and contorted, the pain of them more severe than ever they were before.

"Yes, Nate, sweetheart, I did get burned a little I think. But I got out, Danny, I got out - I had to get back to you two. My big boys."

"Are you okay?" They asked in unison.

"I'm a bit sore, that's all - but I'll be fine, I'm sure."

She studied them both with pride. As different as chalk and cheese but no mother could be more proud. Nate was of slight build, a result of his premature birth, Meggie had always assumed, but he was honest and true and stood up for what he believed in. He shared her faith in God, even though hers had been severely tested of late. But Nate had no such doubts, his belief was unshakeable and certain. He had his father's red curly hair and the same pale complexion and he reminded her every day of Nathaniel; the good, honest reliable man she had married all those years ago.

Beside Nate, knelt Danny. Dark and tanned and broad across the shoulders, with sharply inquisitive emerald eyes, he was destined to be a real heartbreaker. Both tough and resilient, as well as a natural leader, Meggie suspected, but with an easy sense of humour and a mischievous streak, just like Armando. He reminded Meggie of Maria - good and kind and thoughtful but with an iron resolve and a determined will. But for sometime now, whenever she looked deeply into those handsome green eyes of his, she felt a pang of guilt.

"Does it hurt, Mom - are you okay?" Asked Danny.

"I'm fine, honey, I just need to rest a little, that's all."

"What about Red, Mom, did he get out okay?" Said Nate.

Meggie thought of Red, the hideous image of his body engulfed in flames as the ceiling of the diner fell in on him. Then she thought of him rutting on top of her, of his vile glassy eyes and his drooling rubbery lips as he violently raped her. "No, darlin'" She said coldly. "He didn't." Try as she might she could not sugar coat it; the man was a monster and she was glad he was dead.

Both the boys looked shocked at this news and Nate's eyes filled with tears. He put his head down as Megan placed her hand over his, but even that slightest movement caused her to wince with pain and Danny realised then just how serious her injuries were.

"Nate, sweetheart, I know you liked Red - I know he was good to you, but in the end he…" She knew she ought not say more but she could not have her son believing a brutal rapist such as Red was good man. "In the end he proved himself to be a very bad person."

Nate's head shot up and he looked at his mother's emotion filled eyes, reading in them something unsaid. But he was a smart lad, as was his brother. "He hurt you?" He said quietly.

Meggie's heart broke for her boy. "Yes," she said. "I'm afraid he did."

Nate sniffed away the tears and wiped his nose with the back of his hand. "I always knew he was bad, really," he said. "Cos he was always so mean to Danny."

Meggie smiled. "Yes, he was," she said.

"What about Jay, Mom?" Asked Danny, after mulling things over in his mind for a while. "There was a big fight on the basketball courts between the Dukes and the Playboys - do you know if he's okay?"

Meggie looked at the younger of her two boys, her lips buckling with emotion as her own eyes filled with tears. "No, my darlin' boy, I'm afraid he's not."

Danny started to cry. "Jay's dead? The Playboys killed him?"

"No sweetie. He died in the fire, saving me. He saved me from Red."

"He was good?" Danny asked meekly, "He wasn't a bad man too, was he?"

"No, darlin', he was good. He was the best." Then she started to cough uncontrollably, blood spraying from her lips and staining her mother's shawl. Danny ran to fetch her a glass of water whilst Nate did his best to comfort her, but at his slightest touch she whimpered with pain.

As the coughing fit abated, Nate pulled a clean handkerchief from the pocket of his jeans and gently dabbed the blood away from her lips. His face was fixed as he tried to hide his emotions, realising, as Danny had a few moments before, just how gravely ill his mother was.

His brother held the glass of water up to Meggie's lips and she managed to drink a little but even that burned as it trickled down her throat.

"I'm going to fetch Dr O'Dowd," announced Nate.

"No, I'll be fine, sweetheart," protested Meggie, her voice little more than a faint rattle. She suspected, as did her boys, that she had already gone beyond the point when a doctor could be of any use. Especially a drunken sot like Seamus O'Dowd, the local quack, who lived some distance away and would no doubt be found at the bottom of an empty whiskey bottle.

Also, Meggie did not want to be without her oldest son any longer than absolutely necessary. These last moments, for however long they might go on, were so important to her and she wanted to make the most of them.

But Nate would not be dissuaded, he would not give up hope, not if there was even the slightest chance of saving her.

"No, Mom. Danny will take good care of you. Stay strong - I'll be back before you know it." Nate then darted from the room and Meggie heard the front door close behind him as he left the apartment at a gallop.

Danny moved up into the spot where Nate had been kneeling and ever so carefully took hold of his mother's small, frail hand.

She turned very gradually to look at him, seeing his big, emerald eyes looking back at her. Again she saw Maria in them and felt the pang of guilt. He had to know. Before she left this world for good, Danny had to know the truth.

"Danny, sweetheart," she rasped, "be a darlin' and fetch me the leather bound bible in the bottom drawer of my dresser, would you?"

"Sure, Mom. Course," Danny replied, immediately bounding over to the dresser.

The bottom drawer was already open from when Meggie took out her mother's shawl and Danny could clearly see the brown leather bible with a small, silver clasp. He had never seen it before but thought little of it as he lifted it out and carried it back to Megan, kneeling down beside her once more.

"Here it is." He said.

"Danny, my sweet boy," she whispered. "There's something you must know. Something I should have told you many years ago."

"It doesn't matter, Mom. Really it doesn't." Danny was an exceptionally bright lad, certainly nobody's fool, and guessed what she was about to tell him may concern the truth about his parentage. He always knew he was not Irish and presumed he was possibly Italian but he had never asked his mother and she had never told him. "I don't need to know anything, it's okay, honest."

"No, honey it's not. You have to know. It's only right that I tell you - it's what's right in the eyes of God."

"I don't care about God. I just care about you."

"I know you do, honey, and I care about you, too - more than anything, but you mustn't say that about God, you mustn't blaspheme."

"Sorry."

"That's okay, He knows you are. But please, let me tell you what I must before it's too—"

"Okay," Danny interrupted, he could not bear to hear her say 'before it's too late' as that would mean she was going to die and the thought of that was too dreadful to even contemplate. "Tell me," he said. "Whatever it is, it'll be fine."

Meggie smiled at her big, brave boy, knowing only too well that the next few moments might tarnish his opinion of her for the rest of his life, but she had to take the chance. It was the right thing to do. "Undo the clip and open the bible," she instructed. "Inside, among the pages, you will find a letter. It's addressed to you."

Danny glanced at her, a little surprised, then did as instructed. Sure enough, amid the pages of the bible he found a carefully cut-out hollow, a secret space in which he found an envelope addressed with the words *My Son*. Again he looked at Megan, clearly shocked, but she nodded her encouragement and he lifted it out. As he did so, he saw a little gold locket on a fine golden chain, the words *Always and Forever* inscribed upon it. He left the locket in the hollow and placed the bible down on the bed, holding the envelope in his shaking hand.

242

"Open it," Meggie gasped. "Read it. Please."

Danny took a beat then tore along the top edge of the envelope with the side of his index finger. Once it was open, he waited another moment, steeling himself for what the contents might reveal, and then slid out the letter.

He held it in his hand, not quite able to bring himself to unfold the expensive, heavily bonded white paper.

"Please, Danny. You must, sweetheart, it's important," prompted Megan.

Again Danny looked at her, his eyes full of uncertainty, before, at last, he unfolded it and started to read the fine script of the handwritten message it contained.

To my darling son, it began.

My name is Maria Liuzzi and I am your mother. I gave birth to you in Hollywood, California, when I was just seventeen years old and you were taken from me, against my will, a short time later. But know this, I have never stopped loving you and never will.

Your father was a handsome, young Italian named Armando Calabrese, a good, kind man, who I also loved with all my heart - but, my darling boy, I'm so sorry to tell you that he, too, was taken from us both before you were born.

The reason for his disappearance and the reason why you and I were parted is because of my own father, your grandfather, Carlo Liuzzi, a cold, evil, heartless man who had me sent away and your father banished.

It was my intention to escape with you, to take you to safety, somewhere we could live happily together, but if you are reading this letter then you know that I failed in my plan. However, please believe me when I say that I will never, ever stop searching for you, not until my dying breath.

When last I saw you, you were to be taken to a monastery somewhere in Italy and I was destined for a convent in Messina -

243

whether either of us made it to our respective destinations I do not know, but I hope you, at least, are living a happy, wonderful life and this letter, when you are old enough to read it, gives you some comfort and the assured knowledge that somewhere out in the world there is a person who loves you unconditionally.

I know not what happened to Armando, your father, but it is my dearest hope that, one day, we will all be together again.

Whatever your circumstances now, my darling, please know that you were born into a family of significant wealth. Carlo Liuzzi is a rich and powerful man and as his natural heir it is your fundamental birthright to inherit all that he has - and for what he has put you through it is nothing less than you deserve. When I find you - and I swear upon everything I hold dear that I will, you and I will face your grandfather together, united, and demand what is rightfully yours.

Until then, I will continue to think of you and pray for you each day and hope with every fibre of my being we will be reunited very soon.

I enclose with this letter a locket that was given to me on my sixteenth birthday. In it you will find a lock of my hair and a small photograph of me, so you might recognise me when we meet again.

Until that time, Godspeed my darling and I wish you all that your heart desires.

Your loving mother
Maria Liuzzi

Danny, stunned by this startling information, re-read the letter through twice more just to sure he understood everything correctly, allowing it to slowly sink in.

"I always thought you were my mother," he at last said softly.

"I know sweetie," said Meggie hoarsely, "I wish I was, but no. I was your mother's maid - more than that, her friend. Her good friend. She was a lovely, kind woman - what happened... why she could not be with you - it was no fault of hers. It was your grandfather, he—"

"I always thought you were my mother and that Nate was my brother, but maybe that we just had different dads."

"Nate *is* your brother, darlin', in every way that matters - just not by blood, that's all. And your da was a warm, handsome, lovely man, just like my Nathaniel - they were the best of friends the two of 'em."

"The letter said that my dad's still out there somewhere - is that true?"

Meggie rested her hand upon Danny's arm sympathetically, as painful as it was to do so, "Alas, my darlin', he is not - your mammy thought he was when she wrote that letter to you but we found out a while later that he—. Well, that he had died, sweetheart. I'm so sorry."

"How?" He asked abruptly, "How did he die?"

Meggie looked at Danny, straight in the eyes; his expression was set, determined. He had to know, she could tell. No matter how dreadful the truth of it was, he deserved to know. It was his right.

She coughed a little, but it did not develop into anything so violent as the attack a short while before. Although Danny quickly picked up the glass of water and gently held it to her lips once more. She managed to swallow a small quantity down, even though doing so made her throat sting with pain.

When Danny had put the glass down again and Meggie was relatively settled, he said again, "Please, Mom, how did my father die?"

Meggie took a heavy, laboured breath, then said in a wheezy whisper, "He died the same way as Nate's father, my husband - both murdered by Carlo Liuzzi - your grandfather, and his right-hand man, Salvatore Falcone."

"Murdered?" Danny queried, the amazement and shock apparent in his eyes.

Meggie nodded. "Yes. I'm so sorry, my darling boy."

"And my mother? Was she… Is she dead too?"

"No, sweetheart. I thought she was - for the longest time I was convinced Falcone had killed her too, which is why I raised you and brought you up as my own - I know it's what she would have wanted. But then, just recently, I discovered she is actually alive. It's a miracle. She somehow survived. But then I found that—" Meggie paused briefly as she was weak and panting for breath, but also she needed to break through the barrier of her own guilt, to admit to the wrong she had done.

"What, Mom? What did you find - tell me, please."

"I found that… I found that I couldn't give you up, my darling - I couldn't bear it, you see." She started to cry, tears rolling down her burnt face, sobbing as she thought of the terrible sin she had committed and the dreadful penance she had now paid for it.

Danny began to cry too, but he sniffed back the tears and wiped them from his eyes with the back of his hand.

"Does she know? Does she know where I am?" He finally asked.

"No, sweetheart," Meggie sniffled, "I'm sure she doesn't. The Maria I knew would never stay away from you - never wish to be parted from you - not if she knew how close you were."

"How close? What do you mean, 'how close'?" Suddenly Danny was kneeling bolt up upright as this fresh snippet of information was revealed.

Meggie closed her eyes, knowing the impact her words had caused. But he had to know it all now. She had to purge herself of sin if she was to ever find peace.

"I saw her," she said at last, "Just recently - it was how I knew she was alive—"

"You spoke to her?"

"No. I was across the street - she saw me too, I think. But then I ran - I couldn't face her, couldn't tell her…"

"You mean here, in New York?"

"Yes, my darling, here in New York, on Park Avenue - she lives in The Greyling Building with her husband. She doesn't know I've got you. Doesn't know where you are."

Danny was silent as he considered all this. He knelt, with his head down beside his mother's bed, for Meggie was his mother, or at least the only one he had ever known, all too aware that she was dying.

He thought hard about what he had heard, listening to her harsh, laboured breath as she lay there beside him, her lungs rattling in her chest, the sound of it piercing his heart. He could feel her eyes upon him, knowing he should say something to help her feel better but the words would not form in his mouth.

Slowly he opened the bible again and turned to the hollowed out section, his fingers closing around the locket as his eyes fell upon the inscription once more. Always and Forever.

Danny then jumped to his feet, startling Megan who looked terrified by his reaction. Had she lost him? She wondered, did he hate her now? Again, tears welled in her eyes.

"I'll be back soon," Danny said, shoving the locket roughly into the pocket of his jeans just a moment before Nate burst back into the apartment and hurried in through the bedroom door.

Nate was breathless and had clearly been running, sweat and tears soaking his wet face. "I couldn't wake him up!" He yelled, obviously distressed. "Dr O'Dowd was drunk - drunk as hell and I couldn't even get him to open his eyes - it was useless!"

Danny made to move past him. "Where are you going?" Nate asked, "O'Dowd won't come - I tried everything, he doesn't care - he's too drunk!"

"I'm not going to get O'Dowd," Danny replied.

"Where then? Mom needs us, where are you going?"

"Out!" Danny replied sharply, "Just out." And with that he

rushed from the apartment and was gone.

Nate was stunned, confused. He couldn't believe what he had just witnessed. "Danny!" He called after his brother, "Danny, come back!" But he received no reply.

He looked down at his mother laying in the bed, her lifeforce clearly ebbing away, tears dribbling down her scorched cheeks. "I'm sorry, Mom," he said, his heart breaking. "I'm so sorry. I tried, but the doctor wouldn't come and I don't know where Danny's gone."

"It doesn't matter, sweetie," she breathed. "And Danny's just upset, that's all. I'm sure he'll be back in a while, when he feels a bit calmer." Meggie prayed with all her heart she was right, forcing a smile as she continued, "Come, sit down here with me, there's much I need to tell you."

Nate did as instructed and knelt down by her bedside just as Danny had moments earlier. He saw the leather bound bible with the hollowed out section and the open letter laying beside it, unable to prevent his eyes from falling on the words.

Meggie said nothing, allowing him to read it, watching his eyes widen as he did so. It was a hard thing for her to do but there would be no more secrets. Not anymore.

When he had finished reading, he looked up at her, more shocked than even Danny had been. "I… I don't understand?" He said at last.

Meggie coughed. This time it turned into a violent fit; a deep hacking bark that made her shoulders shake and caused thick, black blood to spit out of her mouth. Nate tried as best he could to help her but it was futile, the pain wracking her body too great for him to even touch her. All he could do was wait for the fit to pass.

When, eventually, it had subsided, leaving Meggie even weaker than before, Nate dabbed her lips clean with the cloth and helped her drink some more water. She seemed so fragile as she sipped it down, so small, her body infused with pain.

Then, when she was as comfortable as he could make her, he said again, "I don't understand, Mom, Danny isn't my brother?"

"I'll explain everything, my darling, as best I can," Meggie wheezed, "But first you must know the truth of what happened to your father. About how he died."

And Nate was horrifically enthralled as she proceeded, painfully, breathlessly, to tell him it all.

Chapter Eighteen

Maria had slept little the night before, the image of Megan standing across the street from her the previous day playing over and over in her mind, along with all of the long dormant memories that seeing her had awakened.

She had been up early and had spent much of the day in tears as she thought about her lost son; berating herself again and again for not remembering he even existed. Injured or not, how on earth could she have forgotten about him for so long?

But she remembered it all now, even her fall from the train - or, indeed, the firm kick to the chest from Salvatore Falcone that had propelled her from it.

She could clearly recall dropping headlong into the deep crevasse, over the edge of the bridge, and plummeting through the air before smacking down hard on a rough scree slope; pain exploding through her body.

The speed of the fall caused her to bounce and roll uncontrollably down the near vertical incline, hurtling towards the turquoise waters below. Then her head hit something hard - a rock, she guessed, knocking her almost senseless as she plunged deeply into the water and sank far beneath the surface.

Barely conscious and severely dazed from the blow to her head, the freezing cold water had something of a rousing effect and, as she descended ever deeper, she forced her eyes open and looked up.

Immediately she saw something floating far above her, silhouetted by the dazzling sun which was high up in the cloudless blue sky.

It appeared to be a mass of debris; the wreckage of a small boat, or the remnants of one at least, all ensnared by a tangle of old fishing nets and sea borne detritus. But it was enough to give her hope. Quickly running out of breath, she kicked and swam, desperate not to drown, desperate for air.

Fighting unconsciousness and her aching body battling her all the way, she eventually burst through the surface and gasped for air, grabbing for the wreckage as she fought to fill her lungs.

Seriously concussed, her head pounding and her vision hazy, she somehow found the strength to clamber onto the floating mass of wood, seaweed and netting.

Maria could recollect lifting her head and seeing the horizon as she lay, bedraggled and battered aboard, hearing the waves slapping against her makeshift raft as it carried her out to sea on the tide just moments before the pain in her head dramatically intensified.

And then everything went black. For seven long years.

That one event had not only wiped out a huge chunk of her life but also everything she remembered prior to that point.

Until now.

With her memory having returned, Maria was determined to make those responsible for her suffering pay - no matter what it cost or how long it took.

But first, before anything else, she had to find her son. Without him she was nothing.

All that day she and Delores had worked the phones, calling police stations all over the city, as well as hospitals, housing authorities, employment agencies and any other organisation that might give them some clue as to the whereabouts of Megan Kelly, but they had turned up nothing so far and were still waiting on several call-backs from people who may or may not be able to supply them with a useful lead.

Diego had been helping, too. He had been out all day trawling through immigration and naturalisation records at the National Archives, taking time out of his busy schedule to help Maria search for her son.

He was now back at the apartment with a list of several Megan Kellys within the New York area who had entered the United States during the last nine years but each one would need to be cross-checked and eliminated and all that would take time.

But at least it was a start.

Yet none of them knew Megan Kelly had re-entered the United States nine years earlier under the name Megan Malone so the likelihood of them finding her at all was remote.

Nevertheless, it was late, almost midnight, by the time Maria and Diego finally found the time to sit down for dinner at the small table in their kitchen.

Diego ate hungrily, needing fuel after a long, tiring and very frustrating day, but Maria had no appetite.

She had an ache in her stomach that no food could fill; only the sure knowledge that her son was alive and well could sustain her fully now but so far that knowledge had not been forthcoming. But she knew not to lose heart; today was just the first day of what she was well aware could be a long, drawn-out search.

Yet she could still not get over the sight of Megan and the fearful expression on her face, nor the fact she had disappeared so quickly. Which begged the question, 'why?'

Diego had been a rock over the last thirty-six hours or so, his strength and understanding so important to her as she relayed to him more fully the details of her life before she met him. She had told him all about her father and his murderous, evil ways and of

Falcone, his malevolent, ever constant shadow.

She had been honest about her feelings for Armando, about how much she had loved him and how she so naively believed her father had merely sent him away after finding them together, only to find out later that her lover, the father of her unborn child, had actually been brutally murdered by the man she had previously respected more than any other.

She told of her heartbreak at being banished and the pain of being forced to give up her son. She had also related how Salvatore had tried to rape her on board the Conte Biancamano and the eventual fight on the train that had led to her being ejected from it, which resulted in her being rescued by Diego.

Maria also spoke at length about Megan and her son, Nate. She had told Diego of Nathaniel's fate, too, and how Megan found out the truth of it at the same moment Maria, herself, had learned of Armando's murder.

But, in the most part, she had spoken of Megan in glowing terms, referring to her as a good, honest and loyal friend - regardless of whether she was in her father's employ or not.

Which was what haunted Maria most about Megan's reaction to seeing her. The overriding emotion that Maria read on her face was horror and she could not fathom why somebody she so loved and trusted would react that way to her - even if she had assumed her to be dead. Surely then the reaction would be one of joy, delight in finding that she was, in fact, alive and well.

It was all very odd and just did not seem to add up.

Maria had been pondering this issue all day and was going over it again now, with Diego, as she pushed the food around her plate.

Diego, himself, had no such qualms as he wiped his plate clean with a crusty chunk of Spanish bread - a throw back to his Mediterranean roots where people enjoyed eating in a more rustic way - although his table manners were much more refined in company. But it did not trouble Maria who liked to watch her man eat, it gave her an enormous sense of well being - although tonight her mind was elsewhere.

Finally, when the plate was spotless, Diego swallowed down the last morsel of the delicious bread, sourced by Delores from a nearby deli, and leant back in his chair, satiated at last.

And then the phone rang.

Maria looked at the clock on the wall, it was ten past midnight. "Who on earth can that be at this time of night?" She queried.

Diego looked at the platinum Cartier on his wrist, "It's okay, it'll be Juan Pablo wanting to go through some things - he's been pressing me for a few minutes all day but I've been fobbing him off. I'm sorry, my darling, I have to answer but I won't be long, I promise."

"Don't be silly," Maria replied, smiling appreciatively at her considerate husband, "I've kept you from your work for too long - you've been so helpful today, so understanding. Of course you must take the call. Tell Juan Pablo 'hi' from me. I'll get the dishes."

Diego stood and planted a kiss on his wife's forehead and strode over to where the phone hung on the kitchen wall, snatching up the receiver. "Hello?" He said.

Meanwhile, Maria started busying herself with the dishes. She, of course, had a maid and a housekeeper but they were both off duty at this time of night - and besides, she liked to take care of her husband personally whenever she could. Even though they were fabulously wealthy she still liked to cook and clean up after him - at least some of the time, as it made her feel like a 'proper wife', although they rarely ate at home unless they were entertaining, so it was nice, on occasion, to revel in the mundanity of being a 'normal couple'.

"Oh, good evening, Sam," Maria could hear Diego saying in the background as she carried the dirty dishes over to the sink. Clearly it wasn't Juan Pablo as he had expected but the night porter from downstairs in the lobby. "No, it's fine, no trouble," he continued, "Señora Del Toro and myself were not sleeping. How can I help you?"

Maria was mildly curious as to what Sam could possibly want from them at gone midnight but then this was New York, after all, the city that never sleeps.

"A what?" Diego asked incredulously.

Maria's ears pricked up.

"To see who? Are you sure?"

She turned to look at him now, a quizzical expression on her face.

"That's impossible—"

Maria put down the dish she was holding and wandered over to where her husband stood talking into the phone.

"No. No - it's okay Sam, please don't worry. I suppose you'd better send him up. It's fine - yes, I'm absolutely sure. No bother. Please just put him in the elevator and I'll be there to meet him when he gets off."

Maria watched as Diego brushed a hand through his thick hair, concern etched on his handsome face. "Thank you, Sam," he said finally, "yes, goodnight to you, too."

He hung up the receiver and turned slowly to meet Maria's worried gaze, her mind racing with all sorts of possibilities. "Who is it that's coming up here, Diego?" She asked, "Not the police? Everything's alright with the new hotel isn't it?"

"No my darling. Not the police." Diego replied solemnly. "But a boy. A young street kid. He says—"

"He says what?" Maria interjected urgently, her face expectant and eager yet also slightly fearful.

"He says he's your son."

***

Danny had but a single thought in his mind as he ran from

the apartment and out onto the darkened streets of Hell's Kitchen; he had to save Meggie - or, at least, do everything in his power to try and do so.

However, he would need help.

Normally, he would have turned to Double J, but tragically he was not around to help anymore and there were precious few other people who would even give him the time of day. This meant he had to go further afield, to the only other person he thought might be able to help him - if, indeed, she was willing.

It was getting late now and the streets were dangerous at night, especially for a nine-year old. He had heard tales they were crawling with street gangs, muggers, hookers and drug dealers but Danny refused to be scared and would not be deterred from what he had to do.

He started to run, wearing just a faded T-shirt, a scruffy pair of Levis and his old basketball sneakers. As he headed out of The Kitchen he was perspiring lightly in the heat of the balmy night, the glow of the fire still raging at Red's Diner illuminating the dark sky behind him.

He kept to the kerb, close to the road, on the far edge of the sidewalk, keeping out of the shadows; his youthful imagination running wild with the possibility of someone lying in wait to attack him as he passed by.

Nevertheless, he forced himself relentlessly onwards as he cautiously made his way uptown, the rubber soles of his sneakers slapping on the sidewalk, echoing on the deserted street.

He travelled on up 49th to 8th Avenue, where more people were milling about and the amount of traffic increased substantially; yellow cabs were speeding to and fro and cars of all shapes and sizes lined the street; the houses and store fronts a little more upscale than those of Hell's Kitchen.

His legs were aching and his heart was beating hard in his

chest as he approached Broadway, close to the South side of Central Park and he found himself occasionally ducking for cover if a cop car drove by or if any large groups of people were approaching. The tales of muggers and pushers ringing in his ears again as he pressed on, forcing down any concerns he had for his own safety.

The streets were busy around Broadway in particular, with many suspicious looking characters wandering about and as for Central Park, well that was no place for any person to be alone at night - especially a young boy. Yet, regardless, he made it to Grand Army Plaza without encountering any trouble and from there it was just a short jog to the tall, awe inspiring buildings of Park Avenue.

Once there, he had to reluctantly ask directions to The Greyling Building - carefully choosing someone who looked suitably non-threatening to help him.

Less than an hour after starting out, he arrived at his destination and stood under the dark green marquee of the elegant grey building.

Only then did he rummage in his pocket and pull out the locket. Again he regarded the inscription, *Always and Forever*, desperately hoping the words were as sincere as he had wanted them to be.

Cautiously he opened the locket for the first time, being careful not to let the lock of hair get blown away by the light breeze.

The short, neatly tied length of jet black hair was the exact same colour as his, he noticed, and he held it securely between his thumb and forefinger as he turned his attention to the photograph.

As he saw the likeness of his birth mother for the first time he was staggered by how beautiful she was; just a girl still when the photo was taken, a little before her sixteenth birthday, making her barely seven years older than he was now. Her eyes were the same emerald green as his, her skin tanned and Italian in appearance - just like his.

Yet she was so feminine, so pretty.

He studied the photo and remembered what she had said in

her letter. She had given birth to him just a year after the photo was taken; her lover, Danny's father, had been murdered around that time, too, and she, herself, had been banished by the man who had killed him; Danny's own grandfather.

As much as he tried not to, Danny could not help but feel sorry for her as he studied her image. How awful it must have been to lose everything she loved most; how hard.

But why, if she had loved him so much - indeed, if she was living in New York, a mere stone's throw away - had she not come looking for him?

It was a puzzling question that most definitely needed an answer.

But presently he had to set about saving the woman who had been there for him, who had raised him and cared for him and done her utmost to keep him safe. The woman who lay burnt and battered and close to death in a tiny, three room apartment in Hell's Kitchen.

As he thought of her, his resolve hardened and he pushed his way in through the revolving door of The Greyling Building and marched confidently up to the smartly dressed old man sitting behind the front desk, the soles of his sneakers squeaking loudly on the highly polished marble floor.

"Excuse me, sir," He said politely to Sam, the night porter, his nose barely level with counter top as he stood on tip-toe to speak with the sixty-five year-old black man. "My name is Danny Malone and I'm here to see this woman—" He showed Sam the photo in the locket. "She is my mother."

***

Maria squeezed Diego's hand as they stood shoulder to shoulder, in a nervous state of heightened anticipation, as they waited for the elevator doors to open. They had watched the small lights above it, one for every floor of the building, briefly shine red as the car carrying Danny past swiftly by on its way to the penthouse and them.

At last, in the stylish opulence of the large rotunda, under the impressive glass canopy that allowed a view of the stars, they heard a loud 'ping' which echoed off the curved white walls as the gold doors of the elevator finally slid open.

For a second or two the elevator car looked empty and Maria's hopes were briefly dashed. But then, from the recess beside the doors, next to the keypad, where he had been hesitantly waiting, a nine year-old boy of taller than average height stepped out.

He looked like a street urchin, dressed as he was in his old T-shirt and jeans; his battered sneakers dirty and worn and his tousled black hair sticking out in a boyish manner, giving him a windswept appearance. But he was an extremely good looking child with strong, chiselled features and neatly curving dark eyebrows.

There could also be no mistake as to who his father was as he was the spitting image of Armando. Except for the eyes, they were identical to Maria's; sharp, quick and inquisitive in a distinctive shade of emerald green, exactly like hers.

Maria gasped for breath, quite taken aback by how striking the resemblance was to Armando.

She was temporally dumbstruck, her voice - indeed, the whole concept of speech - suddenly abandoning her as she stared in astonishment. Emotions of joy, wonder and relief simultaneously powering through her as she stood stock still, furiously gripping Diego's hand, unable to move for fear of falling over.

"Welcome," Diego said, coming to her rescue, breaking the silence. As he spoke, he also noted the colour of the boy's eyes and their likeness to Maria's, he could see other similarities, too, where maybe his wife could not - the mouth perhaps and the slight squareness at the tip of his nose. There was no question in Diego's mind that he was staring at Maria's long lost son.

"I'm sorry," he continued, "forgive me, I don't know your

name?"

"My name's Danny." Said Danny, assertively, glancing around him in wonder at the unbelievably large and obviously incredibly expensive penthouse suite in which he was now standing. Amazed by the sight of the circular glass ceiling dome as he raised his eyes upwards. Never in his wildest dreams had he ever imagined such grandeur or that people lived in such lavish style.

It was a whole world away from all he had ever known and he could not help but feel slightly awed by it all.

But he forced his eyes down and focussed on Diego, mildly surprised that the slender, expensively dressed yet rather awkward looking man in the horn-rimmed glasses spoke with a slight accent - Spanish, perhaps.

He then regarded the woman standing beside him, unable to resist any longer after having previously made an effort not to look directly at her.

His immediate impression was how much like the photo in the locket she was, barely appearing to be a day older. Again, he could not help but be staggered by her beauty; her long, dark hair perfectly styled in what he assumed to be the latest fashion. She was slim and elegant, her clothes, which to Maria herself were just part of her everyday wardrobe, were finely cut and exquisitely fitted to her tall, yet femininely curved figure.

She looked nice. In fact, exactly how Meggie had described her to be; a lovely, kind woman.

But he resisted the temptation to be charmed by her, tried not to be drawn to her, fighting against any instincts he had to the contrary. He had come to this place for one reason and one reason alone. And he would not be swayed from his task for a second.

Or at least that is what he kept telling himself.

"Hello, Danny," Maria at last said, struggling to keep a grip on her overwhelming emotions and forcibly holding back the flood of tears that threatened to pour from her brimming eyes.

Her voice was soft, sweet, compassionate - the voice of an angel and Danny suddenly had an almost overpowering urge to run to her and throw his arms around her - it was inexplicable, a feeling quite unlike any he had ever felt before, yet it just seemed right. But he held back and stood resolutely still, rooted to the spot.

Maria, too, wanted to go to him, to take him in her arms and hold him close; hold him and never let him go ever again. But she did not want to scare him away. She was patently aware that she knew nothing of his life prior to his appearance there tonight and did not want to assume anything that may jeopardise this surprising but very welcome reunion.

She had to take it slowly, to hang back and resist the temptation with every ounce of her resolve. Her son had just walked back into her life of his own volition less than 48 hours of her realising he even existed. It was nothing short of a miracle and she would not risk it all now by any misjudged acts of selfish impetuosity.

Instead, she just held out her trembling hand and said, "I'm so pleased to finally meet you. I'm your—"

"I know who you are!" Danny snapped rather too quickly, immediately feeling guilty as he saw the look of rejection on Maria's disappointed face. Before adding softly, slightly ashamedly, "Sorry. I know who you are. But please, I really need your help. It's my mother - I mean, my—" Suddenly he felt awkward, the words dying away, the emotions of the last couple of hours finally taking their toll as a tear ran down his cheek.

"It's okay, sweetheart," Maria said, reassuringly, "How can I help?"

Chapter Nineteen

It had been nearly two hours since Danny had rushed out of the apartment and Nate was extremely concerned as to where he might be.

Yet it worried him more that Megan's eyes had been closed for more than half the time Danny had been gone and Nate's many efforts to rouse her had, so far, been unsuccessful.

He now knelt by her bedside praying.

Nate's faith was stronger, deeper than Megan's had ever been. His belief in God's Plan previously unshakeable. But he had found himself questioning why his mother should be made to suffer so, especially after what she had told him before she slipped into unconsciousness.

In fact, after hearing his mother's terrible story about her life prior to her arrival in Hell's Kitchen, Nate's outrage was so strong that for the first time in his young life he had experienced the desire to physically harm another human being.

Nate had always known his father was a poor Irish immigrant from County Clare who had come to America to make his fortune. He knew, too, or at least had been led to believe, that his father had been killed, although Megan had never elaborated and always said she would tell him about it when he was older. But now she could delay no longer; her son had to know the truth of it all, before she, herself, died - no matter how painful it was to hear.

So, with her life ebbing away, she had told him about his father's murder at the hands of Salvatore Falcone and Carlo Liuzzi, who Nate now understood to be Danny's grandfather.

She could see the anger glowing in her son's innocent eyes as she went on to reveal that Falcone had tried to kill her and Maria, too, on the train to Messina.

Indeed, she thought that Maria had been killed.

However, when Megan then told him how she pushed Salvatore from the train, believing him to have died in the fall, Nate was delighted.

He knew it was wrong in the eyes of God, but he could not help but be pleased by the demise of such an evil man.

It was the incident, he now knew, that led to Megan and Maria being parted for so many years and the reason why she had brought Danny up as her own - as a way of honouring her good friend who she believed had died trying to save her.

Nate, like Danny, had always just assumed the two of them to be half brothers - sharing a mother but with two different fathers - and finding out they were not actually related by blood came as something of a shock. Intelligent as they were, neither of the boys had stopped to calculate how impossible it was for them to both be Megan's by birth, as the dates of their birthdays were only a few months apart. But at nine years old, the mysteries of child birth and pregnancy were still yet to be revealed to them.

Nate, a naturally compassionate boy, felt extremely sorry for Maria and Danny. And for his own mother, too, who he knew was fast slipping away. He was very grown-up for his age, even more so than his brother. Whereas Danny was much more impetuous and passionate by nature, Nate tended to be a deep thinker, preferring to mull over all the facts before forming an opinion.

However, not once since finding his mother laying there in

bed, badly injured, had Nate considered what would become of him if she died. He refused to do it because if he did it would mean it was over; that there was no more hope for her, and that thought alone was just too much for him to bear.

So Nate prayed. He prayed to God for His divine benevolence, begging Him to find some way of saving his mother. Surely she had suffered enough - after all, how much of a part could her small, insignificant death figure in His Great Plan?

He also wondered, too, where on earth his brother could be.

As Nate pondered this, there was a screech of tyres from the street below and what sounded like several vehicles pulling up and slamming their doors in front of the tenement block. It was almost one in the morning and all should be quiet down there by now, not a hive of bustling activity - even after the fire and the gang fight, things should have settled by now. But Nate could definitely hear a flurry of movement and he opened his eyes and listened.

Before long he could hear footsteps on the stairs; the foot falls of several people and the sound of them getting progressively louder, as they trudged swiftly up the last of six flights. Nate braced himself for whoever it might be as the door to their apartment suddenly burst open.

Relief flooded through Nate as Danny ran into the room, although he was immediately followed by a smartly dressed young couple and an older, chunkier man who was carrying a black leather bag - much like the one Dr O'Dowd usually had with him only in much better condition.

"Nate, this lady is my—" Danny started to say breathlessly, but he could not bring himself to say 'mother', especially not in the presence of Megan who looked considerably worse than when he had last seen her. "She's my—"

"Hello, Nate." Maria said softly as she entered the room behind Danny, coming to his rescue. "My name is Maria Del Toro, I am a very good friend of your mother's from a long time ago, and this is my husband, Diego. The gentleman behind him is Dr Evan Sanders, our personal physician. If you would allow him, he would like to take a look at your mother, to see if he can make her a little more comfortable."

Danny nodded at his brother, indicating it was okay to do as she asked. Nate took a beat, then nodded curtly back, moving quickly out of the way. "Sure, thanks," he said.

Promptly, Dr Sanders knelt by the bedside and took Megan's pulse. He then fitted his stethoscope into his ears and listened intently to her chest. A moment later he proceeded, very gently, to give her a brief examination, being as careful as possible not to cause her any more pain. He lifted the bedclothes slightly and immediately saw the mattress below her waist was wet with blood so swiftly pulled the covers over her again to prevent the boys from seeing.

Danny and Nate stood off to the side with Maria, who could see the letter she had written so many years ago folded neatly on the floor beside her leather bound bible. She remembered it now as if it was yesterday.

She also looked at Megan; her good, loyal friend who lay so gravely ill, almost wasted away and barely recognisable as the young, healthy girl she had once known. Indeed, so different from the woman she had seen across the street just two days earlier.

Her injuries were terribly severe and Maria did not need Dr Sanders to tell her what was so blatantly clear to see. Megan was dying and she did not have long left.

Diego stood hovering by the door, ready to be of assistance if required. He studied the scene and came to the same tragic conclusion as Maria. He then turned to look at the two boys. Two ragamuffins dressed in threadbare clothes, worry and fear written deeply all over their angelic faces.

He also took in the apartment, just one of many in this poor, run-down old tenement block; the three rooms no bigger than his and Maria's own dining room. The living space was small and squalid with damp lying thickly on the walls and scratched, tatty, 'make-do' furniture was scattered sparsely here and there. An old couch, a battered dresser, an ancient, second-hand bed - it all painted a troubling picture for Diego.

Life had treated them harshly; no doubt riddled with poverty and hardship in a tough, over-crowded part of the city; a melting pot of racism, hatred and violence. And now the only mother they had ever known, who from what Diego had surmised, had done everything in her power to make their lives as happy and as safe as possible, was about to die.

It just did not seem fair and was all so very different to his own idyllic, very affluent childhood and he suddenly felt incredibly guilty; his whole body infused with an overriding desire to make amends. To give something back for his charmed life, which had been bestowed upon him simply by the luck of birth.

As he considered this, he watched Dr Sanders give Megan an injection in her arm, something, he guessed, to ease her pain.

Then, the old, very experienced physician stood and turned to Maria and the boys, his expression grave as he quietly spoke the words neither of them wanted to hear. There was very little he could do. He had made her as comfortable as possible, given her a morphine shot to ease her suffering, but her life was in God's hands now and very soon she would be with Him.

When Sanders had finished speaking, both boys had tears in their eyes and they went to her bedside and knelt down beside her once more. Maria, too, felt a deep ache in her heart, as she regarded Megan, lying there. How much must her poor, dear friend have suffered to sustain such injuries? She looked at Danny and Nate, also, and felt desperately sorry for them - knowing all too well the pain of losing somebody so loved.

Then, as she looked on, Megan miraculously opened her eyes and turned her head slightly to see her two darling boys beside her.

"Danny, you came back," she said, in a faint, barely audible whisper, her lungs rattling weakly as she fought for breath, "I'm so pleased you did."

"Course I did, Mom - it's just that—"

"It's okay, sweetie, I understand."

"Don't die, Mom," said Nate, tears now flowing freely from his eyes and down his pale cheeks. "I don't want you to go."

But Megan knew there was nothing to prevent that now.

"Oh, Nate. Please don't cry my darling. You mustn't be upset. It's just my time, that's all. I don't want to leave you either but God is calling me and I have to go. You must be strong, the pair of you—" She coughed a little and briefly she closed her eyes again, but it was just for a moment and when she opened them again she added, "You must look after each other now - I'm just so sorry I'm leaving you on your own, to fend for yourselves."

"It's okay, Mom - it's not your fault - you can't help it," Danny said.

"We love you," said Nate.

"And I love you. With all my heart. You're both such good boys. I'm so, so proud of you both - and Danny, please don't think badly of me, raising you - both of you - is the best thing I have ever done in this life."

"I don't, I never could," said Danny, tears streaming from his eyes, too, now.

"You must find your mother," Megan wheezed, "Your real mother - Maria - she'll know what to do - she's good and kind - she'll help you she'll—"

"But she's here, Mom," said Danny, "She's here already, she's who brought me back - I went to fetch her, to ask for her help, she brought the doctor—"

"Maria's here?" Megan asked suddenly, "Here in this apartment?"

"Yes. I'm here," said Maria, stepping up so Megan could see her. "Of course I'm here, how could I not be? How could I not come to you?"

"Oh, my," gasped Megan, bursting into tears. "I'm so sorry - I'm so sorry for what I've done to you—"

"Nonsense, don't be silly. You've done nothing but raise two fine boys."

"I didn't know you were alive - not until a couple of months ago - I was so... so... surprised," Megan said at last. "So surprised and scared - I couldn't give him up you see, I couldn't bear to - I know it was wrong - I know I shouldn't have—"

"Ssh, please - don't be upset," Maria pleaded, "please don't blame yourself for anything. You've done me a great service - you've been a wonderful friend. I was badly injured - for a long time - nine years, in fact. I had no memory of what had happened - no memory of anything at all. Not until I saw you the other day, on Park Avenue - and then everything came flooding back. You see, you saved me Megan, my dear, dear, friend - you brought me back."

"You didn't know?"

"No, not a thing. If I had I would have come looking for you, I swear it - we could have taken on the world together - raised our sons together. I'm only sorry I wasn't here to help you when you needed me most."

It was Maria's turn to cry now. Her big, green eyes filled with tears as her heart broke for what might have been.

Megan slowly reached out her hand and took hold of Maria's, the pain was gone now, the morphine working its magic upon her failing body. She looked proudly up at Danny and Nate, her eyelids drooping, "Look after them," she said, "look after our boys."

Maria swallowed down the lump in her throat. "Of course, my

darling, you have my word."

Megan smiled just briefly before her hand slipped from Maria's, content in the knowledge that her sons would be safe and loved after she was gone.

Then, as Danny and Nate wept for her, she died.

***

A short time later, Maria, Diego, Danny and Nate walked out from the old, dilapidated tenement block and climbed into the back of Diego's waiting limousine.

Max, Diego's burly chauffeur, who had been standing guard over the gleaming Cadillac whilst they were inside, loaded a few small items belonging to the boys into the trunk and then slid into the driver's seat.

As they drove out of Hell's Kitchen, Danny and Nate, sitting in the back of the plush limo, glanced out of the window to see fire fighters still milling about around the smouldering ruins of Red's Diner and the burnt out remains of Loughlin's Oldsmobile, which had also been engulfed by the inferno.

But all they could think about was Megan.

***

As the first glow of sunrise began to show itself in the early morning sky, Max pulled the limo up outside The Greyling Building on Park Avenue and Sam, the night porter, came rushing out to see if he could be of assistance.

As Max held open the rear door, Diego stepped out onto the sidewalk, then helped Maria out, who, in turn helped the two nine-year old boys.

Max then popped the trunk and handed a small, battered suitcase to Sam along with a couple of cardboard boxes.

Nate looked up in awe at the grand building before him and then up and down the long, wide boulevard, already bustling with activity in the pre-dawn light. How different it was from all he was used to. Danny, too, even though he had been there a short while before, could not help but be amazed by the sheer scale of it all.

As they stood there on the sidewalk, Maria looked down at the boys, Danny was nearest to her, Nate next to him and Diego at the far end of the line. She smiled compassionately. "Ready?" she said to them.

They both nodded hesitantly.

Then Maria felt something wonderful and thought for an instant she might cry yet again as emotion flooded through her. But she resisted the urge and took a deep breath to steady her feelings at this most tender of moments.

Danny had taken hold of her hand.

Diego noticed this extremely significant gesture and his heart swelled with pleasure for his wife as he, Maria and Danny walked forward. But then he stopped and looked back to see Nate still standing by the kerb, next to the limo, unsure of quite what to do.

But Diego instinctively knew and simply held out his hand for the boy to take. For a second Nate just blinked, then it dawned on him. *This was God's Plan.* This is what He had intended, it was why He had allowed his mother to die. Because God knew Maria and Diego would be there to take care of them.

After coming to what he considered to be this obvious conclusion, he felt suddenly more at peace and he reached out and took Diego's hand.

Then together, all four of them walked into The Greyling Building, the place that would be Danny and Nate's new home.

Part Two

Chapter Twenty

Hollywood, California 1966

Frankie DeLuca's muscular bulk was wedged in the driver's seat of the sleek convertible - the top down and the wind rushing by; his big, gnarled hands planted at ten to two on the ivory steering wheel as The Beatles' *Day Tripper* blared out of the radio at full volume.

As Ava studied him from the passenger seat of the ultramarine Lincoln Continental, she thought his crinkly hair was slightly greyer and had receded a tad more than when last she had seen him at Spring Break. His punchy, boxer's face showed one or two more lines and his broken nose seemed a little more red, but she could not help but be pleased to see him. Truth be told, he was the only person she had been looking forward to seeing as she flew back from New Hampshire where she had just finished school.

For the last six years she had been attending The Sheldrake Academy for Young Ladies - an elite boarding school founded way back in the late seventeen hundreds. Hardly Ava's idea of 'home' but even the austere halls and crusty, out-dated strictures of that historical old pile had been eminently more preferable than the thought of returning to her real home.

She hated coming home and dreaded it more and more as each term passed - although her time at the school was over now and she would be going off to college in the Fall - which, for Ava, could not come quickly enough.

The thought of seeing her step-father again or that creep Salvatore made her feel physically ill and it was only Frankie that made the prospect of it all slightly more tolerable. Indeed, it did her the power of good when she saw him waving to her in the arrivals hall at LAX, a lop-sided grin on his world-weary face, happy to have been given the task of picking her up.

When he spotted her she was still in her school uniform; a formal blazer and skirt in a nasty shade of grey that was made from an itchy woollen fabric. In addition, the school required her to wear a simple white blouse, a navy 'Sheldrake Academy' tie with their swan's head emblem embroidered on it, thick dark tights and a pair of flat, sensible shoes. Yet even in the drab, unflattering uniform, she looked older, taller - even more beautiful than he remembered; a blossoming young woman.

But he almost did not recognise her at all until she waved at him. The wavy, dark hair Ava always had was now dead straight and shiny blonde giving her the head-turning allure of a young Bardot. She had just turned eighteen but if not for the uniform could easily have been mistaken for someone in their early twenties.

"Wow!" He said as she leaned in and kissed him on the cheek, throwing her arms around his thick neck. "Look at you!"

"I know, it's wild right?"

"Oh, yeah - it's wild alright," Frankie said with a chuckle, shaking his head with mock exasperation, "You go away for a few months and you come back all growed up."

"Miss me?" She asked mischievously.

"Sure, kid. Always. You know that," he replied taking her suitcase from her.

"Yeah, I know," she smiled, "and I missed you, too," she teased playfully - but it was the truth.

"I'll bet. Come on - let's get outta here, you can tell me what you been up to on the way back."

***

On the drive from the airport, Ava had given Frankie a blow by blow account of her final term at the Sheldrake Academy - all to the accompaniment of the radio, which she had re-tuned to a rock 'n' roll station and turned up loud.

She had told him of all her exploits and which of her friends were doing what, leaving him in no doubt she had clearly been popular and had thoroughly enjoyed herself, even though she tried to protest otherwise.

Frankie was also pleased to hear her grades were good and that she had consistently been in the top three of all her classes which, he believed, stood her in good stead for her freshman year at Columbia in New York, where she would be heading to after Summer vacation. It made him so proud.

Frankie had a daughter of his own back in New York but he was never allowed to see her. He and the girl's mother had gone through a very acrimonious split which, sadly for Frankie, had tarnished the image of him in the eyes of his daughter, leaving them irreconcilably estranged.

So Ava had become a natural substitute, although he had to be extremely wary of showing his very fatherly affections towards her in front of his boss.

Their tight bond had grown since that night almost ten years earlier when her real father had been killed. The then nine year-old Ava had cried herself to sleep on Frankie's lap, with him holding her in his arms; the already traumatised little girl not yet knowing Edmund was dead. As Carlo Liuzzi's big, burly bodyguard sat there, with his arms around her, he had been struck by an irresistible and overwhelming desire to protect her - a feeling that had grown immeasurably over the years.

"So what's with the hair, blondie?" Frankie eventually yelled

275

to Ava in the passenger seat, when she had, at last, finished relating her tales of school life at the Sheldrake Academy. Although it was difficult trying to make himself heard above the vocal stylings of Paul McCartney and John Lennon and the noise of the breeze swishing through his hair as he guided the Lincoln along the neatly manicured boulevards of Beverly Hills en-route to the Liuzzi mansion.

"I thought it was time for a change!" Ava shouted back. "Like it?"

"Kid, I love it - it looks real good on ya - but it ain't me you gotta worry about, it's your old man!"

"Hey! He's not my old man - you know that - and screw him anyway - who cares what he thinks?"

"Yeah, kid, I know - and just to be clear, I do!"

Ava giggled as the middle aged Italian American gave her a wry look. "Don't worry, Frankie, I'll protect you!" She said.

"Yeah, yeah - I know you will kid, I know you can wrap him round that pretty little finger of yours, but one day, that ain't gonna work and I'm gonna find myself buried six feet South in the Mojave with a bunch of other stiffs who thought they could get one over on your old man - sorry, I know, I know - your step-father - better?"

"Better. But don't worry, he knows how much you mean to me."

"Yeah, kid. That's exactly what I'm worried about!"

Ava laughed, but she knew Frankie wasn't joking. She had to be careful how much affection she showed him in her step-father's presence as it would not do to make Carlo jealous - and it certainly would not be good for Frankie.

Nonetheless, she did so like to provoke Carlo, to undermine him wherever possible and to get under his skin as much as she dare. Which is exactly why she had dyed her long, dark hair a light, honey blonde.

However, what was intended as just another subversive attempt at irritating her step-father had, quite unintentionally, turned into something she actually preferred.

She looked good as a blonde, better in fact, it suited her and complemented her lightly tanned skin and big, blue eyes. In effect, it had transformed her into the epitome of the 'California Girl' which made all her classmates oh so envious.

Indeed, to them Ava Peyton already seemed to have it all; she was fun, good looking, had a great figure and, of course, an overly indulgent daddy with bags and bags of money.

But they had no idea of the truth, which Ava kept very close to her chest.

In point of fact, she had not spoken to anyone about what she had witnessed when she was nine years old, or the horror of what she went through afterwards, not even to Frankie, at least not since she was a little girl.

Frankie was extremely loyal to her but he was also loyal to Carlo; he had to be as his life depended on it. He had advised her to forget about what had happened - saying that dwelling on things she could not change would do her no good. For her sake and his, he had begged her, forget about it.

So they had never properly discussed that night when her father failed to return, as he promised he would, or how she found him the next morning hanging in the bathroom of his small apartment above the garage.

When she discovered him, his face all grey and cold, she had been utterly distraught, the pain of losing him especially after the events of the night before almost too much to bear. Yet in her heart she knew that Edmund had not committed suicide as she had been meant to believe - even with her grief still so raw, she knew things were not as they appeared to be.

Firstly, there was the typewritten suicide note. Why on earth would he simply not just hand write it - especially as her father did not type or possess a typewriter.

Secondly, the words in the letter itself were not the sentiments of her father - they were clearly not his words, not the way he would have spoken to her - and he certainly would not have requested that she put her faith in Carlo Liuzzi, to rely on him and trust him, not in a million years.

And thirdly, when Ava found her father he was wearing a mismatched chauffeur's uniform - a dark blue jacket over grey pants - not a matching suit of either colour, which was out of keeping with Edmund's high standards of dress.

It was as if he had been dressed by somebody else and hung up for the deliberate purpose of Ava finding him. But whoever it was had not taken the time to do it correctly. It was a sloppy, stupid mistake that caused her to seriously doubt the truth of what she was supposed to see.

Then there was the mystery of whatever happened to Mildred, her mother. The images of that night still burnt indelibly into her memory - the last night he ever saw her - when she had witnessed her with all those men, performing what Ava knew now to be lurid acts of sex.

The very same night she had watched Carlo kill a man right in front of her, when he became a monster in her eyes; a loathsome devil who she hated with all her heart.

Seeing him commit that abhorrent, brutally shocking act had driven an immovable wedge between them, at least in Ava's eyes, resulting in her becoming closer to Frankie, who she came to regard as her protector. But, fond of her as he was, he had never shed any light on the sudden disappearance of her mother. All he would say on the subject was, "It's not my place to tell ya, kid."

However, some weeks later, by way of casual explanation, Carlo told Ava that Mildred had gone away for reasons of ill health - to recuperate somewhere more conducive to her medical needs. Indeed, that was the story he put out to the gossip columnists and the media in general, although he refused to be drawn on the subject any further - by anyone, including Ava - and, under strict orders from Carlo, Frankie was not permitted to elaborate.

But Ava had her own suspicions and could not help but wonder if her step-father had murdered her mother and father, too, like he had that poor man in the library.

She had no proof of it but guessed he probably had, which left young Ava terrified that she might be killed too.

But then she realised, with ghastly resignation, that Carlo adored her. He doted on her; relished spoiling her and showing her off to his powerful friends and she could scarcely do wrong in his eyes. With this realisation it dawned that she would be relatively safe if she pretended to forget all about that fateful night.

And as time went on it became easier to convince Carlo she had.

But, in truth, she would never forget. Not as long as she lived and every time her step-father hugged her, or kissed her or bought her an expensive trinket in a bid to buy her affection, she felt nothing other than absolute revulsion. Yet she put a smile on her face and kept up the pretence of being a loving, devoted step-daughter - it was the only way she knew how to survive.

Yet she did take exception to changing her name to 'Liuzzi', much to Carlo's chagrin. But she would not be swayed and insisted she remained 'Ava Peyton' to honour the memory of her dead father. It was a small rebellion in an otherwise submissive existence.

However, as the years past and she became more mature, more opinionated, she found it difficult to stay so passive to her step-father's overbearing ways and, against Frankie's best advice, she took to acting up and talking back to Carlo - pushing the limits of what she knew she could get away with. But she always stopped just short of making him properly angry as the image of him murdering that young man in the library with that jagged shard of pottery still lived horrifically in her memory.

She also knew her step-father's anger was quick and volatile, usually erupting without warning - something she had learnt the hard way when she was just six years old when he had whipped her with his belt as her mother looked on.

He was dangerous - psychotic even - but Ava had learnt to carefully read the signs now and he granted her much more leeway than he would anyone else - even Salvatore.

Frankie was right, she could wrap him around her little finger - she was Carlo's little angel and thankfully, for her sake, there was very little she could do to dissuade him of that notion.

Even so, Carlo was convinced this surly new attitude of hers was due to him having spoiled her when she was young. He blamed himself and was desperate for things not to turn out as they had with Maria - he had to stamp his will upon Ava, force her to succumb to his authority, before she, too, spiralled out of his control.

He had lost one prized daughter and was damn sure he was not going to lose another.

So, as much as it pained him to be without her, he packed her off to an all girls boarding school, at the tender age of twelve, in the hope it would turn her into an obedient, virtuous and well-mannered young lady.

For Ava, the departure was a welcome one. As much as she hated the stringently oppressive routine at the Sheldrake Academy, it did get her away from her step-father and his pet vulture, Salvatore, for large chunks of the year, which allowed her to feel properly safe for the first time since she was nine.

But she did miss Frankie.

***

As Frankie pressed the button on the intercom beside the enormous electronic gates that blocked their way onto the Liuzzi estate, he noticed Ava had gone suddenly quiet. Her bubbly, carefree demeanour replaced by one of fear and trepidation.

It was the same feeling she always had whenever she returned home - her mind regurgitating memories of Edmund and Mildred and murder. But she fought them down.

Frankie spoke a few words into the intercom, announcing their arrival, before putting a steadying hand on Ava's knee and asking, "You okay, kid?"

She simply nodded and said, "Yes."

"All you gotta do is be his little girl for a few weeks, okay? Put on the act like I know you can. Then, before you know it, you'll be going off to college in New York and you can forget all about him until Christmas vacation."

"I know. I can do it - I can."

"Good girl."

Then, as the gates swung open, Frankie stepped on the gas and the Lincoln swept through them, heading all too quickly up the long driveway towards the huge mansion beyond.

For all her brave words, it was only now that Ava truly contemplated what her step-father's reaction would be to her dramatic change of hair colour and a shiver of unease ran through her. Carlo's famously volcanic temper could be ignited by the most trivial of things, although he had not directed it at Ava since that night long ago when he had whipped her for refusing to go down to the party.

But she was older now and had been away from him for several months. In that time she had grown up and was no longer a little girl by any means, and it occurred to her that maybe his regard for her had waned and, perhaps, his indulgence along with it.

Frankie sensed her anxiety as they pulled up in front of the mansion, "Hey, you look great, blondie - don't sweat it, he'll love it," he said reassuringly just as Carlo opened the front door and strode out to greet them.

At 60, her step-father looked every inch the Hollywood power player; tanned and fit with an impressive, masculine physique that could have been sculpted from a huge chunk of solid granite. His casual clothes - a white open-neck shirt, light grey pullover and pale blue slacks - fitting his tall, broad frame perfectly.

His wavy, swept-back hair was the colour of gun-metal, although now silvery white at the temples and above the ears and the thick, heavy-duty eyebrows and perfectly trimmed moustached were flecked with traces of grey.

But Carlo's dark eyes gleamed and his white teeth sparkled as he smiled widely, delighted to see his 'baby girl' was home.

Trailing in his wake was the tall, slender figure of Salvatore, his limp now almost imperceptible and the dead right hand covered with a smooth black glove.

He, too, was tanned and dressed in much the same style as Carlo, although his slacks were beige and his pullover green with a diamond pattern on the front.

Now 53, his receding hair was still jet-black and greased back, his long, thin face beginning to show slight signs of age with crows feet at the edge of his sly, hooded eyes.

Salvatore was smiling too, his thick, rubbery lips curled up in a creepy, lascivious grin, clearly intrigued by the sight of the newly matured, blonde beauty in the passenger seat of the Lincoln.

"Oh, my!" Carlo said loudly, dramatically, as he approached the open-topped Continental, "Frankie, who's this blonde young woman you've brought home and what on earth have you done with my darling Ava?"

"Sorry, Boss," Frankie replied, hoping Carlo was in as good a humour as he appeared to be, "Ava wasn't there so I picked up Brigette Bardot instead - hope that's okay?"

"Hello, Daddy," Ava said, nervously touching her hair, using the name he insisted she call him, which she despised doing and rarely did, unless she was trying to get on his good side. But she knew how much the name pleased him and feeling slightly trepidacious about her newly blonde locks thought it maybe wise to use it now. "You like it? Please say you do - please - I really think it suits me."

"My darling, I love it!" He said, scooping her out of the car and squeezing her to his chest. "You look so grown up, so beautiful."

Then, still grasping by the her shoulders, her feet barely touching the ground, he thrust her backwards and held her at arms length so he could admire her properly. "Yes, I agree, it does suit you - very much. You have my permission to keep it."

Ava felt her anger stir. She had his permission - how dare he! But she forced it down and smiled sweetly.

"Salvo, my daughter looks a perfect picture, does she not?"

"She, does, Carlo, she looks good enough to eat," agreed Falcone, appraising Ava's new look, his voice soft and heavily accented. As he spoke, a hungry smile spread across his thin, lecherous face, which, with Liuzzi's back towards him, was visible only to Ava. Her stomach squirmed with disgust and again the cold austerity of the Sheldrake Academy seemed decidedly more appealing to her than being back here, alone, in this lion's den of evil. She would gladly have returned to the school in a heartbeat if it was possible. But sadly it was not and Ava feared it was going to be a very long summer indeed before she finally left for college and the freedom of New York.

"Tell me, my darling," Carlo continued, "have you missed me, my angel? It seems like such a long time since I saw you last!"

'No, no, no, of course I haven't missed you, you murdering, psychotic bastard! - why the hell would I?' The voice yelled in her head but instead of uttering it out loud she said, "Of course, Daddy, of course I have - it's great to be home!"

Shortly after Edmund's death, Liuzzi had insisted that Ava stop calling him 'Daddy Carlo' and instructed her, instead, to address him just as 'Daddy'. "After all, I am the only Daddy you've got now, my

283

darling," he had told her with barely disguised glee.

His words had always stuck with her and whenever she used the term 'Daddy' she felt, somehow, that she was betraying Edmund. But sometimes, in order to placate her unpredictably volatile step-father, it was necessary.

"You had a good flight?"

"Yes, it was fine, thanks - I'm just a little tired now, that's all."

"But of course you are. You must rest - get some sleep - we'll have plenty of time to talk later - we've got the whole Summer after all. Frankie—" he snapped his fingers at his underling who had been loitering by the trunk of the car, "—take my daughter's case to her room - and let her rest - none of your gossiping, you old woman."

"Sure, Boss. No problem." Said Frankie meekly.

"Go, get some rest," Carlo said to Ava. "I'll see you at dinner, we'll catch up then."

"Okay - see you later, then," she smiled, but as she went to move off, Carlo caught her by the arm.

"Aren't you forgetting something, my darling?"

"No, I don't think—" she began to reply before seeing her step-father tapping his cheek with his forefinger.

"Oh, yes. Of course," she said with sickly realisation and stepped back, stood on her tip-toes and, with great reluctance, kissed him lightly on the cheek.

"That's better," he said, beaming. "Now, off you go."

Then, with Salvatore at Carlo's shoulder, the two men watched as Ava followed Frankie into the house.

***

They arrived at her room in silence, by way of the grand, sweeping staircase, and she followed Frankie inside who, in turn, put her suitcase on the bed.

As he turned to leave, Ava took his hand and leaned in close, so she could whisper in his ear, "Don't worry, I don't think you're an old woman - I think you're lovely," she said. Then she kissed his cheek in an identical manner as she just had Carlo, but this time the sentiment was sincere.

"Thanks, kid. I know - and the feeling's mutual - but for both our sake's you'd better keep it to yourself."

Then he winked at her mischievously before walking to the door and shutting it behind him, leaving Ava alone.

In two and a half months she would be in New York - away from this place and away from the cloying, overbearing malevolence of her step-father. Ten weeks and she would be gone.

She had been home less than ten minutes yet, already, she could not wait to leave.

Chapter Twenty One

The seemingly endless weeks of her long Summer vacation dragged by slowly at the mansion and Ava tried to amuse herself as best as she could. But the only people she had to talk to other than Carlo and Salvatore or Frankie and Vito, Liuzzi's other underling, were the household staff - all of whom were too intimidated by their employer to speak openly to her.

It was a male dominated, very masculine environment and invariably, at mealtimes, it would be Ava sitting sweetly at one end of the long, mahogany dining table and four heavy-set Italian men sitting at the other. Their conversation was far from scintillating for an eighteen year-old girl and the only sounds often to be heard were those of scraping plates and the occasional clash of cutlery.

It was almost like being back at boarding school except she was the only pupil.

All Ava's friends were from school and the majority of them were still back East so she had no one in Los Angeles with whom she could while away the long hours of each monotonous day - and boys were strictly forbidden.

However, to alleviate the boredom of life at the mansion she had spent some of her vacation at the studio with her step-father.

Accompanying Carlo to the sprawling Gold Star lot was just about the only thing she was favourably inclined to do with him because whilst he was in his office making calls or taking meetings, she was free to wander around the huge backlot - which meant she could visit the various air-craft hangar-sized sound stages and soak up some of the movie magic.

Occasionally Salvatore would lurk nearby, keeping a watchful eye on her but oftentimes she would be on her own, at liberty to do as she pleased and it was at those moments she truly felt free.

She loved the hustle and bustle of the big movie studio; mingling with the extras dressed in their wonderful costumes, seeing the spectacular sets being constructed and being around the busy production crews as they worked.

Quite often she was even permitted to watch a scene being played out by world famous actors which never failed to leave her star-struck. Indeed, she would frequently find herself rubbing shoulders with movie stars as they strolled around the lot between takes.

Had Carlo been a normal step-father and not the murdering psychopath that he was, Ava would have happily envisaged a future for herself working there in some capacity, perhaps even one day taking over the running of the studio from him.

But she would never - could never - work with him and refused to show anything other than a passing interest in Gold Star whenever she was in his presence. She would just not give him the satisfaction - even though she knew this was tantamount to cutting off her nose to spite her face.

So even though she enjoyed being at the studio immensely she feigned indifference which regularly resulted in Carlo heading there without her.

This meant, with little else to occupy her, Ava's time during her ten week break was predominantly spent sunbathing and swimming. Although she was rarely completely alone as Frankie was usually around somewhere looking after Carlo's fleet of vehicles - a job he had inherited from Edmund - and most days he would find an excuse to wander down to the pool for a chat which was something Ava always looked forward to.

However, Salvatore did not always accompany Carlo to the studio either - often claiming he needed to rest for a day or two; blaming his occasional lack of energy on the pleurisy that had blighted much of his earlier life. It was a lie, of course, as Salvatore had not felt better in years. Yet Carlo was recently more sympathetic to Falcone's bouts of supposed ill health after being proven too dismissive of them in the past and did not have any inkling of his friend's duplicitous intentions.

Nonetheless, when Salvatore was around, and Carlo was not, it made Ava feel uneasy. She always got the feeling that he was skulking somewhere nearby, his eyes burning into her, but she was damned if she was going to hide away because of him.

Refusing to be perturbed, she would defiantly lay out by the pool in her bikini; the sun darkening her skin to a glorious copper tone, the sunlight bleaching golden streaks into her long, honey blonde hair.

To keep herself amused and to combat the daily tedium, Ava would read. Before heading down to the pool each morning she would often go to the mansion's completely re-furbished library and choose a book to take with her.

On one such occasion she padded silently into the library barefoot, a pair of shiny black sunglasses perched on her head and a rolled-up towel under her arm as she stood there, on tip-toe, in her white bikini, perusing the higher shelves.

She looked simply stunning; her svelte, athletic figure superbly exhibited in the scant white swimsuit, which made her look incredibly, yet quite unintentionally, sexy. It was easy to see why all her school friends were so envious of her.

Small yet perfectly formed breasts, flat stomach, sculptured hips, a pert, round bottom and long, shapely legs. Whilst the colour of her skin contrasted delightfully with the tiny bikini to complete the overall picture.

Quickly, she selected a leather bound copy of *The Great Gatsby*, which she hoped would keep her entertained for a good few hours. But as she turned to make her exit from the library and head down to the pool, she heard Salvatore speaking in Carlo's study.

Her heart sank as she had assumed he had gone with her step-father to the studio, but clearly he had not.

For a moment she thought he was talking to her and she took a few steps towards the door. Then she realised he was actually speaking to someone on the phone and with relief made to turn back.

But then she overheard him say something which made her stop dead in her tracks.

"Listen, man, can you get me more blow or not?" He was saying, "I got orders for coke a mile long - people like our merchandise, just like we knew they would - but I gotta supply the demand - know what I mean? I gotta know you can deliver on your end."

Ava was stunned. She had led a closeted life but she was intelligent and far from naïve. Salvatore was clearly talking about cocaine - in fact, it sounded very much like he was dealing in drugs. Although why she should be surprised she did not know as he was eminently capable of many vile things.

Silently she crept behind the study door and spied on Falcone through the crack between the door and frame, continuing to listen intently to the conversation as she did so.

"You sure, Bruno - you sure these Wolves have got it covered?" He was saying now. "And what the fuck kind of name is that for an organisation anyway, 'I lupi di montagna' - 'The Mountain Wolves', I mean, come on - are they fucking serious?"

Whoever this Bruno was that Salvatore was talking to was obviously making some sort of excuse about a late shipment but

Falcone was not interested.

"I don't care about glitches or problems with shipping - I just wanna know that they - and that means *you* - can supply my blow."

Ava then saw him nod his head, agreeing with something being said on the other end of the line. He was leaning back in Carlo's leather chair, his feet up on the wide desk.

"Yeah, I can take as much as you got," he said, "just don't give me problems. I got customers with big appetites and money to burn - and that's gotta be good for all of us."

Then Salvatore went quiet, apart from the occasional "uh-huh," and "yeah," as he listened to the other party, before saying, "Okay, Bruno, well if that's what the Wolves are saying then I got no choice but to believe 'em - so I'll expect my delivery by Friday - no later, okay?"

Then the other person spoke for a moment again before Falcone added, "Alright then - but don't fuck me on this, Barca - don't make me have to call again."

He was quiet once more and then, "Okay, good. That's good, Bruno - don't let me down then, alright? I'm trusting you and your faith in these lupi di montagna - capisce?

Bruno obviously replied before Salvatore finally said, "So I'll talk to you next month, then. Ciao."

And with that he slammed the phone down.

Ava was rooted to the spot; not daring to move for fear of making a sound. Her mind racing, trying to digest all she had just learned about her step-father's long serving and supposedly loyal lieutenant.

Salvatore was clearly in league with someone named Bruno Barca, dealing cocaine supplied by a scary sounding organisation called 'The Mountain Wolves' - whoever they were. It all seemed very clandestine, very hush-hush - as if Falcone had purposely waited for Carlo to leave for the studio before making the call.

Her instincts told her this enterprise existed without her step-father's knowledge or blessing - although she could not be completely certain.

Nor was Ava sure what she should do with this new information but she decided to log it in her brain, certain it may prove useful at some point in the future.

As Ava continued to watch, Salvatore swung round in the swivel chair and sat for a moment, back to her, looking out the tall windows of Carlo's study, across the lawn. His elbows were resting on the plush leather arms of the chair, his fingertips pressed together forming a tent shape in front of him, as if contemplating something.

Then, as if having decided, he jumped out of the chair and strode to the substantially sized bookcase that climbed the wall to the right of the desk.

For a second, Ava thought Salvatore was choosing a book - much like she had, to while away a few boring hours, but then she watched in utter amazement as he pushed the spine of one particular book inwards.

Using just his forefinger, he pressed the book into the case by about an inch until there was an audible click. This triggered a mechanised reaction that caused the bookcase to slide gracefully aside - spectacularly revealing a shiny steel door that had been cleverly concealed behind it.

It was like something out of a spy movie and Ava was agog; she just could not believe what she was witnessing as Falcone turned the handle on the thick steel door and vanished behind it to the hidden place beyond. The moment the steel door closed, the bookcase automatically slid back into its rightful position and the depressed book spine popped out so that it sat perfectly in line with the others.

Ava blinked her eyes in shock. She had lived in the mansion since she was a little girl and had never before known, or even suspected, this hidden doorway existed.

But the important question that now consumed her was, where did it lead to?

Tentatively, she crept out from her hiding place and tip-toed into her step-father's study. Silently, very cautiously, she approached the bookcase. She could still see the red-spined book that Salvatore had pressed in - *The Count of Monte Cristo* by Alexandre Dumas.

Ava stared at it for a moment, trying to find some hidden meaning in the title but finding none. Then she pressed an ear to the bookcase and listened intently for a long moment but no sound could be heard.

Again she wondered where the secret door led. Ava had no idea but was resolutely determined to find out.

***

Salvatore had made this same trip many times over the years, usually when he was full of pent up aggression or frustrated in some way - or just whenever he needed a release.

Conversely, Carlo had never been down here, not since that night nine years earlier when he had locked Mildred in her own private prison - sentencing her to a life of solitary confinement with no hope of reprieve. She was nothing to him now, yet kept alive solely at his whim, to ensure she suffered for the shame she had brought upon him.

He had assigned Salvatore the role of jailer and it was up to him how he dealt with her. He was responsible for her food, her clothing, her sanitary needs - everything - and she had become reliant on him for her very existence.

Once a month, Salvatore would supply her with clean linen and stock the larder and refrigerator in her cell. She was given pre-packed meals and had a small electric oven with which to re-heat them. It was up to her to make the supplies last.

By way of cutlery, she was allowed only a spoon.

Should she have the desire to start a fire, a highly sensitive sprinkler system would soak everything in sight.

Should she wish to commit suicide then she would simply be left to rot. But Mildred would not do it - not whilst there was any hope of freedom.

And Salvatore cruelly let her believe there was.

Right from when Carlo had first started his affair with Mildred, before they were married even, Salvatore had wanted her. She had made him ache with desire; her ripe, firm body making his mouth water with lust as he watched her from a distance.

Knowing she had an insatiable, voracious appetite for sex had only fuelled his need for her further but whilst she was Carlo's there was nothing he could do about his cravings.

Then, when he saw her go into the library with those three young boys on that momentous night nine years before, knowing she had gone in there to have wanton, debauched sex with them, it incensed him, made him mad with envy and his resulting actions led to the bloody murder of five people.

Yet it also made Mildred his.

Now he kept her as his pet; an eager, subservient nymphomaniac whom he used as he pleased - made her perform for him as he pleased - and she did it all willingly in the mistaken belief that one day he would set her free.

But she could not be more wrong.

***

Salvatore descended the two flights of narrow, steel steps that brought him out deep under the mansion, two storeys below ground. At first, years ago, the tightness of the staircase with its skimmed concrete walls and mesh enclosed ceiling lights, had made him feel desperately claustrophobic but now he scarcely gave it a second thought.

The slender passageway at the bottom of the staircase was equally rudimentary and only slightly wider than shoulder width however the small living space, or cell, at the end was well lit, relatively spacious and air-conditioned.

The door that accessed the cell was ten inches thick and made from heavy-duty steel. Originally it could only be locked from the inside as it was intended to be a safe room - to protect anyone inside from external threat. But Carlo had removed the lock and welded a new bolt on the outside, so it could only be locked from without.

In the centre of the door, at roughly head height, was a small, square, peep-hole window glazed with toughened bullet-proof glass that allowed a view of the space within.

The cell itself was also constructed of ten inch thick steel and comprised of a living area large enough for a double bed, a television and a basic galley kitchen suitable only for preparing and cooking food. There was also a small shower and toilet which was in a partitioned annex adjacent to it. In addition, there was a walk-in larder with several shelves and a huge, white refrigerator with a freezer drawer.

In short, it was a tight yet functional prison.

As Salvatore approached the door he spied Mildred through the small peep hole in the centre. As usual, she was laying on the bed wearing the shabby silk robe he had provided for her some years earlier.

The robe was open to expose her nakedness and Salvatore was not surprised to see she was busily pleasuring herself. In fact, he almost expected it as sex had become something of an all-consuming obsession with Mildred to the point where she thought about it constantly and masturbated many times a day.

But it was Salvatore whom she craved most and eagerly awaited his visits so that she might once again feel him inside her.

In her deluded mind she thought keeping Salvatore sexually satisfied was the key to her freedom. But, in truth, she had almost forgotten what it was like to be free and her long, solitary confinement had addled her brain, making her easily confused. This resulted in her frequently mixing up what had happened in the past with her life in the present.

What is more, she sometimes mistook Salvatore for Carlo, or Edmund - sometimes even Donnie, Bobby or Wyatt, the three young Texans who had been murdered for having sex with her in the library. On occasion, she would even call Salvatore some random name which, he could only assume, belonged to one of the many boys who had sampled her pleasures before she came out to Los Angeles, when she was little more than a girl.

Nonetheless, he still enjoyed her, revelled in the power he had over her, no matter who she mistook him for.

At forty, and even after all her years of incarceration, Mildred still had an extremely desirable body. However, her skin was almost white now, having been deprived of sunlight for so long, which gave it an ethereal quality. Her hair was still dark but it had lost all of its lustre and had grown long and wild and hung to below her waist. A grey streak, maybe an inch wide, ran from front to back which, when coupled with her alabaster skin, gave her something of a vampiric appearance.

She spent most of her time naked, with very little need for clothing in the constant temperature of her surroundings, although she would often wear the pale pink robe Salvatore had given her.

Her day largely consisted of television, sleeping and masturbation. She would eat whenever she was hungry but had no set mealtimes and with no window to the outside world, had no idea if it was even day or night.

It was a demeaning, tawdry existence but it had become her life and Salvatore's visits were the only thing she had to look forward to.

He slid the bolt and pushed open the thick, heavy door, entering the cell. Immediately Mildred looked up excitedly.

As Salvatore carefully closed the door behind him, she slipped from the bed and on her hands and knees crawled over to where he stood.

She smiled and looked up at him, placing both hands reverently on the front of his pants; the scarred stub, which was all that remained of her ring finger, looking strangely out of place amongst the rest of her long graceful digits.

"I thought you wouldn't come today, that maybe I wouldn't—"

"Shut up!" He barked. "I haven't come down here to listen to your whining."

"No. Of course not," she said obediently.

"You know why I'm here. So let's get on with it."

"Yes," smiled Mildred. "Thank you," she said before obediently unbuckling his belt and unzipping his pants.

"Get on the bed," he demanded and quickly she complied, her excitement barely contained as she dutifully presented her firm, round backside to him.

Salvatore wasted no time with foreplay and set upon her with brutal efficiency but Mildred was beyond caring.

"Oh, yes, Carlo!" She cried with exaggerated pleasure, confusing Falcone with his boss. "Oh, Carlo! That's it, that's it!"

"I'm Salvatore, you dumb bitch," he snapped, already at the point of finishing.

"Of course you are my darling," she said absently, "who else would you be?"

Salvatore sneered with disdain, he could not really care less what she called him or who she thought he might be, as long as she did as she was told. His frustrations from his phone call with Bruno Barca now subsiding, the sexual release easing his earlier annoyance.

How different Mildred was now, how compliant and eager, compared to the first time he had forced himself upon her, just two days after her incarceration, nine years earlier, when he had beaten

296

her mercilessly until she surrendered to his will.

Indeed, he still savoured the memory of her screams as she tried, with futility, to fight him off.

But she had soon come around, soon bent to his demands after he had withheld all food and turned off the lights in her cell for almost a week, leaving her starved and in total darkness.

She soon learned that he was the boss and that she had to please him to earn the things she required to survive.

And now she was his, mind, body and soul - even though she was addled most of the time.

"Will you be taking me away soon, baby?" Mildred asked as he re-fastened his pants.

"Soon, yes. Very soon, Mildred. You must be patient, I've told you."

"I know, I'm sorry. I will be, I promise."

"Good. Now, I've got to be going - I'm very busy."

"Of course, Edmund - you will be in trouble if you don't get back." Again her mind had slipped away. She was getting worse, he was convinced of it.

"It's Salvatore."

"I know, how silly of me. Yes, Salvatore, of course. Will you be back soon, my darling?"

"As soon as I can."

"Please hurry, I can't wait for you for long - I need you, here, you see." Mildred pushed her hand between her legs once more, to show him exactly.

"As soon as I can, I promise," Salvatore said, slightly alarmed by her almost insane thirst for sex and the demented look in her eyes.

Was she finally toppling over the edge?

"Good. I'll be waiting," she said, making an exuberant show of pleasuring herself once more as Salvatore swiftly exited the cell.

"Come back soon, Edmund!" He heard her yell with confused

desperation a moment before he slammed the thick, soundproofed door shut and carefully re-bolted it.

Chapter Twenty Two

Ava had retreated to the top of the mansion's sweeping staircase and was squatting on the top step, behind the thick marble balustrade. From that vantage point, she had a clear view of the study door but could not be easily seen herself.

Her curiosity was driving her wild and she was desperate to know what lay behind the concealed door in her step-father's inner sanctum - a passageway perhaps, or maybe a secret vault - she did not know but was determined to find out.

She had been waiting, so far, for around twenty minutes yet Salvatore had still not reappeared and she was beginning to wonder if there was, indeed, a passageway which he had used to reach some other part of the estate and that maybe he was not going to come out the same way as he went in. But then, just as she was contemplating this possibility, the study door opened and Salvatore stepped out.

He looked flushed and somewhat sweaty as he lit a cigarette and strode away across the tiled lobby, out through the wide front doors and into the glorious California sunshine. A moment later she heard the wheels of his blue Corvette screech as he drove away.

Ava waited a few minutes more before descending the staircase, still in her bikini, her black sunglasses perched on her head; still barefoot as she silently crossed the lobby and slipped into the study.

Her heart was racing as she determinedly strode to the bookcase where, after taking a beat, she put two fingers on the red spine of *The Count of Monte Cristo* and pushed until she heard a 'click'.

Suddenly, exactly as she had witnessed with Salvatore, the bookcase slid gracefully aside to reveal the mysterious steel door. Ava stared at it for a moment, briefly questioning the sense of what she was about to do, before turning the handle and pushing it open. The door was heavier than she had anticipated and much thicker - at least ten inches or so - but she opened it nonetheless. Ava entered onto a dark, very small landing from which she could see a narrow steel staircase descending steeply into blackness.

Beside her, mounted on the roughly skimmed concrete wall, was a small switch box with three switches labelled, *stair lights on/ stair lights off, room lights on/room lights off* and *Bcase open/Bcase closed.* She clicked *Bcase closed* and as the bookcase began to slide shut behind her, she quickly clicked stair lights on, which caused a series of mesh covered ceiling lights to flicker into life - the sort she would have expected to find in an underground tunnel of some kind - functional and sturdy as opposed to modern and stylish. The final switch, *room lights on/room lights off,* was already in the 'on' position, so she left that alone but the word 'room' stirred her interest further.

She closed the steel door behind her and immediately felt the chill on her almost bare body, wishing, with regret, she'd had the good sense to put something different on other than the skimpy bikini. Nevertheless, with her curiosity piqued, she slowly began to descend the narrow, claustrophobic staircase. It was a very tight space, the walls, again, formed from just roughly skimmed concrete, purely functional, nothing more, although Ava was extremely glad of the lights. Had it not been for them it would have been a very different place indeed. Already she was missing the daylight and the fresh air - the stairwell smelled musty and earthy; an oppressive, suffocating odour that made her feel irrationally scared.

But she pressed on, down one steep flight and then another

until she was deep underground in the very bowels of the mansion.

Finally, her bare feet touched down on the cramped passageway and under the dim, industrial lighting, she saw the steel door at the end. 'It is a secret vault', she thought, for a moment, until she saw the glass peephole.

Slowly, very cautiously, she edged closer until she was standing right in front of the door. Ava noticed it was bolted securely, observing that the bolt and socket appeared to have been attached at some later date, as an addition to the original door, seemingly as an afterthought, and had been unskilfully welded on in a hurried, botched fashion.

Nevertheless, Ava thought little more of it before turning her attention to the peephole.

As she looked through the thick glass, her eyes widened in amazement, stunned by what she saw.

It was a tiny apartment.

There was an unmade bed, which had clearly been slept in recently, its sheets pulled back and the single pillow dented; a small kitchen area with empty food packaging on the worktop along with a dirty plate and spoon; and a television set, which was switched on. A threadbare Persian rug lay on the concrete floor and the bare walls appeared to be made from sheets of heavy-duty steel. There were no windows whatsoever and only another mesh enclosed ceiling light, albeit with a seemingly much brighter bulb, to illuminate the small space.

Ava could not believe it. Someone was obviously living down here; kept like an animal, two storeys underground in what was little more than a glorified prison cell. But who on earth could it be? And why, for the love of God, were they locked away down here? It was nothing short of barbaric.

Appalled by the horror of it and heedless of the potential danger, Ava slipped the bolt and pushed open the door. Again, like the one behind the bookcase, it was heavy and thick, made from brushed steel.

As she stepped inside, she heard the sound of a toilet flushing in what Ava realised was a small annex that had not been visible through the peephole.

Then, a moment later a woman appeared from behind the partition, having obviously been using the lavatory and taking Ava a little by surprise. "Who are you?" She snapped. "Why are you here? What do you want?"

Ava stepped back, startled by the woman's appearance and slightly fearful of her unwelcoming gaze.

The woman was ghostly white with dark, wild hair - a long, unkept main that hung below her waist; a singular white streak ran through it which made her look like 'the Bride of Dracula'. She was dressed only in a frayed silk robe and clearly naked underneath.

Like Ava's, her feet were bare.

Ava stared at her, much longer than she politely should, but the woman was beautiful, yet strangely familiar.

Then it hit her like a blow to the chest. The shock of it almost stupefying. The woman was older, paler, far more dishevelled than when she had last seen her, but there could be no doubt.

It was her mother.

"Oh, my God!" She gasped, a hand shooting to her mouth in disbelief.

"Well?" Mildred demanded tersely. "Who are you and what do you want?"

Ava began to cry; shock and relief and horror all mingled into one. "It's me, Mommy, it's Ava - your daughter," she said quietly.

"Liar!" Mildred snapped. "My daughter's nothing like you! Get out!"

"But it is, me, Mommy, it is."

"You're lying. Stop lying! My daughter's only tiny - a little

302

girl - not some blonde slut - not—" Suddenly an idea popped into Mildred's head and her mouth curled with anger, "Wait a minute! Are you here to steal Salvatore away from me? Is that what you're doing here you cheap—"

"What? No. Salvatore? Of course not. Mom it's me, Ava, your little girl - Edmund's little girl. I'm older now, I've dyed my hair—"

"Nonsense! Edmund's dead. Carlo killed him, stabbed him in front of my eyes - I saw it - I saw it - he's dead!"

"Stabbed?" Ava suddenly felt weak. "Carlo killed him—"

"Of course he killed him - you know he did you lying slut - killed him like he killed those three boys, like he killed his first wife - now he's sent you to kill me hasn't he? So you can have Salvatore - so you can steal him away from me—"

"No, Mommy, honestly, please!" Ava was weeping loudly now, her mother clearly unstable, her mind addled. "It's me," she tried again. "I've dyed my hair, I've grown up - but it's still me, I swear it. I'm Ava."

"Liar, liar, liar!" Mildred screamed, her face contorted with rage. "Don't lie to me - don't you fucking lie!" Suddenly she charged forward and struck Ava around the head, then again with her other hand.

Ava raised her arms to protect herself as Mildred punched and slapped and kicked her; crazed, insane and angry.

Mildred's long fingernails scratching three long claw marks across Ava's chest as she tried desperately to ward off the attack.

"How dare you come down here - dressed in just your underwear - dressed like a whore - trying to take—" Then, without warning, her attack ceased and her enraged expression switched in an instant to one of calm confusion - her befuddled mind trying desperately to find some order.

"Wait a minute," she said quietly, "are you Maria?"

"Maria?" Ava replied warily, feeling shell shocked.

"Oh, my darling girl, Carlo will be so surprised to see you, he thinks you're dead - thinks you were killed."

Mildred then tried to hug Ava, who flinched warily before reluctantly letting her guard down, allowing her mother to embrace her. Mildred smelt musky and of unwashed femininity and Ava found herself holding her breath.

"But you shouldn't be here," Mildred continued, suddenly worried, "my husband - well, I'm not sure he's forgiven you—"

"No. Mom - I'm Ava - Edmund's daughter. Your daughter."

"Edmund? Yes, of course - he's my husband, not Carlo but Edmund. That's right, I remember now."

"Yes, Edmund."

"Ah, yes, Edmund," said Mildred wistfully, "a good, kind man. A nice man."

"Yes, he was," Ava agreed, choking with emotion.

"But what about Salvatore?"

"Forget Salvatore," Ava snivelled, "he's no good - he doesn't own you—"

"That's it, isn't it?" Said Mildred, her demeanour switching yet again as she abruptly pulled away from the embrace. "You want him for yourself don't you?"

"No! No I don't!"

"Yes. Don't lie you dirty whore, you want him don't you? You want to spread your legs and let him fuck you!"

"No, please, Mom, stop. Stop it please - I don't want him, I just want you!" Ava begged.

But Mildred was deaf to her pleas and without warning, she lashed out and slapped Ava hard around the face, stunning her and sending the sunglasses that were on her head spinning off.

"You can't have him - do you hear me?" She was yelling loudly at the top of her voice, manic, frenzied. "Salvatore's mine, mine alone—"

Then, quick as a flash, she reached out and tore off Ava's bikini top in one swift stroke, snapping the flimsy straps. "—And none of your fancy, slutty underwear will make him want you!"

Hurriedly, Ava covered her naked breasts with her arm and quickly stooped to pick up her bikini top from the floor, a punch from Mildred landing hard on the back of her head as she bent, dazing her momentarily, and she staggered backwards.

"Get out!" Her mother screamed, "Get out, get out, get out!"

Ava, clutching her bikini top to her chest, tears streaming from her eyes, had no choice but to retreat as Mildred came at her once more.

Swiftly, she scrambled back through the doorway, trying desperately to keep her mother at arm's length whilst attempting to escape her wrath.

Ava flung the bikini top down the passageway then, using both hands, she heaved the door to. Mildred's arms were still grabbing at her madly, the clawed fingernails angrily trying to scratch her - only as the heavy door threatened to crush her flaying limbs did she finally pull them back through.

The moment her mother was free from harm, Ava, using all of her might, slammed the heavy door closed and slid back the bolt, locking Mildred back in her cage.

Then Ava, with her naked back pressed against the cold, hard metal, slipped down to the dusty floor and began to sob loudly, utterly distraught, as her mother repeatedly beat the door behind her with her bunched up fists, the muted rhythm only barely audible through the thickness of the steel.

Inside, as she hammered on the solid, immovable metal, Mildred was raging. She was cursing Ava at the top of her voice; using a stream of vulgar, disgusting words to describe her. On the outside, the abusive diatribe was little more than a faint whisper, but still Ava heard it and although she realised her mother was insane, the words still hurt her deeply.

Holding her head in her hands and feeling heartbroken, bruised and scratched from Mildred's violent attack, Ava wept. She cried solidly and despairingly for sometime until Mildred's tirade eventually abated and no more sound could be heard. Yet still she sat there, virtually naked, on the chilly concrete floor, goosebumps raised on her frozen skin as she digested all she had heard and all she had seen.

Carlo had murdered her father, just as she suspected. Edmund's suicide was a lie.

Yet her mother lived. If, indeed, it was living. Kept as a prisoner, a caged animal; her mind gone, her dignity gone. What sort of an existence was that?

Carlo Liuzzi; murderer. He and Salvatore Falcone; her mother's jailers. God how Ava hated them.

After a long while and shivering with cold, she finally climbed wearily to her feet. She risked another look through the peephole, fearful of what she might see, anxious not to spark another venomous, demented tirade. But Mildred was just sitting with her feet up on the bed, the robe wrapped round her, watching television. Her face was blank and calm, without emotion and Ava felt incredibly sorry for her.

She watched her for a few moments then turned and walked back down the passageway, picking up her bikini top as she went.

She slipped it on as best she could, enough to cover herself at least, but the straps were broken.

It did not matter, she had plenty more.

She climbed the steps with a heavy heart, wishing that, too, could be so easily replaced.

***

Four days later, the three long claw marks on Ava's chest, inflicted by Mildred's fingernails, were healing slowly but they were

306

still sore and inflamed, serving as a graphic reminder of her mother's terrible plight.

Ava had been deeply affected by the traumatic events in the underground cell and was haunted by what she had seen.

She also felt incredibly guilty about her imminent departure for New York - and to actually be looking forward to going, which just seemed so wrong. She fretted about what would become of Mildred in her absence but she had to get away from this place, away from this vipers nest of lies, captivity and murder before she, too, suffered a similar fate to her mother or father.

It was only Frankie with whom she felt safe. Only him she trusted but in just two short weeks she would be leaving him, too.

Her step-father did not know it yet, but Ava had no intention of returning - at least not until he was behind bars and her mother had been rescued.

Mildred needed to be cared for in the safe environment of a psychiatric hospital, where her damaged mind could be given the chance to heal. Perhaps then, at some point in the future, Ava could actually get her mother back.

They had never been close, even when she was a little girl their relationship was often fractious but she would never have wished Mildred's awful fate upon her. Maybe, after all that had happened, if Ava could save her, they could start again; become the mother and daughter she always hoped they could be.

But she temporarily had to put those dreams on hold and just get away. Once she was in New York, free of Carlo's control, she would talk to the police, get them to take action against her step-father and Salvatore who needed to be held accountable for what they had done.

They could both rot in prison for all Ava cared, she would not shed any tears.

But first she had to get away.

Carlo and Salvatore had both gone out - her step-father to the studio and Falcone to someplace unknown, having sped away in his shiny Corvette a short time earlier. But Ava knew they had gone as she had watched them from her bedroom window as they both left the mansion that morning.

Immediately feeling safer, Ava took a long cleansing shower then rubbed some soothing cream into the rosy red scratches that were the only blemishes on her otherwise perfect skin.

Afterwards, she took a long, leisurely time drying her straight golden hair which hung a third of the way down her back, working the hairdryer expertly as she repeatedly brushed her thick locks, always aware that below her, many feet underground, her mother had no such luxury. She pictured Mildred's wild dark hair and the silver streak that ran through it and the guilt seized her again.

She wished she could go back and see her but she had no desire to upset her further. She also felt that Mildred might attack her again - maybe even harm her seriously next time and in the long run that would do neither of them any good. The surest way to see her mother again was to get her step-father put away and Falcone along with him, but she realised that might take some time. Which did little to assuage her guilt.

Nonetheless, when Ava's hair was dry, she dressed in a simple white T-shirt, faded denim cut-offs and a pair of blue rubber flip-flops before heading downstairs to rustle up some breakfast.

The household staff were kept to a minimum nowadays and consisted only of a cook, a maid, and a gardener. Frankie and Vito shared chauffeuring duties and any other tasks that needed to be undertaken, whilst Salvatore was mostly required in an advisory capacity.

However, the mansion appeared to be empty today. The cook had already finished her morning chores and it was the maid's day off. The gardener was cutting the lawns and Frankie was cleaning cars out by the garage block. Vito was at the studio with Carlo.

So Ava had the place to herself. Or so she thought.

It was not until she was halfway through her second slice of toast that she glanced out the window and noticed Falcone's blue Corvette on the driveway. He had obviously returned whilst she was getting ready and she had not heard him arrive.

A cold shiver ran through her as she listened for a clue as to where he might be. But she heard nothing.

Hurriedly, she finished her breakfast and made to go back upstairs, having no wish to run into Salvatore. But she was already too late, because no sooner had she set foot on the bottom step of the grand staircase, than Falcone stepped out from her step-father's private study.

"Ah, Ava!" He said, in an overly friendly manner. "I was hoping to catch you - would it be possible for you to spare me a few moments please?"

"I'm sorry, I'm busy," replied Ava, "maybe later—"

"But I must insist, my dear. It's most important. I won't keep you for long, I promise." His command of the English language was excellent although his accent was unmistakably Italian.

Even though he made her skin crawl, Ava did not wish to cause a scene; she only had to behave for two more weeks and then she would be gone. "Sure, what is it?" She said.

"In here, if you wouldn't mind," said Salvatore, waving her to the study."

"Er, okay." She agreed warily as she crossed the lobby and walked past Salvatore as directed. He followed her in and shut the door.

"Sit, please," he said.

"Hey, I thought this wasn't gonna take long?" Ava was feeling a little uneasy now, what was this all about?

"It's not. Please, sit."

She rolled her eyeballs and reluctantly did as instructed.

Falcone walked around to the far side of the desk and sat down in Carlo's chair, making himself nicely at home.

"You're looking awful comfy in that chair, Salvatore - you know this isn't your office, right?" Ava said, unable resist the dig.

"Of course," he smiled, unfazed, an inscrutable expression on his long, thin face.

"So, what is it? What's so important?"

"Ah, yes. My apologies, I know you're extremely busy," he said sarcastically, his smile widening as he reached into his pocket and pulled something from it.

"I was just wondering if you recognised these?"

Then, with malignant pleasure, he placed her black plastic sunglasses on the desk.

They were scratched and one of the lenses was cracked, but they were definitely hers - the very same ones Mildred knocked off her head down in the cell.

Ava was dumbstruck. She had been so upset by the encounter with her mother she had quite forgotten all about the sunglasses. And now that she saw them again she was shocked - and her face clearly showed she was.

"Ah, good. I see you do. I was hoping you would."

Ava looked at the triumphant sneer on Salvatore's face, knowing she had been discovered.

"I wonder," he continued, obviously enjoying himself, "can you guess where I found them?"

It was pointless her denying it and she stared daggers at Falcone, her lip curling into a snarl as she said, "You know damn well I do. You found them in that cage, two stories below this room, where you've been keeping my mother locked up like an animal!"

He laughed, "Yes, that's correct. Very clever. I trust it was a

310

happy reunion?"

"What do you think, you bastard? You and Carlo might just as well have killed her - her mind's gone - she didn't even know who I was—"

"Oh dear, poor little Ava - you must have been so upset. But yes, Mommy's quite mad, I'm afraid. Although why we should have killed her I just don't know - after all, I've had so much fun with her over the years - I had no idea she could be quite so amenable."

"Bastard!" Ava spat again. "How dare you sit there so smugly - with that shit-eating grin on your face - after all you've done - you and my step-father? You're monsters, the pair of you - and you deserve to be in prison!"

"Please, my dear. Do try not to get so excited."

"I know everything - I know Carlo killed my dad - that his death was no suicide and that you and my step-father hung him up in his apartment for me to find so I would think he'd killed himself—"

"Oh, Ava, my poor, sweet deluded girl, you don't really think it was Carlo or I who hung Edmund up do you?"

"Of course it was, who else could it have been?"

Salvatore grinned, savouring this delicious moment. "Why Frankie of course. Your faithful, loyal lapdog who can do no wrong. Your trusted friend. It was him who hung your father's corpse up for you to find - in fact, now I think about it, it was he who welded the bolt onto to your mother's cell door, too. Yes, that's right - nice, funny, understanding Frankie. Your friend."

"Liar!" Ava cried, "You're lying!" But she could see by the look on his face he wasn't and she forcibly had to hold back her tears.

"Oh, he's got a great many talents has Frankie. Indeed, on that same night he also buried the bodies of four young boys in the desert - you remember them don't you? But of course you do - you saw them fucking your darling mommy didn't you?

"Anyway, Frankie might not have killed them but he's certainly got blood on his hands - theirs and your father's."

Ava's emotions were racing. How could Frankie not have told her? How could she have been so naïve?"

But then she pulled herself together and hardened her resolve.

"I'll go to the police," she said, victoriously, "I'll go to the police and tell them it all."

"Tell them what, exactly?"

"Tell them about my father's murder, tell them about what you've done to my mother - show them what you've done to my mother."

"Oh, my dear girl. You really don't understand do you? Do you really think we'd let your mother be found? Before you could even open your mouth to the police she would be killed. Instantly. Without hesitation. She is worthless and her body would never be found. And as for Edmund, well, good luck with that. There's not a lawman in the land who would find your story plausible - and even if they did, where's your proof?"

"I don't care. I'll still go to the police - I'll make them listen - if not here then in New York!"

"Well, that's your prerogative, of course. But I must warn you, your father has a great many friends in New York - friends who would be happy to silence you on his behalf."

"Carlo would never harm me - you know that."

"Oh dear, Ava. How innocent you are. You are talking about the man who strangled his first wife to death with his own bare hands - the man who sliced off the cock of his daughter's lover and fed it to him as he died.

"Indeed, Carlo even banished his own daughter, his own flesh and blood, who he loved and cherished with all of his heart - as well as his own newborn grandson - without thinking twice about whether he'd see them again.

"So do you really think he wouldn't hesitate to silence you - the lowly daughter of a dimwit chauffeur and a sex mad whore?"

Ava was appalled. She had always known her step-father was a monster but she had no idea of the depths of his depravity.

"But—" Ava spluttered, unable to think of a pithy response.

"Cat got your tongue?" Falcone sneered. "But then, of course, you of all people know how bad Carlo's temper can be - you have witnessed it first hand, after all."

Ava wanted to shout and scream and punch Salvatore but instead she just sat there speechless, realising the truth of her hopeless situation.

"No. My advice to you Ava, my darling, is to say nothing, to anyone, ever. Then - and only then - might you get the chance to live."

She glared at him, boiling with rage, feeling humiliated and helpless.

"Oh, and a little tip—" Salvatore added with glee, "I wouldn't mention this conversation to Carlo, either, my dear. As I don't think it would bode well for your future - or for your dear mad mother's either."

"Bastard." Ava hissed. "I can't wait to get to New York - away from you and him and this vile place!"

"Ah, about that, didn't Carlo tell you?" He smiled delightedly.

"Tell me what?"

"I'll be accompanying you to New York - just to help you get settled in - I do hope you don't mind."

Ava felt as if the bottom had fallen out of her world - "What? No! No, you can't be?" It was too horrific to even contemplate.

"Oh but I'm afraid I am. Your step-father thinks it might be for the best and I tend to agree."

Salvatore had, in fact, recommended it to Carlo the night before - after he found the sunglasses. He had persuaded his friend it might be for the best - just for a month or so, just to make sure

Ava had everything she needed. However, Falcone had an ulterior motive for wanting to go to New York. He needed to speak with Bruno Barca about the shipping problems he was still having with his cocaine consignments - to impress upon him once and for all the importance of getting things sorted out.

Nevertheless, Carlo had agreed that Ava could possibly do with his help to settle in to her new surroundings, and gave his consent for Salvatore to accompany her.

Ava looked at Falcone, his smug, self-satisfied expression taunting her. But she felt utterly helpless, completely void of anyone she could call upon to help her - even Frankie - he, too, had lied to her, withheld vital information. She had trusted him so, relied on him implicitly and now she felt betrayed.

She felt the tears welling up inside her, but she was damn sure she was not going to give Salvatore the satisfaction of seeing her cry.

"You can go to hell!" She yelled as she leapt to her feet and bolted from the room - straight up the stairs to the comparative sanctuary of her bedroom, where she flung herself onto the bed and sobbed uncontrollably into her pillow.

Yet downstairs, in the study, Salvatore was still smiling.

***

That afternoon, after Salvatore had gone out once more, Ava was lying on her bed, her mind replaying all she had been told, when she heard a knock on the door.

"Who is it?" She said, warily.

"It's me, kid," said Frankie, pushing her door open slightly, "Salvo said you wanted to talk to me?"

"No. I don't, get out!"

"Hey! It's me - what's the matter?"

"You mean you don't know? You really don't know?"

"No, hey, I'm at a loss here, kid, give me a clue why don't ya?"

She looked up at him as he shuffled into the room, big and

314

tough but with a heart of gold - or so she had thought. She could not help but start to cry again. She felt so alone.

"Oh, no - don't cry Ava, baby, don't cry - you're breaking my heart here - what's the matter? What's happened?

"I'm breaking your heart?" She snapped, turning on him. "How about you breaking my heart - how about that? I know, Frankie - I know what you did! Salvatore told me this morning. It was you who hung up my dad's body - you!"

"Oh, Christ, kid - Oh God—"

"How could you? How could you not tell me? All these years I thought you were such a good man - all these years I thought you had my back - and then I go and find out you're part of the conspiracy, too!"

Frankie looked bereft, his own eyes watering. "Ava, baby - sweetheart, I didn't—"

"Yes you did! Don't lie to me - I know you did it - I know you helped seal my mother into that tomb of hers underground - that you knew she was right here, under this roof all this time! How dare you - how dare you?" She broke down and wept, her head in her hands. "You betrayed me, Frankie. You betrayed me!"

Frankie was staggering about the bedroom, rocked by what she had said - deeply ashamed that she had discovered what he had been trying so hard not to tell her all these years. Eventually he slumped down heavily on her dresser stool - sat down before he fell down.

"I didn't tell you, kid, cos I didn't know how to. I swear it. After all you'd been through that night - after you and I got so close - I just couldn't tell ya for fear of breaking your heart—"

"But you did break my heart, didn't you?" She wailed.

"But it wasn't intentional. I was trying to protect you - trying to protect myself too. Your step-father - you know what he'd do to me if I told you? And if I was dead how could I possibly be your friend?"

"Friends don't keep secrets from each other, Frankie!"

315

"They do if they're trying to protect 'em - and that's what I was trying to do, kid, protect you, that's all."

"Hmm, well good job!"

"Listen, do you really think I wanted to do that with your old man - do you really think I wanted to hang him up there for you to find? But I couldn't think of a way out - surely it was better that way than I bury him out in the desert, in some unmarked grave, where the coyotes and wolves could dig him up! I tried to give you a clue - I knew you were smart, that you would probably figure it out someday - so I dressed Edmund in a mismatching uniform - to purposely make you suspicious - I knew you'd think he'd never dress himself like that!"

"And what about the suicide note?"

"Hey, I had nothing to do with that - that was all Carlo. All I did was put it where you could find it - but I didn't write it, kid, I swear it!"

"But you did seal my mother into that cell - didn't you?"

"Yeah. I did. I can't deny it. I welded the bolt on, as best I could anyway. But I had no idea that place existed until that night - and when I found out what Carlo was gonna do to your Mom I was sick to my stomach - I couldn't believe it. But he made me do it, kid. He made me - I wouldn't have been here today if I hadn't - I wouldn't have been able to be your friend, Ava, when I knew how badly you needed one.

"Carlo was like the devil that night - murderous, covered in blood - you know, you must remember. Like a mad man. And I feared for your safety. Yours and mine - hell, I freely admit it. He's a psycho - you know he is.

"But when I looked into your tear-stained eyes, it was like I was looking straight at my own daughter - I wanted to protect you, Ava, keep you safe. And so help me, I did the best I could.

"But am I a good man? No. Have I done things I ain't proud

of? Sure. Too many to even count. And do I wish that I'd told you the truth - you bet your ass I do.

"But I never meant to hurt you, kid, I promise - I promise with all of my heart. Please, you have to believe me."

Frankie's eyes were wet, too, now and he looked older than his years; world weary and sad. He sat looking at her imploringly, hoping she could find someway to forgive him.

Ava was silent for a long time as she digested what he had told her. She had stopped crying now.

"Do you know Salvatore's coming with me to New York?" She said eventually, sniffing up the last remnants of her tears.

"He told me this morning. A moment before he went out. I didn't know before that, kid, honest. I'm sorry."

"What the hell am I going to do with him there? I don't trust him, he's evil - he's as bad as Carlo."

"I'll protect you. I swear it. I won't let him harm you."

"How can you - you won't be there, remember?"

"You mean you don't know?"

"Don't know what?"

"I'm coming, too, kid. Not just for a few weeks like Salvo, but for the whole time. I'll take care of you, Ava. I promise."

"You're coming?"

"Yep - found that out this morning, too. Apparently Carlo don't want no harm to come to his little girl in the big, bad city and I'm the guy who's gotta keep you safe. I hope that's okay with you after—"

"You're coming to New York with me?"

"Uh-huh. For the duration. If you'll have me."

Ava looked up at him, staring into his big gnarled face, seeing the emotion in his steel blue eyes, knowing he had done what he thought was best and understanding, at last, why. He definitely wasn't perfect, definitely had a past she did not care to know about. But she knew he had her best interests at heart.

317

He gazed back at her with sad doleful eyes; Frankie DeLuca - a big, loveable, puppy of a man who Ava could not help but feel a deep affection for. Rough around the edges and not the most subtle guy in the world, but reliable and loyal nonetheless.

And when all was said and done, no matter his faults, he was the closest thing to a proper father she was ever likely to have.

"Of course you can come, you big lug," she said, at last. "Now come over here and give me a hug."

***

Two weeks later, Ava kissed her step-father goodbye, forcibly putting on an act so he would not suspect she knew anything. But as she kissed his cheek she made a silent vow to make him pay for his crimes - to see him behind bars if it was the last thing she ever did.

Then, as Frankie took her case and loaded it, along with his own, into the limo, she also said farewell to her mother too. It was unspoken, of course, as Mildred was still locked away in her cell deep underground. But one day Ava swore she would set her free.

However, before then, she was to head to New York and once there anything was possible - she felt it in her bones. With Frankie beside her, after Salvatore had returned to Hollywood, she would start a new life.

With that thought in her mind, she climbed into the limo beside Frankie. Falcone was sitting up front, next to Vito who was in the driver's seat.

She waved briefly to Carlo and then the limo drove away from the mansion, down the long driveway and out through the gates.

Ava did not look back.

Chapter Twenty Three

Manhattan, Upper East Side, New York 1966

D anny stared as his reflection in the mirror and groaned as he studied the black eye. It was a real peach.

There was no getting around it, he was going to have to tell his mother he had been fighting again.

However, Danny knew that even though Maria would make a show of admonishing him, she would not mean it, not really. She never did.

Whenever he came home after a fight, and he had many times, Maria always told him not to do it again, feigning anger, but she could never stay mad at him for long - nor Nate, for that matter.

In the nine years they had been with her, Maria had been fiercely supportive of both boys and stood protectively beside them like a proud lioness, ignoring their minor faults and championing their many gifts, loving them unconditionally.

And they loved her in return.

Indeed, she was much more like an older sister than a mother, but she was their mother nonetheless; Danny's by blood and Nate's by decree - she and Diego had adopted him two years after rescuing the boys from Hell's Kitchen. Diego had also lawfully become Danny's father at the same time.

However, whilst Danny had taken 'Del Toro', as his adoptive

surname, Nate had opted to keep the name 'Malone' in honour of Megan.

But regardless of surname they had become a happy family unit and Diego and Maria had proved to be wonderful parents.

Once the New York Matador was finished, which now stood proudly on Fifth Avenue, hailed as the finest hotel in the city, they had taken the boys with them around the world as they tended to Matador business in many exotic locations across the globe.

In fact the Hermes IV had become almost as much a home to them as the Park Avenue apartment or Diego's palatial family home in Cadiz - or even the villa on Lake Como where they had spent many an idyllic summer.

Accompanying them on their adventures, along with the ever present, ever fussing mother hen that Delores had become, was a carefully chosen private tutor who continued the boys' schooling wherever they went.

Whilst they had both been good students before, each with impressive grades, the tutor Maria hired transformed their skills beyond all previous expectations.

Amongst their other academic accomplishments, and with thanks in no small part to their multi-lingual parents, they were both now able to converse with ease in Spanish, Italian and French.

Nevertheless, for the last two years, Maria and Diego had based themselves permanently in New York where the boys attended an exemplary, very expensive private school.

Both had exceeded the academic hopes Maria had envisaged for them and had finished in the top five percent of all their classes.

But whilst Danny had just started his freshman year at college in the city, Nate had flown to Italy to enrol in the American Seminary in Rome where he was to study to become a priest.

It had long been his dream - or more his natural calling - and Maria and Diego did not stand in his way - in point of fact, neither could have been more proud.

Diego had gone with Nate to see him settled and would return to the States shortly afterwards, but he would miss the boy with whom he had formed a particular bond. Maybe it was because he, too, was of a gentle, philosophical nature much like himself.

Danny would miss Nate, too. He and his brother had never previously been separated and it already felt as if part of his own body was missing - which was the reason why he was feeling so downright ornery at present and getting into so many fights.

Nate had always been a stabilising influence and without him Danny felt slightly adrift.

Unlike Nate, he was not one for turning the other cheek and it did not need much provocation to get him riled - a cross word, a wrong look - was all it took to get Danny's blood boiling. However, he was fighting to keep this hot-headedness under control and knew, deep down, it stemmed from the loss he felt from Nate's departure.

Nevertheless, Daniel Del Toro was fast gaining a reputation as a tough guy on campus.

However, aside from a few minor altercations, he had a large group of friends and was thoroughly enjoying his time at college.

Especially when it came to the girls.

Danny had grown into an extraordinarily handsome young man; dark and tanned with smouldering green eyes and rugged good looks. He stood at just over six feet with broad shoulders and a sculptured, muscular physique that would shame Michelangelo's David. He also had charm in abundance and an easy smile that made many a young girl go weak at the knees.

But Danny took it all in his stride.

However, today, after yet another altercation, he turned on the tap in the men's rooms and cupped his hands under the cold stream of water before splashing his face. He rubbed his cheeks and eyes to wash away the small amount of blood from the slight split in his lower lip, then looked at his reflection again and smiled wryly. The bruises had been worth it, the sophomore who had inflicted them had fared much worse than Danny and would no doubt be regretting calling him a 'dirty wop'.

Danny wiped his face with a paper towel then swung open the men's room door and entered the busy thoroughfare of University Hall as he made his way out into the bright October sunshine of the main quad.

It was late in the day but students were still milling about all over the campus; chatting, laughing, sitting in study groups or just generally soaking up the sun after a long day of learning.

For Danny, the great thing about the Morningside Heights campus at Columbia was that, unlike many other universities, it was quite compact and therefore crammed its many resources into a relatively small area. This meant that everyone had to pass through the main quads which offered Danny a lot more chance of random interaction with people he knew as they crossed from one building to the next.

He also loved it because it was on Broadway, right in the heart of the action, and he would often hang out around there with his friends after school, getting into all kinds of harmless fun.

Occasionally, he would meet up with a girl, maybe even take them to the park for a flirtatious hour or two as they lay on the grass under a tree and studied together.

Afterwards he would ride the subway home - or take the bus depending on how the mood took him or, from time to time, especially if it was raining, Maria would send Max to pick him up.

But today Danny had opted to walk, even though the Greyling Building was over an hour away on foot. But it was a beautiful day and it felt good to be out in the sunshine. The walk would also enable him to enjoy the city; the route home taking him via Morningside Park and through Central Park, before leading on to Park Avenue.

He slung his duffel bag over his shoulder and strolled up College Walk towards Amsterdam Avenue, the warm sun beating down on his tanned neck. He wore only a light, white T-shirt and faded Levis as his rubber soled sneakers fell softly on the scorched concrete sidewalk; his gait confident and relaxed.

Danny was still a little uncertain as to where his future lay, although it was generally assumed he would go to work for Diego when he left college with a view to, one day, taking over at the helm of Matador. This appealed to Danny, of course, as he loved being with Diego and could think of no better mentor.

However, Danny secretly dreamed of a life in California, ideally taking up a position at Viscount Studios which had been owned by Matador for several years now and was turning a healthy profit. But he knew his mother was vehemently against the idea, fearing for his safety and worrying his true identity might be discovered by her own father, Carlo Liuzzi, who was the ruthless head of Viscount's biggest rival, Gold Star Pictures.

Maria was terrified that if Carlo knew of Danny's existence and, indeed, of hers, too, it could result in very serious and possibly deadly ramifications and she had no wish to put her son in harm's way.

As long as Carlo did not know about Danny, did not know about her, they were safe - especially as they lived in New York and her father rarely set foot out of Los Angeles. They had a whole country between them and Maria prayed that would be enough to keep her boys from harm.

Maria had mellowed since taking on Danny and Nate. She still despised Carlo with a passion but her love for her boys outweighed her hatred of him and she had decided to focus her energy on providing Danny and Nate with a happy family home rather than seeking vengeance for what her father had done. His vile actions still stirred incredible feelings of bitterness within her but she swallowed them down. Danny, Nate and Diego were those most important to her now, not her father. She was happy - they were happy - and she was determined not to let Carlo spoil things.

To this end, she purposely stayed out of the spotlight and went to great lengths to guard her privacy - careful to ensure that her face never appeared in the newspapers or on television.

Since regaining her memory and taking on the boys she had taken a back seat in matters pertaining to Matador. She still liked to accompany Diego on his travels around the world, at least as often as the boys schooling allowed, but instead of appearing at her husband's side, in the glare of media attention, she chose instead to stay in the background out of sight.

Diego understood her reasons for this as it was a decision they had made together. It was imperative that Carlo Liuzzi never discovered Maria's existence or that of his only grandson.

And, so far, their strategy had been successful, even though Diego's ownership of Viscount Studios often took him out to the West Coast. Indeed, he had found himself at many a Hollywood soirée where Liuzzi had also been in attendance. They had shared pleasantries, nothing more, and Diego had been careful not to reveal anything about his private life. Carlo had always been charm itself but Maria had warned Diego not to be fooled by the man she had come to think of as the devil.

Danny was aware of his mother's reluctance to let him go to Hollywood and understood her reasons for it, but it did not stop him from dreaming.

Indeed, on such a glorious day it was almost impossible not to let his imagination run away with him as he ambled care-freely along College Walk; his head in the clouds, lost in a daydream of long, sunny days in California.

He turned right onto Amsterdam, his thoughts full of sun-tanned girls in bikinis, letting his feet guide him in the direction of home and not really paying attention to where he was going.

As he hummed The Beach Boys' *California Girls* to himself, he was oblivious to the small group of people exiting Hartley Hall who were now crossing the sidewalk directly in front of him, heading towards a waiting car.

Quite by accident, Danny clattered headlong into one of them; a tall, skinny man, sending him crashing to the ground.

"Oh, my god, I'm so sorry! Are you okay?" He spluttered apologetically, holding out his hand to give assistance. "Please, let me help you—"

"Idiot!" Yelled the man on the ground, slapping Danny's hand away angrily and standing up by himself, brushing dust off his expensively tailored suit. "Watch where you're fuckin' going, you goddamn hippie!"

"Hey, I'm sorry, okay?" Said Danny, not appreciating the man's attitude, "It was an accident, that's all."

"Yeah? Well maybe I'll arrange for you to have an accident, too - I mean, what are you, fuckin' blind or something?"

The man spoke with an Italian accent and had the same Mediterranean skin colouring as Danny. He had a long, lean face with thick, rubbery lips and slicked back black hair that was severely receding. One of his hands was also covered by a smooth, black glove, giving him a menacing, slightly sinister appearance.

Danny could feel his hackles rising as he studied him, "No, I'm not blind," He replied calmly, "- I said I'm sorry, man, what more can I do?"

"I'll tell you what you can do—" The man snarled before suddenly being cut-off by another voice - a female one.

"Salvatore, it was an accident, that's all. He didn't mean it - please, I need to get back - I've got to study."

Danny looked past the skinny man and saw another shorter, stockier man behind him. This one was grey haired and punchy with

325

broad shoulders and a thick, sturdy physique, but it clearly wasn't him who had spoken.

Then the girl stepped out from behind him. Blonde, beautiful, a figure to die for and long, shapely legs. She looked to be about Danny's age and was dressed fashionably in a sleeveless lime crew-neck, green, floral pedal-pushers and simple white pumps.

She looked exactly like the 'California Girl' Danny had been imagining just moments before as he hummed The Beach Boys' song.

As her big blue eyes peered at him under long, pretty lashes, he was quite taken aback by how attractive she was. Her blonde hair hung loosely around her bare shoulders but a white alice band held it back off her lovely face. She had a perfect, smooth complexion with skin the colour of light caramel and plump, pink lips that Danny found almost irresistible.

He was immediately smitten.

"Hi," he said with a winning smile, his altercation with Salvatore immediately forgotten, "I'm Danny."

"Ava. Nice to meet you." She replied. *God, he's good looking,* she thought, *and what a smile* - even though he looked like he'd been fighting. But a black-eye and split lip did not detract from the overall vision, which was both rugged and cool and suddenly, quite unexpectedly, she felt all of a flutter.

"Likewise," said Danny. "You go to school here?"

"Uh-huh, started this fall—"

"Hey kid - enough!" Interrupted Salvatore. "You don't get to talk to her - you only talk to me, capiche?"

Danny's attention was snatched away from Ava and he glared at Salvatore. "Yeah, I understand - but you really gotta lighten up, man, I mean you're attitude's really not cool - know what I mean?"

For a second Salvatore was stunned, then he very nearly exploded. No one ever spoke to him like that. "You no good, snot-nosed punk - I'll fuckin' kill you!" He growled, lunging at Danny before being grabbed bodily by the smaller, stockier man behind him.

"Hey, Salvo - not here. This ain't the place - too many people!" Said Frankie DeLuca, fighting to keep a hold on Falcone.

"Get off me! I don't fuckin' care - no one speaks to me like that - no one - you hear that, punk!" Salvatore raged at Danny as Frankie restrained him.

"Yeah, I hear you, old man," Danny sneered, squaring up to him, unintimidated. "Give it your best shot - let's see what you got!"

"No! Stop it - both of you," Ava interjected, "it was an accident, nothing more. This is silly - you can't have a fight out here on the street, it's just madness."

"She's right, Salvo," Frankie agreed, "you know it. Don't make sense to get into it here - the kid said he was sorry, let's leave it at that, okay?"

Salvatore, at last seeing the sense of what they were saying, stopped struggling and shrugged Frankie off. "Okay," he said. "Sure. He's just a punk kid - what's he mean to me anyway?"

But his eyes, still filled with fury, never left Danny's as he spoke.

Danny, however, eager to impress Ava, obligingly offered his hand to Salvatore. "Look, man, I apologise, okay. I'm sorry - I didn't see you, that's all. I'm glad you're alright. Now let's shake, eh?"

Salvatore considered Danny's hand with disdain for a long moment, then spat on the sidewalk beside him. "Fuck you," he said with disgust, before walking away to the waiting limo, leaving Danny standing there with his hand out feeling foolish.

Frankie looked at him apologetically and shrugged. "Sorry, kid," he said quietly.

"Frankie, Ava!" Falcone shouted from the back seat of the car, "Come on - let's get going!"

DeLuca headed to the car, leaving Ava alone, staring at Danny. She smiled sweetly. "Sorry, Danny," she said softly, "It really was nice to meet you though, honestly."

Danny was captivated by her smile. She was simply stunning; the most beautiful girl he had ever seen. "You too," he said. "Guess I'll be seeing you around campus, huh?."

"Yeah, guess so—"

"Ava!" Salvatore yelled sharply, "Now - this minute - get in here!"

"Sorry," she whispered to Danny before obediently scampering off to the car and climbing in beside Falcone, just managing a brief wave before he slammed the door shut.

A moment later, Frankie pressed his foot on the gas and the shiny limo slipped into the flow of traffic on Amsterdam Avenue.

And when it eventually disappeared from view Danny felt bereft.

***

Ava had been studying at her friend's student residence in Hartley Hall. It was far from glamorous and the rooms were incredibly tiny - there was even a significant cockroach problem - but she could not help but feel slightly jealous of her friend's freedom.

Ava, herself, lived in a brownstone on the Upper West Side which belonged to her step-father, Carlo. She lived there with Frankie, an Italian housekeeper named Nona Rosa and, temporarily, Salvatore, who would be flying back to California within the month - and Ava could not wait. Her existence in New York so far had been nothing like the life she had hoped for. Indeed, with Salvatore watching her every move it had been almost suffocating.

She loved being at the university as within its grounds she could truly be herself. Without Falcone there to watch her every move, she was free to make friends and interact with people without fear of him passing judgement. Ava tried to wring the most out of each day; she had enrolled herself into several after school clubs and groups and went to Hartley Hall with her friend, Susan, as often as she could, ostensibly to study, for as long as possible. Anything to avoid returning to her cloistered life at the brownstone where all she had was her room and her books in which to escape.

Once Salvatore went back to Los Angeles she knew things would get better; Frankie was a push over - and mostly on her side - and Nona Rosa was just a sweet, yet slightly stern, old lady who had looked after Carlo when he lived in New York. She was fiercely loyal to him still but Ava knew how to handle her and was confident that after Falcone left the old woman would lighten up considerably.

Ava just wished Salvatore was already gone.

As Frankie guided the limo up Amsterdam, she sat in the back next to the man she loathed almost as much as her step-father, thinking about the boy she had just met.

Danny.

Her heart skipped a beat as she thought about him. What was his last name? Where did he come from? Where did he live? And, more importantly, the question she now longed to know the answer to, was when would she see him again?

**

Danny, too, was equally curious about Ava and as he walked home, through Morningside Park and Central Park, he could think of little else other than the girl he had just met.

Chapter Twenty Four

Rome, Italy 1966

Diego was now forty-three years old but he still seemed eternally youthful; his floppy hair giving him a boyish appearance and only the slight trace of grey at the temples betrayed his true age.

He stood in the doorway of Nate's room on campus cleaning his black horn-rimmed spectacles on his silk tie. It was a familiar procedure Nate recognised as one of his adopted father's most endearing habits.

Diego had been staying at the Rome Matador for a few days whilst Nate underwent his orientation at the college and familiarised himself with his new surroundings; eager to see him settled before leaving him there, alone, and flying home to New York.

But Nate was well-prepared for life at The Pontifical North American College, or PNAC, as it was better known. Even though he had been nominated for a position there by the Archdiocese of New York, it had long been his goal to study at the seminary, which was situated tantalisingly close to The Vatican.

He believed that being separated from the people he loved and the places he knew would help him form a more intimate reliance on The Lord, allowing him to hear His voice more clearly, which he knew would guide him on the path to becoming a priest. Indeed, Nate could think of nothing better than a life of prayer and study in

Rome - whilst hopefully meeting many like-minded people.

However, it did not make saying goodbye to Diego any easier.

Both of them had tears in their eyes as Diego slid on his glasses before hugging his son for a final time.

No longer did Diego wish for children of his own or, more specifically, children sired by him, as both Danny and Nate had amply rewarded him with their love, friendship and acceptance. Furthermore, he viewed them not as adoptive children but simply as his children. They were his and Maria's and there was nothing more to be said.

However, even though he loved them equally, Danny tended to be more Maria's and Nate more Diego's. It was just the way their respective personalities gelled.

In fact, in another life, Diego himself could have imagined dedicating himself to God. The priesthood had always fascinated him but the business world had appealed that bit more. In truth, Diego's father would never have entertained him entering the priesthood and it was always envisaged that he would one day take over the running of Matador.

Sadly, that day had come sooner than both men expected although Diego had taken up the role with natural expertise but it did not stop him feeling slightly envious of the life Nate had chosen for himself.

In reality, though, Diego would not have swapped his life with Maria for anything. She was his whole world.

After the embrace, he held Nate at arms length and studied the remarkable young man he had become.

He stood before him in his freshly pressed PNAC attire; black slacks, black short-sleeved shirt and a white, fiercely starched clerical collar.

Fresh-faced and pale skinned with curly red hair which he kept closely cropped, Nate was of a slight build but handsome in his own way. He also exuded a natural calm which other people found infectious.

More importantly, his calming abilities had certainly worked on his brother over the years and both boys knew Danny's life would be much more volatile without Nate's influence upon him.

But Danny would have to learn to keep a lid on his anger because for the foreseeable future Nate would be based here in Rome at the American Seminary.

"Take care of yourself, my boy," said Diego. "Eat well and work hard - I'm sure you will."

"I will. I'll be fine, don't worry. Have a safe trip - and keep an eye on Danny, make sure he stays out of trouble."

Diego smiled. "I think we both know that's not going to happen, but I'll do my best."

"I know."

"Well, I suppose I'd better be going."

"Guess so."

"Enjoy yourself - and don't forget to call."

"I won't. Promise. You take care - and try to take it easy - slow down a bit."

Again Diego smiled. "I'll try." He offered his hand and Nate shook it firmly.

"See you," Diego said.

Nate returned the smile. "See you, Dad."

Then he watched as Diego, rather forlornly, turned and walked away.

***

Nate soon immersed himself in life at the college and found it everything he hoped it would be. He was thoroughly enjoying all aspects of his theological studies and was extremely grateful for his knowledge of languages as all his courses were conducted in Italian.

His daily schedule included both morning and evening

332

worship as well as at least thirty minutes of personal prayer which, according to the college, was to help him achieve absolute clarity in his vocation.

Nate could not help but smile at this - not because he thought it absurd, in fact, he welcomed it - but because he knew Danny would think it to be a huge pile of religious mumbo jumbo - to put it politely.

Nevertheless, alongside the college's focus on the spiritual growth of its seminarians, it also promoted friendship and personal growth. The New Men, as they were called, of which Nate was one, were encouraged to bond with their fellow students and 'to build a healthy respect and love for each other whilst living out God's will.'

As a direct result of this philosophy, Nate and his classmates soon became a tight-knit group who could regularly be seen hanging out together on campus.

In particular, Nate had found a good friend in fellow New Yorker, Gino McBride, an Italian-American New Man from Brooklyn who had a fun, out-going personality.

Gino was the same age as Nate but whilst Nate was small and slender, Gino was tall and chunky; some might even unkindly call him fat. He had a tanned, pudgy face with big, brown, slightly feminine eyes and bushy black hair that was almost 'afro' in style.

His room was situated just across the hall from Nate's so they often studied together.

However, when they weren't studying, at prayer or taking part in some other theological activity, the New Men were free to do as they pleased.

This included on campus activities such as football and basketball, for which the college had excellent facilities, or to venture out into the city - which Nate and Gino frequently did on a pair of rented Vespa's

There was nothing better than buzzing around the narrow

streets on the little scooters; the wind rushing through their hair as they took in all Rome had to offer.

However, even though Gino was born and bred in Brooklyn and his father was of Irish descent, his mother hailed from Rome and still had relations there, up in the hills, who Gino visited whenever time allowed.

Gino even asked if Nate would like to accompany him sometime and he readily agreed.

And so it was on an especially glorious Saturday morning, he and Gino headed out of the city on their scooters; Gino's bulky frame and bushy hair looking slightly top-heavy on the tiny Vespa as Nate followed him up into the hills.

The hustle and bustle of the forever frantic and fast-paced capital were quickly left behind as they navigated their way along the windy road and up into the much more tranquil and altogether more rural surrounds of the countryside.

They had been going for some time, travelling higher up into the hills, speeding through many quaint little hamlets and passed numerous tumbledown rustic dwellings; occasionally slowing for a stray goat or a shepherd guiding his flock to fresher pastures, but always moving ever upwards.

The scenery was breathtaking and Nate was overwhelmed by the sheer beauty of it all, quite expecting Gino's relatives to live in a typically rustic little cottage similar to those he had passed along the way - ramshackle on the outside, spotlessly clean and fastidiously maintained on the inside.

But as Gino led the way out of one particularly scenic tree-lined boulevard and onto a stretch of sweeping grassland with panoramic views of the hillside, Nate saw they were heading towards a huge, stone-walled, high-gated compound with a spectacular villa standing in its centre.

The grand structure and its few outbuildings stood at the end of a long, narrow track that was little more than a well-worn cattle path; the only settlement of any kind in the surrounding area.

Gino bumped down the track and slowed his Vespa to a halt outside the solid iron gates. Nate pulled up alongside him, slightly awe-struck by the impressively fortified residence and more than a little wary of the two armed guards that stood either side of the gates.

The men were heavy set, burly types wearing typically rustic attire and floppy cloth caps. Both were heavily armed; a holstered pistol on each one's hip, a bullet belt strapped across each of their chests and at least two knives shoved into each of their thick, leather belts. One of the men carried a twelve-bore shotgun, the other had a machine gun slung over his shoulder.

"Your family live here?" Nate asked quietly, the incredulity in his voice undisguised.

"Uh-huh," replied Gino, a mischievous glint in his eye, "Just what you were expecting, right?"

"Pretty much," said Nate, playing along with his friend's obvious joke.

"Sorry to disappoint," Gino winked before turning his attention to the man with the shotgun approaching him. The pair of them shook hands and exchanged pleasantries, then the guard stepped back to the gate and banged on it three times.

A moment later the gate was opened by another equally well-armed individual and Gino and Nate were ushered into the compound.

The inner sanctum consisted of a large gravel driveway that led up to the house with what looked like lush gardens to the rear, whilst close to where the two trainee priests entered were several sizeable stone outbuildings with neat terracotta roofs.

Inside one of the outbuildings Nate glimpsed a fleet of luxury automobiles including a Rolls, a Lamborghini and a Ferrari amongst others, all highly polished and gleaming.

Beyond the outbuildings there was a large stable block where a muscular groom was removing the saddle from a magnificent black horse which had clearly just returned from a morning ride; a mist of perspiration rising from its glossy withers.

But Nate's attention was quickly drawn away by yet another armed guard who directed them to park their scooters beside a covered lean-to that sat up against the compound wall. An ancient Fiat 500 was parked under this alongside various motorbikes, scooters and bicycles which, Nate assumed, belonged to the obviously sizeable workforce.

The villa itself was large and monastic in style, built in the 17th century, with bleached stone walls and wooden shuttered windows. Before becoming a family home it had been a serviceable and simplistic farmstead and still retained many of the old features. Over the years these had been sympathetically added to, subtly transforming it into something entirely more stylish but without compromising the rustic charm of its surroundings.

However, it remained an incredibly imposing building that reeked of understated opulence and Nate could not help but be impressed - he was curious to know, though, why it was protected by heavily armed guards.

"Sure beats the Lower East Side, don't it?" Gino said, "Heck, this place is bigger than my whole neighbourhood back home - I couldn't believe it the first time I saw it."

"I know what you mean," replied Nate, who had experienced the same sense of awe when Maria and Diego took him from Hell's Kitchen to Park Avenue. It was a whole different world away from what he had been used to so he could understand entirely how Gino must feel about his Italian relative's obvious wealth in comparison to his modest upbringing in Brooklyn.

As Nate climbed off his scooter and pulled it onto its stand, a dog suddenly bounded up to him; an English border collie, which seemed a friendly sort of mutt with a floppy tongue and a waggy tail.

Nate bent down and gave him a good fuss, "Hello, boy," he said, scratching him under the chin and stroking his ears, "Who are you, then?"

A moment later another dog, a shiny Doberman pinscher, ran in and began sniffing at Gino's crotch and shortly afterwards a pointer and a chocolate labrador arrived on the scene; all of them apparently delighted to see their guests.

"Dogs - away!" A sharp female voice shouted and Nate turned to see a tall, smartly dressed woman approaching them. The dogs quickly scurried off, not needing to be told twice - all except the border collie who seemed to be enjoying Nate's attentions rather too much to do as instructed.

"Berto!" The woman snapped. "You, too. Off you go, away!"

Reluctantly, Berto wandered off, but not too far, just in case there was a chance of a bit more fuss.

The woman was now almost up to them and Nate immediately noticed she was wearing a black leather patch over her left eye; a jagged white scar directly above it was also visible. However, apart from these imperfections she was strikingly beautiful with high, sculptured cheek bones, a gently curved nose and well-formed, fulsome lips. Her one good eye was exquisitely shaped and expertly made-up to make the most of its deep brown hue.

She had short, silver hair that was cut in a masculine style yet, on her, it somehow looked extremely feminine.

Nate put her at about 48, certainly no more than 50, but she had the slim, firm figure of a woman half her age. Her curves were shown off to perfection in a cream silk blouse, dark brown jodhpurs and knee length leather riding boots. Around her neck a green chiffon scarf was loosely tied and on her slender hands she wore soft, brown pigskin gloves.

She carried a long, leather riding crop which she raised to

playfully threaten Berto who was still lurking nearby, but he paid her no mind.

"Please excuse my dog," she said in lightly accented English, smiling pleasantly and displaying a row of faultless white teeth, "he seems to ignore just about everything I say even though I love him the most."

Nate returned her smile, "He's no trouble - it's nice to have such a greeting."

"Nate," Gino said, "allow me to introduce my aunt - La Contessa di Montagna."

Nate held out his hand, 'The Countess of the Mountain', he mentally translated.

"Contessa," Gino said, continuing his introductions, "my friend and fellow seminarian, the soon to be 'Father' Nate Malone."

"Father," the Contessa said, taking Nate's hand and shaking it firmly. "Very pleased to meet you."

"It's just 'Nate', please, I won't be 'Father Nate' for some time yet, I'm afraid. A pleasure to meet you Contessa, thank you for having me."

"Not at all. You're most welcome. And Gino—" she said, leaning in and giving her nephew a kiss on both cheeks, "—it's a pleasure to see you, too. Welcome, both of you."

***

After a leisurely tour of the villa's beautifully landscaped gardens, with its ornate fountains and tree-lined walkways, The Contessa led Nate and Gino onto a wide, shaded veranda where a servant poured them wine as they relaxed in comfortable wicker armchairs.

The dogs had accompanied them on their tour and were now laying close by, lazing in the afternoon sun, again, all except for Berto, who had positioned himself between Nate's legs and was currently enjoying an ear rub from his new found friend.

The Contessa was an excellent hostess, albeit rather mysterious. Several times Nate broached the subject of why the villa was so well guarded and what the nature of her business was, but each time she remained resolutely vague and expertly changed the subject. Nate also observed whenever he pursued that line of conversation, the Contessa became noticeably less affable whilst Gino seemed to fidget in his chair rather uncomfortably.

In the end Nate came to the obvious conclusion that La Contessa di Montagna was not all she seemed and thought maybe she was involved in some sort of nefarious activity. Indeed, the idea that she might be the head of the local Cosa Nostra entered Nate's mind more than once - although she was certainly not what he assumed a Mafia boss would look like.

As it was, they spent an extremely pleasant few hours in her company and she seemed genuinely interested in Nate and especially fond of Gino, who was her younger sister's only son.

When the time at last came for the two apprentice priests to leave, the Contessa gave them each a hug and kissed them on both cheeks as was the continental way and made Gino promise to bring Nate with him again. She seemed to enjoy the company of the young men in a very motherly way, having never had the benefit of children herself.

Indeed, the Contessa had never been married and had spent most of her life alone; a strong, formidable woman who had apparently thrived, single-handedly, in a very masculine environment, yet she clucked around these young men like a protective mother hen and Nate couldn't help but take to her even though he had serious reservations about what he strongly suspected she actually was.

Upon arriving back at the college, Nate tactfully voiced these suspicions to Gino; about the high level of security surrounding his aunt and how she managed to live in such fabulous style, and Gino, after furtively looking about him to ensure they were not being overheard, confirmed it.

La Contessa di Montagna was indeed a high ranking mafiosa; the capofamiglia of the local Cosa Nostra, one of the most feared and secretive in the whole of Italy.

The Contessa, of course, had never eluded to as much but Gino's mother had told him. She, herself, had escaped the family business at a young age by marrying her GI lover, after their father died. But her sister, the Contessa, had stayed, taking over from Gino's grandfather, building the family's assets and accumulating enormous wealth in the process. She had also earned a great deal of respect.

Gino told Nate that the Contessa did not have the best of starts in life. When she was just thirteen, he said, she was brutally raped and severely beaten by a passing vagrant. She had been left for dead, blinded, scarred and robbed of any future hope of bearing children.

But she had fought for life, battled against the odds and had emerged as a stronger, more determined individual, vowing never to be so helpless again.

However, the attack on his daughter had all but ruined her father, her severe injuries leaving him guilt ridden for not being able to protect her. In a deep depression, he took to his bed and did not leave it for seven long years, until the day he died, when his two daughters carried him to his grave.

In those seven years the half blind elder daughter grew resilient and resourceful with a will and drive stronger than that of any man. She took the reins, commanded respect and became a legend amongst the hill folk, earning the honorary title of La Contessa di Montagna, whilst Gino's mother simply fell in love, wishing for nothing more than a peaceful life with the American soldier she had fallen for.

Nate considered all this information, then eventually asked, "So your aunt's not really a countess?"

"No," replied Gino, "It's just an honourary name that everyone calls her - 'The Countess of the Mountains' - and her clan, our family, are known as 'I lupi di montagna' - 'The Mountain Wolves' - all because of her and the respect she has earned."

"But who is she then, if not a contessa?"

"At heart, just a country girl who defied the odds to become the woman you met today. But our family name is 'Tartaglia.'"

"And her name?"

"Lucia." Gino said. "Her name is Lucia Tartaglia."

Chapter Twenty Five

Manhattan, New York, 1966

Salvatore Falcone had not thought of Lucia Tartaglia in a very long time.

For many years he thought about her almost daily; that last mental picture he had in his mind of her laying there on the dusty ground, her blouse ripped open and her naked breasts exposed, blood pouring from the gash in her forehead and the delicious knowledge he had just stolen her virginity.

It excited him, titillated him, but then as he grew older, enjoyed many more sexual encounters, the memory of her faded. But today, looking out of his temporary bedroom window at the brownstone, run by Nona Rosa, on the Upper West Side, he saw a dark haired girl of around thirteen who reminded him very much of Lucia.

The girl was playing with her hula hoop in the street below; her youthful body just blossoming into womanhood, just like the girl from the hills south of Rome whom he had desired so when he was just a boy.

Salvatore's excitement grew at the thought of her and as the bedroom drapes flapped casually in the growing breeze he hurriedly slid down his zipper and jerked off. His pleasure made all the more intense as he

spied on the girl just a few feet below his open window. He

watched her salaciously, his dark eyes playing over her small, immature breasts, imagining they belonged to Lucia, whom he had left for dead all those years ago.

His excitement building, he gasped loudly with unbridled exhilaration, startling the young girl who looked up to see Salvatore's face, contorted with rapturous delight, looking down upon her, but she was unaware of what was happening below the window sill, beyond her vision.

Falcone's cheeks were flushed and his eyes were bulging as he stared back at the girl.

Then it was over.

Salvatore emitted a loud, animalistic growl of enormous gratification as he grinned at the girl with evil delight.

Her scared young eyes met his and Salvatore took yet another mental picture, knowing her image, the sight of her innocent face, would stay with him forever, much like Lucia's had.

Briefly, he wondered if Lucia had lived or died but he was indifferent either way and the thought soon passed. It mattered not.

Then he looked on unabashed as the young girl, clearly creeped out by the sight of his leery face staring back at her, quickly picked up her hula hoop and ran off back to the safety of home.

A moment later Frankie called him from the bottom of the stairs, snapping her from his gaze.

He looked at his watch then hurriedly zipped himself up, before sliding on his jacket and heading out of the room.

Lucia Tartaglia was once again forgotten.

***

Ava was already in the car waiting when Salvatore and Frankie eventually came out; Frankie carrying Falcone's cases - finally he was going home and Ava would be free at last.

Frankie would drop her off at school first before taking Salvatore to LaGuardia where he was due to fly back to LA later that

343

morning. When she got home that night he would thankfully be gone.

The morning traffic seemed heavier than usual and it seemed like an eternity before the car eventually pulled up next to the curb beside the 114th Street entrance to the college. It was raining hard now, the heavens had opened shortly after they left the brownstone and Ava had neglected to bring either a coat or an umbrella but she was anxious to get out of the car, eager to be rid of Salvatore as soon as possible.

"Okay, bye then, safe trip!" She cried, rather too cheerfully, as she made a grab for the door handle.

"Whoa! Hold on there, young lady!" Salvatore said. "Just wait. I've got an umbrella, I'll take you in."

Ava's heart sank. "No, please - I'll be fine - you don't want to miss your flight."

"Nonsense. I've got plenty of time. And I must insist. After all, I must say goodbye to you properly."

Ava felt sick. Even now, in these last moments, she still could not be rid of him. But she knew it was futile to protest. "Fine," she said flatly, "Get all wet. It's up to you."

"Indeed," replied Falcone with a grin as he hopped out of the car and hurried to the trunk.

A moment later he appeared at the window next to Ava, a large black umbrella raised above his head. He popped open the door, "Please, my dear, allow me," he said.

Ava grabbed her bag and slid out. Salvatore slipped his arm around her waist and held the umbrella over her. "See, that's much better, isn't it?" He said lasciviously.

"Maybe for you," Ava muttered as the pair of them scurried across the sidewalk in the pouring rain.

***

Danny was running late. Delores was fussing round him,

trying to ensure he ate at least one of the bagels she had just toasted for him. "You growing boy," she said, her Spanish accent still strong, "you need eat, keep up strength."

"I'm fine, Del," he replied, trying to manoeuvre around her, reaching for his leather jacket that was hanging on the back of one of the kitchen chairs. "If I don't go now I'm gonna be late for class!"

"You still must eat - teacher understand."

"No, Del, he won't - he doesn't care if I starve. I gotta go."

As a dejected Delores wandered off to the back of the kitchen, holding the plate of bagels and muttering something about the teacher being 'stupid man' under her breath, Maria walked in.

She was 35 now yet still just as beautiful as the day Danny first set eyes on her nine years earlier.

She wore her hair slightly shorter nowadays in a long, straight 'bob' yet her clothes were as stylish as ever. Today she was wearing a short, plaid mini dress and a pair of black patent loafers. She entered through the kitchen door pulling on a shiny red macintosh, taking in the familiar scene instantly. "Danny, eat a bagel, Delores made them especially for you - don't worry about the time, I'm going into the city so Max can drop you off - you won't be late."

"But Mom—"

"No 'buts' Delores is right, you've got to eat."

Delores raced back to the table triumphantly holding the plate of bagels as Danny slumped into a chair and reluctantly took one.

"Good boy. I love you," said Maria, running her fingers through her son's thick, black hair before proudly kissing him on the top of his head.

"You eat. I'll tell Max to bring the car around," she said, crossing to the phone hanging on the wall.

***

A short time later, Max smoothly tucked the limo in next to the sidewalk on Broadway, just a short dash through the rain along

College Walk from the Morningside campus, to drop Danny out. He and his mother were sitting in the back. "See?" Maria said, "Made it all safe and sound - and right on time."

"Yeah. That's cool, Mom, thanks for the lift," Danny said before adding, "Thanks, Max - don't know what I'd have done without you!"

"My pleasure, Master Daniel," the chauffeur replied, waving a gloved hand as he looked at him through the rear view mirror.

"See you tonight, Mom," Danny said, kissing his mother on the cheek before opening the door onto the soaking wet sidewalk.

"Bye, sweetheart!" Maria said as her son jumped out into the pouring rain, "And no more fighting!" She added hopefully, just as he slammed the door.

***

Annoyingly, Salvatore had insisted on accompanying Ava all the way to the Low Library where she had arranged to meet her friend, Susan, who she could see waiting there for her as they ran up the steps and hurried for shelter under the library's ornately columned facade.

Susan Porter was a strikingly pretty girl with dark brown, almost black skin which she had inherited from her Ugandan mother. Her father was a blonde haired, pale skinned doctor from Oklahoma whose brains she had been gifted with along with his blue eyes, which gave her a stunning appearance. Long and lithe with short 'ironed' hair, she was Ava's best friend and together the pair looked like runway models.

Yet Salvatore did not approve of Ava's dark skinned friend and knew her father would not either. "Why do you wanna be so cosy with that nigger bitch for?" He sneered, almost within ear shot of Susan.

"Because she's my best friend and I love her and it's none of your damn business who I like or don't like - okay?" Ava snapped, shrugging out of his hold on her and turning to face him angrily.

346

"Sure, okay, it's up to you." He replied, shaking the rain off his umbrella, "Just don't say I didn't warn you when she turns on you like all wild animals eventually do."

"You're a racist pig, you know that?" Ava spat with disgust.

"Hey, what did I say? I told the truth, that's all - you see if I'm wrong."

"Bye, Salvatore," she said, stepping away from him. "See you whenever."

"Ava, please, don't be like that. Please, give me a kiss, let me say goodbye properly."

"Not a chance - I'm a big girl now, all grown up," she said, by now half way between Falcone and Susan, "That means I get to do what I want. Goodbye Salvatore - safe flight!"

Salvatore knew there was no way to get her back. He had missed his last moment of intimacy with her, his last opportunity to taste her, at least for the time being, but other opportunities would present themself in due course, he would just have to be patient. And perhaps then they would be alone.

"Very well, Ava. Ciao. I'll see you again soon, I promise!" He said, turning to walk away.

"I really hope not," Ava said under her breath to Susan who giggled complicity as her friend arrived with her.

"Don't say I didn't warn you!" Falcone shouted without looking back, "Never trust a wild animal!"

"What does he mean by that?" Susan queried.

"Nothing," said Ava quickly, "he's just being stupid, that's all."

***

As Danny rushed through the main quad, the collar of his leather jacket turned up, trying without much success to dodge the rain, he was completely oblivious to the man hurrying past him in the opposite direction. The same man he had nearly come to blows with a couple of weeks earlier.

The sinister looking Italian with the black gloved hand had been accompanying the girl, Ava, who Danny had not been able to forget.

Over the past two weeks he had been looking out for her, desperately hoping to see her again, but so far his efforts had been fruitless. Nevertheless, he was not one to be easily put off and resolved to keep on looking.

There was just something about her, and ridiculous as he knew it was, he felt they had made an instant connection. He sensed she felt it too. Or maybe that was just wishful thinking.

Blind faith was more Nate's department whereas Danny preferred to work only with the facts.

And the fact was, he really liked this girl.

***

Salvatore had his head down and the umbrella held at an angle in front of him to deflect the driving rain as he headed back to the limo parked out on the street. He, too, had failed to notice his antagonist from two weeks earlier as Danny dashed by, hurrying to his lecture.

Indeed, Salvatore was too lost in his thoughts of home and getting back to dry, sunny California to notice anybody. The changeable New York weather, and particularly the confines of the cool, damp brownstone were no good for his health. Even in just the short time he had been staying there he could already feel a growing looseness in his chest, fearing the pleurisy that had plagued him some years ago might make an unwelcome return if he stayed on the East Coast any longer.

He coughed at the thought, glad that it was time to finally be going home.

But he had concluded the business he had come here for.

Even though the trip had been made on Carlo's orders, ostensibly to see Ava successfully ensconced at the college, Salvatore

348

had also managed to find the time to iron out the wrinkles in his arrangement with Bruno Barca.

Barca operated out of Brooklyn and had ties to one of the smaller families, but he was keen to make his own mark, be his own man, and had seen an opportunity to earn a huge amount of money.

He had drafted in Salvatore to run things out West and things had been going well, very well, for the last few years.

But Barca had grown cocky and had developed a taste for his own product; it had made him sloppy and careless, his eye not often enough on the ball and Salvatore had to straighten him out.

Barca had been great at sourcing the merchandise and had been instrumental in their initial success but recently he had let things slide, allowing shipments to run late and quantities to be inaccurately accounted for.

It would not do.

Salvatore cared little about who Barca sourced his merchandise from; these so called 'Mountain Wolves', who were apparently so mysterious and secretive.

But no matter how clandestine their operation seemed to be, they were not the problem.

From what he could ascertain, their shipments to Barca were as regular as clockwork and accurate to the very last gram, so there was no point in Falcone airing his grievances to them - even if he knew who to approach, which he did not.

No, it was Bruno who was the problem. And it was he with whom Salvatore had shared his concerns.

Falcone had turned up on Bruno's doorstep unexpectedly in the early hours of the morning.

Barca, short and portly and sporting a long gold medallion, had answered the door in his under shorts and an open silk robe. Under his nose he had two days growth of stubble and a significant amount of white powder, leaving Salvatore to draw the conclusion his business partner had once again been sampling their merchandise.

By the time Falcone left Barca's home, some eight hours later, Bruno had no doubts about how seriously Salvatore took their partnership and was under no illusion about what would happen if he let things slide again.

Nonetheless, in arriving at that conclusion, Bruno had lost both his little fingers and the whore who had been sharing the copious amounts of cocaine found in Barca's bedroom had been gutted and left to bleed out on the silk sheets of his bed.

Suffice to say, Bruno Barca had been brought back into line and Salvatore did not envisage any further problems from him again.

Falcone smiled at how rich he was becoming, without Carlo's aid or, indeed, his knowledge and the satisfaction it gave him was immense.

He was in a self-congratulatory mood as he trotted across the pavement, through the rain, and round to the back of the waiting car without paying attention to the oncoming traffic. As he blindly lowered the umbrella he suddenly heard the blast of a horn and a screech of brakes. Falcone turned, quickly, bracing himself for impact, only to see another limo pull up sharply mere inches away from him.

Salvatore banged down on the car's immaculately waxed hood, "Hey, buddy! Watch where you're fucking going!" He yelled at the peak-capped chauffeur driving.

The chauffeur leaned on the horn again. He then made a hand gesture and shouted something that Salvatore could not hear, before pulling out into the traffic once more.

Salvatore banged on the front passenger door as the limo passed by, then stared into the blacked out side window of the rear passenger door to see if he could get a glimpse of whoever was sitting in back. But all he could see was his own evil reflection scowling angrily back at him.

Maria watched Danny sprinting away through the rain for a moment. He really was so dashing, just like Armando had been; tall, handsome and a killer smile. She was so proud of him, so proud of both her boys.

Absently, she fingered the locket that hung around her neck; the very same one she had left tucked in the hollowed out bible for Danny to find - which had found its way, along with her lost son, safely back to her, many years later. *Always and Forever.*

She wore it now as a mark of respect to Megan and the children she had entrusted to her safe keeping. In one side there was a picture of Diego, her saviour, her husband, the man she loved with all her heart and in the other was a photograph of Megan; the woman who had raised and cared for her son as if he were her own.

Maria was now fulfilling the same role for her and it was a privilege - and the locket reminded her of that.

She thought of Nate, wondering if Megan would have approved of her allowing him to go to the American Seminary in Rome, and came to the conclusion that she would. Maria had pondered this question many times in the past, as had Diego, and both had agreed it was right for him to fulfil his dream of becoming a priest and were confident Megan would feel the same way.

But Maria missed him. She also felt that Danny seemed somehow incomplete without him. His brother's departure had hit him the hardest, hence his mildly delinquent behaviour, namely the fighting which, Maria knew, was just his way of coping with Nate's absence.

But Danny was a battler and, given time, he would get by just fine.

"Just a moment, Max," she said, as her driver prepared to move off.

"Sure thing, Ma'am," he replied, placing the limo back in park as he watched Maria in his rear view mirror rummaging about in her purse, the locket hanging freely once more.

She found her compact and popped it open, holding its tiny mirror in front of her face as she applied a fresh coat of glossy red lipstick.

After studying her handiwork for a second, she snapped the compact shut and returned it to her purse. "Okay, Max," she said, "I'm presentable once more, let's get going."

"You got it, Mrs Del Toro," he replied, chuckling slightly, knowing Maria was never anything less than absolutely perfect - at least in his humble opinion.

He indicated, shifted gears, then slipped smoothly out into the traffic. A few moments later he turned off Broadway and onto West 114th, heading towards Amsterdam.

It was still raining hard and the limo's wipers were doing their best to cope with the downpour, but visibility was at a minimum and Max was having to concentrate hard in order to navigate through the traffic.

Then, out of nowhere, some idiot carrying an umbrella stepped out into the road without looking where he was going, forcing Max to jam on the breaks.

Maria, who had just begun to read the morning paper, was suddenly thrust forward in her seat as Max braked abruptly and blasted the horn.

"Sorry, Ma'am, are you okay?" Her driver asked quickly.

"Yes. Fine, fine. Thank you," she replied, looking up to see what on earth had happened.

Maria saw a man with an umbrella standing in front of the car, he was banging on the hood and shouting something inaudible.

Then, as she looked at his angry face, she was suddenly filled with horror.

Immediately her mind flashed back eighteen years to that

fateful train journey in Italy and her desperate fight with the loathsome creep who had succeeded in ejecting her from the it.

She had hoped never to see the man again; prayed that by some miracle he might even be dead.

But now she was staring at him once more.

Max shouted something at him in return but Maria was too shocked to register what he had said, unable to tear her eyes away and oblivious to all distractions.

As the car started to move once more, the man banged on the passenger door and then glared angrily into the side window, seeming to look directly at Maria, staring into her very soul.

She could not quite believe what she was seeing. But there could be no mistake.

It was Salvatore Falcone, in the flesh.

Chapter Twenty Six

Danny was sitting alone on the steps of the Low Library during lunchtime recess, studying the notes he had made in his morning lecture, trying to decipher his hastily written scrawl and not having much luck.

Unfortunately he would have to go back to the professor later and beg him to run through the pertinent points again - it would not go down well but it would be better to get a reprimand than to fail.

Recently, he had not been able to concentrate on much of anything. Firstly there was Nate; he just could not help but keep wondering how his brother was fairing in Rome. And then, just when he was getting used to life without him, he met Ava - and now he could think of little else other than her.

He had found himself daydreaming throughout much of the lecture; thinking about her once more, curious as to where she was. Surely she was around somewhere, she just had to be.

The sun was shining now, after the heavy downpour of earlier, and the sky was a clear blue once more. Danny was sitting there in a T-shirt and faded Levis; the short sleeves of his shirt rolled up to allow his muscular biceps to tan in the glorious sunshine.

He looked good, like a young movie star, which did little to dispel his growing reputation as the campus heart throb; a fact which was not altogether lost on him. But he didn't play on it. Much.

However, although there was always a string of girls eager to catch his eye, Danny was only interested in one. Yet she was proving to be something of an enigma.

He took the stubby pencil from his mouth and scribbled a few notes on a pad; things he needed to ask the professor, once again berating himself for allowing his mind to wander so during the lecture. He had always been a good student and a quick study but the last few weeks he'd let things slide a little and he knew he must not allow himself to be distracted any more.

Just as he thought that, a shadow appeared over him, darkening the glare of the bright, white paper of his note pad.

He looked up and was amazed to see Ava standing there.

"Hello, Danny. Remember me?" She said cheerfully.

"Sure," he replied, pleasantly surprised yet giving no outward indication that his heart rate had just risen ten fold. "It's er—". He pretended not to remember, trying to play it cool. "Amy, isn't it?"

"Ava," she prompted, slightly disappointed her name had not stuck in his memory.

"That's right. Ava. Sorry. How are you?"

"Great, thanks. This is my friend, Susan," she said, pointing to her companion.

"Hi, Susan."

"Hi, Danny," Susan said knowingly, having heard all about him many, many times from Ava. He was not a disappointment and was exactly as billed - indeed a small part of her wished she had spotted him first. "Good to meet you."

"You, too. Please, siddown."

The two girls readily did as invited. Ava was in a sleeveless purple blouse with dark pink pedal pushers and Susan was dressed similarly but in yellow and orange.

"What's that you're doing?" Asked Ava, nestling in close and peering over his shoulder.

"Ah, this. Nothing, not really. Just trying to decipher my notes from Professor Gordon's lecture - I was kinda distracted."

"His lecture this morning?"

"Uh huh, why?"

"I was there, too. You can borrow my notes if you like."

"You were there? I didn't see you. I looked all over but—" Suddenly he realised he had given himself away and his mouth cracked into wide grin.

Ava smiled sweetly. "You did, huh?"

"Mmm hmm," He said, guiltily, slightly embarrassed.

"Looked all over, you say?"

"Everywhere." He confessed, staring into her lovely face and breathing in her delicious perfume.

"Yet you had trouble remembering my name? That can't be right can it? Very curious indeed," she teased.

"Okay, okay," Danny held up his hands in defeat. "You got me - I've been looking for you all over. Ever since we met - I just— I dunno, I guess I thought we just kinda clicked."

"Clicked?" Now it was Ava's turn to be embarrassed and her cheeks coloured a little. "Really?"

"Yeah. I guess. I hope?"

Again Ava smiled. She looked truly beautiful - even more so than Danny remembered. "Me, too." She said.

Suddenly Susan coughed and stood up, reminding them both she was still there. "Hey, listen, Ava - I, er, just remembered. I've gotta go do that thing, you know, and meet, er, that guy," she struggled, trying desperately to find an excuse to leave them alone.

"Oh, er, yeah. Of course. I remember. You've got to meet Whatsername. Sure. Okay. Want me to come?"

"No. No. It's no big deal. I'll catch you later. You stay here. I'll be fine."

"Sure?"

"Positive."

"Okay. If that's alright with you, Danny?" Asked Ava a little too casually.

"Hey. No problem," Danny smiled.

"Great. Nice to meet you then, Danny," Susan said, backing away down the stone steps. "See you later, Ava."

"Yeah, okay. See you later, Sue - thanks!"

Danny watched Susan skip down the steps and scamper away across the quad, allowing her to get well out of ear shot before he finally turned to Ava and said, *"Whatsername*, huh?"

She giggled prettily, knowing her and Susan's ploy had been rumbled. "Yeah, Whatsername. He's a good guy. You should meet him."

He laughed. "Yeah. I'd like that."

Ava looked at him, still giggling, he really was handsome - every bit as good looking as she remembered. "So, you want my notes, huh?"

"If that's okay?"

"Sure it is."

"Tell you what then," he said, gazing into her big, blue eyes, "What are you doing this afternoon?"

"Nothing really. I haven't got any classes - I was just gonna go to Susan's apartment to study, that's all. Why?"

"Well, I'm free, too. How 'bout we just go to the park, enjoy the sunshine and talk a little, maybe get a soda? Then, later, you can let me have those notes. How's that sound?"

She smiled. "Sound's great. "Let's go."

***

Three hours later they were sitting in a small diner across from Central Park having spent a blissful afternoon together.

First, they had just strolled for a while around the park, chatting casually, getting to know one another, gently flirting and thoroughly enjoying themselves.

Then they planted themselves under the shade of a tall tree and talked some more as they watched the world go by. It was idyllic, they fitted together well and found themselves very comfortable with each other, almost as if they had been friends for years.

But there was an underlying pull, a natural magnetism and neither could keep their eyes off the other.

After a while, they lay side by side on their stomachs as Ava went through her lecture notes with Danny. Their shoulders were touching as she explained everything but both of them were finding it hard to concentrate as the chemistry sparked between them; a frisson of excitement accompanying every gesture, every movement that brought their lips closer together.

But they did not kiss, no matter how much each of them longed for the taste of the other.

There was no rush, they had all the time in the world. Nature would inevitably take its course. For now they were content to just get to know each other.

Both felt instinctively that this was the beginning of something meaningful, something long lasting, so there was no need to force it.

It was going to happen, of that they were both certain.

After the park, they took another gentle stroll and somehow it seemed natural for Danny to take Ava's hand.

They made a strikingly handsome couple as they wandered along the busy street, several people even turning their heads to stare at them as if they were a pair of movie stars. But they were just Danny and Ava, two unknowing kids on the cusp of love.

Eventually they found their way to the small diner; the conversation having slowed now into an easy silence, the electricity between them, the overwhelming attraction, almost palpable.

They eyed each other silently as the waitress delivered their ice cream sodas. Even the waitress could sense the heat between them and she smiled knowingly. "Enjoy", she said with a smirk, as she headed off to the next booth but they were almost oblivious to her presence.

They reached for their sodas in unison, each taking a long, refreshing gulp from the candy-striped straws. Their eyes still locked together.

"So," Ava finally said, taking another sip of her soda, "What is it your parents do?"

"Good question." Danny replied. "The answer's 'a lot', I guess, but mainly hotels - you've heard of the Matador chain, right?"

"Mmm hmm", she replied, sucking seductively on her straw.

"Well that's my dad."

"He works for them?"

"Well, not exactly. He kinda is them. It's his company - started by his father before him."

"Wow!"

"I know. Far out, huh?"

"Yeah, really. And your mom? What does she do?"

"I guess she kinda works with my dad - but mainly she just looks after my brother and me."

"You gotta a brother, too?"

"Yeah, Nate. You'd like him, he's a good guy."

"I'm sure. So you and Nate were a couple of lucky kids then, huh? From a fairly privileged background?"

Danny smiled. "I guess. Well, sort of. It's a long story and I'll tell you about it another time but no, we weren't always so lucky."

"Hmm, intriguing," Ava said. "And a little mysterious. I look forward to finding out more."

Danny continued to smile but there was a wistfulness behind his eyes as he thought about his early days in Hell's Kitchen. Things really had worked out well for him and Nate when they could so easily have gone dreadfully wrong. Who would have thought back then he'd end up going to Columbia University or that Nate would ever be able to go study in Rome.

They had been very fortunate indeed and had a lot to be thankful for.

But he did not want to get into it with Ava now, there would be plenty of time in the future to give her all the details.

"So, Ava Peyton from California," he said, diverting attention from himself. "What about you. What about your folks, what do they do?"

Now it was Ava's turn to smile wistfully. "Another long story, I'm afraid," she said. "My dad died when I was nine—"

"Oh, I'm sorry—"

"No. It's okay. I like to talk about him. He was a lovely, sweet guy. Really kind and gentle - a good father. You'd have liked him, I'm sure - and he you."

"Hey, if he was like you then—"

Ava smiled again, warmly this time, "Yeah, I suppose he was - at least a bit, I guess."

"And your mom? Is she still around?"

Ava thought back to the last time she saw Mildred, regretting now starting this line of conversation and not even knowing where to begin to describe the hell her mother was living in.

"Yes," she said finally. "She lives in California with my step-father."

"Your step-father?" Danny asked. "That guy I saw you with a couple of weeks ago? If that was him then I'm sorry, I didn't mean—"

"No. Not him." Ava said unintentionally sharply. "He just works for my step-father. His name is Salvatore Falcone."

Danny recognised the name but he was too wrapped up in Ava for it to fully register. It sounded familiar but that was all.

"I think I've heard of him before," he said. "Is he well known?"

"I don't know. Maybe. My step-father is though - you might

have heard of him."

"Really? What does he do?" Danny asked taking a sip of his soda.

"He owns a studio out in Hollywood - Gold Star Pictures. His name is Carlo. Carlo Liuzzi."

At hearing the name Danny nearly choked on his soda and started coughing violently. He could not believe it.

Suddenly the name 'Salvatore Falcone' made sense too - he was the man who had tried to kill his mother, Maria.

And Carlo Liuzzi was Danny's own grandfather - the same person who had killed his father; killed Nate's father, too, and sentenced Maria to a life of enforced seclusion in a Sicilian convent.

He had even tried his hardest to make Danny, himself, disappear.

He was responsible for everything his mother and Megan had been through - leaving Maria in a coma and Megan in poverty.

Carlo Liuzzi was the devil.

And he was Ava's step-father.

Danny felt his gorge rise. He was going to be sick. If he did not get some air he was going to throw up right there in the diner.

"Danny?" Ava asked, suddenly worried, seeing the colour drain from his face as the coughing fit finally subsided. "Are you okay?"

"No. Sorry," he spluttered in reply, feeling most unwell. Utterly appalled by what he had just heard and finding it almost too much to comprehend. How could she possibly be the step-daughter of such a vile, evil monster. "I- I- I've gotta go, sorry - I don't feel well. I'm gonna be sick."

"Oh, no. Oh dear. Do you want me to come with—"

"No! He snapped, struggling to his feet. "I'll be fine. I'll see you at school."

He rolled out of the booth they had been sharing, throwing a handful of dollars down onto the table top as he hastily made a getaway, barging open the door of the diner and spilling out onto the street; feeling faint with shock.

He stuck out an arm and hailed a taxi. Almost instantly one drew up beside him and he bundled himself quickly inside.

Ava stood staring after him, completely bemused, wondering what on earth was wrong as she watched the taxi speed off taking Danny away from her.

***

Maria was frantic. After seeing Falcone that morning she had cancelled her plans and returned immediately to the Greyling Building, where she had been pacing the floor restlessly for most of the day fretting about what she should do.

She had also been extremely anxious about Danny and prayed he would arrive home safely.

Diego was in California and would not be back until the following afternoon. She had phoned his office but he was in meetings all day; she would not be able to speak with him until that evening at the earliest.

Maria had determinedly put the past behind her for the sake of her boys, putting them first and denying her thirst for vengeance.

However, in doing so she had stupidly assumed them all to be secure, living their lives in the cocooned bubble of New York, far away from her father and Falcone on the West Coast.

But all that imagined security had come crashing down this morning.

Staring into the eyes of Salvatore Falcone she knew, without doubt they were no longer safe.

Danny was in danger. Her beautiful, precious son must have passed within mere feet of the man who would have so happily killed him all those years ago. Indeed, she, herself, had nearly died by his hand and it was only thanks to Diego that she had somehow, miraculously, survived.

But what was Salvatore doing right beside Danny's university campus? Was he looking for her boy? Had he and her father finally discovered their existence after all this time?

Why else would he have been there otherwise?

Nonetheless, regardless of those questions, it did not alter the fact that up until this morning she had successfully managed to put Carlo Liuzzi and Salvatore Falcone to the back of her mind. She had forcibly removed them from her thoughts so her memory of them did not taint the rest of her life.

But now they were suddenly back at the forefront of her mind and Maria knew she had to act quickly in order to evade them and save Danny.

Over the last few hours she had been racking her brains trying to come up with some sort of workable solution to their situation and at last she thought she had. But it was by no means ideal and went against all her instincts to fight; to claim the vengeance that was rightfully hers - but she had to put her son first. His continued safety was paramount, yet she felt certain the solution she had conceived would not sit well with him either.

But, for now, it was the only way.

***

Danny all but fell into the rotunda as the elevator doors pinged open. He looked dreadful as he staggered, drunk-like, across the marble floor of the apartment's grand foyer. He was still in shock; he just could not believe it. The girl, who just a few hours earlier he believed might be 'the one', had turned out to be the step-daughter of the man his whole family hated most in all the world.

And with very good reason.

He and Ava had genuinely made a connection. They had something - or the makings of it at least and on the strength of just one afternoon with her, he could easily believe they were made for each other - even though such romantic hogwash was not normally his thing.

Nevertheless, there was a definite spark and who knew where it might have led.

But now he would never have the chance to find out.

He could never be with her, not now, not in a million years; the step-daughter of Carlo Liuzzi, his reviled grandfather - how on earth could he.

It sickened him that he unwittingly got so close - and it made him feel worse that he could still not get Ava out of his thoughts even now.

Yet he had to. For his sake, his mother's sake and for Nate's too.

But if he saw her again his resolve would weaken, he was sure of it and that would be fatal.

Danny was a strong, determined and resolute young man but where Ava was concerned, when he thought about her beautiful face and those big, blue eyes, he knew his will might easily crumble.

But if Salvatore Falcone discovered who he was, indeed if word got back to Danny's grandfather that he was alive and well and living in New York, it would put all their lives in jeopardy.

Danny had already had one run in with Falcone and had been fortunate to get away with it but he might not be so lucky a second time.

And the only possible cause for that would be Ava.

For that reason alone he could not allow himself to see her ever again - but that would not be so simple when they both attended the same college - even some of the same lectures.

Danny's head was swimming, he could not think straight but he knew, no matter how much it would hurt, that the only solution was for him to leave Columbia.

***

Maria was standing in the apartment's large, spacious living room staring out of its tall windows at the stunning Manhattan

364

skyline but she was not seeing it, not really, as her mind was lost in her thoughts.

Only when she heard the elevator doors open did she snap out of her trance and rush quickly from the room, desperately hoping that her boy was home.

As she entered the foyer she saw Danny standing there and her relief was immediate. But as she looked closer she saw that he appeared to be ill. He was pale and breathing heavily as if trying to prevent himself from being sick.

He looked up at her, his eyes red and brimming with emotion.

"What's the matter, my darling?" Asked Maria, hurrying to his side, "What's happened - are you okay?"

"No, Mom. I'm not," he replied, his voice heavy with sadness. "I gotta leave college, I gotta get away - we've gotta get away—"

"Why, what's—"

"It's Falcone, Mom. Salvatore Falcone is here in New York—"

Maria felt a stab in the chest at the mention of his name. 'Oh, God,' she thought, the panic rising within her, 'what's happened, has he harmed Danny in some way?'

"—He's in Manhattan." Danny said. "There's a girl I know, who I met at school, her name's Ava Peyton, turns out Falcone's her—" suddenly Danny's voice left him, he could speak no more. The truth about Ava still too shocking to even talk about.

"He's here for the girl - this 'Ava' - and not for you?" Maria pressed.

Danny nodded.

"You're sure?"

He nodded again. "Positive."

"But are you okay? Has he hurt you?"

Danny shook his head and gasped, "I'm fine. I'm alright. But he's here Mom - he's here!"

Maria's thoughts were racing, wondering how her son found

out this information and if he, himself, had been discovered as a result of it. "I know," she said. "I saw him this morning with my own eyes, I couldn't believe it. I've been so worried about you all day - praying he hadn't seen you. Hadn't hurt you."

"It's okay - he doesn't know who I am. Not yet anyway. But if I stay at college any longer he will, I know he will." What Danny did not say was that if he stayed at college he would also find it too hard to keep away from Ava and he could not allow that to happen.

"I know," Maria replied. "I've been thinking the same thing myself - it's the only solution. We'll get away for a while - go live somewhere else—"

"I'll get a job - maybe go work with Dad—"

"No, honey. You need to finish school. Finish your education and graduate—"

"But I thought you just said you agreed with me - that I can't stay at school—"

"I said you can't stay at *that* school. Not all schools."

"You mean transfer?"

"Uh huh. I've been making a few calls, trying to keep my mind busy and off Salvatore Falcone - I think we can get you moved pretty quickly - maybe even as early as next week—"

"But where? What college?"

"How do you like the sound of Harvard?"

Danny looked at her surprised. "Harvard? Are you sure?"

"Mmm hmm. I've spoken to the Dean of Admissions and yeah, I think you're pretty much a shoe-in - you just gotta go for an interview, talk to them a little and tell them about yourself. But your grades speak for themselves. They'd be lucky to have you. The Dean thinks so too."

Danny thought for a moment. Harvard had been one of his top three picks but he had chosen Columbia because of its Manhattan location, yet he'd always wondered if it was the correct decision.

366

He looked at his mother, feeling immediately brighter."Harvard, huh?" He said.

***

Ava could not understand it.

She and Danny had got on so well; they'd had a wonderful afternoon together in the park.

There was a definite spark, she felt, and was certain he had felt it too. She went to bed that evening with a warm feeling in her stomach, a contented, happy feeling, the early stirrings, she had thought, of love.

She was, of course, troubled by his swift departure from the diner; his quick disappearance and his apparent ill health. But she had convinced herself it was nothing more, perhaps, than a tummy bug, or even a touch of food poisoning - she certainly had no idea that she would never see him again.

She had waited on the steps of the Low Library every lunchtime for a fortnight, hoping he might turn up. But he had not and eventually she had to concede he never would.

It was a mystery to her why he had vanished and after finding out his address, she had tried calling his apartment several times but there had been no reply. Eventually, rather desperately, she and Susan had taken a cab to the Greyling Building to see if they could actually see him but they had been told by the doorman that Danny Del Toro was no longer in residence and had given no indication as to when he might return.

Ava had been distraught. She thought she had done something wrong, was convinced she had said something, done something to upset him. Then she started to wonder if the sickness he was suffering from in the diner was something much more serious and that maybe he'd had to leave because of it.

That made her worry even more. She hoped he was okay, that he was going to survive - but she just did not know what to think as she had no clue as to why he had disappeared.

Then Susan had found out through an intern who was working in college admissions that Danny was no longer listed as a student at Columbia and had, in fact, transferred to Harvard.

So he was not ill. There was nothing wrong with him at all. He had just left. As simple as that. With no word, no goodbye, no reason or explanation. He had just gone.

Ava could not claim to know Danny, not well at least. But it did seem out of character for the boy she had fallen for on that glorious afternoon in the park.

But she had clearly misread him. Obviously her judgment of his character, of his intentions, were completely wide of the mark and it made her feel angry. He made her feel angry.

But she also felt dreadfully upset and hideously bereft. It was stupid, she knew, after just one blissful afternoon, but she liked him. She really liked him and she had been convinced he liked her, too.

It would take Ava many months to get over Danny Del Toro, many more before she could even look at another boy as he had left her feeling completely broken.

But fortunately Susan was there to help pick up the pieces.

Chapter Twenty Seven

Carlo Liuzzi had been very busy with studio business whilst Salvatore had been in New York.

Gold Star had several big budget pictures scheduled for Christmas release and had an enormous amount of money invested in them - and even more riding on their success.

Poor box office receipts would hit the studio hard, not to mention Carlo personally who had also sunk a large amount of his own personal wealth into them.

One was a big-budget animated picture; something of a departure for Gold Star who, for the first time would be competing for the 'family friendly' market that was traditionally more Disney's fare.

Another was a hugely expensive sci-fi flick - all special effects, with hundreds of hours and thousands of dollars spent on stop-motion animation for the many monsters and space creatures that featured heavily in the storyline. However, it had run way over budget and had overshot its deadline by over two months. It had originally been scheduled as a big summer release but was now being re-marketed for Christmas.

Thirdly, a sumptuous costume drama was in the final stages of post-production; a big, swashbuckling pirate movie which featured thousands of extras, grandiose locations, fabulous sets and a wardrobe department that had worked almost constantly twenty-four-hour a day to keep up with the gruelling schedule in order to achieve the all-important Christmas release.

Numerous other movies were in various stages of production throughout the huge Gold Star lot so it was an incredibly stressful time for Carlo personally, who was walking a tightrope between making the best possible pictures for the lowest possible price - whilst all the time hoping for the highest possible returns.

To make matters worse, he had been locked in a pitched battle with a rival studio for the rights to a red hot screenplay entitled *Streets of Blood*, which was a Mafia crime saga - a genre which Carlo had first hand knowledge of.

He was desperate for the opportunity to tell the tale, knowing he could do it justice, and had even gone to visit the writer personally to demonstrate just how important his screenplay was.

However, Carlo's enthusiasm had got the better of him and when the writer did not immediately agree to sell him the rights, Carlo got nasty and threatened the poor man.

Needless to say, the writer had decided to go with Viscount Studios and not Gold Star Pictures.

This made Carlo furious and he flew into a rage that lasted the best part of a week.

He hated Viscount; hated the suavely intellectual Spaniard who owned it - who breezed into town twice a month in his private jet before jetting off somewhere else in the world to look after his chain of over-priced hotels.

It made Carlo sick. This was Hollywood, a town run by movie men, not hoteliers, so what right did that fucking spick have to own a goddamn studio in the first place.

The irony that Carlo was both an immigrant and an unlikely movie boss himself was completely lost on him.

But Diego Del Toro was not the only executive he despised at

Viscount. He also had no time for the little Jew who ran the place in Del Toro's absence who, Carlo was loathed to admit, was doing an exceptional job.

Herb Horowitz was a movie man. He had been in the business for years and had worked his way up the ladder to become one of the most successful and respected players in Hollywood. Small, bald and chubby with a big nose and huge black-framed spectacles, Herb had been hand-picked by Diego to run Viscount for him, luring the sixty year old away from a very lucrative, very comfortable role at Paramount.

Diego had promised much and, so far, had delivered on everything. In return, Herb had taken Viscount, which had been struggling amongst growing competition for many years, and built it into something truly impressive. In just a few short years Horowitz had reversed the studio's flagging fortunes as Diego knew he would, although, in fairness, much of the credit belonged to Diego, too, whose original vision was nothing short of genius.

Viscount was now on the crest of a wave with numerous awards to its credit and many of the world's most profitable movies.

Now they had also won the rights to the Mafia movie that had been so desired by Liuzzi.

But Carlo was not one to be beaten and had, at his own expense, commissioned a writer to come up with a rival screenplay.

Carlo had come up with the title himself, *Family Ties*, which he thought was inspired, even though the writer tried to persuade him it sounded like a family melodrama and might not attract the kind of audiences it would need to make it successful. But Liuzzi was having none of it. He knew best.

No expense was to be spared; the budget was huge, the sets lavish and the locations spectacular. He had also hired the hottest names in Hollywood to star in it - paying them way over the odds to persuade them to appear in what was, at best, an over blown, over stuffed B-movie.

Even though the picture would have to recoup an enormous amount just to break even, Carlo was convinced it would - putting Viscount's rival picture to shame.

As proof of this he sunk even more of his own personal fortune into it - paying the stars' travel arrangements and exorbitant location expenses out of his own pocket. He even bought one of them out of their Warner Brothers contract specifically to play what was essentially a supporting role in his movie.

But he had to have the best. The whole production was his baby, and coming in second to Viscount would just not do.

After all, he had been a Mafioso, he knew the life, so was expertly placed to ensure a movie on such a subject was an unqualified success.

Diego Del Toro and Herb Horowitz; a pampered rich boy and an over-the-hill Jew - both would have much to regret after crossing Carlo Liuzzi.

Both *Streets of Blood* and *Family Ties* were scheduled for release in the summer of 1967 and Carlo could not wait to put Viscount Studios in its place once and for all.

***

Carlo was in his study when Salvatore arrived, fresh off the plane from New York.

"Salvo! I'm in here!" Liuzzi shouted, removing his reading glasses and looking up from the Family Ties screenplay upon which he had been making notes.

Falcone hobbled through the study doorway, his slight limp more pronounced due to the confines of the aeroplane, even though he had travelled first class. It would be better tomorrow after a good night's sleep in his own bed and a morning spent on the patio beneath the warm California sun.

He was thankful to be home and already his chest felt better;

the looseness in his lungs that had been mildly bothering him in New York already felt clearer and he made a silent oath not to stay away so long again.

"Hey, Carlo!" Salvatore greeted him with a smile. "How are you? It's good to be home."

"Good to see you, too, my friend. Come in, come in. Sit down, please."

Falcone did as instructed, taking a seat in front of Carlo's heavy wooden desk.

"You had a good flight?"

"I did. Thank you. Yes."

Good. Good - pleased to hear it. But tell me, how is Ava?" Carlo asked anxiously, "How is she settling in? Is Nona Rosa taking good care of her?"

"She is. And Ava is well. She's enjoying school and doing okay, I think. Frankie is watching over her."

"She'll be okay, then?"

"She will. I'm sure of it."

"Does she miss me?"

"Of course, Carlo - like crazy," Salvatore lied, "but she's in good hands - Nona Rosa will make sure she doesn't want for anything. And besides, you're just a phone call away - she knows that."

"Yes. I suppose you're right. It's odd she hasn't called me yet though, don't you think?"

Falcone knew the reason for this was that Ava hated her step-father but it would not be wise to tell him. Instead, he said, "She's eighteen, Carlo. She's made lots of new friends and is also kept very busy studying - they work them hard. These colleges - I had no idea. I thought it would be easy but no - lots of work - too much work!"

Carlo smiled. "You're right, of course. I'm just being a father. It'd be nice to hear from her, that's all. She's my little girl, Salvo, after all."

"I know. Of course. I understand."

"But what about you Salvo? How are you?"

"Me? I'm fine, Carlo. A bit tired but—"

"And your business meeting? How did that go?"

Salvatore suddenly looked up, straight into Liuzzi's evil eyes, momentarily stunned. "Meeting?" He said nonchalantly, trying to keep the guilt from his voice, but already knowing Carlo had found him out. "What meeting?"

"Come now, Salvo," said Liuzzi, from behind his desk, sliding open the top drawer and casually taking out his prized dagger, its jewels sparkling in the late afternoon sunlight which was shining in through the tall study windows. "You know very well what meeting I'm speaking of - the one you had with Bruno Barca."

"Oh, that!" Falcone said, trying desperately to bluff his way out of the situation. "That was just a friendly get together - I haven't seen him in—"

"Don't lie to me!" Carlo yelled loudly, stabbing the dagger violently down into the leather inset of the wide oak desktop, burying the tip by at least an inch.

"I know what you were doing - and I know what you have been doing behind my back for many years! Someone as good as told me - and well, after a little research, it all became clear. I've got many friends, Salvo, did you not remember that?"

"Y-Yes, of course. I-I'm sorry, Carlo!" Salvatore pleaded, "Please—"

"Do you think I'm a goddamn fool? Do you think me an idiot - is that it?"

"No, Carlo, I swear, not that - never. It's just that I wanted something of my own—"

"You mean you haven't got enough! Carlo barked. "I don't give you enough! The life you have here is not suitable for a man of your high standards - is that it?"

"No, Carlo, it's—"

"I've given you everything - a house, a life, money - Christ, I've even given you shares in my fucking studio - what more do you fucking want?"

Salvatore was almost crying now. "I'm sorry," he pleaded, "really I am - I just wanted something of my own - so I didn't—"

"What? So you didn't have to tell me?"

"No! Not that. Honestly. It was so I didn't have to sponge off you all the time. You've been so good to me Carlo. I hate to keep on taking, taking, taking - I just wanted to make something of myself and not have to ask you!"

This seemed to quieten Liuzzi for a moment as he thought about what Salvatore had said. He tugged the dagger free of the desktop; its point still sharp, still keen, as he balanced the weapon in his grip, studying its incredible beauty. He was still awed by the irresistible allure that had bewitched him so many years before.

Carlo remembered again, back to when he was younger, back to that tiny fishing village in Southern Sicily where he was born, where he craved for more - yearned for a better life.

And he had got it. Both the dagger and the mansion he was now sitting in was testament to that.

He looked at Salvatore, his closest friend and trusted lieutenant, sitting snivelling in the chair opposite, clearly terrified about what might happen next.

He regarding him carefully. Could he really begrudge him the desire to want more? To deny him the ambition and the urge to better himself when he, himself, had done exactly that?

Was it fair to forbid it?

Carlo stood up slowly, still holding the dagger, and walked around to the other side of the desk, positioning himself immediately behind Salvatore.

Falcone inadvertently whimpered, expecting at any moment

to feel the cold steel of the jewel-encrusted dagger slicing through his jugular as he had seen it done to many men before him.

Carlo rested the heavy blade on Salvatore's shoulder, watching his friend wince at the touch of it as again he noticed the sunlight playing mesmerisingly on the beautiful stones of the handle.

After a moment or two, he lifted it again and placed the flat of the blade against Falcone's cheek before bending down and placing his lips next to the other man's ear.

"Okay, Salvo," he said softly. "You have your little drug business. But you keep it from my sight, you never let it come to my door and you never lie to me ever again - otherwise I will kill you. Do you understand?"

Salvatore very nearly voided his bowels with utter relief. "Yes, Carlo. Yes, yes - I understand - thank you, thank you so much - I'm sorry, I truly am."

"Hmm, we'll see. In the meantime you better tell your starry clientele to keep quiet - one of them openly asked me on set if you could get him any cocaine - me - can you believe it? If it happens again I won't be responsible for my actions, Salvo, hear me?"

"Yes, Carlo. I promise. I promise I'll sort it out. No one will ask you. No one. I swear it."

"Good." Then we are done for tonight." Carlo finally removed the polished blade from Falcone's neck and walked back around to his own side of the desk.

"So," Salvatore asked warily, "we're good? Everything is cool?"

"Everything's cool, my friend," replied Liuzzi replacing the dagger back in the drawer. "Good luck with your business. I wish you well."

Not for the first time Salvatore marvelled at how changeable Carlo was. There was just no way of knowing how he would react in any given situation. Another day Salvatore knew that his old friend would have cheerfully sliced him up and buried him in the desert leaving the vultures to pick at his bones, and yet, today he had acted almost calmly - at least for him. Falcone knew he had been extremely fortunate to escape with his life - indeed, to still be in Carlo's good graces.

However, he also knew he had just used up his last life.

"Thank you, Carlo. Thank you honestly, from the bottom of my heart. You're a good friend. The best," he said, as he stood to leave.

Liuzzi merely shrugged. "Oh, one other thing, Salvo, before you leave," he said off-handedly.

"Yes?"

"Hadn't you better check on your whore first? Before you go to your bed. I mean, she's bound to be hungry after all this time."

Salvatore stared at his smiling face, the feigned innocence of his expression conveying more than words.

Carlo had kept Mildred captive for nearly ten long years, having locked her in her steel cage deep underground and keeping her imprisoned there like a wild animal. She was less than dirt to him and he cared not if she lived or died - but he did want her to suffer. Whatever her fate should be, whether it be life or death, he wanted it to be as unpleasant as humanly possible.

And his wish had been granted.

"She's not been fed?" Falcone queried.

"It's not my job to feed the animals, Salvo, is it?" Carlo said. "It's yours."

Salvatore had left Mildred some food. Enough for a few days, but he had specifically told Carlo she did not have enough for any longer and would need more. He distinctly remembered telling him.

"Oh dear," Carlo said, with undisguised glee, "had you forgotten?"

Salvatore made no response.

"Yes. I think you probably had. Please - don't mind me - go

check on her - I know how you so like to."

Again Salvatore shot him a look.

"Ah! Another surprise, I see. I told you Salvo. I'm no fool. Of course I knew you weren't just feeding her - you were always gone far too long for that. And I know how you've always lusted after her. But I do so hope it wasn't love as I'm afraid Mildred's not really the loyal kind."

"No. It wasn't love." Salvatore whispered. And it genuinely was not. Very far from it in fact. But it was sex. Very good, very rewarding sex.

"Still, I think she might be in need of a good meal - don't you think?" Carlo smirked.

This was Salvatore's punishment, he knew it. Carlo had found out about the cocaine and because of it he had let Mildred starve - to deprive Falcone of her delights.

It was Liuzzi's reaction to his duplicity.

But what could Salvatore do? After all, it was better Mildred than him.

Nevertheless, he turned to his boss and said, "I'll go check."

"You do that," Carlo replied, sliding his glasses back on and picking up the screenplay once more, immediately dismissing his friend.

***

Salvatore descended the narrow staircase that led down into the bowels of the mansion, the smell already pungent even before he arrived at the bottom.

As he stepped into the cramped hallway that led to Mildred's cell the air was putrid and reeking of death. Falcone pulled the silk handkerchief from the breast pocket of his sports coat and held it firmly over his nose and mouth but it was still not sufficient to keep the stench of rotting flesh from his nostrils.

Tentatively, whilst trying not to gag, he slowly approached

the bolted door at the end of the passage, surprised the smell could escape the confines of the thick metal cage, but it had found a way through the cracks around the door seal and leaked its corrupt odour into the depths of the underground cavern.

Salvatore had been gone for six weeks and guessed he'd left Mildred enough food for five, maybe six days if she eked it out - which, of course, she would not have done without the knowledge it was to be the last of her rations.

She was thin, just a waif, and her health was already in slow decline so she would not have lasted long without sustenance - a week perhaps, probably less. Salvatore estimated she had been dead for around four weeks - giving her tiny body plenty of time to decompose.

As he arrived at the door, he braced himself for what he might see through the little window, knowing it would not be pretty.

But he had to know.

After taking a moment's pause to summon up the courage, he finally put his face against the glass and looked in.

The scene laid out before him was the worst thing he had ever seen in his life; more ghastly, more horrific than he could ever have imagined and immediately he felt his stomach heave. Unable to prevent himself, he vomited violently all over the concrete floor of the passageway, hot puke splashing his shiny brogues.

He wretched time and again but when he was certain his stomach was empty, he risked another look, unable to resist the hideous allure of the macabre vision beyond the thick, steel door.

He heaved again, but nothing came up, the gag reflex unavoidable as he studied with interest Mildred's swollen, rotten corpse.

She was sitting upright on the bed, wearing the pink silk robe Salvatore had given her which remained the only recognisable thing about her.

379

Her hair and fingernails had fallen away and her skin had turned a revolting shade of bluish green. The skin had shrivelled, too, and clung to her skeleton like a thin layer of wrinkled paper. Her mouth had sagged open with the tongue protruding grotesquely, sticking out pointedly between her withered, crumbling gums which, in turn, had caused the teeth to become detached. Decomposition had caused vile green substances to seep through her skin, releasing gases that emitted the offensive, foul-smelling odour which saturated the air in the subterranean bunker. Fluid had also oozed from her lungs, eyes, mouth and nostrils. Large blistering had occurred over the entirety of her corpse, most of which had ruptured and were being feasted upon by hundred of giant bluebottles and maggots - as were her body cavities, which had burst open; their gooey, fetid contents now nothing but a congealed, brown residue on the soiled linen bed sheets.

Briefly Falcone was transfixed, he had never seen anything like it, the scale of decomposition was immense and he studied it with an almost forensic fascination.

But other than a morbid curiosity, he felt nothing. No sadness, no remorse and certainly no regret for the utterly abhorrent way in which Mildred had died - or, for that matter, the way she had lived.

She had fulfilled her usefulness, having proved herself to be an eager accomplice in his more outlandish sexual fantasies and a willing slave with whom he could practice his most debase urges. Yet nothing more.

However, in latter years she had become increasingly delusional and her mental state ever more fragile, ever more unpredictable.

All things considered, Salvatore knew it was good she had died before becoming a hindrance to him.

He decided that Carlo had done them both a favour.

With the handkerchief still held over his nose, he finally, tore his eyes away and walked back down the passageway, thankful he

380

had not had to make the decision to kill her himself, which he no doubt would have had to sooner rather than later.

Not that killing ever troubled him.

As Falcone climbed the stairs, back up to Liuzzi's study, leaving Mildred locked forever in her steel tomb, he did not once think of Ava.

Or, indeed, how she might react to the death of her mother.

Chapter Twenty Eight

Rome, Italy 1968

Young Seminarian Gino McBride, Nate's best friend, was enjoying the sights and sounds of Rome; the bustling city always a hive of activity. It was so European, so continental - so different from home - but he was thriving there.

Since his enrolment as a New Man at the college two years earlier, he had taken great pleasure in immersing himself in his Italian heritage, soaking up the culture and purposely getting to know the place where his mother was born.

Furthermore, he now felt such an affinity with Rome that he had even begun to wonder if his vocation might lead him there once his studies were complete - he certainly would not be averse to it.

He whizzed through the streets on his little Vespa, easily bypassing the jams and traffic bottle-necks that were typical of the city - often accompanied by a cacophony of honking car horns and irate motorists shouting colourful insults at one another.

But Gino, was immune; his bright red scooter keeping him free from such confrontations - as did his black, short-sleeved 'priest shirt' and starched white clerical collar - of which the God fearing people of Rome were always deferential.

Indeed, God had really outdone Himself today, bestowing a truly heavenly morning upon His faithful Roman subjects and Gino raced along, basking in the glory of The Lord's wondrous majesty, feeling privileged to be a small part of it.

As the wind rushed through his bushy hair and the warm sun beat down on his back, its rays tanning his bare arms, he gently twisted the throttle of his nippy machine and it responded instantly.

Weaving in and out of the traffic without a care in the world, he swerved around a stationery Fiat 500, which appeared to have stopped in the middle of the street for no apparent reason. 'Typical Rome,' Gino thought, smiling to himself as he swept past it, completely unaware of the 'Stop' sign that was concealed by a parked van on the side of the road as he shot out, unknowingly, across the hidden junction.

He did not see the bus until the very last minute, but by that time it was much too late.

The large, heavy vehicle ploughed into the tiny scooter, hitting it with a resounding thud, the impact immense and devastating.

The Vespa and its rider were then pulled under and dragged along, trapped helplessly beneath the bus's cumbersome chassis for several yards, to the hideous accompaniment of metal scraping on gravel, as the driver wrestled to bring the unwieldy vehicle to a halt.

But at last, amid a hiss of breaks and the cries of horrified onlookers, it finally came to rest.

The bus driver leapt out and ran around to the front, hoping desperately that there was something he could do to help the poor man on the scooter who had shot blindly out in front of him, giving him no chance whatsoever to react.

But as he looked under the bus, at the mangled wreckage of twisted metal and torn flesh that lay snagged and snarled around the filthy axle, he knew it was hopeless.

He crossed himself and said a silent prayer for the trainee priest who lay dead beneath his wheels.

He prayed the young man's death was instant and that he felt no pain.

He need not have worried. God had been kind to Gino.

***

Nate's heart was extremely heavy as he rode his own scooter up into the hills later that afternoon, so soon after hearing the tragic news of his friend's death himself.

It had still not quite sunk in, it seemed almost impossible for Gino to no longer be there, to no longer be alive; the shock so great that for the first time in his adult life Nate had pause to question his faith.

Why take Gino? He wondered with an incredulity bordering on anger - such a sweet, friendly, caring guy - why him? It just did not make sense.

But Nate's training, indeed his own set of strongly held beliefs, told him Gino's death, just like his mother's, was surely all part of God's Plan.

Yet he was finding it hard to actually accept that 'cover all' explanation.

After having lost a second person close to him in just a relatively short space of time, he was finding it very difficult to believe indeed. It just did not seem right.

He was saddened beyond words by the passing of his friend and the pain of it had shaken his faith to its very foundation.

Nate hoped this unwelcome feeling of doubt would evaporate with the passing of time, thinking it might just be a reaction to the grief that filled his heart.

However, as he wound his way carefully up the mountain road, with tears of raw emotion now streaming from his eyes, he had just the slightest niggle in the back of his mind that his uncertainty in God's Plan may yet gather momentum.

***

Nate had insisted he be the one to inform the Contessa of

384

Gino's death as he felt it only proper.

Over the past two years he had visited her mountain stronghold many times with his friend and had become well acquainted with her. So, out of respect for both the Contessa and Gino, Nate felt the burden of relaying the news lay with him.

Better it came from a friend than from a stranger, he thought.

But it did not make the task any easier.

By the time he arrived at her villa Nate's eyes were dry and he had steeled himself for what must be done.

After a brief delay at the gates, he was shown through to the large courtyard and taken directly to the Contessa who was sitting on the veranda sipping coffee, her dogs laying at her feet, as she perused what appeared to be shipping manifests.

"My apologies for disturbing you, Contessa," Nate said rather hoarsely.

"Not at all, Father," she replied, using the title that had become something of an 'in joke' between them, but she always used it with great affection. "Is Gino here, too?"

"No, I- er, I'm afraid he's not. Not today. I've come alone."

This was most unusual, but the Contessa's face did not register any surprise. Instead she said, "Oh, how nice. Please, sit down, have some coffee."

"I'd rather not, for the moment, if you don't mind, Contessa," Nate replied. I'm afraid I've got some very bad news. And I think it would be better if I delivered it standing up."

"Oh dear. You have? What is it?"

"It's Gino, Contessa. There's been a terrible accident - just this morning - and I'm so dreadfully sorry to tell you—" Nate's legs felt suddenly weak and he began to wish he had accepted the offer of a chair, but he pressed on, knowing if he did not say it now then his emotions would overwhelm him and he'd never get it out. "Gino was—"

"—What?" Interrupted the Contessa, sitting bolt upright in her chair, already suspecting what Nate was about to say and dreading it with every fibre of her being. "Gino was what?"

"He— he was killed, Contessa. I'm so sorry." Nate hung his head, unable to meet her horrified gaze as he fought back the tears, "Gino's dead."

With the words finally out, Nate began to weep, his shoulders heaving, and he slumped into a chair opposite the Contessa. Berto, her faithful old border collie, stood up from where he had been laying and crossed over to Nate, resting his soft head on the grieving lad's lap, almost as if to comfort him.

Lucia Tartaglia looked over at the young trainee priest of whom she had grown extremely fond, her heart breaking for both him and for Gino; the boy she had come to think of as her own.

Her one good eye was moist and a solitary tear ran down her cheek as she thought of his kind, loving face.

But he was now dead and she would feel his loss enormously.

***

For the remainder of the afternoon, Nate and the Contessa consoled each other, with him expanding on the cause of Gino's death, which was, in actuality, just a stupid accident and such a senseless way for him to die.

When there were so many of Nate's countrymen - young boys of just nineteen and twenty - being killed in Vietnam each day, fighting for their country, it seemed so absurd for Gino to have died the way he did. It was cruel and pointless in the extreme, and again Nate found reason to question God's intent.

Nevertheless, whilst he and the Contessa had always enjoyed an easy rapport, on that afternoon they formed a definite and firm bond.

She insisted that Nate should still visit her as often as possible, and he did so regularly, whenever his studies allowed.

Over the months that followed their relationship flourished and became something akin to that of mother and son - or perhaps more of doting aunt and adoring nephew, with Nate never replacing Gino in Lucia's affections but certainly equalling him.

By now Nate was under very few illusions as to how the Contessa made her money and was well aware of the ethical dilemma it put him in, but it was not his place to stand in judgement - besides Lucia had taken Gino's death as a sign.

She had come to believe it was God's way of punishing her; a warning for her to change her ways and to stop plying her deadly trade; convinced she was being made to pay for earning millions of dollars from cocaine trafficking - even though she, herself, had never so much as looked at an ounce of the stuff.

Lucia was merely an overseer, an orchestrator who kept tight control on shipping, distribution and finance. The closest she ever got to the product itself was on her twice yearly trips to Columbia where it was sourced.

In the magnificent drug built mansions there, hidden deep in the jungle, she was wined and dined by members of the fabulously wealthy cartel who were keen to retain her and the highly secretive organisation she controlled as their most valued client.

But since her nephew's passing, Lucia was having a hard time reconciling the morality of it all.

Nate, too, was struggling to come to terms with Gino's death and was wrestling with his own demons.

He was continuing with his theological studies and kept up the pretence of pursuing a vocation within the Catholic Church but he was, in fact, suffering a huge crisis of faith.

As a result, Lucia and Nate became confidants; personal confessors who offered opinions without prejudice or agenda, which brought them closer still even though there was a thirty year age difference.

But their friendship was purely and most assuredly, platonic.

Indeed, Lucia reminded Nate a great deal of Maria; strong, resourceful, stubborn yet extremely generous, too. He had written home many times extolling the Contessa's virtues and Maria and Diego were delighted he was being so well cared for - especially after the tragic death of his good friend.

But what they did not know, what Nate never alluded to, was the struggle he was having with his faith. He just did not feel he could share his misgivings with them, perhaps because he felt more than a little ashamed of himself.

Nate never mentioned either what line of business the Contessa di Montagna happened to be in.

His parents were broad minded, enlightened people but that was possibly too much for them to cope with.

As it was, Nate and Lucia made for a pair of very unlikely companions; a young, trainee priest and a high-ranking mafiosa, but somehow it simply just worked.

Chapter Twenty Nine

Manhattan, New York 1968

Ava sat snivelling silently on a fixed metal bench in the holding pen of the 26th Precinct Station House, just one of many Columbia students being detained there.

Her eyes were still red and stinging from the tear gas and her knees were still sore from where she had been dragged along the ground by New York's finest before being thrown manfully into the back of the police paddy wagon.

She and Susan had been arrested together and now sat huddled in the corner of the large metal cage in the bowels of the station feeling extremely sorry for themselves.

Since the assassination of Dr King just a few weeks earlier, civil unrest had been high in the city, particularly around the Washington Heights area and Harlem. Also, the anti-war lobby had been making their voices heard around the Morningside Heights campus, protesting against America's involvement in Vietnam - which added yet more spice to the volatile boiling pot.

This was exacerbated by a proposed gymnasium at Morningside Park which, rumour had it, was intended to be segregated.

With tensions already heightened over race relations and the civil rights movement quickly gathering momentum within Columbia itself, the proposed gymnasium project was the last straw.

This sparked numerous demonstrations around the university which resulted in students forcibly taking control of both Hartley Hall and the Low Library.

Almost inevitably, these demonstrations led to violence, with the NYPD storming the buildings occupied by the protesters, using tear gas and strong arm tactics to quash the rebellion.

Ava and Susan, who had been protesting peacefully, showing their solidarity to the civil rights cause, had unintentionally gotten caught up in the melee and found themselves, along with 700 other students, arrested and carted off, unceremoniously, to jail.

After a long, wretchedly uncomfortable night, the girls were finally released without charge into the custody of their families - on condition they each went home and stayed clear of any further trouble.

This meant Susan was released into the care of her extremely worried parents and Ava into the anxiously waiting arms of Frankie DeLuca.

"Oh God, I'm so pleased to see you!" She said, hugging him tightly and feeling the safety of his big, powerful arms around her.

"Me, too, kid. You okay?" Frankie asked.

"Yeah, I'm fine. I just wanna get home and take a shower."

Then Ava froze, her body suddenly rigid as she saw Salvatore Falcone lurking furtively by the entrance of the police station.

Her immediate reaction was to recoil, to demand to be taken back to the cell, but Frankie held her firm as he whispered in her ear.

"I'm so sorry, kid. There was nothing I could do. Someone tipped off your step-father - one of the cops on the Carboni payroll - Falcone turned up at the brownstone first thing. He caught the red-eye from LA - I knew nothing about it, I swear."

"I won't go with him!" Ava hissed vehemently. "I won't."

"You got to, kid. It's a condition of your release - the only reason you're free - cos your step-dad told 'em you'd be safe in his care. He got to 'em before I could. I was too late to help."

"I won't go!" Ava said again.

"You've no choice, honey. Your step-dad's got some powerful friends in this city - it's the only way."

"I'll take my chances - go to trial, get a lawyer—"

"—Not gonna happen, kid. It's why Carlo sent Falcone. The pay-off's been made. You either go with him or to jail."

"Then I'll go to jail—"

"—Ava, honey. Listen to me. I've been to jail. It's tough. Real tough. You wouldn't last five minutes, sweetheart, believe me. This is the best way. The best option. Go with Salvo - go home to LA - you're an adult now and once you get there, hell, you can do what you like."

Ava thought about the last fifteen hours, stuck in that holding pen, thinking about the smell and the cramped conditions and the hideously filthy communal toilet without any privacy.

Not for the first time in recent hours she thought of her mother, too, and her tiny cell under the Liuzzi mansion.

Frankie was right, there was no way Ava could stand another moment in captivity let alone God knows how many months in the state penitentiary.

"But—" she began.

"—I know, kid. I wish it could be different."

"Are you coming too?"

"Soon. I just gotta square things away here. But I'll be joining you real soon, I promise."

Ava buried her head in his shoulder and wept, the tiredness of her sleepless night finally catching up with her.

But her tears were brief as she resolved to do exactly as Frankie advised; to go back to LA for the shortest possible time then be gone as soon as ever she could.

Ava had not been home in over two years, not since she started at Columbia, in fact. She had never wanted to return ever again but had always felt a deep guilt over Mildred.

As far as she was aware, her poor mother was still trapped in that tiny cell, the madness slowly taking her over. Maybe now, she supposed, Mildred's spiral into insanity might be complete - and that made Ava feel even more ashamed.

But this time, she promised herself, when she left Carlo's house, it would be for good - and her mother would be going with her.

"Okay, I'll go." She said softly.

"Good girl."

"Just let me say goodbye to Susan first, okay?"

"Sure, kid. No problem."

Susan was with her parents; her mother dark skinned and attractive; her father; pale and flabby and looking suitably grave.

The two girls embraced and promised to keep in touch, even though Susan suddenly seemed more distant than before; the events of the past couple of days tainting her outlook on the way she now looked at things.

Ava knew her friend had been more damaged by their ordeal than she had as the colour of Susan's skin made it far more personal, but in time, she hoped she could put the horrors of the riots behind her.

Yet as they held hands and said their goodbyes, a bored-sounding, heavily accented voice remarked, "For Christ sake, hurry up and put that monkey down - we got a plane to catch and they don't take no pets!"

Ava turned and stared daggers at Salvatore. If looks could kill then he would have died right there on the spot.

As it was he just shrugged nonchalantly, he couldn't care less what anyone thought.

But as Ava turned back, ready to apologise profusely for Falcone's outburst, Susan's appalled parents were already escorting her hurriedly away.

Susan stared angrily back at Ava, tears flooding her eyes. After all the prejudice and racial tensions of the past twenty-four hours, Salvatore's hateful insults were simply the last straw. Furthermore, even though she knew Ava to be nothing like him, she was guilty by association and, in Susan's view, it highlighted the huge gulf between them.

"I'm so sorry!" Ava cried. "Please—"

But it was too late, Susan had already turned away, deaf to anything her friend had to say. A moment later, her parents had pushed her through the swing doors that led out onto the sidewalk, so she would not be forced to listen to any more of Salvatore's racist jibes.

Susan and Ava had been best friends since their first day at Columbia but now, thanks to Salvatore, they would never see each other again.

***

Hollywood, California 1968

Carlo Liuzzi was incensed. His anger had been building for many months, but it had reached its zenith two weeks earlier and had scarcely abated since.

His concern about Ava's arrest had distracted him briefly, but once he had made some calls and despatched Salvatore to fetch her home his thoughts quickly returned to the matter which had so enraged him.

His mafia movie had bombed. His personal baby, his own pet project had been a complete and utter failure.

Indeed, not only had it done badly but it had also earned the dubious honour of being the most expensive flop ever made.

It had been savaged by the critics, derided in the press and laughed at by the industry in general. Furthermore, to quote the great Sam Goldwyn, the public had 'stayed away in their droves.'

To compound Carlo's misery further, his big-budget sci-fi

picture had also flopped, coming in second only to his mafia saga, *Family Ties*, in the list of Hollywood's biggest turkeys.

What is more, his gamble on the enormously expensive swashbuckling movie nor Gold Star's first, tentative foray into animated films had paid off. Neither of the movies had even earned their money back - making the Christmas of '66 the studio's worst ever by some considerable margin.

Carlo had offset the disappointment of those movies' bad reviews and poor returns by being overly optimistic about the summer '67 release of *Family Ties*.

But his hopes had been disastrously misplaced and the resulting fall-out had all but destroyed Gold Star; its fortunes irreparably damaged by such a calamitous run of failures.

Nevertheless, all of that was somewhat historical for Carlo now, as he sat outside the Beverly Hills Matador Hotel, strumming his fingers impatiently on the steering wheel of his dark green Camaro.

For Carlo, it came as a tremendous blow that his movies had flopped and his studio had lost millions. He had also lost a huge percentage of his personal wealth after investing so much of it into the failed pictures.

The humiliation he was having to endure within the industry as a result of it hurt him beyond words. In his opinion it was not just embarrassing but also devalued him within the Hollywood community, significantly reducing his power, and that was terribly hard to accept.

However, what niggled him most; what gnawed at him day in day out and made him angrier than the loss of mere money - or even his own self-esteem - was that Diego Del Toro's Viscount Studios production of *Streets of Blood* - his rival mafia picture - had been an enormous success.

It had been the most successful movie of 1967 and one of the biggest box-office hits of all time. In its year of release, it had become the most profitable, the most critically acclaimed and the most popular among movie going audiences.

All of which had been eating Carlo alive for many months.

But what capped it all, what really did it for Liuzzi, was seeing Diego Del Toro and Herb Horowitz on stage two weeks ago at the Santa Monica Civic Auditorium picking up the Oscar for Best Picture. In addition to that particular honour, Streets of Blood also won Best Director, Best Actor, Best Actress and seven more of the highly-prized golden statuettes, making it equal only to Ben Hur in the list of most Academy Award winning pictures.

And it made Carlo's blood boil.

Diego Del Toro - a fucking hotelier - had won an Oscar - for a goddamn mafia flick!

Since the Academy Awards ceremony Carlo had thought of little else; his ire still not exhausted.

Indeed, he had taken to following the object of his rage around; spending hours just sitting parked outside his hotel and imagining sweet revenge; the jewelled dagger stashed in the glove box, just waiting for an opportune moment to be unsheathed.

If Diego Del Toro wanted mafia, then he'd get fucking mafia.

***

Diego had been in Los Angeles much longer than anticipated, the post-Oscars buzz that had been created by the movie's mass domination of the Academy Awards had generated enormous interest and spawned meeting after meeting about new and exciting projects.

He and Herb Horowitz had been at it flat out for the last two weeks, both individually and together as they tried to accommodate all the people that wanted to meet with them.

In fact Diego had been so tied up with Viscount business that Juan Pablo Clemente, his eminently capable right hand man, and Maria had been handling Matador affairs in his absence.

Juan Pablo had flown many miles around the world in the last fourteen days and had been back and forth to LA more than once with various papers for Diego to sign and to keep him apprised of matters pertaining to Matador that required his attention.

Indeed, he was sitting across from Diego now as they worked together in the Beverly Hills Matador's sumptuous penthouse suite - where Diego had based himself for the duration.

Diego was currently on the telephone to his wife who he missed dreadfully. Maria missed him, too, and was devastated she was unable attend the Academy Awards with her husband to share in his moment of glory. But it would have been just too dangerous.

She knew her father would undoubtedly have been there and she could not risk him seeing her at such a visible, high profile event.

As it was, Diego took Delores, the family's faithful housekeeper and nanny, as his guest. He flew her out on the Hermes IV and treated her in grand style; a designer gown, expensive jewellery and a brand new hair-do.

She looked an absolute picture on the night and Diego was proud to have her on his arm but he would have preferred it if she had been Maria.

Delores had flown home two days afterwards leaving Diego in Hollywood with a diary full of appointments.

But he was tired now. Tired of talking movies and anxious to get home to see his wife. Maria could hear the weariness in his voice as they talked, her heart yearning for him.

However, today was the last day. Diego and Herb had finished the majority of appointments and the few that remained Herb could easily handle on his own. In the last two weeks they had closed some very lucrative deals which would secure Viscount's continued growth for many years to come.

But later that evening, Diego, along with Juan Pablo, would climb into the Hermes IV and fly home.

Maria and Matador needed his attention now as he had been absent for far too long.

***

The plane to LAX had been stuck on the tarmac at LaGuardia for five torturous hours having been delayed as a result of heavy thunderstorms over New York.

This meant Ava had spent the long, arduous wait sitting next to the loathed Salvatore - a truly ghastly situation which she would not have wished on her worst enemy.

She was thankful, at least, that she had been allowed to return to the brownstone prior to leaving for the airport where Falcone had permitted her to throw a few basic possessions into a holdall. Amongst these was a good, thick, book which she had immersed herself in whilst the plane lingered, motionlessly on the ground, so tantalisingly close to the runway.

Nevertheless, the skies eventually cleared and the flight finally made it into the air.

Ava had read and slept a little during the flight but she could not keep her mind from thinking about where she was headed. She dreaded seeing her step-father, indeed, she had hoped never to see him again and could not even begin to contemplate how she might survive the next however many days or weeks under his roof.

She was also anxious about seeing Mildred. It had been so traumatic last time, so gut-wrenchingly awful - the encounter with her mother so shocking, so surprising, that it had left her feeling both bereft and guilt-ridden for many months afterwards. Bereft because it was like losing her mother all over again and guilt-ridden for having left her there in that God-forsaken dungeon; angry, addled and delusional.

No, she was certainly not looking forward to going home.

Yet, as the wheels touched down on the tarmac at LAX, on that typically warm Californian evening in late April, Ava knew she

397

could no longer avoid it.

***

With Juan Pablo as his passenger, Diego was going to drive the short distance to Van Nuys Airport himself in the classic 1951 Porsche Speedster he had bought whilst in California. It was the first opportunity he'd had to drive the silver convertible and he had been looking forward to it all day. However, the journey was only around fifteen minutes long so Diego would have to wait until he got the car back to Cadiz before giving it a proper test drive.

He would leave the car at the airport, where it was due to be shipped out the next day. Diego would not see it again for a couple of weeks when he was next due to be in Spain.

As the valet brought it around to the front of the hotel, a little after 10pm, and parked it just a few feet away, Diego marvelled again at its smooth, clean lines. It was in mint condition, as immaculate as the day it rolled off the production line and he eagerly anticipated his first opportunity to get behind the wheel.

"Drives beautifully, Mister Del Toro," said the young valet as he handed the keys to Diego.

"Thanks Tony. I hope you're right - I haven't had the pleasure yet," he replied giving the boy a generous tip.

"Appreciate it Mister Del Toro, thanks," said Tony, sliding the money into the ticket pocket of his bright red waistcoat.

"Not at all. My pleasure - I'll see you in a few weeks, okay?."

"Sure thing, sir."

Diego and Juan Pablo's luggage had already been forwarded to Van Nuys earlier in the day where it had been loaded onto the waiting Hermes, which presently sat fuelled and ready for take off.

Each of the men had kept only a small valise with them which they stowed on the tiny back seat of the Porsche along with their jackets.

The only additional item Diego carried was the small golden

statuette he had been presented with at the Academy Awards. It had quickly become one of his most prized possessions and he could not wait to show it to Maria and Danny - he might even send a photo of it to Rome as he knew Nate was eager to see it, too.

He laid the Oscar carefully on the back seat, nestling in the folds of his sports coat, next to his valise, where it would be safe until they arrived at the airport.

Then, Diego climbed into the front seat, revved the gently rumbling engine and sped off in the direction of the airport.

***

The gleam of the golden Oscar shining in the moonlight was the first thing to attract Carlo Liuzzi's attention.

He had been waiting obsessively for many hours and had just begun to doze when the glint of the highly polished statuette caught his eye.

It taunted him, teased him, as Diego Del Toro clutched it in his unworthy hands.

A fucking hotelier.

Carlo's temper, which was already burning hot, immediately rose to boiling point as he watched his hated rival clambering into the shiny Porsche, just a hundred yards or so from where Liuzzi sat watching from the front seat of his Camaro.

It was clear Del Toro was leaving town - taking the award with him. The award that in Carlo's twisted mind, rightfully belonged to him - much like the jewel encrusted dagger which he had viewed as 'his' so many years earlier.

And he had to possess it.

Fuelled by rage, driven by avarice, he shifted into gear and when the Porsche set off, Carlo duly followed.

He guessed Del Toro's destination to be Van Nuys, where he knew the wealthy Spaniard kept a fancy private aeroplane.

He also knew Van Nuys was not too far away. So if he was to

act then he must do it swiftly.

***

Diego steered the Porsche along Wilshere and up through Bel Air, the engine purring like a kitten and the warm evening breeze blowing through his floppy black hair.

He was taking the scenic, more round about route, enjoying being at the controls of the beautiful vintage automobile. Aside from being eager to see his family he was in no real rush to get to the airport. So why not make the most of the journey.

With the road deserted, he opened it up as he sped through Stone Canyon heading for Mulholland - relishing the thought of The Drive's wonderfully windy blacktop as he weaved his way towards Sherman Oaks and the San Fernando Valley, completely unaware of the car closing in on him fast from behind, its headlights switched off.

The first Diego knew of the other car's presence and its dangerously close proximity to his own was when its headlights were suddenly turned on.

By this time the car was mere inches from the Porsche's rear fender, the dazzle of the high beam blinding a startled Diego as he checked the rear-view mirror.

"Hey, buddy!" he yelled over his shoulder whilst gesticulating wildly and wondering where the hell the car had suddenly sprung from. "Dip those lights will you! Either go past or back off!"

But it was to no avail, the mysterious driver of the rogue vehicle paying him no heed.

Indeed, quite the contrary, as a moment later the car pulled out as if to overtake but then purposely swung in and side swiped the rear side of the pristine Porsche. It smashed violently into the Sportser's wheel arch, crumpling the antique bodywork grotesquely.

Diego screamed with despair as he fought to keep control of his now damaged classic car. But he had very little time to react before

400

the Camaro rammed into them once more, this time colliding so forcefully with his door that he was jolted sideways into Juan Pablo.

The Porsche slewed dramatically as it veered off the road and bounced along the verge, still travelling at over sixty miles an hour.

"Hey, man! What the fuck—" Juan Pablo yelled at the driver of the Camaro, just as it smashed into them again, stealing his voice away as he grabbed the top edge of the convertible's windshield to steady himself.

Diego was fighting to keep the car on the road as it rumbled over the loose scree of the verge.

They were fast approaching a telephone pole that was planted in the ground up ahead and he jammed on the brakes in attempt to avoid it.

Immediately the wheels locked and the Porsche was sent into a long, controlled skid; Diego expertly steering into it. And even though they were still hurtling along, he thought they might just stop before hitting the pole.

But then the Camaro slammed into them yet again. This time the impact was like a wrecking ball and Diego lost control.

The Sportster's back end snaked wildly, then as the front wheels hit a half-buried rock, it flipped over violently.

Juan Pablo was thrown clear and landed hard in the grassy scrub at the side of the road as the Porsche crashed back down onto its wheels and slid sideways into the pole, with an ear-splitting crunch.

The back end of the German sports car had embedded itself in the splintered woodwork, its rear-mounted engine hissing steam and sparking electrics. Water and oil mixed in a rainbow patterned puddle on the ground beneath the broken automobile and a long, black skid mark stretched back along the road; the smell of burning rubber laying thickly in the warm night air.

Diego Del Toro lay slumped over the steering wheel; the car's horn playing a single, monotonous tone as his chest pressed heavily against it.

One of the lenses in Diego's spectacles had shattered but they still, quite miraculously, remained firmly on his head. However, his eyes were closed, his hair was damp with blood and a long, red line trickled down his forehead and onto his cheek.

***

Carlo Liuzzi smiled as he pulled the green Camaro over a short distance away in front of the totalled wreck of the Porsche.

There were no other vehicles to be seen, with the road both ways completely deserted.

Without haste, Carlo reached into the glove box and took out the beautiful, jewel-encrusted dagger, holding it reverently as he briefly admired it in the moonlight. He never ceased to be awed by its magnificence; the fine craftsmanship, exquisite sparkle and perfect balance. It truly was a wondrous object and a remarkable weapon.

Casually, he opened the door, which creaked on its hinges - the whole right side of the Camaro buckled and bent like a piece of screwed up paper that had been roughly straightened. Great slashes of raw metal were drawn jaggedly along the dark green paintwork and the hood was crumpled.

But Carlo could not have cared less. It was just a car.

He ambled unhurriedly back to where the Porsche still sat hissing and steaming, firmly embedded in the telephone pole. He studied it absently, noting only that it was ruined beyond repair. He had owned one much like it many years earlier but had never liked it. Give him American any day of the week or, better still, Italian - now they really knew how to make sports cars.

Liuzzi's eyes then settled upon the driver; Diego Del Toro. Hotelier, millionaire, studio head and Oscar winner. How dare he even think about coming into Carlo's town and taking over his industry.

And for that unforgivable transgression, the Spaniard would pay a heavy price.

However, as he pushed Diego's limp body back off the steering wheel to silence the infernal blare of the car horn, the hotelier, it seemed, was already dead.

Carlo felt a flicker of disappointment, having been denied the pleasure of finishing him off personally. But then he heard the slightest of groans and realised, much to his delight, his victim was still alive.

He smiled. Grateful he would still be able to have some fun.

Carlo exuded calm, the months of pent up anger all but leaving him now the situation was back firmly under his control.

Murder was his business and he excelled at it.

Del Toro thought he could take over but now Carlo was going to show him who was really the boss.

He tightened his grip on the dagger and held it to Diego's neck, ready to slice through the Spaniard's carotid artery like a knife through butter.

But then something shiny caught his eye and distracted him.

It was the Oscar.

Again its lustrous gleam had attracted him, drawing him to it. It was surely a sign that it truly belonged to him.

The golden statuette lay in the grass on the side of the road, obviously having been ejected from the Porsche when it flipped over.

Momentarily forgetting Diego, Carlo swiftly crossed to the verge and picked up the surprisingly heavy award. Its golden coating shining brightly, its beauty not impaired from its spell in the grass. It was perfect. No scratches, no scuffs - as if it had just been presented to him.

He admired it covetously as he turned it in his hand, finally arriving at the plaque on the base that had initially been hidden from view. Carlo read the inscription:

Academy First Award to 'Streets of Blood'
Best Picture of 1967. Viscount Studios Production
Diego Del Toro, Producer

And his anger flared violently once more.

Then a voice from out of the darkness said, "What happened? Who are you? Where—"

Liuzzi looked up, suddenly startled, his attention snapped away from the gleaming Oscar, as Juan Pablo Clemente stumbled out of the undergrowth, a large lump on his head and blood seeping from a wound behind his ear.

Clearly dazed, Juan Pablo was staring at Carlo in confusion, trying to make sense of things.

But Liuzzi's temper was burning hot once more and he fastened his eyes on Juan Pablo and gripped the dagger firmly. He charged forward and plunged the sharpened blade into the Spaniard's stomach, then twisted it and thrust it upwards, tearing through flesh and ripping through sinew until it came up hard underneath his rib cage.

A horrified look appeared on Juan Pablo's face, his eyes bulging grotesquely as Liuzzi smiled, his evil face only inches away.

Then Carlo pulled out the dagger sharply and Juan Pablo fell away, back into the scree.

He would not get up again.

"Oh my God!" Diego shouted as he saw his friend killed. "No! No! What have you done? What are you doing—" Then he saw the face of the killer and a cold shiver of dread ran through him.

He recognised the murderer instantly as Carlo Liuzzi, his wife's father.

Diego had roused a moment earlier, concussed, with his head feeling as if it was about to explode, yet he was conscious enough to know he had to get free of the car, fearing it might catch fire.

Somehow he managed to hoist himself out and stagger clear of

404

the wrecked Porsche. But he had no time to think about the loss of the car because as he looked up, his eyes focussed on the man who had just killed his best friend.

Carlo turned to face him, still grinning.

"It's you?" Diego gasped. "It's you, you're—"

But then his legs failed him and he fell to his knees on the side of the road, his body too weak, too battered to support his weight.

Liuzzi walked over to him slowly and stood directly in front of him. He was still holding the now bloodied dagger and the shiny, golden statue.

"Yes. It's me. The man you robbed. The man who rightfully deserves this shiny trinket. The man who owns fucking Hollywood."

Diego was breathing heavily. What was Liuzzi talking about?

He looked up at the man towering over him, his glasses slightly askew and one of the lenses shattered, his blurry eyes studying his wife's father, his own father-in-law, with abject terror.

"This is mine, Del Toro, not yours," sneered Carlo. "You are nothing," he said, glancing again at the inscription on the Oscar, his blood beginning to boil once more as his fist closed angrily around the head of the statuette.

Diego gasped, horribly aware of what was about to happen, knowing in that moment the only chance he might possibly have to save himself would be to scream Maria's name and tell Liuzzi that she still lived. But he could not betray her. Could not betray Danny and instead simply accepted his fate.

Looking directly into Carlo's cold, black eyes and summoning as much courage as he could muster, he growled, "And you, you murderous bastard, can go straight to hell!"

Then, through his mop of unruly hair, Diego watched helplessly transfixed as Carlo raised the Academy Award high above his head before swiping it down upon him with almighty force.

The last thought Diego had was of his beautiful wife and the words she had once said to him. 'My father's the devil.'

***

Carlo was only distracted from his evil work when he became aware of headlights approaching.

He had no idea of how long he had been bent over Del Toro's body, clubbing it mercilessly with the Academy Award and stabbing at it with the jewelled dagger. All he knew, as he finally relented from the task, was that he was now sweating and panting heavily and the hotelier's once handsome face was battered beyond all recognition.

With the approaching car's headlights now almost upon him, Carlo rushed breathlessly back to the Camaro, hastily throwing both the dagger and the Oscar onto the backseat before gunning the engine. As the other car pulled up beside the wreckage of the Porsche, the wheels of the Camaro screeched on the tarmac and Carlo sped off into the night.

Chapter Thirty

Vito Spezzano, Carlo's driver-cum-bodyguard, picked Ava and Salvatore up in the limo just after 10.30pm from LAX.

Both were tired and travel weary from their arduous journey and Ava closed her eyes the moment she got into the car and did not open them again until Salvatore nudged her awake as they drove through the gates of the mansion some time later.

After two years, Ava was home.

Very reluctantly, she climbed out of the limo and looked up at the huge mansion; its grand lines and stately exterior belying the horror of what had transpired within its thick walls and beneath its polished floors.

Again, Ava felt the stir of guilt as she thought of her poor mother trapped in the hell hole below, awakening the hatred for her step-father that rarely stayed dormant for long.

She had half expected Carlo to meet her on the driveway and had braced herself for the first awkward meeting with him since she left for college at eighteen.

But there was no greeting. In fact, the house was in total darkness which seemed decidedly odd.

Vito and Salvatore noticed it too. They came to stand beside her, both equally curious as to why the mansion looked so dark.

Then they all heard the strange noise in the distance.

Softly at first, before steadily growing louder and louder; the sound of metal scraping upon metal. Soon it became apparent that the sound was emanating from a car, its engine labouring.

Ava, Salvatore and Vito all stared in amazement as the battered green Camaro eventually came into view, spluttering through the gates and up the long driveway.

As it pulled up behind the limo, Ava could see it was Carlo behind the wheel and a trickle of fear entered her belly. How would he react to her absence, her desertion of him? Indeed, what would his response be to her arrest amid the violent disturbances on the university campus in New York?

As she pondered these things with growing trepidation, she studied the Camaro.

It had clearly been involved in a terrible accident. The whole right side of the vehicle was ruined and the front was crumpled in. The hood had buckled and the fender was hanging off - obviously the result of a heavy impact.

She saw Carlo reach into the back seat and grab something but she could not see what.

Then he pushed open the door with a loud, metallic creak and stepped out of the vehicle.

Ava was shocked by the sight of him. It was reminiscent of that night many years ago when she had watched him stab a man to death with a shard of jagged pottery.

He had been bloodied then, from head to toe, and he was bloodied now.

His hands, arms and shirt covered in it.

In his red-stained hands he held two things, both of them spattered with blood and gore. In his left was a dagger; jewel-encrusted and magnificent; in his right he held what looked to be a club of some kind - metal and gold. Then, upon closer inspection Ava realised with absolute horror it was an Oscar - a blood-spattered

Academy Award, and she put her hand to her mouth involuntarily, the disgust on her face clear to read.

But what really scared her, what really reminded her of that night when she was just nine years old, when her father was murdered and her mother had been locked in a dungeon, was the look in Carlo Liuzzi's eyes.

It was the look of the devil.

Back then, her step-father had not wished Ava to see him as he was and felt genuine remorse that she had witnessed such terrible things.

But now, rather ominously, he did not seem to care.

Carlo regarded her with disdain for a moment. No longer was his gaze one of love or pride - no longer did she feel that he wanted to spoil her or that she could twist him around her little finger as she so easily had when she was younger.

It was apparent that his image of her had been shattered and he now saw the truth of how she truly viewed him, her two year absence and the almost total lack of communication with him in that time virtually screaming it.

His stare was murderous and evil; his bitter disappointment at her obvious desertion of him clear to see.

And it scared her to the core.

He stared at her a moment longer then barked, "Vito - put the Camaro in the garage - quickly."

"Si, capo," replied Spezzano obediently, immediately getting into the battered car.

"Salvo!" Liuzzi snapped again, "Take the girl to her room - I'll deal with her tomorrow."

"Si, capo!" Falcone echoed, grabbing Ava roughly by the arm.

"But—" Ava spluttered.

"—Don't!" Carlo demanded, marching up to her and raising his arm, holding the Oscar threateningly in front of her face, as if he was about to club her with it. "Say another word, Ava - just one more goddamn word - and, so help me, I swear I'll kill you right here on the fucking drive!"

The violence of the man was barely restrained, his true face unmasked and the malevolence of his intent undisguised. Ava was nothing to him now.

She was immediately struck dumb as she cowered in fear, terrified of being bludgeoned by the heavy statuette.

Yet it was not the threat of violence that had silenced her but the sight of the shiny metal plaque on the base of the Oscar where, amid the splashes of dried blood and the tiny pieces of God knows what, she could just read the words 'Del Toro.'

***

Ava sat in her room wide awake. She no longer felt tired but alert and sharp - her mind running over all she had seen.

Why did Carlo have Diego Del Toro's Oscar?

She had seen him win it with her very own eyes, sitting in Susan's cramped little apartment in Hartley Hall, watching the Academy Awards together on her tiny black and white TV. She remembered distinctly because the name, when it was announced, made her stomach do a little flip as she was reminded of the handsome boy she once spent a wonderful afternoon with.

Diego Del Toro was Danny's father.

Yet her step-father had his award. And it was covered with blood.

She couldn't stop thinking about it. Nor of Danny.

And, as it neared ever closer to dawn, she could not help but think about Mildred too.

She had a niggling feeling of doubt that had been growing stronger for the last few hours, a little voice in her head telling her that her mother was dead.

Maybe she read it somehow in Carlo's expression or perhaps

it was just her instincts which were naturally heightened after the night's events. But whatever the reason for her suspicions, she had to find out if they were correct.

The house was quiet now. It was 4.30 in the morning and her step-father and his underlings were all sleeping soundly.

Silently, Ava opened her bedroom door and tip-toed across the landing and down the stairs. Stealthily she crossed the wide hallway and turned the handle to Carlo's study.

There was the slightest of clicks as the door opened allowing her to slip quickly inside.

Immediately, she crossed to the bookcase and depressed *The Count of Monte Cristo*, panicking slightly as the bookcase slid smoothly aside; the soft hum of its mechanism seemingly deafening in the silence of the sleeping house.

A moment later she was behind the secret doorway that led to the staircase.

The stairwell smelled musty and stale and she noticed cobwebs now lined the narrow walls as if the hidden space had not been disturbed in some time.

It did not bode well.

Carefully, anxiously, she descended the stairs and eventually set foot on the slender passageway that led to Mildred's cell.

The glow of the cell's light shone through the spy hole in the steel door and Ava braced herself for what she might see when she looked through it.

Nervously, with a sick, anxious feeling in her stomach, she arrived at the door and tentatively, very reluctantly, risked a look through it.

The scene laid out before her was utterly ghastly and Ava suddenly deeply regretted the impulse to go down there. Even the terrible memory of the last time she saw Mildred was preferable to this, which she knew would stay with her forever.

Instantly her eyes flooded with tears, her heart breaking with unbelievable sadness as she saw the last remains of her mother.

Mildred's skeleton sat upright on the bed, wearing the pink, silk robe Ava had last seen her in. A few remaining straggles of her long, wild hair remained but mostly her skull was bare.

The sheets upon which her bones sat were dirty and brown and lightly sprinkled with the dust of time, as was the rest of her room.

It was clear she had been dead for a very long time.

She knew Mildred must have suffered dreadfully in her last days and dare not even contemplate the nature of her death, suspecting only that it would have been a horrendous end to an appalling existence.

Ava sobbed quietly and said a silent prayer for her poor mother, lamenting how tragic her life had been.

What a terrible waste of all that beauty and intelligence.

In that instant, Ava suddenly came face to face with her own destiny and knew, without doubt, if she stayed in that house, with her step-father and Salvatore any longer, she would end up the same way as Mildred.

Or her beloved father.

Carlo had all but admitted it earlier when he threatened to bludgeon her with the Oscar, scaring her beyond words, leaving her terrified and fearing for her life.

She had to get out. Now, this morning. Straight away before her step-father woke up and made good on his threat.

Taking one long, last look at her mother's skeleton, Ava whispered the words "Goodbye Mommy," then turned on her heels and ran.

***

Five minutes later Ava was back in her room.

Her bag was still packed from the night before. In it, she had five hundred dollars which she had managed to save whilst in New

York, some toiletries and a few items of clothing.

It would have to do.

It was now a few minutes after five. Before coming upstairs she had quietly telephoned for a cab from Carlo's study. It was due to pick her up outside the gates, but not in direct view of the house, at 5.10am.

Hurriedly, she pulled on a pair of faded jeans and slipped her bare feet into her trusty sneakers. Throwing on a denim jacket and tucking her ponytailed locks under a *Jets* cap, she was quickly set to go.

Ava took a last look round at her childhood bedroom in the house that held so many unhappy memories, feeling no regret at leaving it behind.

Then she eased open the door again and snuck down the stairs. Being as silent as possible, she gently unlocked the front door and slipped out into the breaking dawn.

Once outside, she ran as fast as she could down the long cobblestone driveway to the tall, wrought iron gates that barred her way to the street beyond.

The gates were locked firmly shut but that did not deter Ava. After throwing her bag over, she clambered gingerly over them - taking great care not to snag herself on the sharp spikes running along the top.

Once she had navigated them successfully, she jumped down to freedom, her sneakers landing as lightly as a cat on the road below.

The moment she was over, she looked urgently about her for the cab and was relieved to see it parked a hundred yards away on the far side of the spotlessly clean boulevard. After grabbing up her bag she sprinted over to it and threw herself onto the back seat, slamming the door quickly behind her.

"Thanks," she said breathlessly, "thanks for coming so soon!"

"Hey, no problem, sugar pie," replied the large Jamaican

woman behind the wheel, "you in some kind of rush, honey?"

"Yeah, something like that."

"Bad night, huh?"

"The worst."

"Hey, don't worry sugar - we've all been there. Now where is it I can take you?"

"Bus station please. Quick as possible."

"You got it, honey - just sit back, relax - we'll be there in a jiffy."

Ava slunk down on the back seat as the driver pulled away from the kerb and accelerated past the Liuzzi mansion, her heart racing ten to the dozen.

***

Ava boarded the first bus heading out of Los Angeles, unconcerned about the destination so long as it was far away from her murderous step-father.

As it turned out, the bus was going to Flagstaff, Arizona. As good a place as any.

Ava settled down in her seat, pulled her baseball cap over her eyes and quickly fell into a deep, exhausted sleep.

She woke up sometime later when the bus pulled into a truck stop near Lake Havasu, just long enough for the passengers to use the restrooms and grab a sandwich.

After that Ava remained awake, her mind full of the dreadful images of her mother's skeleton and awash with questions about why her step-father was in possession of Diego Del Toro's Oscar and, more importantly, why it was covered in blood.

Also, Ava could not help but wonder what she was going to do now and where she was going to go. She thought briefly about going to Oklahoma and the possibility of maybe spending a few nights with Susan at her parents' house.

Then she remembered what had happened at the police station - what Salvatore had said - and thought better of it. She might no longer be welcome and she could not blame them.

It seemed hard to believe all that happened only yesterday. So much had transpired since then and now here she was on a bus, her future uncertain and without a friend in the world - except for Frankie. But he was in New York - which was surely the first place Carlo would look for her.

Ava had never felt more alone and once again pulled down the brim of her baseball cap, but this time it was not to sleep but to hide her tears.

By late afternoon Ava was in Flagstaff sitting in a diner with a burger and a shake.

The radio was on in the background and Ava listened absently as she chowed down on her burger, surprised at how hungry she was.

Suddenly she heard the radio announcer say the name 'Diego Del Toro' and her ears immediately pricked up.

'...the multi-millionaire owner of the Matador Hotels chain and, more recently, Oscar winning producer of last year's smash hit movie, 'Streets of Blood' was found dead late last night beside his wrecked sports car.

Mr Del Toro, one of two men found at the scene in this gruesome double homicide, had been bludgeoned and stabbed repeatedly in a most brutal attack the LAPD think might have been premeditated.

A police spokesman said initial signs show that the hotelier may have been forced off the road by another vehicle - thought to be a dark coloured Chevy Camaro...'

Ava could not believe it. Everything just suddenly clicked into place. It was Carlo who ran Diego Del Toro off the road; Carlo who bludgeoned and stabbed him to death.

It explained everything; Carlo's appearance, the banged up Camaro - even the blood on the Oscar - Diego Del Toro's Oscar.

Now it all made sense and Ava was appalled. Carlo had killed Danny's father - the only thing she did not know was why?

Nevertheless, she knew what she must do.

She finished her burger and downed the remainder of her shake, then crossed to the tiny phone booth in the corner of the diner.

Picking up the receiver, she dialled the operator and asked to be put through to the Los Angeles Police Department. When at last a woman's voice said, "Hello, LAPD, how may I direct your call?"

Ava replied, "Hi. Could I speak with a detective please? I know who murdered Diego Del Toro."

***

When Ava stepped out of the phone booth some time later, she had told the police everything she knew about both Diego Del Toro's murder and the body they would find hidden in the concealed dungeon at the Liuzzi mansion. They, in return, had promised to fully investigate her claims.

She felt satisfied Carlo would finally get his comeuppance - her only regret was that she would not be there to see it.

Three hours later, she was stretched out on the back seat of a Greyhound bus heading for Boston, her head resting on her small canvas bag - it and its contents representing everything she owned in the whole world.

But at least she was finally free.

***

The LAPD did, indeed, turn up at the Liuzzi mansion late the following morning.

Carlo invited them in, offered them a drink and was geniality itself.

They asked him if he owned a dark green Camaro. He said he did.

They asked if they might see it, he said 'of course'.

Vito showed the detectives to the garage where they found many pristine automobiles; amongst them a Buick Roadmaster, a

Mercury Capri and a Rolls-Royce Phantom IV. All classics.

There was also a couple of limos, a Ferrari, a Maserati and a spotless, beautifully polished, dark green Chevy Camaro, its condition immaculate.

The detectives gave it a cursory inspection but it was immediately clear that the car had not been involved in even the slightest of scrapes.

Quickly losing interest but keeping an air of professionalism, following up fully on the anonymous tip-off from the night before, they asked Carlo if there was a hidden door behind the bookcase in his study.

"A hidden what?" he answered with amazement. "Hell no - where did you get that idea?"

They told him. Knowing it all sounded preposterous and like something out of *The Man From UNCLE*, but they had to be sure.

They said their informant told them it was accessed by depressing a book found on the shelf, *The Count of Monte Cristo*

Carlo laughed. "Well," he said, "I've got the book and you're free to take a look at it."

They did. Indeed, there was a copy of the book, exactly where their informant told them it would be. But that's all it was, just a book. It did not press in, it did not reveal any hidden doors and it did not trigger the bookcase to slide open.

It was just a book.

One final question. Did Carlo know Diego Del Toro?

"Sure! Not well, but I know his work and we met a couple of times at social events - poor guy. Terrible news about what happened."

The police agreed it was.

The detectives apologised for any inconvenience and hated to trouble such a respected member of the Hollywood community, but they had to follow up every lead.

Carlo said, "No problem," he quite understood.

Oh, one last thing. Did he know why anyone might want to implicate him in Mister Del Toro's murder.

"Well I've been having a hard time with my step-daughter recently," he said. "She's at that rebellious age. She got into some trouble in New York recently and, well, she didn't appreciate me dragging her home. Took it quite hard in fact.

"I think she got into the party scene a bit too much, got into drugs. Mind you, what do you expect, hanging out with all those hippies and draft dodgers at Columbia?"

The policemen nodded in agreement. They, too, had kids.

"I'm afraid all the drugs might have damaged her mind," Carlo continued sadly, "So maybe it might have been her. Maybe she was just lashing out at me for trying to help.

"But why she would want to put Del Toro's murder on me God only knows - you'd have to ask her - poor, crazy, mixed up kid."

Was she around?

"No. Did a bunk yesterday morning. I'm worried sick but I don't expect to see her again any time soon."

The detectives said they were sorry.

"Thanks. But what can you do - kids, huh?"

They nodded in agreement, sympathising fully.

Then they thanked him for his time, apologised for disturbing him yet again and went on their way.

Carlo was home free.

However, he was thankful he'd had the good sense to change the opening mechanism on the bookcase - a task he had been meaning to do for sometime. But since Ava's disappearance he thought it prudent to do it immediately in case he should get a visit from LA's finest.

The bookcase was now linked to a button under his desk; the work only completed thirty minutes before the police arrived - hell they might even have driven past the maintenance crew who

418

installed it!

But it mattered not now. The cops bought his story and would not come sniffing around again.

Likewise with the car. A connection of Salvatore's in Santa Monica had supplied him with the brand new Camaro; stolen to order from Philadelphia three weeks earlier and awaiting shipment to the Far East, destined for a wealthy Chinese client.

But the buyer would have to wait for another car to be obtained for him as Carlo Liuzzi had jumped to the front of the line.

All it took was two bags of Salvatore's purest cocaine and twenty grand to sweeten the deal.

They just had to switch the plates.

Simple.

Carlo's own Camaro was now just a small cube of metal buried deep in a downtown junkyard. It had been stripped, wiped clean and crushed - good luck to anyone hoping to find that in a hurry.

Nevertheless, even though Carlo was off the hook, he could not help but think about Ava, wishing he had killed her when he had the opportunity.

Because a little voice in the back of his mind told him that the girl was going to be trouble.

Chapter Thirty One

Cadiz, Spain 1974

Maria regarded herself in the mirror as she dressed. She was forty-three now and had been a widow for six long years, yet she still wore the black clothes of mourning.

Diego's murder, which still remained unsolved, had been a devastating loss and had hit her extremely hard.

She had been in Cambridge, Massachusetts, spending some time with Danny at Harvard when she heard the dreadful news. Both she and her son caught the first flight out to LA desperately hoping it had all been some awful mistake and that they would find Diego alive and well.

But it was no mistake. And a piece of Maria died that day too.

They took the bodies of both Diego and Juan Pablo home to Cadiz and, along with Nate, interred them together in the Del Toro family mausoleum.

Juan Pablo had no close family; his life spent in the service of Diego. It was a fitting resting place for such a dedicated and loyal friend.

The deaths of both men, although Diego's in particular, had hit them all terribly hard. Danny and Nate had been devastated at the loss of their most caring and loving adopted father who had taken them under his wing and treated them as his own; who had shaped them into the good, strong men they had become.

But his death had hit Maria hardest of all.

After the funeral, she retired to her room and did not reappear for several days, the impact of her husband's violent and sudden murder taking a dreadful toll upon her.

Danny and Nate took good care of her and Delores took care of all three of them, even though her heart was breaking too.

Danny decided there and then to drop out of college, whilst Nate took a long leave of absence from PNAC to be with his family, but knew, in his heart, he would not return to the seminary in Rome.

However, Matador was an enormous leviathan of a company and needed someone at its helm. Viscount, too, whilst in the day-to-day charge of the eminently capable Herb Horowitz, needed an objective overseer to guide it safely into the future.

After all, Herb was pushing seventy and would not carry on forever.

Both of these roles had previously been filled by Diego, himself, ably assisted by the redoubtable Juan Pablo. But those men were no longer alive.

The obvious answer, Danny and Nate decided, was for them to take over - but with Maria in overall control - so she would have the final word on everything.

First, though, they had to agree it with their mother.

At the time of Diego's death, Danny and Nate were just twenty years old, yet they were intelligent, multi-lingual, fast-learners who were more than up to the challenge.

And Maria did not doubt it, with the right guidance, the right help, they could do it. However, it was not their abilities she questioned but their readiness to so quickly abandon their studies.

Danny had been doing well at Harvard, with none of the fights or altercations that were so symptomatic of his time at Columbia recurring there. He had knuckled down, settled into a routine and adapted to life without his brother - just as Maria and Diego knew he would.

His grades were excellent, his dedication unquestionable and he was on course for a first class degree.

Yet he was willing to abandon it all to honour his father.

But, he reasoned, it was always envisaged he would work with Diego one day, with a view to taking over eventually, so why not now? Why not get dropped in at the deep end - sometimes that was the only way to truly learn - although not necessarily, he conceded, where multi-million dollar companies were concerned - but he was a quick study.

Maria could not help but agree with his reasoning.

Nate's situation, however, was slightly more problematic. Maria had always known of his deeply religious beliefs and his desire to be a priest and had been incredibly supportive of him, as had Diego who had been a religious man himself.

But Nate explained how in recent years he had been seriously questioning his faith and huge cracks had appeared in his previously rock solid beliefs.

He said that ever since Gino's death he had been having significant doubts and now, after Diego's murder, his belief in God had been all but extinguished.

Maria was shocked, she had no idea, and Nate admitted he had been too ashamed to tell her. But it was the truth and not just a passing phase which he hoped, at first, it might have been.

But the simple fact was, he had lost his faith and no longer possessed the single most important requirement to be a priest.

With that realisation he had become a man in need of a purpose. Something to get his teeth into and build upon - and what better than his father's legacy.

Maria took all of these factors into consideration and gave herself several days to mull them over. But ultimately she knew it made sense.

They were clever, instinctive young men, both trustworthy and honourable - so who better to steer Diego's empire into an unchartered future?

Besides, the boys were always better together than apart.

So it was agreed. Over the coming months and years, Nate and Danny would gradually take over, working together, under Maria's careful guidance and with the help of excellent people such as Herb Horowitz at Viscount and others like him at Matador.

It would be an almighty challenge but Danny and Nate were more than up to the task.

Maria's only proviso was that they should only go to Los Angeles or New York when it was absolutely necessary and, in such circumstances, to keep as far away from Carlo Liuzzi and Salvatore Falcone as possible.

She still feared for their safety, even though they were now grown men with immense power and wealth at their disposal, her chance meeting in New York with Falcone still burning strong in her memory.

As for her father, she dare not think what he might do should he discover that Danny and Nate were her sons. Both sired by men he had killed.

Nor, indeed, what his reaction might be if he found out his only daughter still lived.

Maria already had a rather disturbing suspicion that Carlo may have had something to do with Diego's murder; a niggling feeling that it was him who had killed her beloved husband.

But she had no basis for these suspicions, no proof. Just her own, finely tuned, intuition and she found it extremely unsettling.

Fortunately, no one knew who the boys' true fathers were and to the world in general they were the sons of Diego Del Toro, so there was no reason to believe that Carlo would think differently.

Consequently, whenever Nate or Danny appeared in public - either at the studios in Hollywood or any one of the hotels in LA or New York it was the Del Toro name people associated them with and not those belonging to the lowly offspring of a young Italian gardener or a quiet, Irish chauffeur.

But it did not help Maria sleep any easier.

Nevertheless, six years on from that momentous decision, Maria's faith in the boys' had been completely vindicated.

Both Matador and Viscount were flourishing - stronger and more successful than ever before. Indeed, Herb Horowitz would soon be retiring and the transition, which once would have seemed extremely problematic, was on course to be smooth and trouble free.

Yet Diego's killer had still not been found and it weighed heavily on Maria, Danny and Nate enormously.

But especially on Maria.

She had aged well and lost none of her beauty but there was an enduring sadness about her that she found impossible to shake.

She had become a virtual recluse and rarely strayed beyond the grounds of the villa in Cadiz which had become her permanent residence since losing Diego.

Both boys had offices there which made it easier for them to keep a watchful eye on her, whilst in return, she offered advice and gave them council on matters pertaining to the Matador empire.

However, Danny and Nate also spent a great deal of time abroad, taking care of their various business interests but they tried, wherever possible, to ensure one of them always remained in Cadiz with Maria.

Her perpetual sadness worried them and they knew even though she had Delores for company, she still missed Diego terribly.

As she stood looking in the mirror, she toyed with the locket that had hung around her neck since being reunited with Danny, keeping the image of Diego contained within it close to her heart at all times.

Delores was behind her, fussing with Maria's hair as she regarded the newly acquired dress she had put on for her lunchtime appointment with Nate, Danny and the architect whom she hoped would design and oversee the construction of the new Paris Matador. She had flown him in especially to discuss the project.

The dress she had chosen was stylish and beautifully cut, fitting her shapely figure perfectly and even though it was still mourning black, she looked absolutely stunning.

But her beauty, although not lost on her, was of little consequence, as were the many suitors who frequently sought her attention. But she was not interested.

Maria, although still playing a key role in both Matador and Viscount, had lost all her passion for life outside the villa and the thought of being with anyone other than Diego was simply unbearable.

Only his legacy and her boys were important to her now.

However, both Danny and Nate were keen for her to start living again. Whilst they still felt the loss of Diego deeply, they had managed to move on, no matter how difficult it had been at first. Yet their mother simply had not and they felt so sorry for her.

Delores finished Maria's hair with an elaborate flourish of hairspray and said "Muy bueno," as she admired her handiwork.

Maria turned and gave the old woman a kiss on the cheek, "What on earth would I do without you?" She said gratefully, then strode purposely out of her dressing room to where her sons and the architect were waiting for her downstairs.

***

Danny knew he would be cutting it fine and there was a chance he might be late for the meeting, but he desperately needed some fresh air after a long night spent travelling.

He had arrived in from Kenya that morning where he had

been scouting locations for an upcoming Viscount movie. He had worked and slept a little during the flight but now needed to stretch his legs and get his muscles working again so had decided to go for a run. Mike, however, his ever present bodyguard, was not so keen.

Nowadays, both Danny and Nate had a security team following their every move and each had their own personal bodyguard - Mike, an ex-heavyweight boxer, was Danny's and a former Navy Seal called 'Wes' was Nate's.

It was at their mother's insistence now they were such high profile, wealthy young men and after what had happened to Diego it seemed only prudent.

At first it seemed odd to have them tagging along wherever they went but now it seemed perfectly normal.

Indeed, they had become good friends.

Danny had enjoyed his beach run along La Playa de la Victoria with the light sea breeze blowing away the cobwebs of his journey and the warm waves of the Atlantic Ocean lapping melodically against the sandy shore but as he checked his watch he knew he'd been out too long.

He turned in land, with Mike hot on his heels, and headed down into the narrow streets of the ancient town. After a series of twists and turns he came out into a beautiful open plaza that was milling with tourists and locals alike. Dodging the crowds he darted into another side street and kept going until he came out onto the Calle Del Toro, the street that had been named after Diego's father, and followed it until he came to the gates of the family villa.

He was panting hard now and paused outside the gates to allow his breath to slow; bending almost double and placing his hands on his knees, completely exhausted but miraculously revitalised.

Mike was only a few seconds behind him, sweating profusely and puffing hard.

Neither man had noticed the innocuous little Fiat parked a

few cars away down the tree-lined avenue, nor were they aware of its driver getting out.

"Shit, man!" Mike breathed, "You gotta slow down - I thought I'd lost you there!"

Danny laughed. "I thought you were supposed to be fit?"

"Fit, yeah. Insane, no. It's too goddamn hot to run like that."

"Yeah, I know. Sorry. But I had to get back - I've got that thing, you know, with Mom and the architect—"

"Danny?" Suddenly a female voice said, startling them both.

Immediately Mike was alert and he turned to see a slender woman in a hooded fleece and a baseball cap walking towards them.

"Easy, ma'am," Mike said.

"It's okay, Mike. It's fine," Danny said. "What is it miss? What can I help you with?"

"Danny - it's me!" Said the girl, pushing off her hood and removing the baseball cap, allowing her long, blonde hair to spill out and fall down way past her shoulders. "It's me, do you remember?"

Danny looked at her. The shock and amazement clear to see on his face as he recognised the girl instantly. "My God," he said.

"You okay there Danny?" Asked Mike, concerned, still wary of the stranger approaching, keen to keep his employer safe.

"Yeah, I'm fine, Mike. Fine. You go in. I'll see you in a minute. Everything's okay, don't worry."

"You sure, boss?"

"Positive."

Mike looked far from placated but he did as instructed. He slipped through the gates into the grounds and began to walk up the long shady driveway towards the house. Leaving his charge alone with the girl, much against his better judgement.

When Mike was out of ear shot, the girl smiled prettily, looking slightly embarrassed.

"Surprise!" She said.

Danny was still stunned, yet he could not help but feel a slight rush of delight.

"Ava," he said, "what are you doing here?"

***

Danny could not believe it. Here they were standing in the middle of Cadiz - thousands of miles away from the place where he had last set eyes on her - in a completely different country no less. Yet here she was, the only girl who had ever really meant something, standing right in front of him.

He was utterly stunned.

Ava looked tired, yet still absolutely beautiful - probably even more so now she had fully grown-up. At twenty-six, Danny could not help but notice she had become every inch a woman.

Yet her clothes were simple; a hooded sweatshirt, an old T-shirt, tight, faded jeans and a pair of sneakers that had seen better days. In short, she no longer looked quite so affluent.

She had lost a little weight, too, although not enough to spoil her spectacular physique but enough to give Danny the impression she had fallen on harder times.

He had thought about Ava many times over the years and always wondered what had become of her and whether their paths might ever cross again.

And seeing her now, he knew why she still haunted his dreams.

But then the memory of what she had told him in that diner by Central Park came back to him - the reason why he had left Columbia and forbidden himself from seeing her again.

Her step-father was Carlo Liuzzi.

And the knowledge of that made him harden his attitude.

"I'm so sorry, Danny," she said, noting the change in his body language. "I know it's been a long time and I know you don't want to see me but I had to see you."

"You're here on vacation then?"

"No - not a vacation. Nothing like that. I came here especially to see you—"

"—Just to see me?" Danny was incredulous, yet deep down just a little delighted, too. "But this is Cadiz, Ava, not New Jersey - why on earth—"

"Because I've been looking for you - looking for you for ages. I have something I must tell you." Ava's eyes were brimming with tears, finding Danny after so long was making her feel quite emotional - even more so for what she knew she must tell him.

"Well, you found me. Here I am. What is it you want to say?"

Now it had come down to it Ava's courage was fading, but she knew she must tell him. Knew it for both their sakes. "I don't really know how to make this sound any easier but..."

"But what, Ava?" Danny hated himself for being so brusque, but it was for the good of his family. "It's okay, please just tell me."

"I'm so sorry but I know who killed your father," she finally blurted. "I know who killed Diego Del Toro!"

And then she burst into tears.

***

Sometime later, as they sat on a bench under the shade of a beautiful, bougainvillaea covered pergola in the villa's grounds, Danny could still not believe it.

Ava had told him she had been searching for him for six years. Indeed the first place she went to after leaving Flagstaff was Cambridge, Massachusetts, trying to locate him at Harvard, her last known address for him.

Of course, she knew he would fly to LA after the murder of Diego but she had assumed at some point in the near future he would return to Harvard to resume his studies. But he did not.

She had followed his career avidly since then, but with money scarce she had been forced to find work to support herself, taking any job she could just to save up enough money to get her to Cadiz where she knew the Matador head offices were located. She was certain Danny would show up there sooner or later.

However, with the majority of her meagre income being spent on rent and bills, it had taken her six long years to save for the ticket but at last she had done it.

Ava had flown into Cadiz a month ago and had been waiting for Danny since then. And she finally found an opportunity to approach him that morning.

At first she had told him everything in a jumble; about how she found out that Carlo had murdered Diego; about the beat up Camaro and the bloodied Oscar - and about how she had phoned the police but no action had been taken.

Then, calming a little, she related her own experiences with her step-father. She said how he had killed Edmund and how, right in front of her young eyes, he had murdered a man in his study, with a shard of pottery. Ava then ended her awful tale with Mildred's enforced imprisonment and the dreadful, callous way in which she was left to die.

She was sobbing by the time she had finished, telling Danny she hated her step-father and Salvatore Falcone for what they had done - both to her and to Danny, too, robbing each of them of their fathers.

"I'm so sorry," Ava said, "but I knew I had to find you, knew I had to tell you. What my step-father did - and Falcone - it's not right. They shouldn't be allowed to just get away with it.

"I want to make those bastards pay and I thought maybe you could help."

Danny was silent for a long time as he took in all that Ava had told him, mulling over everything in his mind; all that had happened.

Eventually, he finally said, "Did you ever wonder why I never came back to Columbia? Why I suddenly left New York - or never called you?"

"Sure." She replied, "Always. But it's okay, you don't have to go into it now. You must have had your reasons and I just figured I'd maybe made a mistake, that perhaps you didn't like me as much as I—"

"No. It was not that," said Danny firmly. "Not that at all."

Ava looked at him quizzically, "Why then?" she asked, sensing he wanted to tell her.

"It was because of your step-father. When you said his name - and Falcone's - I already knew them. I'd heard them first mentioned on the night my own step-mother died."

Now it was Ava's turn to look shocked as Danny continued.

"You see, Diego Del Toro was not my real father, even though I loved him like he was - and so did my brother, Nate.

"But my real father was a young, Italian immigrant by the name of Armando Calabrese. His best friend was Nathaniel Kelly, an Irishman - also an immigrant.

"Nathaniel was Nate's birth father. Both had gone to America to find their fortune and met when they were hired as gardener and chauffeur to a wealthy Hollywood studio boss named Carlo Liuzzi."

Ava gasped loudly. "No! But I thought—"

"Please," Danny said, "there's more. Let me finish."

She nodded, dreading what yet she might hear as Danny went on.

"Liuzzi had a daughter, Maria—"

"Yes, I know, she died—"

Danny gave her a look. "Sorry," she said, "please, carry on."

"Liuzzi had a daughter, Maria," he began again, "as you obviously know. She was young, reckless, full of life - much like Armando - and the two began an affair and soon fell deeply in love.

"But Carlo Liuzzi didn't approve. He caught them together and had Armando carted off, locking his daughter in her room.

"Then Liuzzi and Falcone killed my father—"

431

"Oh my God! Danny, I'm so sorry—"

"But Nathaniel found out, maybe disturbed them somehow, I don't know - and they killed him, too."

"Oh, this is too horrible, too vile—"

"Then, upon discovering Maria was pregnant with a lowly gardener's child, he banished her and her baby to Sicily, so ashamed of her that he sentenced her to live out the rest of her days as a nun in a convent. Her child was to be sent to a monastery - never intended to know who his mother was.

"Liuzzi sent Nathaniel's wife, Megan, with her, a nursemaid who had a baby of her own. Her milk would sustain both children until they had reached their destination.

"But Falcone went, too, at Carlo's behest - with orders to kill Megan and her child the moment Maria's baby was delivered to the monastery.

"But something happened, for some reason Falcone decided to take matters into his own hands, and en-route to Sicily he tried to murder Maria and Megan before they ever reached their destination - throwing Maria from a moving train—"

Ava gasped again in horror. "Falcone killed her?" She said.

But Danny ploughed on without answering, "Yet Megan somehow fought Falcone off - and he, too, found himself bundled from the train.

"Megan miraculously made it back to New York, enduring terrible poverty to raise the two children as her own."

Ava looked at Danny, slowly registering her understanding. "You were one of those babies, weren't you?"

"Yes. Maria is my mother. Armando Calabrese was my father - he and Diego Del Toro. Nate is Megan's son."

"So Megan married Diego?"

"No. Maria married Diego."

"But I thought you said— I was always told that Maria had..."

"Died?" Danny asked.

"Yes," she nodded.

"No, Diego saved her but she spent years in a coma. When she came out of it they got married and in time found Nate and me."

"Diego adopted both of us after our mother—" He choked a little, "I mean after Nate's mother, Megan, died."

"Oh my God, Danny. That's incredible!" Ava said, truly amazed. She did not doubt his story for a moment as she knew well what both her step-father and Falcone were capable of.

Then a thought suddenly struck her. "So that makes you Carlo Liuzzi's grandson?"

"Mmm hmm," Danny agreed, reluctantly. "Which means you and me are related—"

"Whoa, there!" Ava interjected. "Just wait a minute - you and me are nothing of the kind. Liuzzi never adopted me - he just liked to call himself my 'father' - he even made me call him 'Daddy'. But my father was Edmund Peyton - a good man from Iowa - and I'm pretty sure no relation of yours!"

Danny smiled a little, lightening the mood. "Well that's a relief," he said.

Ava looked at him and smiled too. He really was handsome. "It is huh?"

"Uh huh," he replied, staring into her big blue eyes.

Chapter Thirty Two

Steven Brownley was mid forties with dark, greying hair, piercing blue eyes, a square jaw and a laconic, easy-going smile. He was slender and supremely fit and looked exceptionally good in the white shirt, tan jacket and beige chinos he had chosen for the meeting.

Incredibly, he was one of the foremost architects of his generation and had earned great acclaim and much respect for his revolutionary designs and influential style. Indeed, some of the world's most amazing structures had been conceived by him.

Maria, after being introduced to his work by Diego, had written to ask him if he would consider lending his considerable talents to the design of a hotel.

The project wouldn't normally have appealed to Steven Brownley but he had been an admirer of Diego Del Toro and had been impressed, too, by his sons' achievements since taking over from him.

Also, Maria Del Toro's letter had intrigued him, as did she, herself - even though he had never seen or spoken to her.

So he accepted her invitation and agreed to be flown to Cadiz to discuss her ideas for the proposed hotel. Paris conjured up all kinds of design possibilities and even though he was loathed to admit it, he was already getting excited about the prospect of creating something elegant and long-lasting there.

Yet, so far, he had not so much as looked at the contract or the woman with whom he would be liaising with if he agreed to take on the project.

***

Maria entered the drawing room and was mildly annoyed to see that Danny was missing from the meeting as she had specifically wanted him to be present.

The Paris hotel project was especially important to her, and the company as a whole, as it had been the last thing for Matador that Diego had worked on personally.

It was he who had negotiated for the land and the rights to build upon it, he who had schmoozed the French government into allowing him to build a new hotel in their capital and he who had originally mooted the idea of Steven Brownley to design it.

However, with all the turmoil caused by Diego's death and the subsequent transfer of power, circumstances had rather gotten in the way and the project had been mothballed indefinitely.

Quite by chance, a few months earlier, Maria had come across some thoughts of Diego's he had jotted down on a notepad outlining his ideas for the Paris building and since then she had made its completion something of a personal crusade.

She had requested the meeting with the architect and had insisted both Danny and Nate be in attendance.

Nate duly was, and greeted his mother with a smile. At twenty six, Nate was still slender in stature and not too tall but he had grown into a good-looking young man with a fresh face and a shock of bright red hair.

He was dressed casually in a blue polo shirt and khaki slacks, as he stood by the antique cabinet that sat up against the wall in the drawing room, pouring two cups of coffee from the pot that had been set out there by Delores for the meeting.

Nate was partially obscuring the man behind him and he

quickly stepped aside to introduce Maria to the architect who had flown in especially to meet with her.

"Señora Del Toro, how nice to finally meet you," said Steven Brownley, offering his hand, his well-educated English accent, soft and deep.

Maria shook his hand, quite taken aback by his appearance. She had expected someone more studious, more scholarly, certainly not the handsome Cary Grant type standing before her.

"The pleasure's mine, Mr. Brownley—"

"Steven, please. And you are Maria, yes?"

"Erm, yes," said Maria, caught a little off guard, "I am."

"Good. That's the formalities out of the way. I believe your son Danny will be joining us too, is that correct?"

"Yes, it is. But I'm afraid he seems to be running a little late - I do apologise."

"Please, no need. I quite understand. I'm sure he must be extremely busy."

"Very," said Nate. "But I know he wanted to be here. Please, Steven, excuse me whilst I go see where he's got to."

"Of course," nodded Steven as Nate walked from the room to leave him and Maria alone.

"Forgive my son, Steven," said Maria. "He flew in from Kenya just this morning and time must have gotten away from him."

"Please don't concern yourself. It's no trouble. And thank you for flying me here to this wonderful villa, the architecture is spectacular - as is the whole of Cadiz, it's a pleasure to come here again to this marvellous old city."

"Ah, you've been here before then?"

"Yes. It's where I met your husband—"

"You knew Diego?"

Steven could see he had touched a nerve. "Alas, only briefly, we met at a party but seemed to hit it off. I admired him greatly. May I say how sorry I was to hear of his passing?"

"Thank you," she said softly.

He sensed her sadness and continued, "I know how difficult it can be to lose someone so close."

"You do?" She looked up at him, staring into his kind eyes.

"Yes. My wife. Eight years ago - breast cancer. She was only thirty-eight."

"I'm so sorry."

Steven nodded his thanks. "It takes time, doesn't it?" He said, immediately understanding what she had been going through since she had lost Diego.

"Yes," she replied simply. "It does."

There was a long moment of silence as each thought about their lost loves, before Maria said, "Diego was a great admirer of yours, too, you know. It was he who first mentioned your name for the Paris project - he adored your work."

"Wow! High praise, indeed. I only hope I'm worthy of it." He looked at her and gave her a self-deprecating smile, finding himself transfixed by her eyes. She was absolutely beautiful, stunning, and he could not help but stare at her.

Realising he had been staring too long, he said, "Forgive me, Maria. You've quite surprised me - I was unsure of what to expect."

"I'll choose to take that as a complement," Maria said with a giggle.

"God I'm sorry, that sounded so rude. Yes, please do take it as a compliment."

Maria was laughing now, something she had not done in a very long time, as she said, "Don't worry Mr. Brownley - I mean Steven, I didn't know quite what to expect from you either."

"Really?"

"Really. In my mind you were a sixty year old university professor - not someone—"

"—Quite so young and dashing, you mean?" He said with an easy smile, mocking himself mercilessly.

"Exactly."

"I hope I'm not a disappointment."

Maria regarded him again, for the first time in years feeling drawn to another man. There was something about Steven she liked - not just the fact he was incredibly good looking and, indeed, rather dashing as he himself had joked, but there was a kindliness about him, too, and he had gentle, sensitive eyes which she found irresistibly attractive.

"Not at all," she replied enigmatically, in fact, quite the contrary."

Steven was just about to say something in return when Nate walked back into the room.

"I'm so sorry, Steven," he said. "I'm afraid something's come up, something quite unexpected - a family matter. Would you mind terribly if we rescheduled our meeting for tomorrow, same time? I do apologise."

"No, not at all, that's quite alright."

"Nate?" said Maria, suddenly concerned, "What's all this about? Is everything okay?"

"Yes. Fine. Honestly - just something which requires both our attention I'm afraid. Nothing to worry about."

Maria relaxed again, although she was a little perplexed as to why the meeting had to be brought to a halt before it had even begun. Not least because she had found herself enjoying the company of Steven Brownley.

"Steven, I'm so sorry for this inconvenience," she said apologetically.

"It's nothing, really. Please do not trouble yourself."

"All the same," she said, "I would be happier if you would let me buy you dinner at least - to compensate for your trouble."

Nate very nearly did a double take, was this his mother talking?"

It was unheard of for her to go to dinner with a man - and many had asked. But she had always politely declined. Now she was the one doing the asking. He was amazed yet pleased. Did this mean she had finally allowed herself to start living again? He certainly hoped so.

"How nice of you. Yes, I would be delighted. Thank you." Said Steven.

"Wonderful," my car will pick you up from your hotel around eight, if that's convenient?"

"Perfect. I look forward to seeing you then." He then walked to the door. "Nate, it's been a pleasure. I'll see you tomorrow. Maria, until tonight, then." And with that he left.

Maria watched him leave then turned to see Nate smiling at her.

"A date huh?" He said knowingly.

"A dinner. That's all," she said, but guilt was etched all over her face.

"Hmm. Sure sounds like a date to me."

"Well I had to placate the poor man didn't I?" Said Maria with mock innocence, "After all, if you're going to cancel meetings right, left and centre, I could find myself getting very fat indeed from all the apologies I might have to make. What's so urgent anyway?"

Nate had been so stunned by Maria's dinner proposal he had almost forgotten what was so important and his face hardened, suddenly becoming grave.

"It's about Diego," he said solemnly, "We know who killed him."

***

Maria followed Nate through into the large kitchen at the back of the villa which doubled as an informal family dining room. In its centre stood a long rustic table in the Mediterranean style with bench seating either side.

On the far side sat Danny next to a striking blonde haired girl of about his age.

439

"Mom, this is Ava," he said. "She's Carlo Liuzzi's step-daughter and she knows for certain that the bastard murdered Diego."

***

Once again, Ava related her whole sorry tale. At first Maria was wary of her and viewed her coolly, but by the time Ava had finished she had warmed to her immensely and felt extremely sorry for her. Maria could also tell Danny was completely smitten with her.

In turn, Maria then filled in the blanks in her own story that Danny had not told Ava, telling it more concisely and from a personal perspective.

What became instantly clear though was that everyone sitting around that table had suffered terribly at the hands of Carlo Liuzzi and Salvatore Falcone - their lives shaped one way or another by the atrocities committed by those two evil men.

Armando, Nathaniel, Edmund, Mildred and Diego - all dead because of Liuzzi and Falcone. Whilst Maria, Megan and Ava had all been lucky to escape with their lives, although each had endured dreadful hardship as a result.

Something needed to be done they all agreed. Which was partly the reason for Ava's arrival in Cadiz; believing there was strength in numbers - and she had felt in desperate need of allies.

"We need to bring them down once and for all," Maria said vehemently. "This has gone on long enough. We have all suffered and hidden ourselves away for too long. We've got to strike now - take the fight to them and make sure they don't hurt anyone else ever again."

"Agreed." Said Danny and Nate in unison.

"But how?" asked Maria.

"I'm not sure, but I think I might have a way," said Ava. "Or at least the beginnings of an idea anyway."

Maria smiled. "Danny, I like this girl - why have I never her met her before?"

Her son smiled back, knowing she was being ironic but pleased

440

she liked Ava so much. "Beats me," he said.

At that moment Delores arrived in the kitchen, "Right, outside everyone," she ordered in her thick Spanish accent, "I serve lunch on veranda in fifteen minute!"

"But Del, we're just having a meeting—" Danny protested.

"No! No 'but' - it's lunch. You need eat to make you strong. You do as I say, otherwise I get Mike and Wes to make you do it!"

Everyone laughed. "Okay Del," Danny surrendered, "you win - we'll take it outside."

"You good boy," Delores said. "I knew you see it my way."

"I don't think we get any choice in that, Del, do we?" Said Nate jumping in.

"No. No choice - in food, I am boss."

"You can say that again," said Maria, "And we'd all be lost without you."

Then she took hold of Ava's hand and added fondly, "Come on, Ava, let me show you the garden where you can tell me all about yourself - we can discuss my father more over lunch."

Ava eagerly complied, allowing Maria to lead her out of the kitchen and into the garden, as Danny and Nate were scooted out behind her by the clearly adoring Delores. It felt so nice to be in company of such a warm and loving family.

**

Danny and Nate sat together at the large outdoor dining table under yet another large pergola as Delores bustled around them setting down platters and plates stuffed with enough food to feed a small army.

From the villa's slightly elevated position, they could see over much of the beautiful old city and out across the bay, the turquoise Mediterranean on one side, the warm blue Atlantic on the other. It was truly an idyllic spot; a fact that was not lost on either of them.

They had, indeed, been truly lucky and each knew, with Ava's arrival, the time had now come to repay that good fortune.

They watched her as she and Maria, their arms linked, wandered happily up towards them, clearly enjoying each other's company immensely.

Nate poured some wine into Danny's empty glass. "You like this one, don't you?"

Danny smiled, "Is it so obvious?"

"As clear as the nose on your face."

"That bad, huh?"

"Uh huh."

"Is it right though?" Danny asked, "You know, bearing in mind who she is, who her step-father is—"

"It doesn't matter about that. If it's God's will then—"

Suddenly Nate clammed up. What made him use that expression? He had given up on God, renounced his religion, so what right did he have speaking about His will?

"God, huh?" Said Danny, interpreting his brother's thoughts and perhaps understanding them better than Nate, himself. "Now there's a thing."

"Ain't it just," said Nate, suddenly deep in thought.

***

As they settled down to lunch the talk got around once more to Carlo Liuzzi and Salvatore Falcone.

Ava then revealed that she and Frankie DeLuca had been keeping in touch secretly for the past six years, at great personal risk to Frankie, himself, who she said she trusted implicitly.

"He's been so good to me," she said. "Like a father really. And I love him. He's sent me money when he could and we've kept in touch through phone calls whenever it was possible. He even put me up in New York for a few weeks in a place not known to Carlo. But it was not safe for me to stay there too long, just in case."

"So you think Frankie might be able to help us?" Danny asked.

"Is that what you're saying?"

"Maybe. He's been feeding me information, keeping me up to date with what's been going on out there and believe me, it's not good.

"Carlo's in debt. Lot's of it. Gold Star has been going through some tough times - a lot of bad pictures and poor investments - him personally throwing a lot of his own money into movies that just bombed at the box office. It's left him with almost nothing."

"Who does he owe?" Said Danny, already seeing her angle, "Maybe we can buy out the debt then call it in? Give the bastard something to really worry about."

"That was my thinking," said Ava. "Hit him in his pocket and destroy his reputation. See how his valuable pride fares then."

"Who does he owe?" Asked Maria, warming to the idea.

"That's the problem," replied Ava, "Frankie says he's borrowed millions from the Carboni crime family in New York - it's who he and Salvatore started out with apparently when they first arrived in The States."

"Damn it." Said Maria. "That could be trouble."

"Not necessarily," chimed in Nate. "I think I might know someone who might be able to help."

"The Contessa you mean?" Asked Maria.

"Yeah, maybe. I'll ask. Can't do any harm, right?"

"Sure," they all agreed.

"But what about Falcone? What about him?" Said Maria. "Has Frankie said anything about him?"

"Not much. Except that he's big into the cocaine business. He ships it into Hollywood from New York and supplies all the big stars - it's making him plenty of money. I think he's doing better than Carlo now."

"Anything else?" Danny said. "Anything else at all?"

"Ava thought for a moment, her mind going back several years

443

to the day she overheard Salvatore talking on the phone in Carlo's office. "Maybe," she said. "I heard him talking to this guy once, from New York, on the phone. A guy called 'Bruno' something?" She thought for a long moment, racking her brains.

"'Barca'", she suddenly exclaimed. "That's it. Bruno Barca - he was Salvatore's guy in New York and he was getting his shipments from some really scary sounding organisation - I'll never forget it cos it sounded so odd at the time. An organisation called 'The Mountain Wolves—"

Nate very nearly spat out his wine. "The Mountain Wolves? Are you sure - did he say 'i lupi di montagna'? - do you remember?"

"Yeah, he did. I'm sure of it. I lupi di montagna - The Mountain Wolves definitely. Why?"

Nate smiled. "Because now I know that the Contessa di Montagna can help us for certain."

***

That evening Maria felt completely reinvigorated. She was confident that together with Ava and the Contessa's help they could finally make her father and his odious sidekick pay for their sickening crimes. She looked forward to the day when she could at last look Carlo in the eye and let him know that she, Maria, the daughter he had thought dead, and Danny the grandson he did not want, were the cause of his catastrophic downfall.

She dressed for dinner in a canary yellow dress by Yves Saint Laurent, which beautifully fitted her glorious form, choosing a pair of Gucci kitten heels and just the right amount of jewellery to set it off to perfection.

As she descended the stairs and walked in to the spacious family room, where Nate, Danny and Ava were all sitting chatting, their conversation instantly dried.

She looked amazing - at least ten years younger than her 43 years and more vivacious and happy than she had looked in a very long time.

It was clear that her long period of mourning was finally over and Danny and Nate could not have been more pleased.

"Wow!" You look fabulous," cried Ava.

"Yeah, wow Mom," agreed Danny, "you really do."

"Thank you," she said, "It's nice to feel pretty again."

"Well you sure look that, Mom," said Nate. "You're looking real good for your hot date!"

"It's not a date. It's just a business dinner. The least I could do for that poor, handsome Mr Brownley after he'd come all this way." She winked conspiratorially at Ava who giggled.

"But don't wait up boys - I might be late!" She said brazenly before waltzing from the room leaving her two sons speechless and Ava laughing at their shocked faces.

She found Max, her faithful driver, out on the driveway, holding open the rear door of her sparkling Rolls-Royce Silver Cloud limousine, its two-tone silver and midnight blue paintwork twinkling luxuriously in the moonlight.

"You look beautiful, ma'am," said Max in his deep Georgia timbre. "Real beautiful."

"Thank you, Max," she said. "You know where we're going?"

"Yes, ma'am. Be there in no time." He replied, closing the door after she had slid comfortably inside the gleaming automobile.

For the first time in years she felt excited.

***

Steven Brownly did not disappoint. He wore a pale grey seersucker suit with a crisp white shirt and a sky blue tie. On his feet he wore polished black loafers. Smart and beautifully turned out.

They dined at a wonderful restaurant overlooking the shoreline and sat at a table on the tiled flagstones of the patio. The sound of the sea carried on the warm night breeze and mingled perfectly with the soft music and lighting of the restaurant to create a cosy and romantic ambience.

Maria and Steven's attraction was immediate and was hard to deny. But they kept the conversation light and mostly business like as they discussed the pros and cons of the Paris hotel project.

Steven was incredibly charismatic as he spoke about his love of architecture and his passion for design and Maria found herself completely rapt in all he had to say, knowing without doubt, regardless of his looks, he was exactly the right person for the job.

Diego had chosen him well for her.

In return, Steven was dazzled by Maria; her looks, her smile and her sparkling repartee. She certainly was wonderful company.

He had dated very little since the death of his wife and in the main had found it hard to engage with women on a romantic level. But with Maria it was different. There was something about her he just took to instantly - a spark which she felt too.

At the end of the evening, Max dropped Steven back at his hotel. "Thank you, Maria, for a lovely evening. I've enjoyed it immensely." He said as Max opened his door.

"Me too," replied Maria. "You're very good company Mr Brownley, you know that?"

"Why, thank you. You too." He replied.

He thought for a moment, not wishing to be too presumptuous, then added, "I'd very much like to see you again if I may - not including our meeting tomorrow of course." He said just to clarify his intent.

"Yes. That would be nice." Said Maria.

"Perhaps you'd let me take you to dinner next time."

"I'd like that. Very much."

"How does tomorrow evening sound - too soon?" Asked Steven tentatively.

"Not at all. It sounds perfect."

"Good. Then I'll see you in the morning for our meeting and

we can discuss our plans for dinner after that."

"I look forward to it."

"As do I. Goodnight, Maria."

"Goodnight Steven." She replied.

And then he was gone. However the feeling of excitement in Maria's tummy had returned with a vengeance.

Chapter Thirty Three

Rome, Italy 1974

Aweek on from Ava's arrival in Cadiz, Nate found himself back in Rome, heading towards the Contessa's villa high up in the hills.

He had left his bodyguard, Wes, back in the city, insisting there was no safer place in all of Rome than behind the thick stone walls of the Contessa's monastic residence.

He would be fine, he said, and reluctantly Wes had agreed to stay behind.

For Nate it was good to get away on his own into the countryside and he felt thoroughly alive as he wound his way up the hillside and through the tiny roadside hamlets.

Eventually the paved road ended and gave way to the well-worn mountain track. This, in turn, led to the familiar clearing above the hillside where the Contessa's villa nestled majestically, surrounded by a spectacular view of the valley beyond.

And, when at last he saw it, Nate felt as if he had come home.

When he had been a seminarian, he had always visited on his trusty scooter but today he was driving a brand new Range Rover which he had picked up at the airport.

However, even in the smooth 4x4 he could still feel the rough, stoney ground under his wheels on the dirt track that led directly to the mountain fortress. It never ceased to amaze him as to why the Contessa owned so many high performance sports cars - from Lamborghinis to Ferraris - because they would be impossible to drive on such rocky terrain.

Indeed, he did not even know if the Contessa could drive as he had never seen her do so. But he guessed, probably accurately, that within the world she lived, a very masculine world, they were an impressive show of power and wealth.

Nonetheless, Nate arrived at the gates and after a brief chat with the heavily armed guards at the gate, whom he had come to know quite well over the years, he was shown through into the compound.

Nate and Lucia had spoken often and seen each other at fairly regular intervals since his departure from the seminary but in recent months his hectic schedule had prevented it and he was looking forward to seeing his old friend.

The first to notice his arrival, however, was Berto, the Contessa's old and extremely fussy border collie. He was at least sixteen now and clearly an old dog but he bounded over to the Range Rover like a puppy when he saw who was getting out of it.

Indeed, Berto nearly knocked Nate to the ground as he slid out of the high seated vehicle and planted his feet on the gravelled forecourt.

"Hello, old friend!" Said Nate bending to give Berto a good fuss, "How've you been, pal? Long time no see."

"Too long." A female voice said as Nate looked up to see the Contessa di Montagna walking towards him, a big smile on her beautifully sculptured face.

The two embraced and kissed each other twice on each cheek, in the affectionate Italian style. Old friends greeting each other after a long time apart.

"You look well, Father, although a little thinner, I think?"

Nate smiled. "It's 'Nate' now Contessa - I never was a 'Father' - you know that!"

"Ah, but you never know - and you always looked like a priest to me. Besides, you call me 'Contessa' when you know full well my name is Lucia."

"Yes, I suppose that is the truth. It's good to see you - I've been away too long."

"Indeed you have and I've been quite lost without you."

"Nonsense - you look like you've been flourishing. How is it you've not aged a day since I met you?"

It was no lie. The Contessa was now fifty-six years old but still looked like a woman in her prime, with a figure most thirty year olds would envy. Only her shortly cropped silver hair eluded to her true age and only the leather patch over her ruined eye marred her beauty.

"You're eyesight is obviously not what it used to be, Father, clearly." She replied, shrugging off the compliment modestly. "Tell me, did you stop by the seminary on the way here?"

"No. There's nothing there for me now," Nate said. Although he was not being completely truthful. The true reason why he had not called in at the Pontifical North American College to see his old tutors was that he was scared. Scared he might discover the decision he had made six years earlier to quit his studies may have been the wrong one.

Over the last week he had felt God speaking to him; showing him with Ava's arrival in Cadiz that He did, indeed, have a plan. A plan which had been invisible to Nate at the time of Gino's tragic accident and of Diego's murder just two years later.

Slowly, it seemed, God's Plan was being revealed and only now was Nate recognising it. And he had been feeling his faith tentatively returning as a result.

"Really?" The Contessa said, not fully convinced of his answer and recognising what perhaps he dare not yet admit to himself.

Nate made no reply except to say, "I'd forgotten how beautiful this place is - it's good the be here again."

"And it's good to see you, too. Come, let's go have some wine and catch up."

***

A short time later they were sitting on a bench by the edge of a huge pond in a peaceful corner of the garden. Teems of goldfish and Koi carp seemed to be flourishing in the dark green water which was alive with the colour of beautifully fragrant lilies.

"I find it very relaxing," the Contessa was saying, "and feeding the fish gives me something to do now I have retired."

"I never thought I'd see the day," Nate said, as he stroked Berto's soft head which rested upon his knee. "Although I had always secretly hoped."

The Contessa turned to him and kissed him fondly on the cheek, "I know, my boy. And you were right to."

Shortly after Gino's death, the Contessa retired from the drug business, passing it over to younger, more willing hands. As capofamiglia she still received a sizeable income which was given in lieu of her respected position but she played no part in the business itself. Indeed, all funds were thoroughly laundered before they ever came close to the Contessa herself so she was, ostensibly, living by legitimate means.

But she was still connected. Still a high ranking member of her clan and would be until the day she died.

And that was something she could not change, although with her belief that Gino's death had been a punishment for her participation in the trafficking of cocaine and other nefarious ventures, it did not sit comfortably.

Yet she had made her peace with it.

"Now then," she said knowingly, "why don't you tell me why you have really come to see me?"

She was as shrewd as ever.

"You mean I can't just visit an old friend?" Nate replied.

"Of course you can. And it's a pleasure to see you. But something's on your mind, I can tell. So why don't you tell me what it is?"

Nate smiled with slight embarrassment. He had wanted to see the Contessa and had genuinely missed her. But he also had important matters to discuss with her and she had seen through him as if he were a pane of glass.

"Am I really that transparent?" he asked guiltily.

"I'm afraid all honest men are, my boy. So come, tell me what it is I can help you with."

"I'm afraid it's rather a delicate subject, one which you might not wish to discuss - one which I'd rather not discuss but—"

"Tush! We are friends. We can discuss anything," said the Contessa, "So go ahead."

Nate thought for a moment about how to begin, then, after taking a sip of wine, he said, "You remember Maria, my mother, Contessa?"

"Of course, how could I forget her. A lovely woman, I liked her very much."

Maria and the Contessa had met when Nate was still a seminarian - he had taken her to the mountain fortress with Gino where they all enjoyed lunch together. Maria and Lucia had gotten on famously, both cast from a similar mould.

They had met again at Gino's funeral and again at Diego's; the Contessa having made the trip to Cadiz especially for Nate, to show her support for him at such a tragic time - as he had done for her.

"Thank you. Yes she is a wonderful woman; caring and compassionate - she took me in when I was a boy - adopted me and raised me as her own. Have I ever mentioned that?"

The Contessa nodded, wondering where this was leading.

"But her father, Carlo, is a terrible, evil man," Nate went on.

"He murdered my father—"

Lucia gasped slightly but allowed him to continue.

"He also killed Maria's lover when she was little more than a girl. Her lover was my brother Danny's father."

"He killed both of your fathers?"

Nate nodded. "Mmm hmm. And just recently we discovered that he killed Diego, too.

"Oh, my dear boy, I'm so—"

"Carlo's step-daughter, Ava, told us. Turns out he murdered her mother and father as well."

"My God—"

"Ava escaped from him, thankfully. And after six years of trying she finally caught up with Danny, Maria and me - to see if we could help her avenge our loved ones."

The Contessa shook her head in amazement. "And are you going to?"

"Yes. Without question. But I'm afraid we might need your help."

"Of course, whatever I can do. What is it you have in mind?"

Nate smiled his thanks and placed a grateful hand over Lucia's. "You might not be so eager once you have heard our plan."

"Oh?" Said the Contessa, immediately intrigued. "Then you'd better enlighten me Father - you've piqued my interest now."

Nate grinned again, knowing he had appealed to the Contessa's mischievous side. But then his face was grave as he said seriously, "Do you know of the Carboni family, from New York? Their head is a man called Carmine Carboni, I believe?"

"Yes, I know them very well. Carmine is my second cousin, on my mother's side. I have a good relationship with him although I do not care for him much. Why do you ask?"

Nate took another sip of wine then began to outline the plan that he, Danny, Maria and Ava had conceived a week earlier.

As she listened, the Contessa smiled.

***

Sometime later, after the Contessa had willingly agreed to participate in the scheme - and after she, in turn, had made some suggestions of her own, Nate at last said, "I wonder, Contessa, if in any of your dealings in the past, you have ever heard of a man named 'Bruno Barca'? He operates out of Brooklyn - or so I've been told."

For a second the Contessa looked mildly surprised, "I know of him, yes. I've never met him, never wished to, but from what I understand he is an utterly loathsome character. Why do you ask?"

"It's just that Ava overheard his name mentioned in conversation once - in connection - if you'll forgive me - with i Lupi di Montagna, The Mountain Wolves, whom I know, of course, to be your people.

"They are indeed," agreed the Contessa. "Yet they do not appreciate people like Bruno Barca bandying their name about - and neither do I for that matter. We are fiercely secretive people, Father, as you know. Very protective of our home and of who we are."

"I understand, that's why it struck me as odd." Replied Nate.

"Indeed. It will not go down well that we are being spoken of so loosely. Tell me, how did Ava come to overhear?"

"That's the strange thing. Carlo's right-hand man - a man who tried to kill not only Maria but my birth mother, Megan, too - is in league with this Barca and was on the phone to him when Ava heard them speaking.

"Turns out that Barca supplies him with large quantities of cocaine which he, in turn, distributes to Hollywood's rich and famous."

For a moment the Contessa looked ashamed as she was confronted once again with the evil trade she would forever be tainted with; the trade which she believed Gino's death was punishment for. "Yes," she whispered. "I know that to be the truth."

Nate lightly squeezed her hand, knowing how repentant

she was and his heart filled with compassion for her. "I'm sorry to unearth such emotions in you," he said.

"You're very kind, Father, but please, do not trouble yourself."

"Nonsense. You are my friend and I care about your feelings."

"You are a very good friend indeed," she replied, placing her other hand over his, sandwiching it between both of hers. "But tell me, who is this man whom Barca distributes his—" she could not bring herself to say the word 'cocaine'. "This merchandise too? This vile person who tried to kill both Maria and Megan?"

"His name is Salvatore Falcone. A murderous, evil—"

"What did you say?" Lucia interrupted, suddenly turning to stare directly at Nate. "What did you say his name was?"

"Salvatore Falcone," Nate replied, immediately seeing the recognition and the alarm written on the Contessa's face. "Why, you know him?"

Lucia involuntarily lifted a hand to her ruined eye, the empty, scarred socket concealed by the leather eye patch; the faint traces of ancient scratch marks trickling out around it like a tiny spider's web.

"Yes. I know him."

Nate could see that the Contessa was visibly shaken, the mere mention of Falcone's name rocking her to the core.

"Forgive me, it was not my intention to upset you—" Nate began, sensing he had delivered momentous news, but the Contessa cut across him.

"I've waited over forty years to hear word of him," she said, "and I will never forget him until the day I die - for he is the person who ruined my face and branded me for life."

Nate remembered the story Gino had told him of how Lucia had been raped as a girl; blinded, left for dead and robbed of any hope she might of had for children, realising only now that it was Salvatore Falcone who was her attacker.

"I'm so sorry, Contessa, I did not know. I never would have

told you - never would have asked you if I'd—"

"No!" Lucia snapped. "You did exactly the right thing, Father. And I am very grateful to you."

Nate was slightly taken aback by her forceful tone, "You are?" He said, a little uncertainly.

"I am." She replied most definitely, a wicked smile now spreading across her face.

"You just leave Falcone to me. I'll handle him."

***

As Nate headed back to Rome almost two hours later, he had no doubts in his mind that the Contessa di Montagna would be every bit as good as her word.

However, as he drove down into the city, he was infused with a rush of renewed faith. God had at last shown him the way, revealing His whole intricately woven plan.

He had purposely brought them all together; him, Danny, Maria, Ava and now Lucia; the final piece of the puzzle. All those who had been affected by the evil of Carlo Liuzzi and Salvatore Falcone, so they could fight them as one.

At last Nate understood and was staggered by the audacity of it all, awed once more by the wonder of The Lord. He had set them all on a righteous crusade to battle evil and overthrow the devil.

And Nate knew, in his heart, that God was on their side.

For the first time in years he wanted to pray; to offer thanks and seek guidance and suddenly he found himself heading not to the hotel but directly to the American Seminary in Rome.

His belief in God stronger, more positive than ever before.

Chapter Thirty Four

Cadiz, Spain 1974

Danny and Ava had been almost inseparable in the week they had spent together.

Now they had no secrets from each other they had quickly become incredibly close and that brief spark of attraction both had felt so many years before had suddenly grown into a burning flame.

Since her arrival in Cadiz they had enjoyed many long walks - either hand in hand through the streets of the ancient city, strolling contentedly around its beautiful parks or just meandering barefoot along the beach.

But they were never far from the protective gaze of Mike, Danny's huge, black bodyguard who could always be found lurking nearby, discreetly watching over them.

At Maria's insistence, Ava had been given her own suite of rooms at the villa. Maria had also taken her shopping, delighting in buying her a whole new wardrobe full of wonderful clothes; treating Ava much like she would a daughter.

Delores had fussed around her too. It was good to have a young woman around to take care of again.

But in the main it was Danny who spent most time with her and he had cancelled all appointments for the specific purpose of it.

They could not get enough of each other and their budding

romance had very quickly blossomed into something much more meaningful.

Indeed, in all the time they had been apart, neither had been able to forget about the other.

As the days drifted by, they were falling ever deeper in love; an emotion which had been making itself known since the day they first set eyes on each other at Columbia.

As yet, however, their burgeoning romance had progressed no further than innocent hand-holding or a stolen goodnight kiss; each taking it slow, wanting to savour the moment when they would finally consummate their relationship.

And the anticipation of it was delicious.

Nevertheless, after receiving a phone call from Nate in Rome, all thoughts of love were temporarily forgotten as the serious planning of Carlo Liuzzi's downfall took over.

And then, all too soon, Danny and Ava were preparing to leave Cadiz; readying themselves to put their dangerously high-risk strategy into action.

***

The Hermes IV had been decommissioned shortly after Diego's death, every inch of the aircraft reminding Maria of the happy times she and her husband had spent on board.

Yet, the fact remained she was now a hugely wealthy widow with a personal fortune that easily ran into the tens of millions. On top of that, she also sat at the head of a vast corporation with almost limitless resources at its disposal.

So, in place of the Hermes she had bought a brand new Boeing 747 - an enormous wide bodied aircraft which was the only privately owned one of its kind in the world.

It was way over the top and far bigger than even Maria imagined it would be but it was important to her that her family were as safe and comfortable as possible whenever they travelled.

Indeed, it was so large that Danny and Nate had christened it *Matador One* as it easily outshone The President's own *Air Force One* which was a more inferior 707 - and the interior design was certainly more luxurious.

Within the 747's vast interior there were four large, luxuriously appointed double bedrooms, each with its own private bathroom; two sumptuous sitting rooms with giant, wall-mounted TV screens; a state-of-the-art screening room and editing suite; several offices - one each for Danny, Nate and Maria with additional ones for their support staff - who shared the use of six individual overnight cabins; a security office complete with a spacious dormitory and rec room for the security team - although Mike and Wes each had their own private cabin - equipped with a single bed, a television, shower and in-flight communications system. There was also a huge conference room and a comfortable bar area in which to relax.

In short, it was a spacious and comfortable home in the sky which doubled as a magnificent airborne office.

However, whereas the 747 was ideal for long haul flights, it was not so convenient for short haul, so Maria had also invested in two identical Learjets, each emblazoned with the Matador colours and the 'charging bull' logo on their tail fins - much like the 747.

Nate had taken one of the Learjet's to Rome - just a short hop away from Cadiz, whilst Maria had taken the other back to Paris with Steven Brownley to inspect the site for the new hotel.

Which left the 747 for Danny and Ava as they set off on the long evening flight back to California.

Once the wheels were up and it was safe to move around the cabin, Danny asked Ava if she would like to go to the screening room with him to watch a rough cut of a new Viscount movie. She said she would love to and for an hour or so they sat in the darkness together watching what turned out to be a rather compelling drama.

Ava was very knowledgeable about the movie industry and

Danny was extremely impressed; she clearly had a passion for it as well as an innate understanding of its complexities which he had, until that point, been unaware of.

After the movie, Danny had to jot down his thoughts and do a little work in preparation for his arrival in Los Angeles so left Ava in the capable hands of Delores who, along with Mike and two additional members of the security team, were accompanying them to the States.

Delores settled Ava into one of the plush staterooms at the stern of the plane and told her to ask should she need anything.

Ava was not particularly fond of flying but onboard the luxurious 747 she felt somehow safer. She was also tired and with at least another ten hours flying time ahead of her she decided to get some sleep.

She took off her clothes and folded them neatly next to the robe Delores had laid out for her on a comfy looking chair, and slid between the cool silk sheets of the enormous double bed.

She snapped off the bedside light and almost as soon as her head touched the soft feather pillow she was out; the dull hum of the big four-engined plane lulling her into a deep, dreamless sleep.

***

Two hours later Ava was awoken with a jolt.

The plane was jumping and bouncing around as it hit a patch of particularly violent turbulence. In the darkness, Ava could see the heavy rain as it lashed against the window and the black, angry clouds which had obliterated the moon.

She was suddenly scared and felt very alone within the vast interior of the massive aircraft. She switched on the lamp beside her bed as the plane lurched dramatically once more, the light flickering on and off intermittently as Ava held on tightly to the bed.

Her clothes slipped from the chair as a wardrobe door swung open then almost immediately slammed shut again.

460

After several minutes the plane at last seemed to steady but Ava was still terrified and fearful of staying in her room alone.

Tentatively, she slid out of bed and staggered like a drunkard over to the chair; clutching hold of the robe before unsteadily slipping it on.

A moment later she was out of her stateroom and standing in the main body of the aircraft. The lights had been dimmed for the night flight and everything was quiet. *Was she the only one awake?*

She crossed the wide aisle, her bare feet sinking into the deep-pile of the luxurious carpet, as she lurched towards the stateroom opposite hers, which she knew to be Danny's.

The motion of the plane had calmed considerably now with just a minor jolt here and there as it safely navigated its way through the storm. But still Ava knocked lightly on his door.

There was no reply so she turned the handle and the door swung open. The room was similar in size to hers and equally lavish in its design although the decor was definitely more masculine.

Danny was asleep in bed, his face towards her; his dark hair, which he had grown to shoulder length in the fashionable style, spread out on the clean, white pillows.

Ava closed the door softly and approached the bed, watching him for a moment as he slept.

Somehow, he seemed aware of her presence and he opened his eyes. "Ava?" he said groggily, blinking as he focussed on her standing there. "Are you alright? Is everything okay?"

"Um, yes," she said, slightly embarrassed. "Didn't you feel the turbulence?"

"Yeah, a little, but I fly so much I guess I'm used to it by now. Reckon I could probably sleep through anything. Did it scare you?"

She nodded. "A little, yes."

"Don't worry. We're perfectly safe - a bit of turbulence won't hurt us."

461

"I know, but—" suddenly she felt utterly stupid. "Sorry, I shouldn't have disturbed you, it just shook me up a bit that's all. Please go back to sleep, I'll be fine."

"Hey, don't be silly," Danny replied. "Come here, I'll keep you safe." Danny sat up in bed, clearly naked under the sheets and his top half now visible to Ava as he propped himself up on the pillows.

My God he's something, Ava thought, instantly forgetting about the turbulence as her gaze wandered over his muscular torso.

But her eyes betrayed her and the mood unexpectedly changed as the air between them became more sexually charged.

Ava hesitated for a second as something primal stirred within her; the fear now gone, replaced by something altogether more base and decidedly more urgent.

Danny felt it too.

She recognised the hunger in his eyes which was now reflected in her own and suddenly she wanted him more than she had wanted anything ever before.

She stood before him and slowly opened her silk robe then let it slip from her shoulders onto the floor, baring herself to him wantonly.

Danny looked at Ava like a wolf eyeing a sheep, his mouth watering in anticipation of her.

She was spectacular; her long, blonde hair hanging loosely around her tanned shoulders; her breasts round and firm, her waist gloriously narrow with generously curved hips and a toned, flat stomach.

Finally Danny's eyes were drawn to the strip of neatly trimmed hair at the junction of her long, slender legs and he involuntarily licked his lips.

He looked at her and smiled. She stared back at him with an expression unashamedly carnal as he pulled the sheet aside and invited her into his bed.

Ava paused for a moment as she took in the splendour of his naked form, her loins aching for him.

But in that instant the plane lurched again as it hit yet another patch of turbulent air and she fell forward into his waiting arms.

Suddenly their lips were locked together, their hot tongues eagerly seeking out the other's as they kissed with the dramatic desperation of long held desire.

Moments later, their bodies were writhing together in a wondrous frenzy of animalistic passion as the plane bucked and pitched through the raging storm outside.

Yet neither gave a damn about the storm now. All they cared about was each other and as the 747 journeyed on through darkness they made love long into the night.

***

They awoke a few minutes before landing at LAX; Ava snuggling blissfully in Danny's embrace, her back resting against his chest.

He held her tightly as the plane touched down, one arm locked protectively around her waist, the other braced against the padded bed head as the 747 streaked along the runway, its wheels rumbling on the tarmac beneath them.

Neither Danny or Ava wanted to move from the bed, reluctant to be parted from the other before absolutely necessary and as the huge aircraft taxied to a halt they made love once more.

Afterwards they showered together and when they emerged back into the bedroom Ava was surprised to find her clothes had been laid out on the bed.

Danny smiled, "You can't get much passed Del."

"No, I guess not. God, I suddenly feel so slutty - what on earth must she think?" Ava replied feeling a tad embarrassed.

"She'll think nothing. Del loves you - just like I do."

Ava grinned. "You love me?"

"You know I do," said Danny, sincerely. "Since the day I first saw you."

Her cheeks flushed a little. "And I you," she said.

They kissed once more and then reluctantly got dressed.

Ava was sitting at the dressing table brushing her hair by the time Mike knocked on the door and Danny opened it to let him in.

"Morning, Danny, morning Ava," he said, greeting them as if it was perfectly natural to find them together. Indeed, everyone had seen the way they looked at each other so it came as no surprise and was immediately accepted.

"Car's here when you're ready, Boss." Mike said, "I've squared everything with immigration so we're all set when you are."

"Thanks Mike, we'll be there shortly," replied Danny as he shrugged on his jacket and straightened the collar.

"No rush," the burly bodyguard said as he left the room.

Danny looked at Ava over her shoulder in the dressing table mirror. "Still wanna do this?" he asked, referring to the plan they were about to set in motion. "There's still time to back out if you don't."

Ava looked back at him, her mind set. "Not a chance," she replied firmly. "Let's get those bastards."

Danny nodded in agreement. "Yes, let's," he said.

***

Paris, France 1974

Maria and Steven Brownley had formed an easy working partnership and found their ideas for the Paris Matador were very much in tune.

She had taken the penthouse at the George Cinq, just off the Champs-Élysées, whilst Steven had been booked into a deluxe suite two floors below.

However, a corner of the penthouse had become their makeshift office and the pair had spent many hours discussing all aspects of the

464

project. They had also poured over Steven's rough sketches - which he had been working on, and continually tweaking, since accepting the commission back in Cadiz.

He would soon return home to his offices in London to draw up a first draft of the plans, implementing all the features he and Maria had agreed upon, but for the time being they still had business to conclude in France.

They had a meeting with the Heritage Secretary in the morning and another with the Planning Officer in the afternoon. After that they had to interview contractors, speak with utilities companies and meet with transport officials to discuss the many new roads that would have to be constructed to carry commuters to and from the proposed building.

It was a hectic schedule and Maria would have loved to dedicate more time to it, particularly as the project was so close to her heart, but her time frame had been unavoidably curtailed due to matters that needed her attention in Los Angeles.

Matters which Maria had waited many years to see settled.

Nevertheless, she had enjoyed her time with Steven very much and romance was definitely blossoming even though, so far, it had not moved beyond platonic. But Maria was keen to take it slow. She liked Steven and could even see a future for herself with him next to her, yet she could not risk something happening to him as it had to her beloved Diego.

And for that reason she could not allow the relationship to progress any further until her father and Falcone had been dealt with once and for all.

When she no longer feared their reprisal; when they no longer haunted her very existence, then she could take things further with Steven.

He was a good man and he would wait but Maria hoped that day would come soon.

Indeed, shortly she would be leaving for Los Angeles to join Danny, Ava and Nate - who was also due to meet them there soon.

However, it troubled her more than she let on that both her boys, and Ava too, were deliberately putting themselves in harm's way.

She just prayed they all knew what they were doing.

She hoped she knew what she was doing, too.

Because after over twenty five years of letting him believe her dead, Maria was once again about to dance with the devil.

Chapter Thirty Five

Hollywood, California 1974

The star-studded event had been a major part of the Hollywood social calendar for the last five years and was a charity dinner funded by Viscount Studios to raise money for widows and orphans.

It had been conceived by Maria shortly before the first anniversary of Diego's death after realising just how fortunate she had been to be left so financially secure. Whilst it was scant compensation for the devastating loss of her husband it did, at least, relieve her of all the money worries many women of less affluent means would possibly face. Indeed, such was the case of her long suffering friend Megan who had been forced to bring her boys up in near poverty.

So she had coerced Herb Horowitz's kind-hearted wife to inaugurate the First Annual Viscount Charity Gala; a grand, black-tie dinner to which the great and the good of Hollywood would all be invited - at the price of five thousand dollars a plate.

Edith Horowitz was amongst the social elite in Tinseltown and she soon enlisted the support of her A-list friends who were keen to add their considerable weight behind the event - especially when Edith told them who the charity's famous patron was.

By this time, Maria Del Toro had become something of an enigma in Hollywood; a mysterious, Garbo-type figure who famously shunned the limelight and obsessively avoided being photographed.

Indeed, few could claim to know Maria personally but many wished to and with her name attached to the gala, interest was instantly drawn to it, quickly making it the hottest ticket in town.

However, other than funding the event, Maria herself would play no part in the gala and would not be in attendance, even though Matador would be the charity's main benefactor.

Danny had assumed the role of President of The Charity at his mother's request and, it seemed, he was almost as big a draw as Maria would have been - as the enormous sums of money raised at the first gala clearly testified.

It was a huge success and each one thereafter had been even more triumphant. Invitations to the glittering events were highly prized and had become a measure of a person's social standing within the Hollywood community.

Everyone who was anyone wanted to be in attendance and not to be invited was tantamount to being ostracised.

As was the case with Carlo Liuzzi who had never been invited.

Even in more prosperous times an invitation to the gala had never been forthcoming and the obvious snub had always niggled him.

What did Edith Horowitz have against him?

And as for that goddamn Del Toro woman - who he'd never even seen let alone met - it wasn't like she knew he had killed her husband so what the hell had he done to piss her off?

Nonetheless, for the first couple of years that the event had been held, Carlo had been conspicuous by his absence - particularly because he had been a major player at that time.

But not any more. Now, with his fortunes on the decline, he feared that he had been forgotten about altogether and the reality of it weighed heavily.

Not only had he lost his hard-earned place in the Hollywood hierarchy - where he once stood unchallenged at the top, but his precious pride had been damaged, too, which had wounded him deeply.

Carlo had descended into a dark fugue; his behaviour over the last few years becoming increasingly more erratic and his violent mood swings flaring frighteningly more frequently - for just the slightest of reasons.

After one such violent outburst, Vito, his trusted subordinate, had been seriously beaten; a broken jaw, a broken nose and a ruptured spleen being just a few of the many injuries he had sustained as a result of his employer's wrath. His crime had been to interrupt Carlo whilst he was speaking.

After a lengthy stay in hospital Vito had returned to New York, unfit for anything much; destined to spend the rest of his miserable life having to piss in a bag and living off disability hand-outs.

Only Salvatore and Frankie remained. Frankie being forced to take on the role of chauffeur, cook, housekeeper and any other job that needed doing.

Salvatore, on the other hand, was prospering, his extremely lucrative cocaine business thriving. What is more, his and Liuzzi's roles had seemingly reversed with Carlo heavily reliant on his former lieutenant's money to maintain the pretence of affluence.

His personal fortune had dwindled to almost nothing and Gold Star was only still in business because Carlo had borrowed extensively from the Carboni family for whom he had once been such a bright light. Indeed, back then he had the golden touch of Midas himself.

But that was a very long time ago.

Now Carlo was into them for millions and they were fast losing their patience.

Liuzzi needed a break and he needed it bad.

Gold Star had now become synonymous with low budget, fast turnaround B-movies, all of which yielded very little return; the studio having slumped to the minor leagues as a result of Carlo's reckless mis-management and over indulgent vanity projects which had cost the company millions.

But Carlo didn't see it that way. In his mind he was a visionary, a movie genius with celluloid running through his veins.

He was convinced he only needed the right opportunity to get him back on track.

And that opportunity had just landed in his mailbox.

***

Carlo knew what it was the moment he saw the envelope, his only slight annoyance being that there was an identical one next to it addressed to Salvatore.

But he quashed his resentment, deciding to focus on the positive, determined to see it as an omen - a sign that he was finally on the way back.

He ripped open the envelope and pulled out the heavy black card which was ornately printed in gold foil:

The Viscount Charity for Widows and Orphans cordially requests the pleasure of your company at their Sixth Annual Charity Gala.

Carlo's chest swelled with pride as he studied the invitation for a long moment, rubbing his thumb narcissistically along the line that read: *'Mr C Liuzzi'*. He was back in the fold and his return to the top was surely just a formality.

Although he happily skipped over the line which required guests to make a five thousand dollar donation to the charity. The money was of little consequence now - besides, he would see that his donation was paid by Salvatore.

Carlo felt he had already wasted enough money on the upkeep of widows and orphans.

Nevertheless, on the evening of the gala, Liuzzi felt excited.

He studied himself in the mirror; tall, broad shouldered, still powerfully built and handsome although his hair and moustache

470

were more silver than black now. Yet he still looked every bit an icon of Hollywood's golden age.

And tonight, it was determinedly so as it was vital to send the right message.

As he tied his silk bow-tie, he thought for the first time in many years of his daughter, Maria, who used to tie it for him and suddenly his excitement was marred.

He felt a rush of bitterness towards her; remembering her unforgivable betrayal of him - of how she had slept with that lowly gardener, becoming pregnant by him, shaming Carlo beyond words and almost ruining everything he had worked so hard for.

He had loved her with all his heart; his little girl, his pride and joy - but she had ruined it with her deceitfulness leaving him no other choice but to kill her lover and banish Maria and her bastard offspring for good.

But then she had died; killing herself and the child by jumping from a train into a ravine, smashing to their deaths on the rocks below, their bodies apparently washed away into the ocean.

As Carlo remembered it now he thought it was possibly for the best. What hope was there for her anyway? A tainted woman who had given herself away so freely, saddling herself with the bastard of a dirt poor immigrant. No good could ever have come of it and Carlo satisfied himself with that.

Then he thought of his other little girl. Ava.

Another bitter disappointment and yet another betrayal. After everything he had done for her, everything he had given her, she had proved herself to be treacherous and false. She had even tried to have him put in jail.

If it wasn't for his own quick thinking he might even have found himself rotting in some cell for the murder of Diego Del Toro - the hotelier who liked to play at being in the movie business.

Carlo evaded arrest but Ava had disappeared without trace.

He had looked for her, sent word out to everyone he knew, calling in favours with the police and his connections in New York, yet she had never shown up, which bothered him somewhat.

Maybe she was dead.

If she was then it would certainly be one less thing to worry about.

Carlo was done with daughters. Next time, if there was a next time - and at sixty-eight who could be sure - then he would like a son. Boy's were surely less trouble.

Again he thought of Maria and of the boy child she had given birth to under that very roof, remembering the baby's cries just moments after it was born and the small bundle in Megan's arms a few minutes later as she showed Carlo his grandson.

Liuzzi closed his eyes and tried to picture the baby's face but he could not; he had only glanced at it briefly at the time and now he could not recall the image.

All he knew was, had the boy lived, he would now be twenty-six years old and Carlo could not help but wonder what he might have looked like.

***

By the time Frankie DeLuca pulled the limo up to the red carpet that stretched from the kerb to the grand entrance of the Beverly Hills Matador, Carlo had once more forgotten all about Maria, Ava and his illegitimate grandson.

Furthermore, with the flashbulbs popping and the crowd cheering as he stepped out of the luxury, chauffeur driven limousine, he felt fuelled with renewed vigour and the thrill of fresh opportunities.

On his arm was twenty-two year old starlet, Madison Kane, who had gratefully accepted Carlo's invitation whilst sucking his cock under the desk at his Gold Star offices; seeing both his cock and the charity gala as an ideal opportunity to boost her fledgling career.

472

Salvatore, who had arrived several minutes earlier in a hired limousine, had already gone in, another young actress by the name of Lana Shaw, his date for the evening. Lana was seriously addicted to the coke Falcone supplied her with and would happily agree to anything he asked for the chance to get more of it.

Neither man cared a damn for their respective dates but it did their egos good to be seen with such desirable women.

Once inside the glamorous venue, which was being held in the hotel's magnificent ballroom, Carlo and Salvatore quickly found their tables which were large and round and decorated with exquisite floral centrepieces and flickering candelabras.

Falcone and his date had been seated alongside six other guests, all of whom looked well over eighty with faces that were intended to make them look under forty - however, in all cases, the plastic surgery had been a resounding failure.

Carlo, meanwhile, found himself sitting at the table of famous Hollywood movie star, Virgil Nash and the actress Victoria Wild who he had brought along as his date. Next to them was Herb and Edith Horowitz and next to them, Carlo was somewhat surprised to find an extremely handsome young man who appeared to have arrived alone.

A man he instantly recognised as Daniel Del Toro.

***

Frankie DeLuca glanced in his wing mirror to see Liuzzi standing on the red carpet, where he had just left him, smiling triumphantly with his arm draped around Madison Kane who, in turn, was busy posing for the cameras in a low cut gown, lapping up the attention.

After carefully navigating through the hordes of people flooding the street in front of the hotel, he steered the limo around to the side entrance.

Once there, in the darkened alley, away from the media and the masses and the general hubbub surrounding the event, he parked up in front of a black, unmarked panel van.

He turned off the engine and relaxed into his plush leather seat. He could do nothing now but wait.

A moment later, he glanced in his rear view mirror to see a woman emerging from the passenger seat of the panel van.

Frankie smiled as she walked towards him.

***

Whilst Frankie was outside in the alley, Ava was waiting impatiently upstairs in the luxurious penthouse of the Beverly Hills Matador.

She realised now that it had been a huge mistake to stay with Danny as he got ready for the party in the hotel's most exclusive suite, especially as he had now gone down to host the event below, leaving her alone and effectively blind to what was happening.

It made perfect sense for Danny to stay at the hotel, in fact, it was only to be expected. As one of the owners, he always stayed there whenever he was in town. Furthermore, he was hosting the event downstairs in the ballroom so it would have been rather odd if he had chosen to stay somewhere else.

But there had been no reason for Ava to be there other than the fact that she and Danny could simply not get enough of each other.

Yet, with all that was at stake, with all that was in play, it had been a serious lapse in judgement on both their parts.

She knew now she should have been with the others, which would have been the much safer choice. But it was too late now and Ava was pacing the floor nervously, waiting until 10.30pm, the time she and Danny believed to be safest for her to leave.

That was when all the guests were due to be at their tables starting on their entrees, thus leaving the lobby clear.

It was a long nervous wait but when the time finally came, Ava rushed out of the room, across the foyer and into the penthouse's

474

private elevator, immediately punching the button for the ground floor as soon as she was inside.

A minute later, as she stepped out into the fabulous opulence of the hotel's grand lobby, she saw many people in fine evening wear still milling about and not seated at their tables as expected.

However, the only person she recognised was Salvatore Falcone who was standing mere yards away.

"Shit!" She exclaimed under her breath, suddenly panicked. Uncertain of what to do, she froze as the elevator doors closed behind her, leaving her stranded in no-man's-land, in full view of anyone who cared to look her way.

She stared, temporarily fixated, despising the very sight of Falcone who had changed little in the six years since she had last seen him. A few more lines, a sprinkling of grey, but still thin and wiry and still wearing the black glove over his dead hand.

Fortunately, he did not see her as he stood talking to his rather trashy looking date who Ava vaguely recognised as the actress Lana Shaw - 'actress' being a generous term for her strictly limited talent.

Nevertheless, Lana already looked fairly wired as Salvatore surreptitiously handed her a small glass vial which contained a very suspicious looking powder.

Ava, however, quickly regaining her composure, had no time to study it more closely and certainly no wish to be seen, so swiftly made a dash for the restrooms which were completely empty - all guests supposedly occupied with their delicious gourmet starters.

Ava ran into one of the stalls, her mind racing, wondering how on earth she could make it safely out to Frankie without being spotted by Falcone.

However, as she pondered this, someone else entered the restroom and a second later she heard the door bang on the cubicle next to hers.

Then, after a moment or two, heard the distinctive sound of

475

someone snorting cocaine.

Instinct told her it was Lana, come to get a quick hit as Falcone waited for her outside.

As Lana vacuumed up the addictive white powder, Ava stood stone still, trying not to make a sound but desperate to escape the confines of the small enclosure she had been forced to retreat to, knowing she was already behind schedule.

"Holy crap, now that's what I'm talkin' about!" Lana exclaimed from the cubicle next door as the high quality narcotic charged into her system, giving her a massive rush.

Then Ava heard the rustling of satin and the sound of the toilet seat dropping down as Lana hoisted her dress and peed. After what seemed like the longest pee ever, Lana at last slipped the lock and opened the door.

Thankfully Ava could finally get out of there and back on schedule.

But it was not to be.

Lana giggled mischievously as she tottered over to the restroom door and silently opened it. Then she took a furtive look around to check no one could see, before grabbing Salvatore by the arm and pulling him inside.

"Hey, whaddaya doin'?" He laughed.

"What do you think, baby? That coke's made me real horny and I want you."

"You do?" Falcone could not hide the incredulity in his voice, nor his delight.

"Uh huh. I can't wait, baby. I gotta get me some."

Fearful of being discovered, Ava pressed her hands against the cubicle partition and silently eased her feet up onto the edge of toilet, so her feet could not be seen from outside.

It was just as well because a second later Salvatore bent and checked underneath each stall.

"Hey, what you doin?" Asked Lana.

"Just making sure we're alone, that's all," he replied.

"Don't sweat it, honey," Lana assured him, "there ain't nobody here except l'il ol' me - and besides, who cares, I work good with an audience."

Salvatore smiled salaciously, "Yeah, I bet you do."

Ava groaned inwardly as she then heard Lana hurriedly fumbling with Falcone's zipper.

But the dread of what she was about to hear was nothing compared to the terrifying thought of what Salvatore might do if he found her there.

Worse still, because of her foolishness, the plan was already in danger of failing.

She held her breath, trying not to give herself away, but she need not have worried as Salvatore and Lana were too busy blundering noisily into the adjacent cubicle - Falcone hurriedly attempting to lock the door whilst his lusty date lifted her dress and wrapped her legs around him; her back pushing hard against the thin divide that separated them from Ava.

The next few minutes were possibly the most uncomfortable of Ava's life; squatting in disgusted silence on the narrow rim of the toilet as Salvatore and Lana heaved and groaned noisily on the other side of the flimsy wall, slamming violently against the partition with alarming force.

Ava was certain the wall would give way, fearing at any moment Salvatore would burst through into the cramped confines of her tiny compartment.

But the partition held firm. And, at last, as Ava's feet began to slip on the porcelain toilet, Falcone and his drug-addled date reached a loud, all-consuming climax that echoed powerfully around the deserted walls of the smartly tiled ladies room.

As Ava desperately tried to keep her feet from slipping, she heard Salvatore and Lana's breathless panting as they recovered from the throes of their vigorous exertions.

Then came the sound of his zipper being done up - just a split second before Ava's foot squeaked noisily off the edge of the toilet bowl and slapped loudly onto the mosaic floor; her elbow and shoulder clattering thunderously into the partition as she lost her balance, the sound of it resonating deafeningly around the large empty space.

For the briefest moment everything went quiet, everyone staying utterly still. Then a loud, heavily accented Italian voice growled "Who the fuck's there?"

Ava said nothing, the panic flooding through her, knowing that at any second she would be confronted by Salvatore.

"Did you enjoy that, honey?" Lana yelled bitchily, "Did it give you a kick?"

Ava ignored the jibe, more concerned about the sudden scrambling next door as, too late, she attempted to escape from her cubicle, but she had locked herself in and was now trapped inside.

"Who the hell are you?" an angry voice demanded from above and instinctively Ava looked up to see Salvatore Falcone glaring down at her from over the top of the partition.

He did a double take as he saw her face, almost unable to believe his eyes - the surprise in them clear to see.

"Who is it, baby?" whined Lana in a sickly, nasal tone, "Who's the dirty eavesdropper?"

"Shut up!" Salvatore snapped at his date. Then, after taking a beat, he said with an evil grin, "Well, well, well - Ava Peyton! Fancy seeing you—."

Before he could finish Ava lunged for the door.

"Oh, no you don't my girl," Falcone shouted, instantly dropping back into his own cubicle and sliding open the latch at the exact same time as Ava.

As she bolted out of her stall, Salvatore grabbed her tightly around the waist, forcing her over to the sparkling row of hand basins opposite.

"You know her?" Lana squealed, "you know this fucking woman?"

"Shut up, Lana!" Falcone barked again. "Get back to the ballroom - tell Carlo I've got a present for him!"

"Don't you talk to me like that you—"

"Just fucking do it, Lana!" Falcone yelled, wrestling to keep hold of the madly struggling Ava. "Do it now - quickly!"

"Fuck you!" shouted Lana angrily, "You don't give me goddamn orders. Do it your fucking self!" Then she flounced off dramatically, throwing open the restroom door in an exaggerated show of hurt, leaving Salvatore and Ava alone, struggling wildly by the hand basins.

Ava slapped him hard around the face, gleefully dragging her nails across his cheek.

But he ignored it, indeed, he seemed to enjoy it as he grinned even wider and held her more firmly.

"That's it, you little tease - fight me, fight me as hard as you like - but it won't do you no good cos I gotcha now and I ain't never gonna let you get away again!"

"Get off me!" Ava cried, beating her fists against his chest and kicking desperately with her feet. "Get off me now!"

"Not a chance, little girl - you, me and Carlo are all gonna go back to the mansion," he sneered. "You might even get to spend some more time with your mommy!

At the mention of Mildred, Ava felt a surge of strength shoot through her whole body and she lashed out with a balled fist, striking Salvatore squarely on the chin with an almighty blow.

Immediately Falcone released his grip on her as he rocked backwards, his legs wobbly and shock registering in his eyes.

"Don't you dare mention my mother you evil, murdering

bastard!" Ava spat, before kicking him hard in the balls.

Salvatore winced in agony, his eyes bulging as he doubled over with pain.

But Ava was not done. As he went down, she punched him hard around the face, her fist connecting with his jaw with a rewarding crack.

Falcone was dazed and felt the darkness closing in around him, but he was determined not to be beaten by a woman - not again. Not this time.

Ignoring the crippling ache in his balls, he stood up straight, spat out a gob of blood and growled. "You're gonna die for that bitch."

However, at that moment, the restroom door banged open behind him and somebody entered.

"Not now!" Salvatore shouted, "This restroom's busy!"

"So I see," said the intruder.

Salvatore was surprised to hear it was a man's voice that replied but he was not fazed.

"Beat it buddy," he snapped, still with his back to the door, his eyes fastened on Ava. "Men's Room's down the hall!"

"It's not the Men's Room I'm looking for, Mr Falcone," replied the man, addressing him by name. "It's you."

Salvatore was clearly taken aback by this and he turned slowly, blood trickling from the side of his mouth and four red scratches down his cheek, to see three men standing there.

The man in the centre, obviously the one who had spoken, was of slight build with tightly cropped red hair and dressed in a beautifully tailored tuxedo. The two large men either side of him were heavy-set Italians, both in peak physical condition; also dressed in tuxedos, although theirs were strictly off the rail.

They were clearly connected, Salvatore could tell, although to which family he did not know. As for the smaller guy, he was harder to read, but he had the look of an accountant or a lawyer or something of that nature.

"Who are you and what do you want with me?" Falcone demanded.

"You're Bruno Barca's business partner, correct?" Said the red-haired man.

"So this is about Barca?" Salvatore asked, seeing no sense in denying it. "Is he what this is about?" *What had that fool gotten him into now?*

"Not directly," said the red-haired man. "But he benefits from the merchandise shipped to him by the party I represent - as do you. And that said party thinks it's about time the two of you met face to face."

"Face to face?" Said, Salvatore, "You mean Now?"

"Yes. Now," the man insisted.

Falcone looked around and glanced at Ava who shrugged, seemingly amused, before he turned back to the red-haired man. "Can't it wait - I'm kinda busy, as you can see."

"I'm sorry," said the man coolly, "but you seem to be under the impression that it's a request. However, I can assure you it's not."

As Salvatore stared at the stranger, he sensed something familiar about him, something he could not quite put his finger on. But before he had time to think on it further, the red-haired man's two burly associates stepped over to him and took hold of his skinny arms.

"Hey, get off me, what the fuck you think you're doing?" He protested. "Do you know who I am?"

"Oh, we know exactly who you are," replied the red-haired man, "and precisely what you've been up to, which is why the party I represent wants a word with you."

"Look, believe me, whatever Barca's done, whatever mess he's gotten us into, I can straighten it out, I promise," Salvatore pleaded.

Yet the man merely shrugged, clearly knowing something he

didn't.

A feeling of dread stirred in Falcone's belly. But he had to save face in front of Ava, even though inside he was starting to panic.

Turning to her, he said, "Looks like you got lucky tonight, honey. But don't worry, I'll catch up with you again soon."

Ava smiled widely and said, "I wouldn't be too sure of that if I were you."

Salvatore had no response, as he recognised the truth of what she had said; his eyes suddenly full of fear, and as the two large men led him silently away, he looked despairingly back at her to see her grinning victoriously.

The restroom door banged behind them as they went, leaving Ava alone with the red-haired man."

"Thanks for that," she said. "For a moment there I thought I was dead."

"Hey, no problem," winked Nate, "that's what family is for, right?"

She smiled at him fondly, "Yeah. I guess it is," she said. "Nicely played, by the way."

"Thanks," said Nate, "sorry I couldn't get here sooner."

"But how did you know I was in here in the first place?" Ava queried.

"Frankie was worried so asked me and a couple of the guys I brought along to come look for you," Nate said.

"I saw you come in here as I walked into the lobby but just assumed you were using the restroom, so stupidly let my guard down.

"As I waited for you, I got distracted by several of the charity's main supporters and sort of lost track.

"Then I saw Falcone get dragged in here by his date, but by then I couldn't get away - people were shaking my hand, all of them trying to talk to me - I was surrounded.

"A few minutes later I saw Falcone's date come out alone and I knew you were in trouble, so I just left everyone, grabbed the guys, and headed straight here - sorry - I should've been quicker."

"Hey, that's okay - you saved my life, Nate. He was going to kill me."

"I know. But still."

Then after a second, he added, "Come on, we both ought to be going."

Ava, gasped, suddenly remembering the plan having momentarily forgotten it after her encounter with Salvatore. "Shit, yes! We gotta go - we gotta go now".

She pecked him on the cheek, "Thanks again," she said, as they both headed for the door. "And if I don't get a chance to say it later - take care of that bastard for me, would you?"

"Don't worry," Nate replied firmly. "I will. You have my word."

Ava smiled and then they were gone.

***

Nate and Ava emerged into the alley a couple of minutes later. In front of them was parked limousine and a dark panel van.

A worried Frankie DeLuca immediately jumped out of the limo. "Come on, kid," he said to Ava, tapping his watch. "We gotta go!"

However, at that moment, the rear door of the limo opened and the woman who had been patiently waiting inside it with Frankie stepped out into the alley.

"No. Wait!" She said. "I want to see. I want *him* to see."

Nate looked over at Maria. "You sure, Mom?"

"Positive. Let him see both of us."

Nate glanced at Ava who nodded, equally firm in her resolve.

"Okay," said Nate. "Wes! Open it up!" He shouted.

A second later, his huge, six foot three, ex-Navy Seal bodyguard jumped out of the panel van and slid open the side door to reveal

Salvatore Falcone sitting on a dirty blanket, bound and gagged; the two burly Italians watching over him, their guns trained on his head.

Maria took Ava by the hand and walked over to the side of the van, directly in front of the door opening where Falcone could see her close up.

"Hello, Salvatore," she said. "Remember me?"

Salvatore's eyes widened with total disbelief. He recognised Maria instantly and the shock he felt at seeing her alive was etched all over his horrified face. *Surely it could not be.*

Yet there she was, in the flesh, standing before him.

She had changed little over the years, his mind suddenly flooding with images of their past. Images of her in the pool house with her lover, Armando; images of himself attacking Maria onboard the Conte Biancamano and the image of her as he pushed her from the train - seeing her last as she plummeted over the edge of the bridge into the ravine.

She was supposed to be dead. He was certain he had killed her.

But she was most definitely alive.

Moreover, she was hand-in-hand with Ava Peyton and it was obvious the two of them were in cahoots together. Carlo's daughter and Mildred's inexplicably united.

How the hell did that happen?

He was utterly amazed and had he not known it already, he knew now for certain that he was in deep trouble.

Maria smiled. "Of course, you know Ava. I'm hoping she will soon be marrying my son, who, I'm sure, you will also remember."

Ava shot her a glance, smiling with love and pride for the woman she had grown to admire greatly, delighted by the prospect of marrying Danny and becoming her daughter-in-law.

But Maria had not finished.

"You see, Salvatore, for all your best efforts to kill us - we have thrived. You have made us stronger, tougher than ever before - and now you and my murderous, disgusting father are going to pay for all you have done.

Falcone started shaking his head, trying to cry out beneath the gag, pleading for mercy and struggling wildly. The tears building in his terrified eyes.

"I can't hear him, can you, Maria?" Ava said dryly.

"No. I don't believe I can," she replied.

Then she turned back to the pathetic, whimpering creature before her. "Goodbye, Salvatore," she said. "And this time it really is goodbye, I'm afraid. In fact, I can personally guarantee you will not be seeing either of us ever again."

Then she nodded to one of the big Italians who, upon her signal, coshed Falcone over the back of the head.

He slumped down onto the van floor into darkness. Out cold.

***

Maria quickly hugged Nate and wished him 'good luck'.

He then climbed into the panel van with the Italians and Wes, whilst Maria and Ava slid into the back of the limo which Frankie was driving.

A second later, both vehicles were on the move.

Everyone still had much to do.

Chapter Thirty Six

As the plates were cleared away from their first course, Danny carefully eyed Carlo Liuzzi; the man who had killed his father and step-father. The Devil, as his mother referred to him.

He could see little of himself in his grandfather, except the skin colouring and maybe the broadness of his shoulders, but everything else was completely alien.

Danny was revolted by the man and would rather have be anywhere than in his presence making 'light' conversation about nothing much. What he wanted to do was punch him, pummel his face until it was little more than mush whilst screaming at him 'You killed my father!".

But he could not. It was vital to the plan that he remained calm.

So he smiled courteously, laughed at his jokes and chatted to him as if he were a man he admired rather than one he so desperately wanted to kill.

They chatted about movies and movie stars, about the harity, the venue and many other things; the whole table involved with the conversation; Danny geniality itself and Carlo exuding the old Hollywood charm he could turn on so easily when required.

However, as their entrees were cleared away, the diners began to talk amongst themselves rather than addressing the table as a whole.

Herb and Edith Horowitz were in deep conversation with movie stars' Virgil Nash and Victoria Wild - and Madison Kane was hanging on every word hoping that some of their stardust would rub off on her.

Carlo was sitting beside Edith, talking to no one in particular as he took a leather bound cigar case from his inside jacket pocket. Five, thick Cubans sat inside. He slid one out and then, as an after thought, after noticing Danny staring at him, he offered one to Diego Del Toro's son. What could it hurt to be sociable. The boy knew nothing.

Danny took one, "Don't mind if I do, thanks," he said, then hotched his chair closer to Carlo's. "You know, my father was a great admirer of yours," he lied.

"He was?" Carlo seemed somewhat surprised.

"Yes. Said you were one of the great movie men of Hollywood." Ava had told Danny exactly how to appeal to Liuzzi's ego.

"He did, huh? Well he got that right," agreed Carlo immodestly, whilst offering Danny a light from his expensive gold lighter.

"He always wished he could be more like you - said you had a natural gift for picking hit movies." This was pushing it a bit considering Carlo's present circumstances and his past history for burying money into catastrophic flops, but Danny needed to oil him up, get him nice and pliable.

"Sounds like your old man got it about right. What about you? How you enjoying things at Viscount - they're doing pretty good I'd say?"

"Hotels are my business, Carlo - may I call you Carlo? Danny enquired as he puffed heavily on the big cigar to get it lit.

His grandfather nodded.

"Great, and I'm Danny. But like I was saying, Carlo, I'm into hotels - they're what I know, it's what my company knows and we do it pretty well, as you can see—" he gestured to their opulent surroundings. "—But movies? Hey, I haven't got the slightest clue - and no interest either." This was a complete fabrication; Danny had infinite knowledge of the movie business and was greatly involved with the affairs of Viscount, but he had no intention of telling Liuzzi that.

"Truth be told, Carlo, I'm sick of all this studio business - all these big events and charity fundraisers - I want to get back to what I know - concentrate on Matador, that's where my future lies."

Carlo's interest was immediately piqued. "What are you saying? You're looking to get out?"

"Between you and me," Danny said, lowering his voice conspiratorially, "Yeah - and as soon as possible. There's people out there far more qualified than me - much better placed than me - to take the thing on."

Liuzzi raised an eyebrow, puffing deeply on his cigar, his mind already awash with possibilities as Danny continued.

"In fact, I've got a couple of meetings set for tomorrow with movie men, just like yourself, who can't wait to get involved."

"How much are we talking about?"

"Why, you looking to get in?"

"Maybe - depends on the price."

"Hey, listen. I'd like nothing better than for you to get involved but I've already promised to give these other guys—"

"How much?" Liuzzi interrupted, sensing a chance to get back into the big time, relishing the opportunity to get into Viscount - Christ, with him in control the results could be stratospheric. He'd merge the two studios - Gold Star and Viscount - hell, they'd be the biggest studio in Hollywood. Bigger than Paramount, bigger than MGM, bigger than them all.

Carlo's imagination was running away with him as his glittering future played out in his mind.

"Come on, what would it cost? Fuck those other guys - you're talking to me now. Give me a figure."

"Are you serious?" Danny asked, reeling him in.

"As a heart attack."

"Okay, well, it's gotta be pretty sizeable, there's plenty that would pay a fortune for the kudos that comes with sitting at the head table."

"Fuck the kudos," Carlo said impatiently, "How much?"

"Well, we've been flirting around the twenty million mark—" Danny smiled inwardly as he saw Carlo involuntarily wince at the huge sum. "—The other parties are looking to get it for a little less but if you want it - if you want it instead of them, then twenty million's the amount that'll guarantee it."

He was studying Liuzzi again, seeing the cogs whirring in his brain as he tried to work out how he could get the money together.

Then Danny launched the hammer blow.

"But I'll need to know tonight - we'll need to get something in writing before tomorrow otherwise I'm gonna have to let one of the others in." Danny tapped his chest, indicating his inside jacket pocket. "I've even got the paperwork with me."

This should have raised Liuzzi's suspicions; given him pause for thought at the very least. But he was excited, desperate.

Reckless.

Danny could see the hunger in Carlo's eyes; the lust for power, the need to get back on top at any price.

"I need to make a few calls," Liuzzi said, suddenly rising from the table.

"Sure," Danny said, "Of course. I quite understand."

"Please, come with me."

"I'm sorry?"

"Come with me, back to my house. We can do the deal there once I have made my calls."

This took Danny by surprise. He had expected Carlo to be

eager but not quite this impulsive.

"But it can wait until after the meal can't it?" He said, trying to buy time. "Why not enjoy the food first - have a good—"

"No." Carlo snapped. "If you want twenty million then come with me now. Bring the paperwork - we'll do the deal at my place."

"Hey, Carlo, listen - that's great, but we can do it here later, upstairs in my suite. No need to go to your house, we can—"

"I said, No!" Liuzzi's anger flared briefly, but he forced it down. The violence of the man lurking ever closer to the surface, but he had to quash it. This was important. This meant everything - he had to keep a steady head.

"Everything okay, gentlemen?" Virgil Nash enquired, after hearing Carlo's tone.

"Fine. Yes. Thank you," Liuzzi nodded curtly. 'What fucking business is it of yours, anyway?' he wanted to say, but refrained from the urge.

Nash looked at Danny who nodded his agreement. "Great," he said. "Everything's swell, Virgil, thanks."

Placated, the handsome movie star turned back around and continued his conversation with Herb and Edith.

Danny, on the other hand, was starting to feel a little anxious.

"You can get the money tonight?" He said, again trying to stall for time, trying to prevent Liuzzi from returning to his mansion so soon. "You sure? It's late, the banks are closed."

"You bet I can - if I can make those calls." He bragged. "Now do you wanna do the deal or not?"

Danny had no more cards to play and he had run out of options. "Sure," he replied, rising from the table, his height matching his grandfather's. "Why not, let's do it."

"You, going somewhere, honey?" Madison asked Carlo.

"Mr Del Toro and I have got some business to attend to, Maddie. Salvatore is around somewhere, he'll take care of you I'm sure."

"Please, allow me," Virgil Nash said, chipping in once more.

'Why can't he just shut the fuck up?', Carlo thought, but instead said, "Thanks, that's very kind but I'm sure my associate will be along shortly.

"Nonsense," chimed in Edith Horowitz, "We'll take care of her, won't we, Herb, don't you worry, Mr Liuzzi."

"Thank you, Mrs Horowitz, much appreciated - and my apologies for leaving so early," replied Carlo, smoothly, using his considerable charm.

"You off too, Danny?" Asked Herb.

"Yeah, I'm afraid so, Herb - but you all have a great night. Sorry to be such a party pooper but this can't wait.

They exchanged a few more pleasantries, Danny desperately trying to eek out the time whilst scanning the enormous room for Mike who was nowhere to be seen.

However, he soon found himself unable to delay any longer and after saying their goodbyes Danny and Liuzzi finally walked out of the ballroom.

"You got a car here?" Carlo asked. "My driver's not due back for another couple of hours."

"Yeah, sure. Down in the parking lot, under the hotel."

"Great, let's go get it."

Danny wanted to tell somebody, anybody, to send some sort of warning, but it was impossible, Carlo was right beside him and he could not get away.

Danny would have felt safer had Mike been with him but he was somewhere in the ballroom, not expecting his boss to be making an early exit from such a high profile event.

So he would just have to go it alone and wing it.

But he knew that was an incredibly dangerous strategy.

***

491

Twenty minutes later, Danny and Carlo Liuzzi were sitting together in a gleaming Ferrari Daytona heading towards the Hollywood Hills en route to the Liuzzi mansion.

"Drives nice," Carlo remarked.

"Yep, you can't beat a Ferrari," Danny agreed.

"You're right there. Give me Italian any day. Better than all that German crap - those piece of shit Mercs and Porsches—"

"My father was driving a Porsche on the night he was killed!" Danny snapped, his mouth working before his brain had engaged.

But he had been unable to stop his anger from flaring as he thought of Diego, acutely aware that the man who had murdered him was sitting by his side.

Carlo glanced at him, a little surprised by the outburst and, for a brief moment, a glimmer of doubt drifted through his mind, was this a set-up?, he wondered.

But then his greed and his desire for power crushed it. The kid was obviously still upset by the death of his old man. Understandable Carlo supposed. But then Diego Del Toro had no business being in Hollywood in the first place - so just maybe he got what he deserved.

Liuzzi smiled inwardly at the delicious irony of the situation. He had killed the kid's father six years ago and here he was now about to complete the biggest deal in cinema history - by buying Viscount off Del Toro's clueless kid. How lucky could a guy get?

"Yeah, well," said Carlo, "Maybe he would have stood more chance if he'd been driving something better."

As he spoke, he watched Danny for any reaction to assuage any remaining doubts he had about the boy's intentions.

Danny had to fight with all his might to resist the urge to pull over and beat Liuzzi to death - right there on the side of the road, just as Carlo had done to Juan Pablo and Diego.

But instead he gripped the steering wheel and kept his face emotion free, knowing he was being watched.

"Yeah. Maybe you're right," he said flatly.

Then, purely out of spite, Carlo added, "I hear the guy who killed your old man had a Camero. They're fine automobiles, Cameros - had one myself once. Not as nice as this though. Like I said, you can't beat Italian."

"No. You sure can't," Danny replied, seething. Christ, Liuzzi was something. A real cold piece of work.

"And it wouldn't kill you to step on it a bit," Carlo sneered, "These babies are meant to be driven fast - not like some little old lady."

Danny had been driving purposely slow, trying to make the short journey as long as possible, no matter how much he hated the man next to him.

It was vital they did not arrive at the mansion too soon. But now he felt as if he had little choice.

"Sure thing," he said, pushing his foot down and feeling the Ferrari respond instantly, "You're the boss!"

Carlo laughed as the surge of speed forced him back in his seat, the Ferrari's high-performance engine rumbling beautifully as Danny shifted through the gears. "You can say that again, boy!" He said delightedly.

A short time later, they were driving up the sweeping driveway of the Liuzzi mansion.

Danny just prayed he had delayed long enough.

***

Forty minutes earlier Maria and Ava had stepped out of the limousine driven by Frankie onto the driveway of their old home. Both dressed in jeans and flats, ready to go to work.

Each of them had spent a good portion of their youth living within the mansion's austere walls but at different times; an unhappy coincidence that united them, as did their hatred for the man who had ruined both their lives.

The purpose of their visit there tonight was to find proof. Proof that Carlo had imprisoned Mildred, leaving her entombed below in the tiny cell under the mansion and proof that he had also killed Armando and Nathaniel.

Maria knew it was a long shot as they were murdered so long ago, but maybe there was some trace - anything that would prove Carlo Liuzzi murdered them; something tangible that they could go to the police with.

The LAPD had found nothing when they visited the mansion after Diego's murder. Ava had told them about the secret doorway behind the bookcase but they had not discovered it - Carlo had altered the mechanism somehow, making her story look like a complete fabrication - a fantasist's wild ravings.

The information she had given them was completely discredited, leaving Liuzzi to carry on with his life unpunished and free from investigation.

Frankie had been feeding Ava information since the morning she left six years earlier, keeping her abreast of everything that was going on within the Liuzzi household - with both Carlo and Salvatore.

Frankie had told her how Carlo had grown more manic; becoming careless and sloppy with matters related to the running of his business; never taking the time to bother with the details anymore but, instead, rushing in headlong, with misjudged impetuosity.

And that was a flaw Danny was presently attempting to exploit.

Yet even Frankie had not been able to discover how to reveal the secret doorway - or find out if it still existed.

But Ava was certain it did and somehow she was determined to find it.

As far as Maria and Ava knew, they had a time frame of around two hours to work within, they would have had slightly longer but Salvatore had delayed things somewhat.

It would have to do.

They crossed the threshold hand-in-hand after Frankie opened the door. "Let's work quickly ladies," he said, "we don't have much time. I gotta be back at the hotel by one o'clock sharp."

They nodded. Yet it felt incredibly strange for both of them to be back there, particularly Maria who had been away for over twenty-five years. Yet it had not changed.

The decor remained the same; a new carpet here, a new set of drapes there, but basically the same as the day she left.

She looked up the wide, sweeping staircase towards her bedroom where she had given birth to Danny. Then she glanced down the long corridor to the kitchen where she and Armando first began their love affair - over a stolen cookie in the pantry. She smiled at the memory.

Her poor, beloved Armando and Megan's good, honest, husband, Nathaniel - both killed in the grounds of this very house.

Just like Edmund, Mildred and God knows how many others.

This gothic mansion really was a hell - presided over by Hollywood's very own devil.

And it was about time he paid for his heinous crimes.

"Okay, sweetie," Maria said, "You take his study - try and find that goddamn door mechanism - and I'll start at the pool house and then head to the garden store. There must be something there - there's gotta be. But if not, we need to know how to open that secret doorway."

"Gotcha." Ava replied. "Good luck - I'll meet you back up here shortly."

Maria lent in and hugged her. "Happy hunting," she said, before heading off outside, a flashlight in her hand.

***

Ava and Frankie worked in tandem, beginning with the books on the bookshelf, systematically trying to push each one in to see if it activated the sliding mechanism.

But none did.

Then they tried pulling each book out, but that failed too and time was already ticking away.

Next Ava started moving pictures and ornaments, being careful to replace them in the exact same position, but again that yielded nothing.

Frankie, meanwhile, busied himself with inspecting the framework of the bookcase itself to see if there was some sort of concealed latch but again it proved fruitless. So he set about tapping on the wall around the bookshelf, checking for other hidden panels.

Ava, growing more frustrated with every wasted minute, then crossed to Carlo's big, heavy desk and started sliding open drawers. It had four down each side; large to small from the bottom up.

Both bottom drawers contained files and paperwork - contracts, scripts and various other documents - certainly no secret buttons. Neither did the next two up, or the two after that.

Then she pulled open the topmost right-hand drawer and was surprised to find a gun; an automatic, she thought, which was sitting next to a pack of bullets, a half empty bottle of malt whiskey and two crystal tumblers.

Very carefully, using just her index finger and thumb, she lifted the gun out and whistled to Frankie.

"Look what I've just found," she said.

"It don't surprise me, kid," he said, looking unimpressed, "I got one just like it in my drawer upstairs."

"You do?" Ava said, slightly appalled.

Frankie smiled and shrugged, "Hey, what can I say, I ain't always been the good, upstanding citizen standing before ya!"

She laughed. "No. I guess you haven't."

Frankie went back to his work and Ava put the gun back in its place, being sure to leave it as she found it, before sliding the drawer shut.

Feeling exasperated, she finally opened the topmost left-hand drawer and was staggered by what it revealed.

Sitting on a rich, red velvet cushion was a long curved dagger in a jewel encrusted scabbard. It was beautiful, unlike anything Ava had ever seen; diamonds, rubies and emeralds all exquisitely inlayed into the delicately carved golden handle.

Yet it was not the dagger that amazed her, it was the object lying next to it.

The irrefutable proof that Carlo Liuzzi had, indeed, murdered Diego Del Toro - the very object he had used to bludgeon Maria's husband to death.

Because next to the dagger, lying on its side, was Diego's Academy Award; still smeared with the dried blood of the man who had won it.

Ava could not believe her incredible discovery and for a moment was struck dumb. However, the sound of a car parking up outside in the driveway soon snapped her out of her astonishment.

She looked at Frankie, her eyes wide with panic, seeing he had heard it too.

"Quick!" He said, "Hide!"

"What about you?" she exclaimed in a terrified whisper.

"Don't worry about me, kid, I'll be fine - I'll try to get out and warn Maria - but you gotta go, now!"

"Be careful - please!" she begged as she slammed the drawer shut and darted from the room, bounding across the lobby and heading upstairs, taking the steps three at a time - only just making it to the landing as the front door opened.

"You can make yourself comfortable in the library while I make a couple of calls," she heard Carlo say as he entered the house, "I'll get Frankie to fix you a drink."

Who's he talking too? Ava wondered, had he bought Madison Kane back there?

Then her question was answered and her heart sank, as she heard Danny say, "Great. Sounds good."

Immediately Ava was fearful for him. What the hell was he doing there?

Danny was supposed to get everything done back at the hotel - that was the plan. But something had obviously gone wrong and now he was back there, in the lion's den, putting himself in serious danger.

Did he know she and his mother were still there?

And what about Maria? Did she hear the car? Did she know her father had returned?

***

Maria went down to the pool house first, everything immediately familiar even in the darkness and she barely needed the flashlight to guide her way.

The pool was exactly as she remembered it; the same mosaic pattern in the bottom that formed a big gold star with the initials *CL* in the centre.

Her father, ever the egotist.

Silently she crossed to the pool house and opened the door. Once inside she snapped on the light, exposing the room where she last saw Armando, the place where they had made love; where Danny, their beautiful son had been conceived.

Suddenly Maria was overcome with emotion as she thought of all she had lost, of all her son had missed. Two husband's, each a father to him, both killed by the same man.

God how she hated him.

The large space had been completely reupholstered since she had last been there and everything looked pristine and clean. A new floor had been laid and fresh paint had been applied to the walls - probably many times over the years.

If there had ever been any trace of what had happened to

498

Armando there then it was clearly now long gone - or trapped under layers of paint and solid marble tile.

To even look for any remaining evidence would be futile.

She lingered there a few minutes longer, relishing the memory of her lost love; her young, handsome, Italian man with the wide smile and the happy-go-lucky personality. Gosh how she had loved him.

But the coma had robbed her of his memory for seven years and by the time she awoke he was long gone. Just a spectre of the past.

But tonight she was going to rectify that. She was going to find justice for him, and for Diego and for all the others.

If it was the last thing she ever did, she would avenge them.

Maria snapped off the light and made her way to the tennis courts which were some distance away across the wide expanse of lawn upon which she had played when she was a child.

When her mother was alive and her father was her hero. My, how things had changed.

Her mother had died when she was very young. Indeed she could barely remember her and still did not know, to this day, what had happened to her. Had Carlo killed her too?

It was certainly possible. As she continued to walk, Maria clutched the small gold necklace, the one with her name inscribed on it, that her mother had given her as a Christening present, which now hung beside her cherished locket.

What would her life have been like had her mother not died? She wondered.

It was a question without answer but even though she was in a wistful mood; old feelings and memories stirred up by her return to the house, Maria knew she could waste no more time dwelling on the past.

She was there for a purpose and, with that in mind, stepped

up her pace a little as she strode across the lawn to the tennis courts.

Once there, she used the flashlight to navigate her way down to the garden store using the old wooden steps, which were now somewhat rickety and dangerous.

Nevertheless, she negotiated them safely and quickly opened the door to the outer chamber. When inside, she flipped on the light to reveal the small area that was used to keep spare nets and tennis paraphernalia. It appeared most of the garden tools were still kept there as forks, spades, rakes and various other equipment lined the cinder block walls.

Minding her step in the cluttered space, she hurried across to the store room a few feet away, seeing immediately that it was bolted shut. The bolt and socket were both old and rusted and had clearly not been used for many years; a fine mesh of cobwebs covering them.

The bolt was stiff; the rust having almost fused it permanently locked but, after tucking the flashlight under her arm and using both hands she at last managed to slide it judderingly aside, allowing her to pull the creaky door open.

Tentatively she entered, using her flashlight to locate the light switch.

The bulb flickered a few times before it eventually remained on to properly illuminate the unfamiliar room.

Maria had no recollection of ever being in there before so it was all new to her.

It was a fairly large space with a low ceiling and seemingly ancient tools hanging on various hooks and scattered about the floor. A couple of hosepipes, a large net which Maria guessed was once used for fishing leaves out of the swimming pool, a sit-on mower and a heavy lawn roller amongst other things, all covered in a thick layer of dust.

What immediately caught Maria's eye, however, was a heavy chain that was coiled like a sleeping python on the floor in the centre of the room; a long strand of it stretching from the main stack and hooked onto a solid wooden beam that ran along the entire width of the ceiling. The hook itself looked to be made of thick steel with a sharp pointed tip.

At first glance the chain seemed to be streaked with rust, but upon closer inspection it appeared to be red paint that had dulled over many years.

Then, with horror, Maria realised it was blood. "Oh my God!" She exclaimed out loud. Was that Armando's blood? Had he been chained to that beam?

It was too awful for Maria to contemplate, but she guessed he probably had.

Even though the bulb lit the room, the illumination it provided was insufficient to penetrate the shadows, so Maria used the flashlight to inspect all the dark spaces not previously revealed to her.

She systematically studied every part of the room, trying to find any other evidence that would conclusively prove Armando had been killed there - something the police would find hard to refute.

She eventually shone her light into the furthest corner of the room, highlighting nothing more than an old bucket and a ragged mop. She was about to move on, when behind the bucket she noticed what appeared to be the toe of a boot.

Maria rushed over and shone her torch down behind the bucket. Sure enough, there was a pair of tatty work boots concealed behind it. What is more, inside the top edge of one, in a scrawly script, she could clearly see the name Armando Calabrese written there.

Maria gasped loudly and burst into tears. She remembered those boots, remembered Armando wearing them - remembered him kicking them off before each time they made love.

There could be no doubt.

As she wept, she noticed with terrible realisation that the boots were liberally splashed with dried on, decades old blood. She then also noticed a red stain on the dusty concrete floor; a macabre trail that led from the boots to a large circular mass directly under where the chain was hanging from the beam.

Was that where Armando begged her father to let him marry Maria? Was that where Carlo had answered by severing her poor lover's testicles, as Salvatore had taken so much pleasure in telling her?

She knew in her heart that it was.

Maria knelt down on the cold floor and placed her palm flat on the enormous red stain; her shoulders heaving as she sobbed for the boy she had loved with all her heart.

Maria had been down there much longer than intended by the time her tears finally dried and she knew she had to be getting back to the house. It surely must be almost time for them to be going.

So, reluctantly, she rose from her knees, switched off the light and left the garden store.

As she strode purposefully back up the lawn towards the house, she felt as if she had finally said a proper goodbye to Armando.

She had also found the proof she needed to put her father away for good.

Chapter Thirty Seven

Carlo opened the library door and shouted loudly, "Frankie!"

"Right here, Boss!" His underling replied, rising from an armchair and feigning a yawn, quite startling Liuzzi who had not expected him to already be in the room.

"Oh, there you are," he said, "what are you doing in here? Sleeping by the look of things."

"Sorry, Boss. I ain't getting any younger - thought I might get a coupla hours shut-eye before going to pick you up - why you back anyway?"

Carlo did not appreciate being quizzed, he certainly wasn't answerable to an oaf like Frankie and it was none of his business anyway.

"That's nothing to do with you. You just get your lazy ass up and make this nice young fella a drink - I gotta make a couple of calls."

Only then did Frankie see Danny standing behind Carlo in the doorway; realising instantly plans had gone array.

"Yeah, sure Boss - evenin' Sir," Frankie said, greeting Danny.

"Evening. My name's Del Toro - Daniel Del Toro, pleased to meet you," said Danny.

"Frankie DeLuca. Likewise." Said Frankie introducing himself for appearances sake, but both knew all too well who the other one was.

"Yeah, yeah, enough with the niceties," interrupted Carlo, "just fix the guy a drink for Chrissakes!"

Frankie looked at Danny for his order, desperate to warn him that Ava was still in the house and his mother was somewhere in the grounds, but he could not as Carlo was still standing between them.

"Whiskey, please, straight up," Danny said.

"Whiskey, yeah, right. Er... I think we got a bottle in the kitchen—"

"Jesus, Frankie! For fuck's sake - there's a bottle in my desk drawer - top right. Go get that before our guest dies of thirst. There's a couple of glasses, too."

"Right, okay. Sure Boss. Will do - sorry. Back in just a sec, Mr Del Toro."

"Hey, no problem," replied Danny with an easy smile.

Frankie crossed the room and used the adjoining door to enter the study. He then made his way quickly to the desk and pulled out the top right hand drawer.

Immediately he saw the gun and placed his hand upon it, thinking he could maybe tuck it in his belt in case things went badly wrong. But as he was about to lift it out, Carlo turned to look at him, "Come on!" He barked, "we're both thirsty here!"

Thinking better of it, Frankie moved his hand from the gun and grabbed the bottle of malt whiskey beside it, along with the two glasses. Then quickly scurried back to the library, neglecting to shut the drawer.

He poured the two men a drink, still trying to find an opportune moment to warn Danny, but one was not forthcoming before Carlo said, "Right, Frankie, you come with me. Let's leave this young man alone for a few minutes while I call New York.

"Mr Del Toro - Danny - if you'll excuse us - we'll be back in a short while."

"Of course," Danny replied. "Please, take all the time you need."

With that, Carlo nodded and strode off towards his study, Frankie following close behind.

As the two of them entered Carlo's office, Frankie was told to close the door.

In compliance, Frankie turned and took hold of a handle on each of the double doors. As he slowly closed them to, he looked directly at Danny, who was staring imploringly back at him from the other room, desperate for some sign as to the whereabouts of Ava and Maria.

Yet all Frankie could do was shake his head slightly, to indicate that all was far from well.

***

The moment Frankie closed the door, Danny began to pace. What the hell was he doing there - was he crazy!

This wasn't the plan.

The plan was to keep Liuzzi busy back at the hotel - to get him to sign the papers - allowing Maria and Ava enough time to find the proof they needed.

If all went well, Carlo would have unwittingly brought about his own calamitous downfall without ever knowing that Maria and Ava had even been at his home.

Frankie would have just picked him up from the Beverly Hills Matador as arranged - after first delivering the girls back safely to the side entrance of the hotel.

Then, in the morning, they had intended to present whatever evidence they found to the LAPD, using all of Maria Del Toro's considerable clout, which would supposedly lead to Carlo's imminent arrest.

By which time, of course, he would undoubtedly know of Danny's deception but by then it would be much too late.

Danny was most definitely not supposed to be at the mansion

and his mother and Ava were supposed to be long gone.

But here they all were. Danny in the library, the two women God knows where but somewhere within the house or gardens.

Danny had to keep calm, to play things out, keep Carlo's attention away from the fine print as he signed the documents then, with luck, persuade him to return with him to the party at the hotel.

It was the only way he could see of them all making it out safely.

But it was a high risk strategy.

And first Carlo had to come up with the money.

However, the Contessa di Montagna had assured them that would not be an issue.

All Danny could do was wait and pray that Ava and his mother were out of harm's way.

***

Ava was hiding behind one of the large marble columns on the spacious landing, trying to peer over the balustrade where she could see both the study and library doors on the far side of the wide lobby. Yet both were closed so she had absolutely no idea where either Danny, Frankie or Carlo were.

They had entered through the library, although she assumed Liuzzi would make his calls in the study - but would the door between the two rooms be shut? Dare she risk opening the door to the library to see if Danny was in there alone?

It would be foolish to do so, she had to admit.

Should she then risk sneaking downstairs to warn Maria?

Again, probably best not as it could put all of them in even more jeopardy if she was discovered.

She would just have to trust Frankie. He said he would find a way to warn Maria and Ava did not doubt that he would if he possibly could.

In the meantime she, herself, would just have to wait and hope Carlo did not decide to come upstairs.

Frankie sat patiently in the corner of Carlo's study as his boss phoned Carmine Carboni in New York and pleaded with him to lend him a further twenty million dollars, so he could buy himself into Viscount.

Carlo was a different man when speaking to Carboni; reverential, respectful, complimentary. Liuzzi was a powerful man, or at least he used to be, but Carmine was his mentor, his former boss and head of The Family with power of a very different kind.

Liuzzi was waxing lyrical about the Viscount deal, telling Carboni how it had just fallen into his lap, how it was a monumental opportunity and how the kid, Del Toro, didn't know just how dumb he was to be giving it up.

The deal had to be done tonight otherwise he would miss out - some asshole not worthy of the chance would steal it out from under his nose - and it would be gone.

But Carlo wanted it, wanted it real bad and surely Carmine could see the sense of it, see the money to be made from it.

Frankie heard Liuzzi say that, 'yes, he was aware he already owed the Carboni Family ten million, and that he knew he hadn't, so far, repaid any of it. But this was a sweet deal - maybe the biggest in the history of motion pictures and the returns could easily triple if not quadruple the amount invested in maybe less than two years. Hell, with a couple of hit movies it could double in less than six months.'

Liuzzi and Carboni danced around for a while, Carlo making promises that he had no idea he could keep and Carmine making him jump through all the hoops to let him know exactly who was in charge.

But eventually, after much pleading, after making many assurances, the deal was finally done.

Carboni would instruct his bankers in Geneva, where it was

already morning, to transfer the money immediately into the already considerable Viscount coffers. All they required was the account number.

"Hold on," Carlo said to Carmine, before saying to Frankie, "Open the door will ya?"

Frankie did as instructed, to reveal Danny sitting in the library looking calm and relaxed, although feeling anything but.

"We're gonna wire the money from Geneva directly, okay? You got the account details?"

It just so happened he did - rather too conveniently - but Carlo was too hyped up, too excited, to notice. All he could think about was gaining control of Viscount and becoming the big man once more.

"Sure," Danny said, knowing this was where things could go horribly wrong.

He took out his pocket book and flipped over a couple of pages, then read a number out loud which Liuzzi, in turn, related to Carboni.

"Yeah, Carmine, I'll hold, no problem." Carlo said into the mouthpiece. Then to Danny, "They're doing it now - should only take a few minutes. You might as well gimme that paperwork while we wait."

"Okay, why not."

Danny was sweating slightly as he walked from the library into the study, taking the folded legal papers from the inside pocket of his tuxedo jacket, praying that Liuzzi would not read the contents of the document.

Risking everything, he flattened the paperwork on the heavy desk, "Just sign here and here," he said, leafing through the pages and showing Carlo the two dotted lines which required his signature.

Liuzzi lifted his reading glasses out of his breast pocket and flicked them open, sliding them up his generous nose as he absently perused the document.

Then he picked up his gold-plated fountain pen, cradled the receiver in the crook of his neck and signed his name with an elaborate flourish on the designated spaces.

He did not read a word of the text, such was his haste to make Viscount his.

However, little did he know that Carmine Carboni had long since had enough of him; sick of his violent mood swings, his wild spending and his poor judgement.

Indeed, Carboni had not actually lent him a cent and was merely acting as a broker for a third party, one Contessa di Montagna, who had already bought Liuzzi's ten million dollar debt from her second cousin, Carmine, as well as authorising the additional twenty.

And by midday tomorrow Carlo's entire thirty million dollar debt would have been sold by the Contessa to somebody else. Someone who was eagerly awaiting the moment when she could call it in.

That person was his daughter, Maria Del Toro, who along with her two sons and Ava - and, of course, the generous co-operation of Lucia Tartaglia, had orchestrated this whole elaborate ruse. Specifically designed for the purpose of ruining Liuzzi - financially, personally and legally.

And it was wholly deserved.

But for now, Carlo was enjoying his major coup.

He picked up his whiskey tumbler and raised it to Danny, "To the continued success of Viscount. May its glory years be ahead!" He toasted.

Danny had left his whiskey in the library, but said, "I'll second that."

A moment later Carmine came back on the line and Danny watched as Liuzzi's face spread into a wide grin.

"That's great Carmine, real good news, appreciate it."

After exchanging a few more words, Carlo eventually hung up. "That's it, it's all done," he said. "Say hello to the new king of Hollywood!"

"Wow! Congratulations," said Danny. "That was quick."

"Hey, I don't fuck around, kid. When I want something, I geddit - know what I mean?"

"Yeah. That's what I figured. No messing around - you saw your chance and you took it - not even thinking twice about it."

"You got that right," Carlo said, glugging down the remains of his whiskey. "Hey, Frankie, go get that bottle would ya - and this man's glass - we got some celebrating to do!"

As Frankie wandered off into the library as ordered, he heard Danny say, "Listen - why don't we go back to the hotel - back to the party? We can celebrate there - make the announcement - what better place to do it?" He was desperate to get Carlo out of the house, as far away from it as possible, to allow Ava and his mother to get clear - also to keep his eyes off the documentation - because the moment he read that then the game would be up.

Frankie could see what Danny was trying to do. The kid was smart, it was a good move. Maybe they would all get out of there alive after all.

"Hey, great idea, Boss," he said, returning with Danny's drink and handing it to him. "You go back with Mr Del Toro here and I'll pick you up later as planned."

He could see that Carlo's gigantic ego was already playing out the scenario in his head.

He was thinking about the glory he could derive by announcing the deal to the great and the good of Hollywood, all packed in to that one fabulous venue - show them that he, Carlo Liuzzi, should never have been written off, that he was back on top - and they had better remember it from now on.

"You know, that's heck of an idea," he said. "Let's do it. Let's make the announcement tonight. Why not - it'll be the perfect opportunity."

"Great," said Danny with immense relief. "Sounds good. Let's go."

Carlo was smiling, feeling happier than he had in a long time, already imagining the expression on the faces of those that thought he was finished. Who would have thought it would be Diego Del Toro's son who made that possible? Carlo could scarcely believe it, but it was true. He had done it.

He was back.

He pulled off his glasses and put them down on the paperwork then screwed the top back onto his expensive fountain pen.

"You know? I thought this was gonna be a good night," he said, placing the pen back down on the table.

As he did so, something caught his eye. The lens of his spectacles, upon the document, magnifying a particular portion of the previously unread text.

'...*agree to pay this donation in exchange of becoming President of the Viscount Charity for Widows and Orphans...*'

Carlo paused for a moment and frowned.

"Hey, what's this—" he said before Danny butted in, immediately fearing the worst.

"—It's nothing, come on - let's go celebrate. You'll have time for that later. Let's go make the announcement," he said opening the door, not seeing Ava crouching down behind the column at the top of the stairs, looking down.

"Wait!" Carlo barked, grabbing up the paperwork and sliding his glasses back on his face. "What the fuck have I signed here?"

Danny knew the game was up but he continued on innocently, "The agreement - it states you have taken over, that's all."

"No. That's not all. Taken over what? That's what I wanna know," growled Carlo, furiously scanning through the legal jargon

511

on the contract, trying to decipher all the bullshit.

"Viscount." Danny replied, hearing the obvious deception in his own voice. "You've taken over Vis—"

"I've taken over the fucking *charity!*" Liuzzi bellowed.

"That's right," Danny said, "That's what we've been talking about all night, isn't it - I thought you understood—"

"Liar! Don't you try to fool me, boy! Who the fuck do you think I am? It says here that I've just agreed to take over as President of some charity for widows and fuckin' orphans - why the hell would I wanna do that?"

"Sorry, but I thought—"

"You thought you could con me boy. That's what you thought - you fuckin' snot nose brat! Con me out of twenty million dollars to become the head of the Viscount Charity not Viscount Studios!"

"I never once said it was for the studios - not once - it was you who assumed—"

"I assumed nothing - you purposely tried to deceive me - admit it!"

Danny said nothing as Carlo continued to rage.

"Do you know what you've done to me? Do you know who it is that I've just borrowed twenty million bucks from? What he'll do to me when he finds out what—" Suddenly Carlo saw that Danny did know. He saw it clearly. That was the whole idea.

He glanced down at the table, smiling at his own stupidity, seeing the open drawer next to him, where the gun lay.

"It was never about the studio—" Danny said.

Suddenly Carlo snatched up the gun from the open drawer and aimed it at Danny. "Not another word, boy. Or I'll kill you just like I killed your old man!"

Upon hearing the confession, all attempts to fool Carlo evaporated as Danny's temper boiled over. "I know you did you evil sonofabitch! I know you fucking killed him, you murdering, bastard—"

"Careful, boy - don't fuckin' test me."

"Or what? Or you'll pull the trigger? Well go ahead, you won't get away with it this time - too many people know I'm here, too many people know just what you've done. You're going to prison, Liuzzi - going to prison for a very long time and personally I hope to God they fry your bones in the electric chair!"

Carlo smiled. The boy had pluck, he'd give him that.

But he still had to die. He raised the gun, "Say 'hi' to your old man for me," he said.

Then he pulled the trigger.

***

Ava saw the door open, then heard Carlo shout.

Immediately she knew it had gone wrong. That Liuzzi knew.

She realised he had discovered Danny's deception. And fear filled her belly.

Then she remembered what Frankie had said about having a gun in his drawer.

Silently she padded along the landing and slipped into Frankie's bedroom. It was sparcely decorated; just a bed, a wardrobe and a bedside cabinet.

She rushed to the cabinet and quickly opened the top drawer. In it she found a few personal items; a picture of his estranged daughter - who lived with her mother in New York, who he had not been permitted to see in many years; a picture of Ava, too, in a little frame, kept where Carlo could not see it - the girl Frankie thought of as his other daughter - just as she considered him to be her true step-father.

There was also a few other nik-naks, an old watch, a ticket stub for a Yankees game - and a gun. Just like the one in Carlo's study.

Swiftly she lifted it out and hurried back along the landing, clutching it in her grip, scared that it might go off but determined to protect Danny and Frankie at any cost.

She had reached the top of the stairs when she heard the gunshot and suddenly the bottom fell out of her world.

***

Frankie saw Carlo raise the gun, saw the familiar look in his evil eyes - the insanity of the man rising suddenly and violently to the surface.

He knew instantly what Liuzzi was going to do. And he could not allow it.

How would Ava cope if she lost Danny? It would be just too much for her to bear after the loss of Edmund and of Mildred. Too much after of all her years of searching for Danny - the man, Frankie now knew, she loved with all her heart.

In that instant, in the split-second it took for him to think it, he flung himself selflessly in front of Danny, feeling the bullet rip into him as it struck like a sledgehammer.

Frankie went down hard. Landing with a crunch, sprawled awkwardly in the doorway between the hallway and the study.

Danny stood over him in shock, horrified at what Frankie had done; by what Carlo had done.

"You bastard!" He spat. "You've killed him - you've killed your own man—"

"Ah, so what?" Carlo sneered. "He was always too goddamn soft - too sympathetic to—"

"To who?" Said Ava, suddenly appearing in the doorway and pointing the gun out straight, aiming it firmly at Liuzzi. "To me, Carlo? Is that who you mean? Was Frankie always too sympathetic to me?"

"Ava?" Liuzzi was visibly stunned. Clearly shocked by her sudden and unexpected appearance.

As was Danny who had desperately hoped she was long gone; that she had got out along with Maria - so she would not have had to witness Frankie's death or, indeed, his own.

Yet she was there nevertheless, and she had a gun.

"That's right, me." Ava said, tears streaming down her face as she stepped carefully over Frankie's prone form, not allowing herself to even look at him for fear of breaking down; her heart aching for the loss of her dear, sweet friend.

"Me - the girl whose father you murdered, whose mother you imprisoned," she continued, " - the same girl who is now going to take great delight in killing you for shooting Frankie - this lovely, gentle man who cared for me like I was his own."

For a moment Carlo was staggered.

But he recovered quickly. "I always suspected you might prove to be trouble," he said.

"You got that right, Daddy Carlo," Ava sneered.

He smiled. "You gonna shoot me, Ava, is that it?"

"Bet your goddam ass I am."

"Careful Ava," Danny said warily. "Watch him."

Again Carlo looked surprised. "You know this guy, Ava?"

"Know him? Yeah, you could say that. I love him, how do you like that?"

Carlo's face hardened as she went on. "You know who he is don't you? Know whose son he is—"

"Ava," Danny warned, concerned she might reveal too much.

Carlo smiled again. "Ah, you love him? Now it all makes sense. And yes, I know who he is. He's the spoilt brat of that worthless hotelier I killed. So what?

"You thought you and your little boyfriend here would try and trick me, did you? Maybe give me a little payback?"

"Why not." Said Ava, sniffing away her tears for Frankie. "You deserve it. You're a murderer, a psychopath. And it's about time you paid for your crimes!"

"Okay, well, if that's what you think, you just go right ahead.

515

Pull the trigger - see what happens."

Ava was confused, why was he being so calm?

"You see," Carlo went on, "I can guarantee you two things. The first is that I can kill your boyfriend here before you can even rustle up the courage to pull the trigger - and the second is that your gun won't fire."

He saw her uncertain expression. "You see, Ava, unless I'm very much mistaken, that's Frankie's gun you're holding there in your shaking hand - a gun I know to be empty. How do I know that? Well because I keep the bullets for it here in my drawer. You think me stupid enough to let a treacherous oaf like DeLuca keep a loaded gun in my house? Please, give me credit for something."

Ava looked from Liuzzi to the gun and back again. Then squeezed the trigger praying to God to hear a loud bang.

But it just clicked.

She pulled it again with the same result. And again. And again.

But each time nothing but a click.

Carlo was right. The gun was empty and they were screwed.

Liuzzi laughed. "You should see your faces the pair of you - such a picture. Now please, both of you, step over to the bookcase other wise I will kill you. Oh, and Ava - drop the gun, there's a good girl."

Danny put his arm protectively around Ava as she did as instructed, the empty gun landing on the carpet next to Frankie's body with a dull thud.

Then slowly they crossed to the bookcase, Liuzzi's own gun trained on them at all times.

With his free hand he reached down and pressed the concealed button that was mounted under his desk top and there was an audible 'click' as the bookcase slid smoothly open to reveal the hidden door.

"Goddamn it," Ava groaned under her breath, "It was under the desk!"

"Right. Inside," Carlo ordered. "Ava, I believe you know the way. I think it's about time Danny boy here met your mother. What do you say?"

"Fuck you!" She replied.

"My, such a dirty mouth - maybe it's a good job you were not my real daughter after all. Now inside.

As Ava reluctantly opened the thick steel door, then led Danny onto the small landing and down the narrow staircase towards the dungeon below, Carlo snapped on the light and followed.

None of them noticed Frankie's head move or heard him groan.

Chapter Thirty Eight

Maria heard the gunshot as she approached the veranda at the rear of the house.

For a moment she froze, knowing the sound had come from inside. Immediately she was fearful for Ava, what had happened?

Stealthily, yet quickly, she sneaked around to the front of the house and immediately saw Danny's Ferrari in the driveway parked next to her father's limousine - that she and Ava had arrived in earlier, driven by Frankie.

Her heart sank. Why on earth was Danny there?

However, the moment she glanced in through the study window she knew.

Her father was home. Standing in his study, a gun in his hand, pointing it at Ava and her son.

She then watched as Ava fired, confused as to why her gun made no sound - and why it was that Carlo still remained on his feet.

However, Maria soon realised why when she saw her father smiling. It was a smile she had not witnessed for over twenty five years, yet the sight of it made her feel physically sick.

Maria then watched as the bookcase miraculously slid open, just as Ava said it did, horrified as she and Danny then vanished into the space beyond with her father following menacingly behind, the gun held firmly in his hand.

She darted round to the front door and quickly slipped inside, running over to where Frankie was laying, clearly in some pain, between the lobby and the study, blood pumping from a hole just below his shoulder.

Maria hastily ripped off her hooded sweat top, leaving just her T-shirt on underneath, and pressed it against the wound to staunch the bleeding. "Are you okay, Frankie?" she asked in a whisper, crouching beside him, "Please say you are!"

"I'm okay, sweetheart," he groaned painfully, "But Liuzzi's got Ava and Danny - they went down there." He indicated to the concealed staircase.

"I know. I saw. I'm going in after them."

"Wait, honey! Take my gun. There's bullets in the top drawer of the desk - fetch them for me and I'll load it. You can't go in there unarmed - he's crazy!"

Maria knew he was talking sense and did as instructed.

As quickly as possible, Maria helped him to his feet and with his hands weak and shaking, Frankie loaded the gun.

He handed it to her. "Be careful," he said. "Please, save Ava - don't let that bastard kill her."

"I won't. I promise. Call the police - tell them to come quickly."

"I will."

"Sure you're okay?"

Frankie nodded. "Go get him."

Maria nodded back. Then she was gone.

***

They reached the narrow passageway at the bottom of the stairwell which was dusty now and thick with cobwebs.

"Please," Danny said to Liuzzi, knowing what they were about to encounter in the cell beyond. "Don't do this - let Ava go. Take me but not her - she's been through enough - don't make her come face to face with her mother after all this time - please."

519

"Carlo smiled. "Ah, how gallant. I can see what you love about him, Ava, I really can. He's definitely a keeper - but no, Danny, I won't be letting her go. Either of you. Now open the fucking door!

Ava was crying now. Mildred's skeleton was inside the cell and she had no wish to see it again - and definitely no desire to be locked in there with it.

But it was futile to protest.

Danny slid the bolt and opened the door.

It smelt fusty and rotten inside. Of death and corruption.

Ava's eyes were closed as she gripped Danny's hand. "It's okay, I'm here," he said softly comforting her. "It's not too bad, honestly."

"Wow. Ain't he just the sweetest," sneered Carlo sarcastically, prodding her in the back with the barrel of the gun, forcing them both inside.

"It's okay," said Danny again, ignoring his grandfather. "Don't worry."

Slowly, Ava opened her eyes and looked about her.

Mildred's bones lay on the bed but they were almost clean now except for a layer of dust. The pink satin robe draped around her skeleton disguising most of it from view.

The bedclothes were soiled but the scene was nowhere near as horrific as the last time she had witnessed it - or maybe it was just that she now knew what to expect.

But she clung onto Danny's hand, drawing strength from him.

"Killing us won't do you any good Carlo," Danny said. "The deal's already been done. You've just signed away your life. Tomorrow morning your debt to Carboni is going to be called in - not only the twenty million you've just borrowed, but the ten million you already owe, too.

"You see, Carboni was only acting as a middle man and has already sold your debt on - as was previously agreed long before you even walked into the gala tonight.

520

"And soon it will belong to Viscount - lock, stock and barrel.

"If you'd taken the time to read the small print, you'd know that you've just signed Gold Star away as collateral. By tomorrow lunchtime it'll all be gone, swallowed up by Viscount - and you'll be ruined."

Carlo smiled. "And who is going to call this debt in if you two are locked down here where no one can find you, eh? Who's gonna find that piece of paper I just signed when I burn it? You didn't think it through, did you boy?"

Now it was Danny's turn to smile, accepting his fate but happy Liuzzi would finally get his comeuppance. "Actually, Carlo, I think it's you who hasn't thought things through.

"You see, those very organised, very thorough bankers in Switzerland keep meticulous records of their transactions - everything recorded in triplicate. Indeed, for a sum so large as twenty million dollars, well you can just imagine the paper trail involved.

"And even if that was not the case, then I think the organisation who currently owns your debt, who, incidentally, make the Carboni Family look like a bunch of playful puppies, might take exception to you not paying them."

The smile slipped from Carlo's face, his lip curling into an evil grimace, knowing Danny was right.

"Think you're clever don't you, boy?" He said. "But tell me this, who do you expect to run Gold Star or Viscount with you and Ava buried down here?"

"Oh, sorry, my mistake," Danny said quite casually. "I think I may have forgotten to tell you. I have a brother."

"A brother?"

"Yes. Do you remember twenty six years ago, you had a chauffeur, Nathaniel? Well he had a son."

"Nathaniel?"

"Yes. You killed him, along with a young gardener - if that

helps to jog your memory."

"What? You and your brother are Nathaniel's sons - is that it? Is that who's gonna run my company - the sons of a goddamn worthless chauffeur? Please gimme a break - it was bad enough you being the son of a fucking hotelier!"

"No. You don't understand. My brother is Nathaniel's son. Not me."

"You're right, kid, you got me - I don't understand," Carlo snorted derisively. "Nathaniel was your brother's old man but not yours - so you are Del Toro's snotty brat - or maybe that's a lie and maybe you're the goddamn gardener's? Who gives a fucking damn."

"You're right. I am Diego Del Toro's son and proud to be. But I am also the gardener's.

"My birth father was Armando Calabrese - the man you killed for the crime of loving your daughter!"

"What?" Carlo couldn't believe it. "What's that you're saying now?"

"You heard me well enough. I am Armando Calabrese's son. Your own grandson."

Carlo was suddenly confused, his thoughts a whirl. "What do you mean - that can't be true. It… it can't be—"

"My mother is Maria Liuzzi - your daughter - the woman you condemned to Hell twenty-six years ago - and now I'm here to make you pay for it you murderous, evil sonofabitch!"

"No!" Carlo cried, unable to believe what he was hearing. "You're lying - you must be—"

"Look at me Carlo. Look into my eyes," Danny raged. "Does it look like I'm lying - tell me that I am!

Liuzzi did as instructed. He looked into Danny's deep green eyes and saw Maria staring back.

"You see it, don't you, Carlo? You see the resemblance."

"Oh my Christ," Liuzzi said softly, unable to comprehend what

522

he was seeing or what he had been told. But knowing without doubt it was the truth.

"Yes, that's right, Grandfather. I am the child you forbade your daughter to name to prevent her from finding me - yet now I have three names - please, feel free to choose one.

"I am Daniel Calabrese. Daniel Del Toro and, God help me, Daniel Liuzzi, too - your own flesh and blood!"

Carlo was reeling, rocked to the very core, his arms dropping to his side, the gun no longer trained on Danny and Ava as he tried to compute the immensity of what he had just been told - what he had seen for himself with his own eyes.

Danny was his grandson.

Carlo's mind flickered back to that night so long ago, when the nursemaid, Megan, had presented Maria's baby boy to him.

He had longed for a son of his own yet had only been granted one precious daughter. She had given him a grandson - a male heir - but he was the bastard son of a lowly immigrant, a nobody with no hope of a future.

Yet there Danny stood; tall, broad, handsome. Fabulously wealthy, far more successful and better respected than Carlo had ever been.

What a fine man the boy had become. And how wrong Carlo had been.

"But… but you're - you were supposed to be—"

"Dead?" Said a voice behind him. "Just like me, you mean?"

Liuzzi span around and saw her standing there in the doorway.

She looked just as she did when she was sixteen; the same dark, shoulder length hair, the same striking green eyes and the same beautiful face. She was even wearing the same gold locket he had given her on her sixteenth birthday; he remembered it distinctly.

And the engraving upon it; Always and Forever.

The woman standing before him was his daughter, Maria.

And she had Frankie's gun pointed squarely at him.

"No!" Carlo said, backing into Danny and Ava as if seeing a ghost - staggering like a drunk, terrified of what his eyes were showing him. "No. It's impossible - it's not true! It can't be. It can't be. You're dead. You're both dead. You died years ago."

"No Father. That's just what you thought. But I'm alive, so is Danny, my son - your grandson - we both lived - no thanks to you."

Carlo started to sob. "No. I won't believe it - I can't believe it - this is a trick. You're fucking with my mind - how can you be here - *how can you be here!*"

"I'm here because Diego Del Toro, the good, kind man that you murdered in cold blood, saved me and because Megan Kelly, the woman you ordered to be killed, saved your grandson.

"We're here because we fought to survive, because you forced us to choose between life and death - and we chose life."

"What? No—"

"Tomorrow," Maria continued, "I'm taking your studio - your precious Gold Star - all legal and above board - signed over by your very own hand."

"You are gonna own Gold Star?"

"Yep. Call it compensation for the hell you put us all through. But don't worry, the twenty million is still going to the widows and orphans - I figure it's the least you can do. After all, you've been responsible for creating a few."

"You're giving it all to a goddamn charity?" Carlo was incredulous.

"Uh-huh. Every dime. But tonight, my dear, loving father, you are going to jail - and that's too damn good for you!

"Danny, Ava, step away from him would you, so I can keep a closer eye on this sonofabitch while we wait for the police to get here."

They did as instructed.

But then, as quick as a flash, like a pouncing tiger, Carlo grabbed Ava and wrapped a thick arm around her neck, instantly lifting his gun and pressing it to her temple.

"Drop it!" He shouted at Maria. "Drop the gun now or she dies - you know I'll do it!"

Maria knew only too well that he would. There was nothing she could do. She paused for just a moment longer then dropped the gun on the cold ground.

"That's my girl," Carlo said triumphantly. "Thought you'd got one over on me didn't ya - thought you could get the better of me. Well you couldn't."

Maria stared at him, hate burning in her green eyes, powerless to assist Ava whose face was etched with fear.

She was going to die. They were all going to die.

"Get back there, against the bed!" Carlo ordered Danny and Maria, "Do it now, quickly!"

They did as instructed. Liuzzi backing away with Ava towards the door.

A second later he was standing in the threshold between the cell and the passageway, his arm clamped like a vice around Ava's neck whilst Danny and Maria looked on helplessly from the edge of the bed where Mildred's ancient bones lay

"Well played," Carlo said. "Well played to all of you. You did a good job and you nearly got me. But you should have known better than to underestimate me.

"Now, I'm afraid you've all gotta die. For real this time - no more play acting! And well, it looks like my darling step-daughter's first."

"No!" Danny shouted desperately as Liuzzi adjusted his grip on the gun, closing his finger around the trigger as he pushed the end of the barrel into Ava's ear.

"No need to say 'goodbye' boy - you and your mom will be

joining her in the afterlife real soo—"

Suddenly, his voice disappeared and he made a slight gurgling sound.

Immediately his hold on Ava loosened and she quickly wriggled out of his grip, scampering safely aside as his hands dropped, the gun slipping from his slackened fingers and clattering on the ground.

Carlo's eyes were wide with shock, his jaw slack, as he slowly, painfully, reached behind his back and with immense difficulty and terrible agony, tugged out the long, metallic object that had just been thrust so fatally into him.

Swaying precariously on his feet, he brought it back around, allowing Maria, Danny and Ava to see the jewel-encrusted dagger, the blood-soaked curve of its lethal, double-edged blade, forged centuries before from the finest Damascus steel, which he now held in his open palm.

Even now he was still awed by the beauty of its carved golden handle, embedded with the diamonds, emeralds and rubies that were sparkling at him enticingly in the flickering light of the cell

He smiled wistfully as the light played upon it, his own blood dripping thickly from its murderous blade.

"It's beautiful, isn't it?" He said, in a whisper.

Then Carlo took several unsteady steps towards Danny and Maria before he at last fell forward.

He landed face down on the cell floor, his arms still by his sides, his legs apart, the Turkish dagger skittering across the floor and coming to a halt by his daughter's feet.

The dagger that had killed Armando, Nathaniel, Edmund and Diego.

She looked down at her father. The devil. Blood spreading in a large pool beside him as it oozed from the deep jagged wound in his back.

Carlo's eyes were open and unblinking, his evil face frozen in the shock of death.

He would never hurt anyone ever again.

Frankie DeLuca slumped against the door frame, blood seeping from the bullet hole high in his chest, looking pale and exhausted and still clutching the ornate scabbard of the dagger he had just plunged into Carlo Liuzzi's back - which he had found in his boss' desk drawer.

"Are you guys okay?" He asked breathlessly, a moment before collapsing.

And Ava ran to him.

***

By the time Danny and Maria came up above ground the LAPD were swarming everywhere. Squad cars were jammed haphazardly in the driveway, their sirens silent but their lights still flashing blue in the early morning light.

A couple of ambulances were also at the scene and a few minutes later the medics brought Frankie up on a gurney, Ava dutifully by his side and holding his hand.

His wound was bad but they expected him to make a full recovery.

The police questioned Danny and Maria for sometime who, in turn, presented all the evidence they had against Carlo Liuzzi; the bloodied Oscar, the blood-stained work boots and the bejewelled dagger - with a curved blade that, in time, would be found consistent with the fatal injuries sustained by Juan Pablo Clemente and Diego Del Toro.

It was conclusive and irrefutable.

And although Frankie had stabbed Liuzzi in the back, the police were convinced he had done it in defence of Ava and the others. He would not be prosecuted.

There was some question over the legalities of the document found on Carlo's desk which ultimately signed Gold Star Pictures over to Viscount Studios. However, no duplicity could be proven and, after hearing Maria's amazing story, the police reckoned it was the very least she deserved - especially as she was effectively donating twenty million dollars to the protection of widows and orphans.

As for the Liuzzi mansion itself; with no other heirs and no record of a will, the ownership passed to Maria, Carlo's immediate next of kin.

In time it would be torn down leaving no trace of the horrors that had taken place there - the land sold off piecemeal to developers.

Mildred's remains would be buried next to her mother and father's back in Iowa. Maybe she would, at last, find some peace there.

However, in the meantime, the final act was yet to be played out.

Chapter Thirty Nine

He woke up in the dark, unable to see anything at all, a blindfold tied tightly over his eyes, a balled up rag stuffed roughly in his mouth.

His head throbbed, pounded, the blood rushing to it as he dangled upside down, his arms and legs bound so that he was completely unable to move.

He could hear muted voices, nothing he could pick out particularly, but the odd word - and they were definitely speaking in Italian.

Salvatore Falcone could remember nothing after seeing Maria and Ava standing together at the side entrance of the Beverly Hills Matador.

He remembered his fight with Ava in the restrooms, remembered the red-haired man and his two burly associates - and them bundling him into the van outside but anything after his confrontation with the two women was a total blank.

He was still stunned at seeing Maria. How the hell had she survived? He was convinced he had killed that bitch long ago but she had somehow lived.

Ava, too. The pair of them together, clearly conspiring, plotting and desperate for revenge.

Well they had got it.

But what now?

He had not seen Maria in a long time but he was certain she was no killer, nor Ava. They were definitely strong, resourceful women capable of many things - but murder? Salvatore doubted it.

He took a little reassurance from that.

Especially as Maria said she would never be seeing him again.

So what then? What was going to happen? A beating? Maybe. A warning? Possibly. But anything more? Probably not.

He felt his confidence build somewhat. Although it did trouble him as to who the red-haired man was - and, more importantly, who the two large Italians were.

What was it the red-headed guy said about Barca? 'He benefits from the merchandise shipped to him by the party I represent - as do you.'

But the coke was shipped from Columbia? Although Barca's contact was in Italy, Salvatore distinctly remembered because they had some weird sounding name like The Woodland Foxes or The Mountain Lions or something along those lines.

But he couldn't be in Italy, could he? Surely not.

And why all the cloak and dagger stuff? Why the rope and the gag? Obviously all that had something to do with Maria, too. But what?

The red-haired guy said the contact wanted to meet him 'face to face.'

Which begged the question, 'Who the fuck were they and what the hell did they have to do with Maria and Ava?'

At that moment Salvatore heard a door creak open and footsteps approaching him.

"Okay, get rid of the blindfold and the gag," a woman said calmly in fluent Italian.

"Si, padrona." 'Yes, mistress'. Replied a gruff male voice.

The handkerchief was pulled unceremoniously from Salvatore's mouth allowing him to draw in a deep lungful of air. He coughed a little at finally being able to breathe properly again.

Then the blindfold was pulled off and Falcone had to blink to adjust his eyesight to the glare of the naked bulb that was shining brightly in the centre of the room.

He could see four, maybe five figures standing around him, their faces silhouetted against the light in the background.

He was in a room of some kind, a cellar maybe, with heavy stone walls that looked years old and rustic in nature. The ceiling was low and curved and also made from stone - like something out of a medieval movie.

Was it a dungeon?

He was hanging upside down, suspended by a rope attached to a winch above him, his head no more than twelve inches from the dusty flagstone floor, making it difficult to properly focus on those standing over him.

Eventually his vision cleared sufficiently so he could at last make out the red-haired man. He was dressed differently now, more casually in an open-neck shirt and jeans as he peered down at him.

"Welcome to Italy," Nate said.

"Who the fuck are you?" Salvatore asked gruffly, his throat still dry from the gag.

"Me?" Nate said with a smile, speaking in faultless Italian. "Well, I'm glad you asked. My name is 'Nate Malone' - which I'm sure will mean nothing to you whatsoever. However, when I tell you that my mother's name was Megan Kelly, then I think you might have some clue?"

Salvatore looked quizzical. The name somehow familiar. Then he remembered. "Megan? Maria's maid, Megan - is *that* who you mean?"

"Ah, yes. I see that your memory of her is faint - but yes, she was my mother. My father, of course, was Nathaniel Kelly - who you will probably remember as the man you killed on the same night that you and Carlo Liuzzi murdered Armando Calabrese - Maria's lover."

Suddenly Falcone's bowel's shifted. That was why he was here.

"Listen, I can explain," he said desperately. "That was all a long time ago - and it was all Carlo, not me - he's the one who made me—"

"Please. Don't lie. I know the whole sorry story. I also know how you tried to throw my mother and Maria off a train on the way to Messina."

"But they lived!" Salvatore exclaimed. "Maria lived and so did Megan - well she was alive when I last saw her, I swear it! In fact it was her who threw me from the train - it's how I lost the use of my hand!"

"Yes, I know. But that still does not excuse what you tried to do to her or, indeed, what you did to Nathaniel."

Salvatore began to weep softly. "It wasn't my fault - I was just acting on Carlo's orders - I swear it. Please! Please don't hurt me - it was a one off - just a mad moment - I was fearful for my life - Carlo's insane, he would have killed me. But I had never hurt anyone before then and I've never hurt anyone since - please, you have to believe me!"

"But I don't believe you, Salvatore. And we both know it to be a lie. You've hurt many people, Maria, Megan and Ava among them. I even have the proof standing here with me." Nate said, his face hard and determined.

"What proof? There is no proof - just Maria's and Ava's word against mine - they're lying I tell you - show me this proof 'cos no such thing exists!"

"I am the proof, Salvatore," a woman's voice said. "The living proof of your violent nature and of your murderous, raping desires."

Falcone squinted at the woman who had just stepped forward to enable him to see her better.

She was tall with an excellent figure and short, silver hair. She also had an eye-patch with some slight scarring on the skin around the edges of it.

Aside from the patch she was an incredibly beautiful woman and Salvatore recognised something familiar about her.

He felt dread stir in the pit of his stomach but could not help but ask, "I know you, don't I?"

"Yes, Salvatore. You know me. You know me well - better and more intimately than I would like - but yes, you know me."

"But how, when?" Although he was just starting to put the jigsaw pieces together in his mind, his fear building steadily.

"Many years ago, when I was just a girl - just a few miles beyond where we are at present - in the hills South of Rome—"

"Lucia?" Salvatore suddenly said, incredulously, immediately experiencing a terrible sense of foreboding.

He recognised her fully now as clear images of the last time he had seen her flooded back into his brain; snapshots of her tender young breasts - exposed through the rip in her torn dress - and images of the large, bloody gash above her ruined eye as he rutted on her, stealing away her virginity.

Delicious memories that he had called upon for self gratification many times in the intervening years.

Yet now they betrayed him.

"Ah. I see you do remember. Yes, it is me, Lucia Tartaglia - the innocent young girl you raped and left for dead when I was just thirteen years old."

Then Lucia dramatically ripped off her eye-patch and thrust her face down towards Salvatore's, showing him the empty socket and the horrific scar where her eye used to be.

"You left me with this as a keepsake of our time together," she snarled.

"Oh my God, oh my God - Lucia, I—" Salvatore whimpered, tears springing from his eyes, knowing for certain he was in very deep trouble.

"Do you know how long I've been looking for you?" The Contessa di Montagna asked him rhetorically.

"All my life," she continued, "Ever since the day you robbed me of my youth, of my ability to have children - and of my face."

Salvatore was crying, trying desperately to twist away from her but merely dangling like a puppet on a string in front of her.

"And now I have found you," The Contessa said with immense satisfaction.

"Wh-what are you gonna do to me?" Falcone pleaded. "Please tell me! Lucia, I'm sorry - please—"

"Silence!" She shouted. Then quietly, her face calm once more, she added, "All in good time, Salvatore. That's the beauty of having you here with me - we've got all the time in the world. Lots and lots of time to get properly reacquainted."

Then she walked away, leaving Nate and three of her guards in the room with Falcone, weeping and snivelling and contemplating his own fate.

He watched helplessly through tear-filled eyes as Lucia left the dungeon and closed the heavy door behind her.

Then he looked up at Nate, a pleading, desperate expression on his cowardly face.

And Nathaniel and Megan Kelly's only son smiled back.

"You won't know this," said Nate bending down and speaking to him in a conversational tone, but I was once a deeply religious man - I was even studying to be a priest.

"But I lost my faith.

"I thought God had somehow forgotten me, that He'd let men like you and Carlo Liuzzi get away with murder whilst good men like my father suffered in your place.

"But then God revealed his whole stunning plan to me - breathtaking in its scale - a plan that brought many people together, uniting us in a common bond - pitting us against a shared enemy who we could vanquish only together.

"He showed us the way to defeat the Devil, Carlo Liuzzi, and you, his faithful Hound from Hell - and that is exactly what we've done.

"My faith is renewed. I am re-born and I will never doubt Him again - I know now, for certain, that He is on the side of the righteous and the worthy.

"Which, unfortunately, does not bode well for you, my friend—"

"Please!" Salvatore whimpered, "Don't kill me - please don't kill me!"

"Killing is a sin," Nate continued, "and as a man of faith once more, it would go against all I believe in to commit such an act."

"Thank you - thank you!" Falcone cried with relief.

"However. I'm afraid the same cannot be said of The Contessa - Lucia or, indeed, these gentlemen beside me."

"No - you can't let them! You can't—"

"Oh, but I can, Salvatore - as this is God's Plan, not mine. And it is not my place to interfere. I must simply trust in The Lord to see that justice is done.

"Now, if you will excuse me, I have business to attend to with The Contessa—"

"No! Please don't leave me!" Falcone shrieked, "Please - not here with them—"

"Goodbye, Salvatore." Nate said, before turning and heading for the door.

"No - please, come back! If you are a man of God forgive me - please forgive me!

But Nate could not offer him absolution as he was not a priest.

***

Nate walked up the ancient stairs from the old dungeons that had been built centuries earlier, deep under The Contessa's monastic villa.

He stepped out into the sunshine and was immediately greeted by Berto, the old collie who accompanied him back to his car where Lucia was waiting for him.

"You've got the papers?" she asked, referring to the documentation that signed Liuzzi's debt and the ownership of Gold Star Pictures over to Viscount Studios which she had previously bought from Carmine Carboni on Nate's behalf.

"Yep. In my pocket, thanks for doing that."

"Pah, tis nothing! It's I who should be thanking you and your family for delivering Falcone to me."

"The least we could do. What will you do with him?"

"Do you really want to know?"

"No. I guess not."

The Contessa smiled, "No, that's probably for the best, but suffice to say he will pay dearly for his crimes."

"Good. Then, for now, I will be going."

"I'll see you soon?"

"Count on it, Contessa," he said, kissing her on both cheeks, "Now that I'm back in Rome you'll be seeing more of me than you can possibly stand."

She laughed. "Well that will certainly please Berto!"

Nate chuckled as he climbed into his Range Rover, " Yes. I'm sure it will - see you!"

***

The Contessa and Berto watched Nate driving away, back to The American Seminary in Rome where he was due to resume his studies - nearly eight years after he had started them.

However, she had no doubts that very soon she would be calling him 'Father' for real.

When the gates of the compound closed, she gave Berto a brief fuss, her faithful old dog revelling in the attention, before she strolled back into the cool interior of the large villa, making her way leisurely to the enormous farmhouse kitchen.

Without any rush, she crossed to the knife drawer and took her time selecting the biggest, sharpest carving knife she could find.

When satisfied she returned to the dungeon where her men had already stripped Salvatore completely naked.

They had re-gagged him, so he was powerless to cry out, but had left the blindfold off purposely to enable him to see all that was about to happen.

Falcone's eyes flew wide when Lucia re-entered the room. His terrified screams muted by the balled up rag in his mouth as he saw what she had in her hand; his whole body dancing wildly on the rope as he hung upside down in the centre of the cold, dank dungeon.

"Hold him." She said to the three big men guarding him and they immediately did as instructed.

Slowly The Contessa walked up to him, Salvatore now frozen with fear, tears streaming from his terrified eyes, as she reached out and took hold of his flaccid penis which was hanging limply down towards his bare navel.

The same piece of disgusting flesh that had robbed her of the right to bear children.

As Lucia squeezed it tightly, Falcone reacted violently, his body jerking, trying to escape her malevolent grip. But the men forced him still as The Contessa lifted the shiny steel blade, the generous width of it gleaming under the singular bulb that illuminated the room.

The Contessa looked down into Salvatore's horror filled eyes, "They say the first cut is always the deepest," she said. "And trust me, this is just the first of many."

She then stretched his penis out sharply and offered up the carving knife.

Epilogue

Paris, France 1980

Maria's twin grandsons were dressed in their Sunday best for the opening ceremony; their proud parents, Danny and Ava, trying to keep them clean until at least after it started. But the mischievous four-year olds were not making it easy.

At least their little girl, Meggie, was being good; the pretty two-year old sitting on Grandad Frankie's lap, being fed chocolate buttons at regular intervals by Delores who had, rather surprisingly, begun a courtship with Frankie after nursing him back to health. The pair had been almost inseparable ever since.

Sitting next to Delores, keeping Meggie amused by blowing raspberries and pulling faces was Father Nate Malone, dressed in his best black cassock and starched white clerical collar. He had flown in especially from his diocese in Rome which had been under his pastoral care for the past two years - after spending the previous two serving the community of Hell's Kitchen, New York.

Next to Nate was his good friend, The Contessa di Montagna, looking spectacular in a white figure-hugging dress and a beautiful diamanté eye-patch. It was hard to believe that Lucia was now in her early sixties as she was still utterly stunning.

Lucia was now one of the five major share holders in 'Golden Viscount Productions' - the enormous production company that

538

had been formed after merging Gold Star and Viscount together - which had quickly become the largest and most successful studio in the world.

Maria, Nate and Danny were also chief shareholders and Ava had been made an equal partner as a wedding gift from her devoted mother-in-law.

It was now primarily run by Danny and Ava together, who had become a remarkable team - both personally and professionally.

Maria had taken over as Head of Matador, and ran it with the help of Danny and an incredibly loyal group of assistants who did much of the travelling on her behalf.

Maria, herself, much preferring to spend time at home with her family or with Steven than flying off around the globe on business. But her finger was well and truly on the pulse and The Company was most definitely thriving under her experienced leadership.

She and Steven had tentatively begun their romance six years earlier, before all that transpired with her father and Falcone. But afterwards they had allowed it to blossom and, in the fullness of time, they had fallen deeply in love.

Steven had proposed in the Spring of '77 and they had married six months later in Cadiz. They were now blissfully happy and spending their time between Steven's home in London and Maria's main residence in New York. Vacations were spent either with the family on Lake Como or with Nate in Rome - where they always made time to visit The Contessa.

Nevertheless, they were presently in Paris for the long awaited, much anticipated Grand Opening.

The Paris Matador had taken much longer to complete than anyone ever imagined and had been fraught with difficulties almost from the very start; the whole project getting hideously bogged down in Parisian 'red-tape'.

But finally, after all the meetings, after all the revisions and after all the long hours spent trying to make it the most elegant hotel in the world, it had finally been completed, just two months earlier.

And today was its Grand Opening.

The building stood proudly in the city centre, complementing the surrounding structures perfectly; harmonising beautifully with the overall 'feel' of Paris. Its gleaming glass spires reflecting the elegant architecture of the neighbouring buildings.

Maria stood behind the lectern on the wide, sweeping steps that led up to the exquisitely designed entrance and delivered her speech to the gathered audience. When she had finished she crossed to the magnificent abstract sculpture of a charging bull, very much in the contemporary style; an image synonymous with Matador Hotels and the man who had first envisaged building one in Paris so many years before.

Underneath was a plaque concealed by a small curtain with a pull cord opening.

Maria said a few more words and then proudly revealed the gleaming marble plaque.

It read simply:

This hotel is dedicated to the hard work and kind nature of Diego Del Toro.

A wonderful man, a perfect husband and a loving father.

Then everyone stood and applauded.

THE END

About The Author

Kris Lillyman is based in Northamptonshire, England and has worked as a freelance graphic designer and illustrator for over twenty-five years. He is married with two grown up children.

In addition to adult thrillers, he also writes and illustrates children's books - to find out more about these, please visit: **www.krislillyman.com**

Alternatively, search 'Kris Lillyman' in iTunes, Amazon, Barnes & Noble or most other online bookstores.

www.ingramcontent.com/pod-product-compliance
Lightning Source LLC
Chambersburg PA
CBHW020822030726
47496CB00001B/43